YORDIM

YORDIM

Leaving the
Promised Land
for the Land
of Promise

MICHA LEV

WOODBINE HOUSE · 1986

Library of Congress Catalogue Card Number: 85-052008

ISBN: 0-933149-03-4

Book and Jacket Design: Sicklesmith & Egly
Illustration: Margaret Finch

Manufactured in the United States of America

1 2 3 4 5 6 7 8 9 10

The quotation that appears on the first page of
Chapter Twelve is excerpted from *Sabbath: Its
Meaning To Modern Man* by Abraham Joshua
Heschel, published by Farrar, Straus, and Young,
New York, 1951.

No character in this novel represents or is based on
an actual person. All personalities are imaginary;
however, the actual historical events are real.

To My Father
in loving memory

ACKNOWLEDGMENTS

No book is the work of only one man. Begun in Israel and completed in America, this novel represents more than ten years of research, experience, and writing during which time literally hundreds of kindnesses were extended to me. Though I am deeply appreciative of them all, space allows me to mention only some of the most significant.

Invaluable guidance and encouragement were given to me by Zvi Shneer, Yitzhak Zuckerman (Antek), and other members of Kibbutz Lochamei HaGhetta'ot during my months of residence and study there. To the collective staffs of the Museum of the Ghetto Fighters, Yad VaShem, the libraries at the Hebrew University of Jerusalem and at Haifa University, and the Zionist Archives I owe particular gratitude for their expert assistance.

The organization of information and thought involved in the writing of this book could not have been accomplished without the support and interest of many generous people both in Israel and in America. I am deeply grateful to: Riva Friedman and Sandra Frager, for unpaid professional preparation of the early drafts; to Drs. Eugene and Anita Weiner, my selfless friends, for accomodation and inspiration; to Barry Fierst, for his informed comments and exacting eye; to Sandy Wiesenthal, for monumental support by example; and to Terry Rosenberg and Diana McGonigle, for their invaluable help and immeasurable contributions in reviewing and preparing the final manuscript.

I owe a special debt to: Henry Robbins, of blessed memory, who believed in this book and in this writer before either was ready for publication; and William Yarrow, my editor and friend who gave unsparingly of his talent and his time, and whose collaborative genius has made this book a reality.

Finally, my deepest indebtedness and gratitude to my greatest source of counsel, support, and inspiration—my wife, Debra.

Micha Lev
Washington, D.C.
1986

CONTENTS

PROLOGUE

*"And the children struggled
together within her."*

GENESIS 25:22

PROLOGUE

HAIFA • MAY 1975

THEN MIRYAM SCREAMED.

It was as though some dark spirit, some ghoul inside her, had bound her hands, propped open her eyes, and forced her to witness past horrors. Robbing graves, exhuming souls, it marched lost loved ones before her, and she watched them plummet, one by one, into the abyss.

"Barukh! Barukh!" she cried.

"It's all right, Miryam. You were dreaming," Barukh Lvov, her husband, said groggily. "Calm yourself, it's just a dream." His words surfaced like air bubbles as his mind slowly rose toward consciousness. What time is it? he asked himself, squeezing one eye open and looking at the clock on the bed table. 4:30 A.M. In another hour they would have to get up to go to their store and open before the early risers stopped by to pick up a Friday morning paper or play the Sportoto football pool. 4:30 A.M. Dawn was early enough to wake up.

He had become used to being jolted from a sound sleep by Miryam's nightmares, and the urgency with which he first had responded had changed into a caring matter-of-factness long ago. Tonight her screams had exploded his sleep like depth charges. What was her dream about this time? Without lifting his head from the pillow, he turned over and saw Miryam sitting bolt upright.

"We lost them, *lost* them!" Miryam cried out. She seemed to be telling no one in particular, talking more to the darkness than to Barukh. Then, almost whispering, she repeated, "Barukh, this time we lost them."

3

Though he could not see clearly in the dark bedroom, Barukh sensed that Miryam was staring through the blackness. He sensed that her eyes were stretched wide, that her brows crowded her forehead; he could feel her body tightening. She was gasping and her lips were quivering. Barukh felt the bed trembling.

"Miryam, you're home, I'm right here, stop shaking," he said gently. "It's finished, the dream's over, tell me what happened."

Miryam did not hesitate. "We turned out the lights and buried the boys," she told Barukh who lay listening beside her, his head pressed hard on his pillow. "We hid them where no one would find them, then we sealed them into the deep hole you dug underneath the floorboards, under the boards which the little rug covers and with the coffee table on it." Her voice was almost inaudible, little more than breath. "After a minute they came pounding their fists on our door. We listened and stood like two trees in the room. You were there with me; we were two trees. Then the doorjamb shuddered. They would find us. We didn't breathe. I was sure they would kick down the door and storm in, but instead they turned away and left. We could hear their boots rock the stairwell.

" 'It's a trick,' you said, 'they'll be back.' But hours passed and nothing happened. 'How long can boys live in darkness?' I asked. 'As long as they have to,' you told me. We waited until we could wait no more, then together we rushed to get them. We lifted the floorboards and shouted down, 'Come out, all's clear.' But no head surfaced, no one answered.

" 'They fell asleep. Don't worry,' you said, quickly easing yourself down into the hole. I knelt down and leaned over the opening, then lit a Sabbath candle and handed it down so that you could see, but suddenly roaches, repulsive black waves of them, scuddled up and out of the hole, pouring over the place where I was kneeling, and crawling around my knees. I cringed but didn't scream or move. Instead I stayed there just waiting for you and

4

the boys to come up, waiting there with open arms, empty arms, and watching the roaches coming. It was a horrible black rush of them that seemed to have no end.

"Finally, thank God, the roaches were gone and you reappeared, but alone. Your face looked like death, your eyes were hollow. Never before had I seen you like that. In utter despair, you tore through the little room like a madman, ripping up floorboards and searching for any hidden spaces, any unmarked graves, but you could find nothing. 'Where are they?' you cried out, 'Dear God, give them back!' Then I screamed too, 'Please God, not the boys!' Barukh, Barukh, we hid them too well and this time we've lost them!' "

Miryam was trembling more violently now than before. Her breathing was shallow and uneven. Barukh could see that retelling the dream had not helped her at all. It had instead let the dream draw her back in. "Miryam, the boys are fine," he told her. "Nissim and Yossi are fine, just fine, and dreams are dreams. You know that. Now, please, let's try to get some sleep."

Miryam tried to calm herself and folded her hand into his in the darkness. "Barukh, I know they're fine," she whispered, "but these dreams, they feel too real."

This dream had been like the others, and like the others she had believed it. Maybe something had happened or was about to happen to Yosef or his wife, Rivka, or little Dorit half a world away in America. Maybe Nissim was involved in some secret and dangerous mission that he could not discuss at home. She wanted to believe that it all was unfounded, that her nightmares were far too frequent to be linked to real premonitions, but her memory was so full of actual horrors that any imagined tragedy, no matter how improbable, entered the realm of possibility. The evil she had witnessed and suffered provided a base for her fears and for these dreams. Barukh understood this. His was a similar history.

"Barukh?"

"What?"

"Did you hear any planes?"

"When?" he asked. "Now? It's not even five yet."

"No, I mean *before* I woke you up." Her tone was searching. The last war had shattered her sense of safety in Israel. Nissim had driven off to the Sinai that afternoon, hours before the Phantoms flew over. He had barely kissed her and hadn't even told her where he was going. Then two months passed, two months of hand-wringing before she saw him again. She had been certain that he would not come home again, that she would never hold him or hear his voice again. Thank God I was wrong, she thought. I hope I'm always wrong. Yosef had been in America then and did not come back for the war. She had been glad at his absence. It had answered her private prayer, for she believed that odds played a part in a family's fate and that God would not have let both sons live. Yosef and Rivka were safer there, she decided, and there could be no better reason for their leaving than to get Dorit better care there. So it had bothered her only a little that other mothers had called Yosef a deserter when he didn't fly back to fight. Too many neighbors lay in too many graves. Yosef had been smart, she thought, and Nissim had been lucky. But then she pictured Nissim's best friend, Avi Farkosh, who had been like a third son to her. He had died in the Sinai on the war's third day. It had been Avi's burial that had reawakened the dark spirit inside her, and since that day after Yom Kippur a year and eight months ago, restful nights had become infrequent for Miryam and so for Barukh.

"No planes," he answered groggily, "only your dreams."

"I'm sorry," she said gently and stroked his head. "Go back to sleep. I'm fine now."

Barukh sank quickly back to sleep, but Miryam still sat up beside him in the bed, her mind unable to shake away the question, How do these dreams keep finding me? Perhaps what she called the ghoul was really a messenger for the Angel of Death. Perhaps he was sent to claim her soul, forcing her back into the abyss. But this was nonsense, she told herself, foolishness. "Barukh?"

"Hmmm?" he muttered without moving.

"Are you asleep yet?"

"I would've been," he said, turning over but not opening his eyes. "Think about Nissim coming home. Before you know it he'll be here."

The thought of Nissim's arrival calmed her. Shabbat would be lovely, much fuller with him home. "Barukh?" she said again softly. "Is chicken all right with you?"

"Chicken?" he mumbled half-asleep, repeating the only word he had heard.

"For dinner," she said, "with kugel and salad." She could tell that Barukh had fallen back to sleep while she was talking and she smiled at herself for going on anyway. "You get some rest," she told him softly. "God knows we both need it."

The even cadence of Barukh's breathing washed across her mind, but she would not let herself drift into dreams again tonight. Instead, she sat counting the minutes until dawn, listening to her husband sleeping.

There were no street lights on HaTishbi Street and the bedroom window was black. Miryam watched and waited for daybreak. Suddenly, in the darkness, she imagined lights were flashing in the room. Her arm felt hot as though volts were surging through it. She could feel it swelling and throbbing and burning. Nissim will be home today, she told herself. Her heart was pumping with such power that she felt it pounding her chest and her back, banging back and forth between them, rebounding and expanding inside her. The flashing lights were neon numbers, blinking, throbbing. A neon dye was in her veins. She looked down and realized the light was coming from inside her. With effort, Miryam

calmed her breathing and gradually the vision stopped. There was
no more throbbing, no more burning, no neon dye. The window
was still black, Barukh was still sleeping soundly, and the tattoo
on her forearm was indistinct in the darkness.

BOOK ONE
Departures

"Deliver him from going down . . . I have found a ransom."

JOB 33:24

One

YOSEF LVOV, TWO YEARS IN AMERICA, leaned over and stuck his head in the Westinghouse oven. He could not really check the inside walls because his eyes were pressed too close to them to see anything clearly, and the lighting did not help either. The little bulb at the back of the oven was lit, but whichever way Yosef turned his head it seemed that his curly hair and beard blocked the bulb from lighting the spot he was inspecting. It was like trying to look at the back of your neck in a mirror directly behind you.

He had heard stories about peanut butter smears on a refrigerator door costing one tenant five hundred dollars and of dustballs in a bedroom corner costing a neighbor his full security deposit. He could not afford to be another story.

A thousand dollars. That's what having no debts had cost him two years ago when he and Rivka had applied to Spring Glen to be tenants in the summer of 1973. The landlord had told them, "No debts, no credit; no credit, bad risks; that'll be three months' rent, up front." A thousand dollars cash. Even the sound of the figure had overwhelmed Yosef and Rivka, just arrived from Israel with two-year-old Dorit and only enough money to manage the first few months' living expenses. So if making this oven sparkle meant reclaiming that thousand dollars, then six-foot-four-inch Yosef was going to bend and scrub until the walls gleamed.

Beads of sweat dripped down his forehead and his cheeks, rolling down into his dark brown beard. The hair across his forehead and at the back of his neck was matted with perspiration. His leather Nikes, worn without socks, were stained with

11

sweat on the tongue of each shoe. A wet, expanding line ran like a tie from the collar of his T-shirt to a vanishing point inside his jeans.

Yosef, smelling of sweat and ammonia, reached next to his knee for the roll of Scott Towels, tore off three sheets, and gave the walls a last wiping. Then, satisfied that all the grease was gone, he pulled his head out to glance at his watch. Almost seven o'clock. He had been working in the apartment since four and the last hour had passed without his noticing. Rivka would be waiting, he knew, and once again he would be late. I can't be every place, he told himself. Rivka has to understand that.

Maybe Rivka and he should reconsider this move they were making. Maybe Dorit would be happier here. Continuity was very important for a child, especially for a four-year-old, especially for a child like Dorit. They had already moved her across the world, and this apartment had been a good home to her, to them. It had been their first home in Philadelphia, and the glass doors to its little balcony had been their window on America. But it was too late now to change either their minds or their plans. Their lease required them to vacate today.

There were two more rooms to check. First he entered the bathroom to see that the tub had no ring and that the sink was not spotted with toothpaste. Everything should have been spotless and it was since he had scrubbed them both until they shined this morning. Even the mirror above the sink showed no signs of having been splattered with soap and Listerine morning and night for the past two years. How easy it was to destroy the evidence, Yosef thought, to erase the record of their living here. How easy it was to undo history or at least confuse it.

Yosef crossed the hallway, walked into the small bedroom, and began inspecting the bare white walls. Strangely, the room looked not larger but smaller without Dorit's furniture in it. A jagged blue mark on the far wall drew Yosef's eye. Beneath the blue patch was a jagged half-moon of white, a speck of black inside it. This was all that remained of Dorit's favorite decoration, all that remained of the life-size Cookie Monster decal with the blue body and ping-pong ball eyes placed above the headboard of her crib.

Yosef looked at what remained of the decal and, using his fingernails, began scratching away the last traces. Yosef kept scratching, finding the blue cellophane more stubborn and difficult to remove than he had expected. The landlord would see it as a serious blemish he was sure and would not know or care that it had held a special significance for a little girl. But maybe that was the way it should be, that memories moved with the people who made them, rather than staying in the places where they were formed.

The last piece of blue cellophane was curling at the edges but stubbornly sticking in the middle. One last hard yank would peel it. Then the walls would be clean of color, devoid of life.

Yosef gripped the curled edge, clenched it in his fist, and gave a powerful tug. Too easily, without any resistance, the strip pulled loose from the wall. The sudden force sent Yosef's arm flying and spun him around until, with a terrible shattering, his elbow went through the window behind him. "Damn it!" he screamed as the glass splintered onto the sill and fell across the bare floor. It was only his shirt, long-sleeved and rolled below his elbows, that protected him from getting cut. "Why does it always happen when you're almost there?"

Carefully he eased his elbow out of the jagged hole in the storm window and took a second to think about how to hide the damage. He pulled down a white linen shade, until it covered the window's upper half. Then he slid the broken windowpane up and locked it in place and slid the screen panel down to the lower half where the broken window had been. The white shade now covered the broken pane. If they find it, Yosef told himself, I'll tell them that's

how it was since we moved in. Then taking a broom, he carefully swept every last shard and splinter of glass onto a piece of old
cardboard he was using as a dustpan.

Finished, he stepped back from the sill and stood in the center
of the empty room, feeling stupid for having cleaned so hard, having paid such attention to detail, only to blow the whole enterprise by rushing into negligence at the last instant. Pay attention!
he told himself.

He headed quickly through the hallway and into the master
bedroom where he scanned the walls and floors for marks and
dustballs. Finding none, he returned to the front door. Seven-thirty
already. A full thirty minutes had blinked by and Rivka expected
him in less than an hour. Yosef took the door key out of his jeans
pocket, walked out of the apartment, and double-bolted the door.

"Morning," someone said. "Heard you cleaning since real
early."

Surprised, Yosef looked up. It was his across-the-hall
neighbor, Mr. Wilkins.

"Good morning," he said. "I am just finishing from four
o'clock."

"You went to a lot of trouble, my friend," Mr. Wilkins told
him.

"Of course, a lot of trouble, but a lot of money. We're moving and I need my security back."

"For nothing, a lot of trouble for nothing. You'll get your
deposit back. Don't worry."

"You are so sure?" Yosef asked.

"Trust me. In the ten years I've been here, I've never seen them
check."

"It's impossible. I've heard the stories."

"So have I and believe me, they're just that — stories. But look,
it's not like you killed yourself for nothing. Clean never hurt
anything, right?"

Mr. Wilkins picked up the *Philadelphia Inquirer* from the mat outside his door, unrolled the rubber band from the paper, and stepped back into his apartment. "So long, my friend. And listen, don't worry about money. If you're gonna worry, worry about worry."

Yosef was surprised at having been called his friend. Americans were funny that way, using terms of affection they didn't mean, giving advice no one wanted. For two years they had lived less than ten yards from each other, but Yosef had never seen the inside of Mr. Wilkins' apartment, only his name on the mailbox downstairs. His friend. Yosef moved quickly into the stairwell and listened to his footsteps echo as he descended the metal steps.

Outside a yellow cab was waiting. His.

A moment later it pulled out of the lot and was rolling down a steep hill. A right turn at the bottom of the hill brought the yellow cab to the curb in front of the Rental Office. Yosef slid out from behind the wheel and walked in.

Inside there was a line at the large counter that served as the reception desk. The rental office had just opened for business, and four people were waiting for a short woman with bleached hair and a forced smile to finish unlocking the drawers behind the counter. "Pardon," Yosef said as he moved to the front of the line. He was in a hurry and had no time for waiting. "Pardon." To him lines were not facts to be accepted, but obstacles to be overcome. They were just the tools of bureaucracies to cut people into conforming shapes. In Israel he had felt the same way, too much sameness, too many agencies, too many rules.

"Pardon," he explained to the people behind him, "but my wife is pregnant and it could be any minute."

The people in line listened to his story, their faces expressing doubt and disapproval, but only one man said anything.

"We're all in a hurry," the man said to Yosef, "but if

your wife's into labor, go ahead."

His statement seemed to ease the others' impatience, but still the air was thick with displeasure.

The woman finished unlocking the drawers and now faced Yosef across the reception counter. "Good morning, may I help you?" she asked.

"Yes, please. I am coming to return my keys," Yosef answered.

"Your name?"

"Lvov, L-v-o-v. Joseph Lvov," Yosef told her.

"Apartment number?"

"438."

"And all the keys are here?" she asked, picking up the keys he had laid on the counter.

Yosef nodded.

"Yes, here are the mailbox keys, both sets, good," the woman said. "Now, if everything is found to be in good order—"

"Why wouldn't it be?" Yosef asked.

"Well," the woman began, studying the bearded, sweaty man confronting her across the counter. He looked to be about thirty years old. Tall as he was, he had to be at least 225 pounds and looked like a Jewish lumberjack in his unbuttoned red plaid shirt with the braided Star of David hanging from a thick gold chain. She compared him with the two men in business suits behind him. "Let's just say that we have had some trouble in the past with other, um, tenants. Sometimes our standards differ."

"The apartment is clean," Yosef told her emphatically.

"I hope it is," she said.

"When do I get my security back?" Yosef asked after a moment. He could feel himself growing belligerent at the woman's patronizing tone.

"Mr. Love, there is no reason to raise your voice," the woman said. "Your security, as you call it, and I take it that by that you

16

mean your security *deposit,* will be mailed to you, in whatever portion, when our people complete their inspection of the premises."

"What does this mean 'in whatever portion'?" Yosef asked.

"Depending on what additional cleaning will need to be done, like scouring the oven and cleaning the windows, the management company will determine how much of the deposit you gave us will need to be deducted for extra cleaning costs," she told him. "The rest will be mailed to you in a check. Do you understand now?"

"I understand you too much," he told her.

"Good, Mr. Love," she said, "then let me just check our records to see that there are no outstanding balances on your account."

"Lvov," Yosef corrected her. "Mr. and Mrs. Joseph Lvov. L-v-o-v. Everything is paid up to date."

The people who had let Yosef go ahead of them in line were growing impatient. Yosef could feel them exchanging disapproving glances behind him.

"My wife is pregnant and I must to hurry," Yosef told the woman, wanting both to remind the people behind him of why they had felt sympathetic toward him and also to finish dealing with this woman's officiousness.

"It's my responsibility to check the records and also to see that we have a forwarding address," she said, slowly turning the pages of a large loose-leaf notebook. "As I mentioned before, in the past we have had people like yourself from other countries pack up and go back home without giving us any clue as to where to reach them."

"We are moving only across the city," he said.

"Yes, well, just in case," she told him. "Ah, here it is. You should get a check in the mail within the next several weeks. Have a nice day. Next please."

Yosef stood there a moment, astonished and offended. She

had wished him a nice day in a tone less sincere than he would use in talking to Dorit's goldfish. Was that how it was? He wanted to tell the woman what she could do with her phony concern for him, but Rivka was waiting and so was Dorit and he would be late enough as it was, so he marched out of the rental office and slammed the screen behind him. "Pardon."

Hurriedly Yosef walked over to his cab and noticed that something about the front seat looked different. The three cartons he had stacked on the passenger side had fallen over. He opened the door. The driver's seat was soaking wet. Water was splattered on the inside of the driver's door. A heavy, moldy smell hung in the cab.

"Not the goldfish!" he shouted. "What a goddamn day." He had placed his daughter's fish and glass bowl on his seat when he had gone to return his keys. This was the pet Dorit had not trusted yesterday to the moving men. Her father, she said, would take it. The stacked cartons must have fallen and knocked the fishbowl over.

Only an inch of water remained in the bowl and there was no goldfish. It wasn't on the floor or seat. Maybe it had fallen into the crack at the back of the driver's seat. How long could I have been in the Rental Office? he asked himself. A few minutes? He reached a large hand into the crack but couldn't reach in far enough to feel anything.

Quickly he leaned over and flipped open the glove compartment. An empty yogurt container lay there among the maps, pens, receipts, candy wrappers, and assorted tools. He felt through the mess until he found a gummy plastic spoon. He pulled it out, spilling some papers on the seat, and began probing the crevice for the fish, but after a few tries he gave up, realizing that even if he could find the fish he'd kill it getting it out. Anyway, odds were it was already dead.

What will I tell Dorit? Yosef wondered. This was her fish,

it was dead and buried in his cab. He hadn't killed it exactly, but he had lost it. Well, they aren't expensive, he thought. At twenty-nine cents each I'll buy her a dozen and that'll make up for it. But what kind of pet was a goldfish anyway? he asked himself. You couldn't even hold it without taking its life in your hands. In Israel pets were luxuries. Any pet was an extra mouth, an extra expense any way you looked at it. His family in Israel had had only enough money to buy food for the people in it. His pets had been the salamanders which he and his brother Nissim had plucked off the outside walls of their apartment building, and the tomcats that roamed through the garbage cans at the top of the walk by day and then wailed by night in the giant wadi behind HaTishbi Street. In America it seemed everyone had pets, and they treated them better than people. It all seemed so strange and misguided to him. But Dorit loved her goldfish.

Yosef moved the empty bowl onto the floormat on the passenger side and took a pair of sweat socks from a carton in the back seat. He began wiping the front seat vigorously. But the socks weren't soaking up much water and he didn't have time to waste on this. So he tossed them into the back and sat down behind the wheel on the wet, stale smelling seat. After strapping himself in, he started the car and gunned the motor. Dorit would have to understand. Things die.

Maybe he wouldn't tell her.

OUT ON THE MAIN ROAD, stop signs were replaced by traffic lights and gradually the distances between intersections lengthened, until the road expanded to four lanes and the speed limit increased to forty-five miles per hour. This was a stretch where Yosef could make good time, maybe even make up some time if he could wriggle out of the considerable traffic heading toward Center City. Crowded by cartons and sitting on a wet seat,

Yosef could not remember having driven in a more awkward or uncomfortable position. Not even in '67 during the war, when he had driven artillery transports under fire into Kuneitra.

The drive home was uneventful, but long. Traffic had been no better than his worst fears. Throughout the trip his thoughts had been of Rivka and Dorit; what he would tell the one, what he would tell the other. The drive had passed in a blur of stories and apologies and now he was almost home.

The yellow cab turned down Louise Lane and slowed in front of a large split-level house in the middle of the block, The house was set well back from the sidewalk by a large lawn. A long picket fence, visible from the street, enclosed a sizable yard in back. The house had chocolate brown siding with beige shutters. A big picture window made it possible to look into the sunken living room when the drapes were open, as they were now. Beyond the cushioned window seat, the room was furnished with teakwood coffee tables, a leather upholstered sofa, and lounge chairs on thick-pile, burnt sienna carpet. Track lights ran along the ceiling. Beyond the living room and also visible through the picture window were white louvered doors that opened into a den.

The yellow cab slowed, turned into the wide driveway, and pulled into the two-car garage. Yosef could not drive into this garage without being amazed by its spaciousness. It was like a smaller house attached to a bigger house and he couldn't get used to the idea of having two houses for one family. More than that, only cars were living in it. In Israel this garage alone would be called a "villa" and people would stand in line to buy it.

Yosef checked his watch. 8:50. The crosstown drive had been bumper-to-bumper and he was almost a full hour late. Wasting no time, he got out of the car, taking the empty fishbowl with him. To carry it inside or leave it anyplace where Dorit might find it would only complicate things, so he opened the trunk, reached back into the deepest part, and put the glass bowl behind his basketball. Then he closed the trunk and headed into the house.

A side door connected the garage to the house and led through a short hallway to the kitchen. This door made it possible to get out of the car and go into the house without going outside. The knob was locked, so he knocked. In a second Dorit ran to the door and opened it. She came up only to her father's hips, and her long straight hair, the same brown as Yosef's, was worn in a ponytail, but was so fine that it kept slipping out of the hairband.

"Abba, Abba," she said with excitement. "You're home. Ema, he's home," she shouted. Then she looked at how disheveled he was, his matted hair and stained T-shirt, and said, "Shalom, Abba. Were you at your work?"

He picked her up and hugged her. "Sort of, sweetie," he told her.

As he held her, she ran her little hands over the thickest parts of his beard. "Your beard is soft, Abba," she said.

"You like it?"

"Yes, it's nice, like my pillow."

"Your pillow?" he asked. "But your pillow doesn't have a beard."

"Abba," she giggled, "you're silly."

"I know it."

"You have a beard because you're a boy and boys have beards and men do too but you're a man *and* a boy, so you have a big beard, right?" she asked him.

"Right, sweetie," he answered, "and you're a girl. Right?"

"Right, and Bradley and Dana and Jennifer have beards and all of my friends at my school have beards, right, Abba?"

"Not exactly, sweetie. Only men can have beards."

"Right, because your beard is soft. And Abba, you know what?"

"What?" he asked softly.

"Your hair smells yucchy," she said, scrunching her face. "You smell like feet."

"Like feet?" he said, and twisted his nose as though to smell himself. "Well, you're right about that, little smartie." He smiled and put her down gently. "There was a lot left to clean in our old apartment."

"Right, Abba, and you got yucchy," she told him. Then she hugged him around the legs and felt that his pants were wet. "Abba, you're wet!" she laughed. "You had an accident!"

Yosef, who had been shushing her as she said this, bent down beside his daughter and hugged her again. She could not see the soft smile on his face. "Shhh," he whispered in her ear, "quiet. Don't tell anybody. Okay?"

"It's okay. I wet my pants, too, sometimes."

"Shh. I don't want Ema to know. It's a secret. Okay?"

"Okay," she whispered back to him, "but why couldn't you hold it in?"

Yosef smiled. He was thinking of how to answer Dorit when Rivka called from the kitchen.

"Nice of you to make it," she said loudly. She was standing at the sink, a tall woman with straight jet black hair and strong features, her sleeves rolled up to her elbows and a dish towel slung over her shoulder. The Formica counter beside her was piled with upside down glasses and pots ready to be dried. The kitchen floor was littered with open cartons filled with more glassware and cooking pots. In the sink was a large plastic basin overflowing with hot water and soapsuds. Steam rose around Rivka's face as she tried to move the loose strands of hair from her face by jutting out her lower lip and trying to blow straight upward. Finally, she wiped the strands of hair away from her eyes by using the back of her soapy hand. "You were supposed to be here an hour ago."

"I hit bad traffic."

"The traffic's always bad. You left an hour too late to get here."

"What's your problem? Where do you think I was? Atlantic City?"

Dorit was still sitting on Yosef's knee as he squatted beside her. "Abba, can I have my fish now?" she asked.

He looked at her softly, pausing a moment, then said to her, "Honey, I wish I could but—"

"I know why you're late. You stopped off at the playground and got in some basketball game again, didn't you? Dorit, is he sweaty? I can't do it all myself, you know."

"All *yourself?*" Yosef shouted back.

Dorit was perched on his knee, and his seat was beginning to itch from the wetness. He was upset at Rivka's complaining but was glad for the interruption. How much was there to do here anyway? This new house of theirs came fully furnished; appliances, closets, everything. It was ready to be lived in without bringing any more than a suitcase and your toothbrush. So what was she complaining about? They had a great deal, an incredible one, housesitting for Professor Barsky of the History Department while he was in Oxford on sabbatical. It even was costing them less in rent than they had been paying at Spring Glen. A furnished house for less than an empty apartment. "I don't know what you're screaming about."

Rivka did not respond right away, and after a second's silence, Dorit asked, "Abba, where's my fish? I made a place for it on the window in my new room. Please get it now. I miss it."

Yosef looked at his daughter and paused. She looked so small, anxious, innocent. "I would if I could," he told her, "but when I got there it was . . . dead, honey."

"Dead?"

"Yes, honey. I tried to save it, but some things even Abba can't fix."

Dorit looked up at him, her eyes wide and welling with tears, then looked down at the floor. "I knew I shouldn't have left it there," she said softly. "It got lonely and got dead."

"No, honey," he told her, holding her gently around her tiny waist. He could feel her little body tensing and tightening as she pressed her head against his chest. "It wasn't your fault," he said. "Fish can't die from that."

"*I* would, Abba," she told him, and started crying loudly.

He hugged her and kissed her gently on top of her head. "I know you're sad and so am I," he said. "And we'll go get another one, together. Promise."

"Dorit, are you crying?" Rivka called from the kitchen, stopping her washing for a moment but not moving away from the sink. "What's going on out there?"

"Ema, my fish got dead," Dorit called, still sobbing and sitting on Yosef's knee. "Abba couldn't fix it."

"What? I can't hear you," Rivka called back.

"Everything's under control," Yosef shouted toward the kitchen. "The goldfish was dead when I got there this morning and we're talking about buying a new one. Right, Dorit?"

Dorit nodded silently, her ponytail wagging and her head rubbing against her father's T-shirt.

Rivka shook her head and resumed sudsing a large pot in the sink. "It wouldn't be a real move without a casualty. Dorit, sweetie, I'm sorry, honey, but it'll be okay, you'll see. We're all here, right? You, me, and Abba. And we'll get you another goldfish tomorrow."

"No, today!" Dorit cried. "I need my fish!"

"I know, honey," Rivka called back. "Okay, maybe Abba will take you when the pet shop opens."

Dorit looked up at her father and pleaded, "Please, Abba. Can you?"

"All right," Yosef said. "*If* you stop crying, I'll take you." He could feel her sobbing begin to subside and in seconds she was no longer crying. "I'll take you sometime today," he said gently, "if I get home from class before the shop closes. Okay?"

"Okay, Abba," she whimpered, and he wiped the last tears from her cheek.

"Are you two going to spend the rest of the day in that hallway or are you going to give me a hand?" Rivka called. "Who knows when people will drop in. I want the place ready to show them."

Holding Dorit's hand, Yosef walked into the kitchen. "This place was ready to show them yesterday, Rivka," he said, "before we even moved in. But if it's not clean enough for you, then you clean it."

"What do you think I'm doing, Yossi?"

"Making everybody crazy," he answered, "including yourself. Relax a minute, back off, take a breath. People are allowed to breathe, you know."

"I'll spend all day tomorrow breathing, but today I'll get this house ready to show our friends."

"Who? Oded and Varda? Shimon and Rakhel? What other 'Americans' have you invited over?" he asked.

"What do you mean 'Americans?'"

"They're *yordim* and you know it."

"*Yordim?* You think they're here to stay?"

"Haven't they been here for years already? What makes you think they'll go back to Kiryat Yam or Bet HaKerem? They won't admit it, but they'll be here forever."

"No, you're wrong. They're no more *yordim* than we are. So what if Rakhel and Shimon have been here six or seven years — that doesn't make them *yordim*. Shimon finished his studies and got a job here he couldn't turn down, a job he could never have had back in Haifa, but now that he's got it he'll land an even better one back home. They're going back, probably when we do, and the same with Oded and Varda. I hate it when you call them *yordim*. Would you want to be called that?"

25

"Okay, Rivka, you're right. They're not *yordim*. They've gone beyond that."

"What do you mean?"

"Now they're Zionists."

"What's that supposed to mean?" Rivka asked him.

"It means that instead of planning to go back, they only dream about it."

"You're impossible, you know? Leave me alone."

Yosef was becoming uncomfortable. The itch in his seat was becoming severe. He had to change out of his wet pants and put on some dry underwear before he was going to do anything else. He picked up Dorit and carried her into the hall.

Putting her down by the steps he said, "We'll go to the pet shop later. Okay?"

She nodded and looked up at him as she leaned against his leg. "Abba, why did you wet your pants?" she asked.

"Yossi," Rivka called from the kitchen, "you're going to be late for your first class anyway so bring me the next load of cartons before you leave, would you?"

Yosef used the interruption to ignore Dorit's last question. "In a minute," he shouted, "I have to go to the bathroom." Then he winked at Dorit and started upstairs.

Dorit tried to wink back at him but could only close both eyes at once. "Abba," she said in a whisper loud enough to stop him midway up the stairs, "Ema didn't even notice."

He smiled down at her and winked. "Right," he whispered. "She never does."

"And I won't tell her. I won't. I promise," she said, raising one finger to her lips as a sign of silence.

"Good girl," Yosef replied. "Now go give your mother a hug." Then taking three stairs at a time, he reached the top of the stairs and disappeared behind the bathroom door.

Two

FOLDING THE DETAILED COMMAND MAP and putting it away, Nissim Lvov knelt down on one knee and smoothed the sand in front of him. He drew deep lines with the blunt end of his pen. Sixty soldiers, some kneeling, some standing, were huddled around him in a close circle. Major Lvov saw his eyes in theirs, fixed sharply on the ground, fixed on the sand and on his pen and on the diagram he was carving.

Black binoculars hung from the thin black leather strap around his neck. He was wearing dark green combat fatigues and heavy, laced black leather boots tied just below the knees. His collar brushed against a two-days' stubble that darkened his handsome face. Nissim had last shaved in his parents' Haifa apartment, just before sitting down to the meal before the Yom Kippur fast. He and his parents had attended services together at the corner synagogue, he and Barukh in the men's section, Miryam watching through the white sheet that curtained the women's gallery. Not that Nissim had prayed. Prayers were something you propped yourself up on when you lost faith in men, in your friends.

Friends. The major scanned the faces around him until he found Avi Farkosh. Two days ago, on Shabbat afternoon at one o'clock, just minutes after the Yom Kippur silence was shattered by air raid sirens signalling the Egyptian attack, Nissim turned on Galei Tzahal, the army radio station, and heard orders to report immediately to Sharm el-Sheikh. He packed, dressed, and drove his jeep to Avi's apartment. Together they sped toward this war. From Carmel Beach south to the Country Club junction out-

side Herzliya the throttle was pressed to the floor, and the jeep raced through traffic lights like a silent ambulance.

By the time they reached the Geha junction, the road had become clogged with vehicles. Jeeps, cars, huge convoys of munitions trucks and artillery trailers, armored personnel carriers from the central depots, and Egged buses filled with reservists—all followed the same route to the Sinai. Even the shoulders of the highway were blocked by the wide loads and heavy traffic.

"We're already late for this goddamn war," Nissim said, frustrated to find no way out of the gridlock. "If it's anything like '67 it'll be over before we get there."

"That'd be fine with me," Avi said. He reached into his backpack and pulled out his khalil. "At this rate we won't be there till late tonight." Leaning back in his seat, he pointed the khalil toward the cloudless sky and began playing "Ein Gedi." The gentle notes from Avi's instrument floated up amid the roar of the hundreds of motors and the groans and screeches of the truck gears and brakes, amid the choking clouds of exhaust fumes and dirt.

"I guess I might as well get used to you playing that wooden dick," Nissim joked. "You've been blowing on it since we were in kindergarten."

"I brought it as a spare," Avi said, pausing a moment between verses. "For Shoshanah, in case they blow off my real one."

Nissim smiled and Avi returned to his playing. The two of them had attended high school, middle school, grade school, and even gan together. Not to mention their three-year stint in Tzahal, Israel's army. Always they had served in the same unit, in the same gidood, in the same tank. They even looked somewhat alike. In fact they looked more like brothers than Nissim and Yosef Lvov did. Both Avi and Nissim were about 5'10", dark skinned, and brown haired. Yet Avi was stockier than Nissim, not as thickly muscled, but heavier and much more hairy. Dark hair covered his arms and legs and back, and tufts of brown curls rose from his chest almost to his thick full beard. Nissim's face was clean shaven.

The traffic showed no sign of letting up, and Nissim could find no opening to steer his jeep through. "What else have you got in your backpack there?" he asked Avi. "What did you grab for your war kit?"

"Same as last time," Avi said, interrupting the Matti Caspi song he was playing. "Last time" had been in '70, during the War of Attrition, when he and Nissim had fought together on the Suez front. It had never escalated into a full-blown war. No air raid sirens had sounded across the country then.

"Some Elite chocolate, a picture or two, two paperbacks."

"Books. We're going to a war and he's taking books. Where do you plan to read them?"

"In traffic," Avi answered, smiling, "and if this keeps up I'll finish one on the way there and the other on the way home."

"Hell you will. On the way home you're driving."

"Don't give me that stuff. I'm driving when we get there," Avi said. "You can drive there and back. And about the books, it wouldn't hurt if you'd read one once in a while."

"I'll tell you what. You read enough for both of us."

"When this thing's over, I'm going to convince you to come back to Haifa and get your degree. Hell, maybe Tzahal will send you."

"Maybe. When do you graduate Haifa U.? This June?"

"Yeah, if we get this over with fast," Avi told him. "The plan is for Shoshanah and me to tie the knot in the middle of June, then the two of us will take off on tour for the summer. Europe, America, Canada."

"Honeymoon deluxe, eh? I'll make you a deal," Nissim said. "You teach me how to play that thing and I'll play chauffeur next summer."

"You're on!" Avi returned to playing his khalil, piping a medley of Israeli songs, thinking of Nissim accompanying them on their honeymoon, as they made their way down to the Sinai. Eight *hours later, in darkness, Avi asleep beside him, Nissim pulled into the base.*

HOLDING THE PEN UPSIDE DOWN *in his fist, Nissim carved two more grooves in the sand, then drew an X where the two lines intersected.*

Suddenly the ground shook beneath him. For hours the distant rumblings had been growing louder, more eruptive, more rhythmic. Cannon flashes lit up the cold desert night. The Egyptian tanks were near. Too near.

"Four teams, four tanks to a team," Major Lvov shouted to his men. "The sun will be up soon. Let's move it!" With a swipe of his hand he smeared the map in the sand and erased it as the circle around him disbanded.

In seconds the major's tank was rattling over hillocks and high dunes, climbing and falling at severe, sudden angles, leading a battalion of sixteen Pattons. The major stood exposed in the turret looking ahead through binoculars. Inside the lower hatch, Farkosh steered while the gunner and the loader unracked shells. As they rolled forward, the landscape rolled toward them so that they seemed to be moving at double speed, until they came to a steep ridge. Beyond the ridge, huge clouds of sand and dirt billowed skyward. The clouds grew thicker as an endless wave of sand-colored Egyptian tanks, led by an infantry brigade, poured across the ridge. Emerging in columns three tanks wide, they rolled forward toward the Pattons. Nissim counted them as they emerged. Fifty tanks, sixty, seventy-five. He had never before seen so many tanks in a single formation. And the infantry were carrying bazookas and antitank missiles.

"Fire in five," he yelled to his men. "Avi, start rolling." Nissim watched the Arab tanks pour toward him.

"Fire!" Israeli missiles whistled through the air and blasts sent

sand and shards of metal flying everywhere. Shells were unleashed
as fast as the men could unrack them. The Egyptian tanks had
rolled forward while the Pattons had hidden behind the hillocks,
lying in wait to spring an ambush. Teams Aleph and Bet were
attacking from both flanks as Team Gimmel blasted from the front-
side angle. The enemy force, confused and surprised, closed
quarters instead of fanning out, and almost every shell the Pattons fired was hitting. Team Daled quickly circled back through
the cover of sand and cannon fire to a position behind the enemy
formation. Now all four teams were firing, and still the enemy
tanks had not answered the attack.

"All right, close in!" Nissim shouted to Avi as their Patton
began rumbling forward. Nissim refused to go down into the tank
shell and close the hatch above him. War was something you met
head-on, with your eyes wide open. He looked through the thicken-
ing clouds of sand, straining to see the enemy who was now so
close in front of him. Avi, sitting tense inside the driver's cell,
could see nothing but smoke through his periscope and Nissim
was blindly directing him forward. Suddenly two Pattons went
up in flames; within seconds a third exploded. The enemy force
had opened fire. RPG bazooka shells, cannon blasts, Sagger
missiles.

Nissim screamed instructions to Avi as their Patton surged
ahead. There was a flash, a monstrous blast, then nausea,
weightlessness, sand. Nissim was lying face down. Avi, his men,
his tank, where were they? He turned himself over, wiped the sand
from the corners of his mouth and eyes, and picked himself up.
What had happened? From fifty yards away he saw his Patton,
whole but blurred, and not moving. Cannons were blasting all
around it and the detonations were deafening. Why was it sitting
there, firing no shells? Where was Avi? Nissim started running
but the sand under foot kept making him stumble. It swallowed
his strides like quicksand. His Patton had taken a hit and since

he had been standing exposed, the force of the blast had sent him flying fifty yards through the air. The hatch of the upper turret was still open, but the driver's hatch was closed. Nissim kept pummeling his legs, trying to sprint forward, but the sand would give him no grounding, no traction. His boots sank deeper with every stride, and the major kept tripping and falling. Now he spotted the gunner and the loader as they hoisted themselves out through the upper hatch. Thank God they're alive. Keep coming, bail out! Nissim got up and tripped again. Avi, where was he?

Just then the lower hatch opened and Nissim watched Avi struggling to lift himself out. "I'm coming," the major screamed as he ran two steps forward and stumbled again. Farkosh pulled his head and shoulders through the hole then spread his arms out for leverage, pressing his palms back against the outside of the tank shell to help him wriggle the rest of his body through. He's all right, keep pushing, I'm—. A shell whistled over Nissim's head and he pressed his body and face to the sand. When he lifted his eyes, the Patton was burning. Flames were shooting out through the upper turret and a funnel of black smoke rose above the burning tank. "Avi!" Nissim saw that Farkosh was caught with only half his body through the exit hatch, the sleeves of his fatigues on fire and flames spreading quickly. "Keep coming, keep moving, Avi!" he yelled, but his friend did not move. He couldn't. The khaki sleeves had burned away, and his arms, exposed and with the hair on fire, were melting onto the hot metal of the tank shell. His flesh fused onto the Patton, pinning Avi in a tortured pose. Nissim watched in horror as the flames moved from Avi's uniform to the tufts of chest hair coming out of his collar and then to his face, setting his beard ablaze. The curly hair crackled and recoiled as it burned. Nissim ran forward, stumbling still, but he was too far away and too late. He wanted to look away but something inside would not let him. Avi, his best friend, was on fire, his spread arms fused to the smelting steel, his eyes wide and white, his helmet welded to the top of his head, his perfect white teeth clenched in a grotesque smile. Inside the tank was a raging inferno. From the driver's hatch flames began shooting out, rising over Avi from behind. They looked like a giant lion's mane, enveloping his head in flame. He seemed a grotesque hunter's trophy, mounted while still alive. Nissim saw a dying friend, crucified in fire.

Slowly Avi's features began to melt as though his face were made of wet clay. His nose collapsed then disappeared, and the sockets of his eyes dissolved so that his eyeballs rolled inward toward one another until they almost touched in the middle of his molten face. "No!" Nissim shouted. "No! No! No!" Nissim shouted and kept shouting, even after the dream had ended.

THE DARK GRAY WOOL BLANKETS and white sheet were bunched in a heap at the foot of his army bed, leaving the lieutenant colonel's legs uncovered. Even in May the nights in Ashkelon were cool, and tonight the lieutenant colonel's bunk was especially chilly, but Nissim Lvov had worn only underpants to sleep. Since the last war he had made a point of underdressing for the weather. He'd come to like the feel of little bumps rising all over his body. He seemed to find a kind of comfort in being cold.

His hand groped groggily across the metal bed and onto the little white stool that served as his barracks bed table. In the darkness Nissim lifted the little round-faced alarm clock that sat there, and held it up in front of his eyes. Through the glass he read the luminous dial. It was four o'clock in the morning, Friday. The alarm wasn't set to go off for another hour, and later today he'd be heading home to Haifa for Shabbat leave.

It already was twenty full months since Avi's death, not even two full years since that battle on the third day of the war. It seemed both too long and too short a time. In that same battle in which the Israelis stalled the Egyptian advance, in which Avi was killed, more than half of the men in Nissim's battalion either lost their lives or were seriously wounded. Nissim somehow avoided injury, going on after Avi's death to lead his men in combat, never allowing himself to yield to the cynicism he felt building inside him, fighting bravely and with vengeance until the cease-fire took effect.

He rolled out of his bed and dragged himself to the sink. He reached through the darkness for the switch that turned on the bare light bulb above it. Then he opened the spigot, cupped his hands under the rush of cold water, and splashed several handfuls into his face. After wiping his eyes with a stiff white towel, he looked at himself in the frameless mirror that hung on the wall. Nothing had changed in the last seven years, Nissim thought. Nothing except for the full dark beard which he had worn for the last twenty months, which he had grown since the war. For an instant in the mirror he saw flashes again of flame-gutted Pattons and faces on fire, but he shook them away and cleared his eyes, focusing again on his own image. Little had changed besides his beard. He was still as trim as he had been at eighteen and was stronger. The same features stared back at him now, the big hazel eyes, the straight Roman nose, the short, dark, burly hair. But Nissim knew that something was different, something had changed. The world had done it, the last war had done it, Avi's death had done it.

Nissim was twenty-five years old now and for all of his adult life an army camp had been his home, a mobile post his mailing address. Every morning for the past seven years, he had awakened before dawn in some army barracks like this one. Soldiering had been full-time duty, his way of life, and since 1971 when his three-year required service had ended, it had been his chosen profession. For him the job of "soldier" was like that of doctor or lawyer, writer or artist. It was at first a belief in your mission, your calling, and then a belief in your talent and acquired skill. Soon you became aware of the absence of absolute answers, of the unknowable, infinite body of knowledge. You realized that your chosen science didn't have all the formulas, and it became for you a precarious game of self-confidence and self-delusion. There was a constant tension between your fear of failure and dreams of fame. You came to see that all success was luck and all credit was pretense. It became a dangerous business of experience and illusion, a shell game you played with credentials, and always you were waiting to hear that someone had found you out, that someone had discovered that you were less than they thought you to be. For Nissim it had been an all-consuming venture. He had been an army workaholic, as high-powered as the most ambitious executive, and had risen to the rank of *Sgan Aluf,* Lieutenant Colonel. But military life felt different to him now. He was tired of the deadlines and protocol, tired of the standards and codes and inspections, and most of all tired of enforcing them. He had been through enough wars and mobilizations to last him for a lifetime. Maybe the letter came today, he thought. The forms asked for my home address. Maybe it's waiting in Haifa.

The army itself had changed drastically during the past year and a half. The way the war had ended, with Russia and America moving in and demanding that the encircled Third Army, the same Arab force that had launched the Yom Kippur offensive at the Canal, be brought water and food in the desert, that they be protected and then released—this had broken his men's spirit.

"We're allowed to fight but not to win," they told each other, "which means we're only allowed to die." Morale had steadily declined until now it had reached a new low for *Tzahal.* Nissim remembered when wars were decided by better tactics and better soldiers, when they were won in the field and not in distant seats of power. He remembered when superior training meant better odds, better chances of walking home whole.

But now it was computerized weapons, smarter buttons. It

had become a high-tech Armageddon, and suddenly soldiers were just incidental. He remembered feeling like no more than a stunt-man in his Patton during the last war, like a stand-in for the movie's big-name star whose contract called for taking no risks. He had felt like a nameless player in a mechanized Western, testing out weapons for America against the East's latest arsenal. Worse, he had felt like a pawn, a faceless soldier-robot controlled by a foreign master, just another automaton in another metal shell. He felt used, exploited, and only a little less bitter now than he had at Avi's funeral.

After finishing at the sink, he began dressing. He put on his green khaki uniform, buckled his belt, laced his boots, then made his bed. In seconds the sheet was smoothed and tucked, the woolen blankets stretched taut as a painter's canvas.

Next to the alarm clock on the white stool by his bed were a pack of cigarettes and a box of matchsticks. Nissim took out a cigarette, let it dangle between his lips, then struck one of the wooden matches. As soon as the cigarette was lit, he walked to the sink and doused the match with cold water. "Twenty-five is still young," he said out loud, pausing there and looking at himself in the mirror above the basin. His beard had grown a little rag-ged, with new stubble climbing too high on his cheeks. He switched on his battery-powered electric shaver, laid his cigarette on the rim of the sink, and began shaving his neck just below his beard. The battery-powered shaver had been Shoshanah's gift to him eight years ago, in '68 when he and Avi began their three-year national service in *Tzahal*. She had given Avi the same gift, the same model. "I like smooth skin on a man's face," she had said. "Nissim, this is to keep yours as smooth as it is, and Avi, you have enough hair everywhere else. You don't need to grow more on your face." She had always wanted Avi to shave off his beard, but he never had.

Suddenly the image of Avi on fire slipped like a slide into

Nissim's mind. He could feel revulsion rising inside him, a revulsion with which he'd become too familiar, a revulsion that intensified then transformed itself into guilt. Why me? he asked himself. Why'd *I* survive it? He thought of his parents, of Barukh and Miryam tormented even now, thirty years later, by having survived Treblinka and Belsen. Why them? Why me?

After a moment Nissim cleared his head and focused again on the bearded face in the mirror. His eyes were staring back at him, first blankly then intently, making him wonder if the image in the mirror wasn't studying *him*. He put down the shaver and picked up his cigarette, taking a deep drag and then blowing a thick cloud of smoke toward the mirror. It would be good to see Barukh and Miryam tonight, he thought. The last Shabbat he'd spent at home was more than a month ago. Maybe he'd take Shoshanah out to the Cinemateque and afterwards tell her about his application.

The smoke cleared, and he looked at his face in the mirror again. Had his eyes lost some of their intensity, some of their conviction? he asked himself. Maybe a little, he admitted. No, a lot.

Three

THE SABBATH OBSERVANCES in Barukh and Miryam's home were both traditional and interpretive. For twenty-seven years they had ignored most of the prescribed rituals and felt considerable ambivalence not only about those they did not observe but also about those they did practice. Both Barukh and Miryam had grown up in orthodox Jewish homes. Barukh's father had been a Talmudic scholar in Lodz, Poland, but it had been Barukh's decision that religious traditions and rituals would be honored only selectively in the Lvov household. After Hitler, he could not embrace the religious faith or fervor of his ancestors. Barukh had not taken Nissim or Yosef to synagogue except for special holidays and the day of each boy's Bar Mitzvah. Praying was fine, he believed, but prayers didn't save any lives. He had seen the most pious Jews carted off with the nonbelievers, and he had seen his own father packed in a train to Treblinka. In Barukh's view, religion connected a man to his family, it connected you to other men, not to God, if there were a God. Shabbat for him was family time, a safeguard against nervous breakdowns and heart attacks. It was a time of forced relaxation, of no schedules or appointments or business emergencies. It was a time for sharing, for being together, a time for deepening family bonds. Love for family saved lives, thought Barukh, for he had seen it.

"Nissim, it's after five already!" Miryam shouted through the open living room window. "It's almost time to light the candles."

"I'll be up in a minute," Nissim answered. "My jeep gave me

some trouble on the way here. I almost had to push this thing up the mountain."

"You'll have plenty of time to fix it tomorrow," she told him. "It's time to come up now, and you haven't even showered."

"I'll be right up as soon as I fix this," Nissim shouted, working on the car as he spoke. "It'll take me just a few more minutes."

"Nissim!" Miryam called down, her voice much sterner, "I want you to stop what you're doing right now. The candles won't wait."

"Then light them without me. I've got to finish what I started here."

Nissim liked to work on cars, to solve mechanical problems, and he was good at it. Many times he had helped repair army vehicles in his division. Even as a very young child he had accompanied his father on housecalls and had served as his unofficial apprentice. From Barukh he had learned to trust his own hands.

Barukh looked out from the living room's large window. Straightening the black beret on his head, he smiled down at his son. I'm fifty-three years old, he thought. He smoothed his thin grey moustache with two fingers. Twenty-five years in a store. Twenty-five years of selling hardware, of repairing toasters and vacuum cleaners, of fixing short circuits and unblocking drains. A quarter of a century, half of my lifetime. And my son? Twenty-five years in a store? Or will he spend his whole life in *Tzahal?*

Barukh resented his daily routine. He wanted to perform more lasting deeds than selling hair dryers, disposing of ruptured boilers, snaking clogged sewage from toilets. But his hands had bought him freedom. He was his own boss, albeit over a small kingdom. A little shop. Even ten people couldn't stand in it at the same time. Business could be better, he admitted, but all things considered he and Miryam had not done badly. Their income had been modest but adequate. Better good and a little, than bad and a lot, he told himself.

"Nissim," he called down through the open window, "you've been out there with your jeep since you got home today. You haven't said two words to your mother. She's been cooking all day getting ready. Now she's asked you to come in here. Let's go."

Nissim bounded up the three flights of marble-chip tile stairs until he reached the door to his parents' apartment. Miryam was standing at the entrance.

"Go hurry and shower. I want to light the candles on time," she said stiffly.

"I'm going," he said to his mother. "You know, Ema, I spend all week meeting deadlines. I don't need any more when I get home."

"Go shower, Nissim."

After Nissim had showered and changed, the three Lvovs sat down to Sabbath dinner. At the table's center, two candles glowed softly in their silver candlesticks. On Barukh's plate, a pewter goblet was filled to the brim with sweet red wine. Two braided challah loaves, topped with toasted sesame seeds, lay beneath silk covers.

Miryam had cooked and cleaned all afternoon to ready the apartment for the Sabbath. As had been her custom, she had prepared two full-course meals, one to serve to her family and the other to freeze for a family in need. But the second dinner she cooked was really for her second family, for the family she had lost to Hitler and the camps. Packing the meal into plastic containers each Friday and putting them into her freezer was like lighting a memorial candle for her loved ones who had perished. She had found that the double preparations and the doubled recipes enhanced the Sabbath's meaning for her. After Shabbat she would give the second meal away.

Barukh in his beret lifted the goblet of wine and rose in his place at the head of the table, as Miryam in a white scarf and Nissim in a black yarmulke stood with him. Poised to chant the Sabbath Kiddush, Barukh scanned the photographs that stood in gilt frames on the large oak bookcase across the room. There were two pictures of Nissim, one in which he was standing alone in uniform at his Army graduation ceremony from basic training, the second with Avi and Shoshanah, the three of them in bathing suits on Carmel Beach, embracing. There was a photograph from fifteen years ago of Miryam and him standing arm-in-arm in front of their store. They had posed for the snapshot a little too stiffly, too conscious of the camera, he thought. There was Yosef and Rivka's wedding portrait from 1969, and beside it a photo of Dorit at her third birthday party. He could not look at that picture without smiling.

Barukh Lvov began the blessing over the wine. *"Barukh atah Adonai Elohaynu Melekh ha-olam, boray p'ree ha-goffen."* But his attention was not on the words he sang; it was on the scene before him. In a sweeping glance he took in his wife and son, an array of roses and carnations on the white-clothed table, a tureen of steaming soup soon to be served, the Sabbath candles, and the frames that stood like miniature people on top of the bookcase across the room. Pictures. Somehow tonight he could not keep his eyes off them. He studied the one of himself and his brother Avram standing in front of a huge ship which was docked at Haifa Port. They both stood in the April sun, Avram dwarfing him in height and girth, Barukh's arm almost tearing out of its socket from reaching to prop itself on his brother's shoulder. Had it really been more than twenty years since Avram's funeral? For a moment it seemed only months, and he thought himself back to Europe.

Thirty-two years ago, a boy of fourteen, Barukh stood in the lineup at Treblinka, awaiting the dreaded shower. His brother Avram and he had been separated the week before and had not seen each other since. The SS guard, a tall blonde twenty-year-old, ran his eyes up and down Barukh who, feverish with typhus, stood 5'2" and weighed only 50 pounds.

By whatever quirk of conscience, the young guard offered Barukh the chance to flee into the bordering forest. If by the count of ten, Barukh was still in view, the guard vowed to gun him down. But if he was out of sight by then, his escape would not be reported. No Gestapo posse would search to bring him back. Without thinking, Barukh propelled himself through a hole in the fence and vanished into the forest.

This sprint to sudden freedom was followed by months of horror. Barukh's mind became an exposed nerve, twitching at the slightest sound. He lived on berries, scavenged food, and hope, surviving until the end of the war by hiding in abandoned buildings.

After the war he made his way to England where his mother's cousins lived. He located them in Manchester, and they took him in. But Barukh had no identity papers, so they adopted him formally as their son. Within days of his arrival, he became a British subject, living with his cousins in England, and joining the British arm of the Haganah, the Jewish underground. Then in 1946 he booked his passage to Haifa as one of a British tour group.

In Palestine his missions for the Zionist underground were constant. Using Haifa as his home base, he carried out assignments with vengeance and abandon. In April 1948, as the British Mandatory troops were withdrawing from Palestine, the Haganah raced the Arab militia to seize control of Bet HaNajadda, the perimeter post that controlled the northern approaches to the city of Haifa. As soon as the British soldiers vacated the command station, a fierce battle erupted between the Jewish and Arab forces. Barukh joined the Haganah fighters who seized Bet HaNajadda, but during the battle's first minutes a bullet lodged in his upper leg, and he was rushed for treatment.

While Barukh lay in the hospital, a letter arrived from England. His cousins, keeping their promise to him, had searched for surviving relatives. "Your brother Avram is alive," they wrote. "He survived two years at Theresienstadt. When the camp was liberated, he sailed for Palestine, but his ship was turned back at Haifa. The last thing we heard was that he was on Cyprus with a child."

Upon his release from the hospital, Barukh contacted people who had known his brother in Europe and in Cyprus. He found out Avram's wife had been ill on the boat from Europe and had died while in Cyprus. Only Avram and his little son, Yosef, had made the passage to Israel. After long months, Barukh's search ended joyfully and tearfully at the transit camp in Tiberias. From there Barukh took Avram and Yosef back to Haifa. And in December 1948, Avram served as best man at Barukh and Miryam's wedding.

For a time, before Nissim was born, they all lived together in their HaTishbi Street apartment, Miryam serving as mother to Yosef while Avram and Barukh worked odd jobs. Then Avram rented a place of his own, not far from Barukh and Miryam's flat, and during their years as neighbors he and Barukh grew closer than brothers.

Looking at Avram in the photograph, Barukh was struck again by the resemblance between Avram and Yosef. They looked more like brothers than Avram and he did. Both Avram and Yosef were big, broad shouldered, thick limbed, bearded. Did he and Nissim resemble each other as much? His eye returned to the picture of his son in uniform and then to the grown man standing with him at this table. No, he told himself. And staring at his son, he finished chanting the prayer over the wine.

After chanting the Kiddush, Barukh drank some of the wine, and sat down. Miryam and Nissim sat also. Slowly the pewter goblet passed around the table, from father to mother to son, and when Nissim drank, his parents watched him. At times during the past months, his eyes had looked to them as ornamental and impassive as marbles. They had noticed something different in them, in the way he seemed to show concern or even excitement only with a conscious effort. Before the last war he had not been this way.

It had always been Nissim who would lift their spirits, who would be first to smile and last to yield to dark thoughts. But since Avi's death Nissim had grown quiet. Barukh and Miryam understood this. Both of them had battled a similar silence, a similar withdrawal into themselves during the years after Europe. Witnessing it in Nissim they worried and grew sad. They remained apprehensive for they knew that the war with despair was as threatening as war itself, that in both cases a person could lose himself beyond reclamation.

"So how was your trip?" Miryam asked, intent on drawing Nissim out of his silence and into conversation. She took his plate and filled it with a chicken wing, a large portion of tzimmes, and two squares of raisin kugel.

"Same as always, except for when my jeep stalled out at the foot of the mountain," he told her.

"You haven't been home since Pesach. That's already over a month ago," she went on. "I thought that maybe it would feel special to you to be home again after so long away."

"Four weeks isn't so long," he said, thinking of Avi. "Please pass the Tempo."

Barukh handed the large bottle of cola to his son. "What your mother meant was that we're glad you're home," he said.

Miryam took over from Barukh. "It's not like we see you every day. We want to know how you're feeling about things, what you're doing, what you're seeing."

"On my trip home?"

"That would be a start," Miryam told him.

Barukh looked over at his son, casting him a knowing glance. "By the way, Miryam," he said, "everything's delicious." He tilted his soup bowl toward him and spooned out the last drops. "How are things in Ashkelon, Nissim?"

"Under control."

"Meaning what?"

"Meaning no change."

"Is the alert still on?"

"If it were, I wouldn't be here," Nissim answered his father. "Everyone's just waiting to see how much of the Sinai Kissinger and Sadat are going to lop off. It's quieter right now. That's how I got time to come home."

"We shouldn't give back one inch," Barukh said. "What would *we* be getting back if *they'd* won? What other country in the world gets attacked, almost slaughtered, fights back and wins, and then is forced to give back what they fought for?"

"Only us," Nissim said. "Politics, everything's politics. We should have an army of diplomats, not soldiers. They could talk nice to the Soviet T62's and the Sagger missiles, and after they all got blown away, then we could bring in other diplomats to sit in some tent and bargain away what they died for."

"I don't blame you for feeling bitter," Miryam said, "but it's never been any different. In '56 when we were eating rations, look what we had to give back in the Sinai, and what did that buy us? Nothing."

"Morale must be pretty low," Barukh said.

"Lower than even right after the war," Nissim told him, "and falling. Who can blame them? How can I tell my men they're wrong? It's like the whole thing was one big pointless waste, like Avi died for nothing. We fight the wars, we put our lives on the line, but when the smoke clears none of it matters. We don't even call the shots. America does. Kissinger does. We might as well make him prime minister."

"Look," Barukh said, "no one said anything should be easy. It never has been, least of all here. Maybe something more permanent will come out of the Sinai talks this time."

"I wish I believed that," Nissim said, finishing the soda in his glass and reaching for the Tempo bottle.

"Nissim, you haven't touched your chicken," Miryam said, lifting the serving bowl of tzimmes. "Maybe you want a little more of this?"

"No thanks. I'm fine."

"He's fine," she said to Barukh. "You're fine. Well, you don't sound so fine to me."

"You want me to eat more tzimmes, I'll eat more tzimmes," Nissim said, putting down the Tempo bottle and taking the serving bowl from his mother. He forked some tzimmes onto his plate.

"They don't feed you in Ashkelon. Eat."

For a few moments the three of them sat quietly, their eating precluding conversation, and Miryam listened to the silence, seeing it as flattery.

"Anything new at the store?" Nissim asked, glad to direct attention away from himself.

"No, nothing, the same old story," Miryam answered, passing the kugel plate to Barukh. "Your father keeps working too hard and won't say no to anybody who tells him he's in trouble. Yesterday alone he made three housecalls. The Kalfons' clogged toilet, Mrs. Goren's toaster that cut off her electricity, the Kassifs' burst hot water heater. He didn't come home till after nine last night. And he was up again before dawn this morning."

"She should talk," Barukh said to Nissim, wearing a guilty smile as he spoke. "She was the one who woke me up. But I'm not the one with the high blood pressure. Sure, it was a busy week. That's how we've been eating all these years."

Miryam shrugged and looked at Nissim. "They're all busy weeks, but a body will listen to a mind for just so long."

"True," Barukh said. "Did you take your pills, Zeisa?"

Miryam wore the perturbed expression of a child who has been outsmarted. "Yes, I took them when Nissim got home. Now how about you two taking more to eat."

"I want to leave some room for dessert," Barukh told her.

"And I'm still working on this tzimmes," Nissim said.

"Well, you know there's plenty more here if you want it." Miryam looked across the candle flames and studied her husband. The bald spot on his head was larger even than it had been six months ago, but only she knew it. Is that how we age? she wondered, looking at his beret. Is that how we hide it? He looks handsome tonight in this light, she thought.

Nissim sliced a piece of chicken and forked it into his mouth. "What do you hear from my cousin?"

"You mean your brother?" Barukh said.

"I mean Yossi, who hasn't answered one of my letters for two years now." Nissim had never really accepted Yosef as his older brother. He always had seen him as his big cousin, as family, as his only living relative besides Barukh and Miryam, and this had been enough to give him a special bond with Yosef, even if not always an affectionate one. In 1953 when Nissim's uncle Avram died, Yosef had been eight years old and Nissim had been only three. One year later, to avoid any problems with the custody of their orphaned nephew, Barukh and Miryam legally adopted Yosef, making him their second son. To Nissim, his cousin's adoption seemed a sort of necessary charade to give Yosef a greater sense of security and belonging. But it also had created considerable confusion in defining the new relationships in the Lvov family. The aunt and uncle became mother and father, the nephew became the older son, the cousins became brothers. Yet in Nissim's mind these role changes happened in name only. He had tried to play the younger brother convincingly, hoping that Yosef would come to believe that the signing of a legal document

47

could give him a new identity, but he knew that Yosef believed it no more than he did.

"Yossi's written us regularly and you know it," Barukh said. "Written *you.*"

"He knows that we read every letter to you," Barukh went on. "For him I'm sure it's the same as writing to you."

"Well, it isn't for me. And anyway he doesn't write a word of those letters; everything's in Rivka's handwriting. She writes every line," Nissim said. "He talks a blue streak, but he won't write one sentence."

"He's been busy in America. Studying, working, taking care of a family," Miryam chimed in. "It's not easy. But you know he's been thinking of you."

"Right," Nissim said. "He's just too busy. I've heard how rough life in America is."

"We got a lovely air-letter from them this week," Miryam said. "I'll give it to you to read after dinner. They're moving into a new place; not an apartment, a house. They have it for the year, until June when Yossi finishes up and the three of them come home."

"They have their own *house?*" Nissim asked. "Their own villa? It must be costing them a fortune. Yossi must be raking it in."

"I don't know," Miryam said. "Rivka didn't go into it, but it's some kind of special deal."

"When are they moving in?" Nissim asked.

"They're there already. I have their new address and phone number in the kitchen."

"God, I hate this distance," Barukh blurted. "Next week's Dorit's birthday, she'll be five years old, and we haven't seen her since she turned three." He looked over at the photograph of his granddaughter on the oakwood bookcase, then looked at Miryam. "Don't let me forget to mail her the dress first thing Sunday morning."

"I'll remind you," she said. "Don't worry about that. Having

Yossi half way across the world has been hard enough, but not seeing Dorit — every time I think of that child I . . . ." Miryam stopped, tears welling in her eyes. "I just hate not being able to hold her. Sometimes I wonder if she'll even remember us."

"She'll remember us," Barukh assured her, "and we'll remember her birthday by calling her and wishing her *yom huleddet samayakh* in person," Barukh said. "Well, by phone in person. Just hearing her voice will be a present for *us* on *her* birthday."

Nissim looked down at his empty plate. "Any mail come for me?" he asked.

"Something came a few days ago," Miryam told him. "I put it in the kitchen. There's a pile on top of the refrigerator."

Nissim put down his knife and fork, stood up, and began stacking the soup bowls from around the table, doing it slowly so as not to draw attention to the curiosity consuming him. "I'll carry these into the kitchen," he said.

After dropping more than putting the soup bowls into the kitchen sink, Nissim reached on top of the refrigerator and took down the pile of letters there. He leafed through the envelopes and almost reached the bottom of the pile before he found one addressed to him in English. The letter had come. He took a breath and began to tear it open when Miryam came walking into the kitchen, carrying more plates from the table.

"Did you find it?" she asked as she turned on the faucet at the sink.

"I found it," he said, quickly folding the envelope in half and tucking it into the back pocket of his jeans.

"Well, I'll finish up in here. You go back in and keep your father company. He misses not having you around more often, but he'd never tell you that. Well, go on. I'll bring in dessert in a minute."

"So, was it there?" Barukh asked as Nissim walked back into the room and sat down at the table. "Anything interesting?"

"It was there," Nissim answered, "but I didn't have time yet to read it."

"So read it now. We have all night to talk."

"I'll read it later. Anyway we don't have all night because I set it up with Shoshanah to go to the Cinemateque."

"What time?"

"I told her I'd pick her up after dinner," Nissim explained, seeing the disappointment on his father's face.

"I see. Well, what time do you plan to head back to the base tomorrow?"

"Don't really know yet. I figure sometime after lunch. So, Abba, tell me more about the store."

"There's not really much to tell . . . ."

While Nissim and Barukh continued talking, Miryam busied herself in the kitchen, slicing one of the two apple cakes she'd baked. Never did she serve any cake whole because she could not resist treating herself to snitches of her own baking. Through the years she had learned to cut her cakes into slices or squares so that no one would notice the portion she had eaten, and every year she had gained a few pounds until now at fifty-five she was thirty pounds overweight. Of course, her family and close friends had found her out long ago, but they went along with the deception. They knew she considered being thin a disease, no matter what the fashion designers were saying. It was something to be combatted, not desired. She was glad to be heavy.

Now the cake plate was filled with generous slices of warm apple cake and Miryam broke off the end of one more slice before carrying it to the table. "If I ate my own baking," she said as she walked into the dining room, swallowing the last crumbs in her mouth, "I'd weigh a ton in no time. But you two enjoy it. I made it for you."

Barukh and Nissim smiled at one another. "You can join us at least for half a slice," Barukh told her.

"No, I've been good all week," she said, "and I don't want to spoil it. You two aren't on diets like I am." She put two slices on each of their plates and left her own plate empty.

"So who else do you know in Philadelphia besides Yossi and Rivka?" Miryam asked Nissim.

The question seemed to come out of nowhere, and the way she had phrased it stunned Nissim. "What do you mean?" he asked.

"I mean did you open your letter? It's not every week you get letters in English from Philadelphia."

Nissim straightened himself in his chair. "I haven't opened it yet," he said.

"So open it now," she told him.

With his dinner knife he slit open the envelope, removed the typed page of stationery from inside, and read it to himself. He could feel his parents watching him. He could feel their eyes on his face, on *his* eyes, on his thoughts.

"*Nu?* What does it say?" Miryam asked.

"It says they want me to come there," he told her, looking up from the typed page for the first time. "They want me in Philadelphia, beginning in late summer."

"Late summer?" Barukh asked. "Which summer?"

"This summer," Nissim said softly, looking into his father's eyes.

"*This* summer? I don't understand," Miryam said, becoming visibly upset. "They want you for what? And who is 'they?'"

"The University of Pennsylvania," Nissim told her. "They want me to come there to study."

"How did they find you?" she asked. "How did they get your name?"

"They got my name from me."

"From *you?*"

"I can't stay in the army forever," Nissim said, looking past his mother at the picture of himself in uniform on the bookcase. He remembered how Avi and he had talked of travelling around the world, crossing borders as tourists, not as "tankists." They had planned to jet to America and spend more than just a few whirlwind weeks there. Every April they had talked of booking tickets and every May they had put off their trip for another year. "Some things just don't wait," he went on. "I need to get away for a while, to get some perspective on my life. Going to America to study will give me the chance to do that."

Barukh and Miryam looked at each other, then lowered their eyes almost in unison. Their silence was heavy with memories of Nissim, of Nissim and Yosef as young boys at home, as young boys playing out back in the wadi, on Carmel Beach, in the apartment. Barukh fingered his wine goblet, spinning its thick stem slowly. Miryam wiped some hair off her face and stared at the Sabbath candles.

"Why America?" she asked. "Why so far? If you want to go to school what's wrong with Haifa University or the Technion?"

"Like I said, I need to get some distance on things," Nissim answered.

"If you want some distance, why not go to Beersheva, to Ben-Gurion University?" she asked.

"Because it's not the same and you know it."

"Of course it's not the same," she said. "One way we never see you, the other at least we get to see you for Shabbat once in a while and holidays." Miryam was so distraught that she picked up two slices of apple cake and put them on her plate. "What if I told you your father isn't well?"

"I'm fine," Barukh volunteered quickly.

"What *if*, Nissim?" she repeated.

"I'm feeling fine," Barukh said again, surprised to see his wife break off a large piece of cake and put it in her mouth. "Please calm yourself, Zeisa. You're the one he should worry about."

"Calm *myself*? My son is going away, I'm trying to put up a fight, and you're taking *his* side! You feel fine? Wonderful. I feel like someone just blew a hole right through me." Miryam swallowed the cake in her mouth and drew a deep breath. "You want him to go?" Miryam asked, breaking off another piece. "You want to talk with your son only through the mail? You want to sit around this table just staring at his picture?"

"I don't want him to go any more than you do, but he's been on his own for seven years already. He's got to live his own life, Zeisa. Look at him. He's twenty-five. He's old enough to make his own choices."

Miryam looked at the cake in her hand and, suddenly realizing what she was doing, put the piece down on her plate. "Twenty-five!" she shouted, turning to Nissim. "Your father and I have been married *twenty-seven* years, we haven't travelled farther than Eilat in all that time, and you don't see *us* suffering, do you?"

"It's different for you," Nissim responded. "You both knew other worlds before you came here. I didn't."

"And you should thank God every day for that," his father told him. "Don't make blessings curses."

"You know what I meant, Abba. All I know about living is what it's like here, and to be honest, right now I'm not thrilled by the prospects. If I'm going to ever see what it's like somewhere else in the world, then I've got to do it now, while I'm young enough, before I have to settle down."

"I understand, Nissim," Barukh said.

"You understand?" Miryam jumped in. "Sometimes I think you don't understand anything. Listen, Nissim, you want to leave the army? With my blessings. You want to get your degree? Nothing would make me happier. It will give you more of a future, a profession. But to let you run away from us and from Israel, from *HaAretz*—"

"Wait a minute," Nissim cut off his mother in midsentence.

"Who's running away? I'm just going to America to study. You're talking like I'm going for good."

"Everyone says they're just going for this or that *before* they go," Miryam continued, "then when they get over there they meet someone or find some job and one year runs into the next—until they never move back. How do I know you won't marry an American, maybe a *shiksa,* and she won't want to live here?"

"Miryam, you're getting carried away," Barukh said gently.

"Maybe she won't want to leave *her* family," Miryam went on, paying no attention to her husband. "Anyway Shoshanah will be crushed, or doesn't she know about it yet?"

"Know about what? My wedding or my leaving?" Nissim asked, casting a knowing grin at his father.

"Have you told her you're going yet?" Miryam asked, not sanctioning any interjection of humor.

"No, Ema. I plan to tell her tonight."

"Do you know how crushed she'll be if you leave, too?" Miryam asked, concern cutting deep lines across her forehead. "Wasn't it enough for her to lose Avi?"

Nissim's expression turned stone serious. "It was enough for me to lose Avi," he said.

"And for us," Barukh said quickly, shooting a disapproving look at Miryam across the table. "You know that we want what's best for you, and that we want you to be close by. I think the message is clear enough, Miryam. Now the decision is Nissim's."

For a moment no one said anything. Barukh picked at his slice of cake, Nissim checked his wristwatch, and Miryam stared at the candle flames.

"What will you study?" Miryam asked, breaking the silence. Her tone was much softer now, sounding as if she were trying to numb herself.

"Computers, Ema," Nissim answered. "Everything is computers now."

"And you'll study in English? I don't remember you getting such good grades in that in high school." She spoke in a slow-paced monotone.

"I did well enough."

Miryam's hands, which she held clasped together, closed into one large fist in her lap. She could feel her neck and shoulders tightening. They were beginning to throb. "It's final already. I know it," she said, a distant look in her eye. Then she focused on Barukh's face across the candles. "How long will you be away, Nissim?" she asked.

"Four years, Ema," he answered softly.

The Sabbath candles cast a pale light on the bookcase and on the framed photographs of the family that stood across the top shelf. Miryam imagined the flames were *yarhzeit* lights, memorial flames, and memories of both boys as children flashed across her eyes. Years? She wanted to reach across the table and cup her hands around Barukh's, but he was too far away. Years? Tears welled in her eyes and she was powerless to stop them.

"I know it sounds like a long time," Nissim said, seeing his mother's anguish, "but if they grant me a few advanced credits and I take courses through the summers, I'll finish in three years, same as Yossi. And *he'll* be back already next summer, before you know it."

Miryam hesitated before she spoke, trying to stop herself from responding but unable to keep silent. "Did you hear that Barukh? Same as Yossi. Nissim," she said, looking at her son with an intensity that seemed to push back her tears, "God knows I'll be glad to have Yossi back, but don't go. Please."

Nissim stood up and moved toward Miryam, searching for some way to calm his mother.

"Nissim, Nissim, you're my only child," she sobbed.

Barukh looked at his wife and sat silent, thinking about his dead brother's son.

Four

TRAFFIC HAD BEEN PRETTY STEADY for a Sunday morning, but things were slowing down as noon approached and more hackers got into the curb line at Thirtieth Street Station. A metroliner from New York was due to arrive in ten minutes, and until then there would be few new fares walking out of the terminal. Leaning against the driver's door, Yosef Lvov stood beside his cab and talked to an older cabbie smoking a stogie and dressed in a red Hawaiian shirt and blue leisure slacks.

Pigeons and sparrows flew back and forth across the Philadelphia skyline, some pausing on top of the towering statue of William Penn, others coming to roost in the eaves above the train station's carport. Large concrete columns, thick as Roman pillars and supporting the outdoor roofed expanse, rose to four stories above the idling taxis. Yosef and the fat older man talked, their words echoing over their heads, their voices mixing with the sounds of cars and birds.

"And worse than anniversaries is birthdays, 'specially the women's," the older cabbie said. "Hell, whatever you do you're in trouble. God help you if you forget it and God help you if you remember it different than they wanted. Truth is Joe, I should know, I've had enough experience."

Yosef didn't mind being called Joe, though Jocko was the only person who called him that. Less than a year ago, when they met for the first time, Yosef had explained that Yosef was Hebrew for "Joseph," and Jocko had taken it from there. No one should get used to being called by his given name, Jocko had said, because it left a person open to "taking hisself too serious." That was why his friends called him Jocko. His real name was Ralph, Ralph Giacomelli.

"Fifty-five years," Jocko went on, patting the large, gold belt buckle that seemed to be holding up both his paunch and his pants at the same time. "And look at this, will ya?" He ran his hand over the balding circle at the back of his head. "I'm gonna have to buy me a goddamn beanie." He took a puff of his cheap cigar and blew the smoke in circles toward South Street. "Jesus Christ, Joe! I'm fifty-five and fading. Double nickels."

Yosef was smiling, amused by Jocko's way of expressing himself and confused by Jocko's use of English. "Today my daughter is one nickel," he told Jocko.

"It's Dorit's birthday? Is that Dorito five today? Then what are you doin' here?"

"Same as you. Working." Yosef unbuttoned his red plaid shirt in the unseasonably warm air, baring his "Property of Temple University" T-shirt. His Levis were sticking to his legs and his sneakers were making his feet sweat in the humidity. "Who else is going to pay for the present I bought her?"

"You're right," Jocko said, "and look at me talkin'. I'm standing here shootin' the breeze with you while my wife's in church with her sister cussin' me out for not being next to her. But wives and kids is different, you know? The bigger ones is supposed to understand, and the little ones—heck, ain't she havin' a party?"

"Sure, but not for another hour," Yosef told him.

"Joe! How many times is she gonna be five? What're you doin'? You oughtta be home blowin' balloons. What'd you buy her?"

"It's in my trunk. A very big present." Yosef walked around to open the trunk of his cab and show the huge box to Jocko, but a flow of travellers began pouring out of the station through the metal-framed glass doors.

"Looks like we're off to the races, Joe," Jocko said, moving around to the passenger side of his cab and opening the rear door for a college student. "Hey, have a great party," he called.

"Thanks," Yosef answered as he watched Jocko slide into the driver's seat and slowly pull out of the station. Yosef's cab was next in line.

Maybe he should go home now, he thought, and not worry about ringing up one more fare. Rivka, of course, would be livid at him for not listening to her last night and this morning when she had asked him please not to work today, not even for the half-day which he had said was all he would do. "It's basic math," he had told her, "I've got to put in the hours to take home the money, and the only one paying my downtime is me." Time versus money, he thought to himself now. Everything in his life seemed to come down to that. More of one for less of the other, and he always seemed to be needing more of both.

A heavy set black woman exited the station, lugging a large suitcase and carrying an oversized imitation-leather handbag on one arm. She was dragging and pushing the suitcase, and it was apparent from the look on her face that she was both in a hurry and in need of assistance. Beads of sweat had gathered across her forehead and above her upper lip.

"Excuse me, miss. A taxi?" Yosef asked as he walked over to her.

The woman said yes, releasing her grip on her luggage and letting Yosef take it from her.

"Where to?" He opened the rear door of his cab and waited as she squeezed herself into the back seat.

"Overbrook," she told him, short of breath. "Lancaster Avenue and City Line . . . please."

"No problem," he said, closing the rear door and lifting the lady's large suitcase to carry it back to the trunk. It would take a good half-hour to get to Overbrook with clear sailing, and then it would take at least that long back again to home and Dorit's birthday party. Yosef checked his wristwatch. It was already ten past noon, and the party was called for one o'clock. He thought about handing the lady her luggage and ushering her into the cab behind him, but Yellow Cab Company policy prohibited any driver from turning away a fare, any fare, once he declared himself "on duty." It was too late to back out. Resignedly but quickly he opened the trunk. One glance inside showed him there was no room for her suitcase. A spare tire, two sets of jumper cables, the pneumatic jack, and a metal toolkit took up almost half the trunk; Dorit's birthday present filled the other half. It was a huge rectangular package wrapped with bicentennial paper, liberty bells and American flags all over it. "Dorit will understand," Yosef muttered to himself, forcefully closing the trunk. Moving fast, he carried the suitcase back around to the passenger's side and, explaining to the woman that his trunk was full, lifted the heavy suitcase onto the front seat, leaning it forward against the meter. Then he hurried around to the driver's side, started the motor, and sped out of Thirtieth Street Station.

"What number on Lancaster Avenue?" Yosef asked the woman as he drove down the ramp to the Schuylkill Expressway.

"No number," the woman answered, wiping the sweat from her forehead with a crumpled white Kleenex. "Lankenau Hospital."

"Hospital?" Yosef asked, looking more closely at his passenger in the rear view mirror. "Are you feeling sick?"

"I am," she said, "but it ain't for me. My mother had a heart attack . . . and they called me to her."

"How long ago did they call?"

"This morning. I caught the first train out." She took the Kleenex, which had begun to fall apart from the wetness, and wiped more sweat from under her eyes. "I'm staying here as long as it takes. I just pray the Lord Jesus lets her hold on."

Yosef thought she was wiping away tears. "It will be okay,

miss," he said, pressing his foot down on the throttle. "I will get you there fast. We will make it." He drove silently for a second, then decided that conversation would make the trip pass more quickly. "Does it smell in here to you?" he asked, taking an aerosol can out of the glove compartment.

"Yeah, it does," she told him. "Like fish or something."

He sprayed the citrus-scented air freshener in the cab. "From where did you come?" he asked.

"Newark," she said, pronouncing the name as one syllable. "I been living there since I finished high school. I went to Overbrook. That was some twenty years back already, but Philly's always been home to me." She rolled the wet Kleenex into a ball and stuffed it into the ashtray on her armrest. "Yeah, got married straight out of high school and moved where my husband's family's from. Thought I was moving across the world when I left here. Where *you* from? You don't sound like you're from Philly."

"No, I am not," Yosef said, his eyes smiling into the rear view mirror. It seemed every passenger asked him this question, and he had devised a game to make answering it more interesting. "You guess," he told her.

"I don't want to insult you," she said, "you know, by guessing wrong or something."

"Don't worry, you can't insult me," he assured her. "Guess anywhere. I like all peoples."

"I ain't good with accents," she said, "and I ain't good with guessing. I don't know, somewhere in Europe? You from Italy?"

"No," he said, "I don't talk Italian. Go east."

"East? I ain't much on directions neither. Spain?"

Yosef did not bother to correct her. He had played this game enough times to know that Americans didn't know the geography of their own country, let alone of the rest of the world. "No. Go south," he told her.

"Mexico?"

"No. Go *way* east."

"Let me look at you better," she said, leaning forward, an intent look in her eyes. "You from Egypt?"

"Close," he said, smiling. Everyone in America seemed to take him for any nationality but his own, seemed to take him for everything but what he was. "Go north."

"I ain't gonna guess it," the woman said. "Just go ahead and tell me."

"Israel," Yosef said proudly.

"Oh," she said, "I should have knowed from the star."

Yosef fingered the Star of David on the gold chain around his neck, then looked back at the woman in the mirror. "Why from this?" he asked. "Are all blacks living in Africa?"

"What's that supposed to mean?" the lady asked, a sudden edge of sharpness in her voice.

"Miss, calm down," he said evenly, turning his head around and looking at her while driving. "This star is only Jewish, and not all the Jews are living in Israel; that's what I am saying."

"I know that," the woman said, still sounding ruffled but calming down. She reached into her handbag and pulled out another Kleenex. "How long you been over here?"

"Two years," Yosef answered.

"What did you come here for?" the woman asked, raising her voice, not realizing until she heard her words that he might misinterpret her meaning and take offense. Her tone became friendly. "What brought you over here?"

"I came to study at Temple," he answered. "I drive this cab at night to pay my bills and on weekends. The rest of the time I am going to classes and studying."

"Don't they have universities over there?" she asked.

"Sure, miss," he told her, "but here they also have a special program for my daughter."

"You got a child? How old is she?"

"Five. And today is her birthday."

"Happy birthday to her. I can't hardly remember when mine was that little, but all I know is it don't last long. You carry a picture?"

Yosef flipped down the visor and removed a laminated photograph from the pocket on the visor's underside. It showed Dorit standing with Rivka on the balcony of their Spring Glen apartment. Dorit was still small for her age, both in height and in weight, and standing next to Rivka who was kneeling, her slightness seemed even more striking. Dorit had been a preemie, born two full months before term, and she had spent ten weeks in an incubator in the neonatal intensive care nursery at Haifa's Rambam Hospital before Rivka and Yosef had been allowed to take her home. For the first year of her life there had been grave concerns about her health and about her mental abilities. The doctors had spoken to Yosef and Rivka about developmental delays and how the growth of Dorit's mental capacities depended largely on the amount of stimulation which they could give her. Only time would tell, the doctors had told them, but that would mean *their* time, their involvement.

Rivka had been told of special methods for infant stimulation which were being explored and applied throughout the world, and she had discovered that an especially intensive new method was being used in Philadelphia. The method entailed a full-day partnership between parent and child with a strictly prescribed program of physical and intellectual stimulation exercises. She had convinced Yosef that this special program was critical for Dorit, that "a few short years there might make the difference between her living or not living a normal life." America knows more, she had thought. America has more and can do more. America has the answers to questions Israel hasn't even asked yet. Rivka would be Dorit's parent-partner. She had promised not to complicate things by trying to study or by trying to find even a part-time job. Yosef would be free to finish his Bachelor's degree, to pick up where he had left off before the 1967 War. He could study at a university in Philadelphia, full-time if he could handle it, and he could work at whatever job he wanted so the rent and other bills could be covered.

Yosef had agreed with Rivka's reasoning and almost immediately had served notice to Sharp Ltd., resigning from his job as district salesman. Rivka and he had come to America for Dorit's sake, for her future. They had relocated halfway around the world for the special care that America offered. Yosef had changed his life for her, had changed his own life in hopes of improving hers, and looking through the clear plastic at her smile in the snapshot on his visor, he had no regrets about coming, at least not where she was concerned. Her progress had been amazing, and today she was five years old.

Yosef studied the photograph, then handed it back over the seat to the woman.

"Strange for a man built big as you to have such a small built child. But she's a cute one. My oldest boy was the littlest one in his grade till he hit twelve, then he sprouted up like they do, you know, and now he's 'bout tall as you." She paused a moment, wiping her face with the tissue again and looking at her wristwatch. "Did my mother take a shine to that boy! Always been her favorite." She handed the photograph across the front seat to Yosef, a sad look in her eye. "You have other family here?"

"No," he said, thinking about how Miryam and Barukh had "taken a shine" to Dorit, thinking of yesterday's phone call from Israel when they had sung her "Happy Birthday" three different times. He had lost count of the number of times Miryam had said "we miss you." "My only family's there," he told her.

"Must be lonely," the woman said. "I know *my* mother couldn't take it. She 'bout had an attack back when I moved to Newark.

Lord forgive me, but I ain't so sure it didn't bring *this* one to her. It don't make no matter if it's Newark or L.A. or anywhere if it ain't Philadelphia. All she knows is we ain't together and I ain't next door." She paused, took a deep heaving breath, and cast a worried stare out the window. "That woman best be battlin'."

Yosef and the woman drove without talking, just watching the scenery for a while as the cab sped along the expressway. The pop songs on the radio, with their thrusting beats, were background music for the varsity crews racing in their sculls down the peaceful river, their multiple oars swinging back and forth in graceful pendular rhythms.

"What about those Flyers?" Yosef asked, breaking the silence. "Do you think they will win the playoffs?"

"I ain't much on hockey, but my husband loves to watch them boys fight," the woman answered. "He says they're gonna win it again, just like last year, and more people are gonna run out into the streets than the first time. Last year they had two million people partyin' all night in this city."

"I remember," Yosef said. "I was driving through it. But many streets were blocked with people so I parked my cab and joined them. It was really something! But if they win the Stanley Cup again, I will stay at home."

"They have hockey over in Israel?" she asked.

"No," he said, almost laughing. "In the whole country we don't have even any ice."

"No ice?"

"I don't mean for sodas," he explained, still smiling. "I mean we have no ice skating."

"Oh, I get you," the woman said. "Do you plan to go back there, or you gonna stay here?"

"I am going back next summer," Yosef told her, slipping the photograph back into the visor pocket, "after I finish my degree."

"To visit, or you moving back?"

"Moving back," he told her.

The WFIL disc jockey was playing the Sunday countdown of top forty singles and had finally reached the number one song. It was Elton John's "Philadelphia Freedom." Yosef had heard the record at least a hundred times since the pop music stations played it every hour, but he still couldn't catch all the words. Maybe it was the singing style, maybe it was just the English. *"I used to be a rolling stone, you know, if the cause was right. I'd leave to find the answer on the road . . . ."* Yosef was tired of everything being a conscious effort for him where language was concerned. It was a constant drain on his energy. Even talking to this woman was a task, having to concentrate at the same time on understanding what she was saying and on "where she was coming from," as the Americans said, and on not asking stupid questions or giving stupid answers, while sounding natural and relaxed.

"Do you miss it?" the lady asked, still staring out the window as she spoke.

"Israel? Sure," Yosef answered. "Of course." He missed home, Haifa, things familiar. He missed being able to drive past billboards and scan them in a glance or to understand the lyrics of songs he half-listened to on the radio. He missed the kiosks plastered with Hebrew handbills and piled high with Hebrew newspapers. But he missed more than just the language.

"You come from a city?" the lady asked.

"Yes," Yosef answered, "Haifa." He pronounced the *H* as though he were clearing phlegm from his throat. "In some ways it's like Philadelphia." He saw similarities between the two cities. Both were major cities relative to the other cities in their countries. Both were known for their shipping ports, and both had a slower pace of life than you found in the largest, most important cities in both countries. Tel Aviv was like New York, he thought,

Jerusalem was like Washington, D.C., and he was in Philadelphia, near the center of things, but not *in* it. I live in the Haifa of America, he told himself.

"All I ever hear 'bout Israel, except what I hear from my preacher, is 'bout bombs and people dyin'. Don't take me wrong now, but it don't sound like someplace *I'd* want to be stayin'."

"From here everything looks different," Yosef said, noting the sign to City Line Avenue and pulling into the exit lane of the expressway. "They show on the news here only blood and funerals. But that's what they show for every place. Even for Philadelphia. On the TV every night it looks like there is war in America. In Israel we think everyone is going with guns in the street here. It's not like that at all when you're here, and the same is for Israel." Tomorrow was *Yom HaAtzma'ut,* Independence Day, and he wanted to describe the celebration that would take place back home, but it seemed too difficult to do in English. "In Israel it is very beautiful, I think," he went on, "and it is different there from here." He pictured the crowded streets, the accordionists hugging and squeezing their instruments, circles of people beginning to form, holding hands and spinning to the music, colored lights swaying on wires overhead, children running through the throng and banging unsuspecting adults with plastic hammers that beeped with each bopping. There would be the midnight campfires on Carmel Beach after the louder formal partying ended in downtown Haifa. He thought back to two years ago, to May before the Yom Kippur War, the last Independence Day for which he'd been home, and he realized the pain of not being there this year was even stronger than last year. "In Haifa we have the mountain and the sea," he went on. "It is very peaceful, with many beaches, and with not so many tall buildings. People there care about each other, you know? Everybody knows everybody. Here I think people don't care so much."

"That's a fact!" the black woman agreed loudly. "Here you got your family if you're lucky, and that's it. Everyone else'd as soon watch you fall without so much as blinkin'. But that's just the way life is in the city." She looked down at her watch, then lifted her eyes. "What time's your watch say?"

Yosef glanced at the Marriott Hotel as he sped past it on City Line Avenue, then checked his watch. "Twenty-five after. We'll be there in fifteen minutes."

The woman checked her watch again and played with the winding mechanism to no particular purpose. "The Lord didn't make no tougher woman," she said, speaking out the window. She ran five spread fingers straight back through her hair. "They put her in one of those special units, with special rules on visiting."

"Don't worry," Yosef said, "the rules don't go for family. They'll let you right in."

"Damn straight they will! Or I'll show them not to mess with my mama's daughter," the woman said, becoming combative even at the thought. She reached down into her large handbag and took out a wallet, which she unsnapped and folded open. On one side of the middle section were clear plastic holders filled with her driver's license, some credit cards, and some photographs. She sat still a moment, staring at her mother in a full-family picture. "Mama, don't be quittin' on us, hear?" she said softly, not lifting her eyes.

The yellow cab raced down City Line, Yosef speeding through traffic lights even after the signal turned yellow. Finally they reached the intersection of Lancaster Avenue in Overbrook. Hardly slowing to turn into the Lankenau Hospital entrance, Yosef pulled up to the main door and lowered the meter arm to stop the clicking numbers. The meter registered $6.80. It was twenty minutes to one. The woman reached into her handbag, pulled out seven dollar bills, and handed them to Yosef.

A twenty cent tip? Yosef thought. After that long a ride and making that good time? For twenty cents I'm late to my daughter's birthday? But maybe she can't afford any more than that. He decided not to make an issue over it.

"It says six-eighty," the woman said, holding an open palm across the seat. "I gave you seven."

Yosef could not believe his ears. In disgust he handed her two dimes, then jumped out of the cab and walked quickly around to the curb side to lift the heavy suitcase out of the front seat and onto the sidewalk. The lady was in a terrible hurry, and so was he. As he opened the front door on the passenger's side, the woman opened the back door and began with obvious effort to wriggle her large body out. Slowly she wedged herself through the doorspace and stepped one foot onto the sidewalk. She tried to take a step, but the heel of her shoe caught on the curb. She crashed onto the pavement, her kneecap absorbing the full brunt of the fall. She was writhing on the ground, crying out in pain. "Gotta see my mama, gotta see my mama," she moaned.

Yosef rushed to her, bent over her, and used all his strength to lift her up, propping her against the side of the cab. "I'll get you to your mother," he told her. "It will be okay." He stopped a gentleman in his fifties who was walking out of the hospital's main entrance and asked him to please stay with the injured woman while he went for assistance.

Less than a minute later, Yosef came running out through the hospital's doors, pushing a vinyl wheelchair. The woman was still leaning against the cab, looking as though she might collapse any second, and she was alone. "Bastard!" Yosef muttered to himself, realizing what had happened. "What kind of man would leave an injured woman?" Quickly, but with great care, he eased the woman into the wheelchair and, carrying both her suitcase and her large handbag in one hand, pushed her inside the hospital. "We'll get to your mother in a minute," he told her, wheeling her through the wide white corridors to the Emergency Admissions desk.

There a nurse asked the woman for her medical insurance information and wrote down a description of how the injury happened. Yosef waited with the woman while all the forms were filled out and the information was processed. Finally a doctor came and asked one of the orderlies to wheel the woman back for X-rays.

"We'll take care of her from here," the nurse said kindly to Yosef.

"You are sure you don't need anything else from me?" he asked.

"No, you can go," she said.

"She has to see her mother," he told the nurse. "She is in your hospital with a heart attack. She doesn't want to wait."

"Yes, I know. We'll take care of that, don't worry."

"Here is her suitcase and her bag," he said, sliding them both around the Admissions desk. Then he turned and strode out of the room, walking back quickly through the corridors, listening to his footsteps echo off the sterile floors.

IT WAS ALREADY ONE-THIRTY when he reached the merge onto Wissahickon Drive. He would be later getting home than he had thought. Rivka would be livid when he walked in and Dorit, though distracted by her friends and her presents, would probably be just as angry. Worse, she would be disappointed in him. Thank God for the big wrapped box in the trunk.

Wissahickon Drive with its snaking turns, narrow lanes, and lack of shoulders was a driving challenge to Yosef. Staying within the tight white lines was difficult for a car as large as his. This cab's more a tank than a car, he thought. Even travelling at the twenty-five miles per hour speed limit it was difficult, but Yosef now was taking the curves at forty, and his cab was shifting dangerously between the two lanes. The scenery on both sides of the Drive was distinctive. Only inches removed from the right-hand lane was a solid strip of mountain that walled in the roadway for most of its length, and on the left side was Wissahickon Creek, as tranquil and idyllic as a nature preserve. Yosef navigated the twisting bends one after the other and, looking at the mountain through the passenger window, he thought of Mount Carmel and of Haifa. Compared to Mount Carmel this mountain was more like a hill. It was smaller than that even, certainly a poor excuse for a mountain. Poor excuse. He heard the phrase repeat in his mind, and he was no longer thinking of the mountain or whatever the wall of rock was through his window. He was thinking of his daughter's party, of being late again, of disappointing her, and of his poor excuse. What could he tell Dorit? So what if he had taken a woman to a hospital? He shouldn't have given the complication a chance to happen. He was thinking of himself in the fall of 1973, several months after Rivka, Dorit, and he had arrived in Philadelphia. He had been in America when the war broke out, but it had been a poor excuse.

On Saturday, October 7, Yom Kippur Day, 1973, the three of them had awakened early in their Spring Glen apartment, and Yosef had turned on KYW, the all-news station, as he did first thing every morning. They were planning to go to Congregation Adath Tikvah for services, but when they heard the newscast's lead story all their plans changed.

"In today's top story: War in the Middle East."

The heaviest and most severe fighting since the 1967 War broke out this morning along Israel's front lines with Egypt along the Suez Canal and with Syria in the Golan Heights on Yom Kippur, the holiest day in the Jewish calendar. Israel acknowledges that Egyptian forces have established posi-

tions in the Israeli-occupied Sinai Peninsula. Cairo
radio says Egyptian forces shot down eleven Israeli
planes and sank four Israeli naval vessels. Golda
Meir in an impassioned speech to the nation called
the attack an "act of madness." Defense Minister
Moshe Dayan described the fighting as "all out war."

Their world had spun upside down and stopped.

"I have to go back," Yosef had said to Rivka that morning,
"I have to be there." She understood, protesting only that she and
Dorit should go with him. It would take only one or two days to
pack up. They would leave and go back for good. But after an
hour of practical talking about lost tuition and Dorit's needs and
cancelling leases and losing security deposits and the reasons they
had come to America in the first place, he and Rivka had realized that he should return by himself. Israel would need every
soldier and even if the war should end abruptly like the last one,
he would be there. After serving, he would come back to the
States, back home to his wife and daughter, wherever "home" was
for now.

Instead of going to the synagogue, they had stayed by the
phone all that day, trying to place an overseas call to Barukh and
Miryam for a full report on what was happening. All of the international phone circuits to Israel had been busy and, frustrated
at not being able to get through, Yosef had repeatedly dialed the
number of the Israel Consulate in Philadelphia to tell the consul
that he wanted to return immediately to fight in the war. That line
was busy, too. Finally that night they got through to Haifa and
Barukh told them that Nissim had left for the Sinai. Barukh and
Miryam had not heard from Nissim yet, of course, and were worried about him beyond words. Yosef told them that he would be
flying back as soon as the Consulate in Philadelphia gave him
his orders. He expected their call momentarily. Miryam had said

that Rivka and Dorit needed him also and that he shouldn't rush back before the smoke of the first few battles had cleared. If this was the same as in '67, it could be over before he stepped down off the plane, she said.

After hanging up with Miryam, Yosef had dialed the Consulate again, not caring how late the hour was, and this time the line had not been busy. The woman who answered told him that only "essential personnel" were being called up at the moment and that, since his most recent Reserve duty had been in Communications, he was not in this first group. She would not accept his protests about being "essential" or about his having served as a driver in the war before this one. "We'll call you as things develop" was how she had ended the conversation. He had continued calling daily, abandoning his studies, his meals, his sleep. For whole days he sat at home with the television and radio turned on, waiting to follow the latest bulletin about the war, cradling the phone. Days passed, weeks, but no one called. Then one day he realized that he had missed the war.

Some days he felt guilty for being alive. Some days he thought it would have been better if he had just paid his own way back, that it would have been better if he'd taken the savings he didn't have or else borrowed the money to buy the plane ticket. Hell, it was only one way for one. *Tzahal,* he knew, would have covered his return passage after the war. At least he would have been there. At least he would have done something decisive, taken some definite action instead of just sitting in Philadelphia and waiting for the phone to ring. At least in dying he would have felt blameless. Nissim had earned the right to keep living by fighting, by laying his life on the line in the Sinai, he thought. All of Yosef's friends had seen action in the war. Some had lost limbs and eyes and friends, some had lost their lives. He had not written to any of them, or their families. How could he? What could he say to them? Would they have let him explain his absence? Would they have believed him? Which friend's mother would accept his condolences and believe that he had cried as long and as bitterly as she had? He just could not face the parents who had been like parents to him and who had buried their sons in his absence. It was hard enough facing himself. At times he wished he were buried beside them or, better, in their places.

Rivka could testify to that. Living with him for the past year and a half had been no party. In his remorse he had punished her for his own disappointment with himself, and he kept punishing her in ways he had come to recognize but still could not control. Little ways, like asking her why she wore her hair in a particular style, joking about her weight, questioning the way she dressed when they went out together. He seemed to always keep her waiting, unintentionally but predictably. By now it had become a pattern. The only question in Rivka's mind was whether he would be there at all. But Yosef kept on killing himself, like to-day, racing desperately against time, trying to turn it back if necessary or at least to hold it still, so that he might arrive home on time for a change. Did Rivka understand all this? Did she know how guilty he felt for treating her so unfairly, so uncaringly? She had gambled on him, had linked her hopes to his dreams, and look at the return she had gotten. Look at the ride he had given her. She was suffering for his shortcomings, his own miscalculations. She deserved worlds better than this, worlds better than the ones he had shown her so far. He loved her and, more, he respected her. He hated himself for making her the victim of his anguish. But this state, he told himself, was just temporary. Beginning to-day he would change it, beginning with Dorit's party.

He braked for the red light at the end of Wissahickon Drive, then pressed down the gas and picked up speed as soon as the signal turned green. Soon he was driving through Germantown and was only minutes from home. He glanced at his wristwatch and pressed down the throttle. The time was a quarter to two.

"Forty-five minutes late," he said out loud, "God damn you, Yossi!"

"HAPPY BIRTHDAY!" Yosef belted out as he walked through the door, cradling a huge patriotically wrapped box in his arms. "Isn't anyone going to help me with this monster?" He flashed a winning smile at Dorit and made a straight path into the living room.

Dorit was sitting on the living room carpet in the middle of a small circle of ten five-year-old friends. All but three were classmates of hers in her special-needs nursery program. Two were playmates from the neighborhood, and one, Orly Hazon, was the daughter of Oded and Varda Hazon, an Israeli couple in their early thirties whom Yosef and Rivka had befriended during the past year in Philadelphia. Across the room Oded and Varda sat on the sofa with Rivka, watching the children enjoy the party. Both Oded and Varda were heavy smokers. The ashtray on the glass-topped coffee table in front of them was filled with ashes and Marlboro butts, and the room was filled with smoke. In the center of the circle on the carpet, next to where Dorit was sitting, were two piles, one of torn and crumpled pieces of colorful wrapping paper, the other of boxed gifts the paper had covered. Dorit turned to see her father, shooting him a look that was both sad and angry. "Where were you, Abba?" she asked him.

He stopped before reaching the circle of children, put down the large box, and lifted his hands in apology. "Traffic, like always," he told her, not wanting to explain about the woman and the hospital, "but I'm here." Then he lifted the giant box again and carried it over to her. "This is for you, from your mother and me," he said gently, leaning down and kissing her on the top of her head. "Happy birthday, sweetie." Looking at the two piles inside the circle he realized that all the other presents had already been opened. "You can save this one to open later," he told Dorit, winking at her as if to say he knew a secret reason why waiting would be better. "Why don't you play with these and share them with your friends. Then we'll open this one, last." He gave the same wink again.

"Okay," Dorit said, winking back at her father and smiling at him. Then she turned to her circle of friends, telling them they could help her break in her new toys. Instantly they descended upon the pile, each child trying to be first and all of the children shouting at once, "Can I play with this one, *please?*" Somehow the bedlam sorted itself out and the children began playing civilly together.

Yosef walked over to join the adults. "Shalom," he said to Oded and Varda. "They all seem happy. Thanks for helping hold down the fort." Then he turned to Rivka, who was glowering at him. "I know you're mad; sorry I'm late," he whispered to her, leaning over and putting an arm around her shoulders, "but wait'll you see our present." He flashed her an innocent smile, then turned again to watch Dorit playing.

"*Your* present," Rivka whispered back sharply. He had told her nothing about this gift. She had also bought Dorit a present and was planning to give it to her as a surprise immediately after the party. Maybe she would give Dorit her gift when she opened Yosef's. "They finished with the cake and candles fifteen minutes-ago," she went on, "and I took some pictures for Barukh and Miryam so that they and *everyone else who couldn't be here* could see what her party looked like." Rivka stripped his arm from her shoulder and rose to walk into the kitchen. "I've still got work to do. Excuse me. At least for *her* you could've been here."

"I *am* here," he said, raising his voice to a loud whisper. "Look, if I wasn't out there driving that cab, you wouldn't have the money to pay for this party. There wouldn't be any party." He sat down in the leather lounge chair near the sofa.

"People make parties, Yossi," Rivka shot back, still glowering at him and no longer worrying about whispering. "Family makes parties. Money doesn't." She excused herself to Oded and Varda and walked out toward the kitchen.

Yosef watched Rivka leave, and as she reached the entrance hall his eye continued past her into the dining room, where the cake and ice cream portion of the party had been held. The room was plastered with birthday decorations. The blue and white crepe paper streamers that crisscrossed the room joined the blue Stars of David and the little plastic Israeli flags to celebrate Israel's impending birthday. Dorit had picked out the Sesame Street paper plates and matching cups, featuring Cookie Monster and now puddled with melted portions of ice cream slices and spotted with sticky fingerprints. At one end of the room was a big poster Rivka had drawn in different colored markers. It read "HAPPY BIRTHDAY DORIT" in English; at the other end was a matching poster that said the same thing in Hebrew.

Turning to Oded and Varda, he stuck out his chin and leaned toward them. "Take a shot," he said, "it's open season on Abba."

"Calm down, Yossi. Varda never hits men with beards," Oded said, "which is why I'm thinking of growing one." One of eight sabra children in a family from Morocco, Oded was dark-complected, of medium height and build. His face was distinct for its small eyes and for the large space between his two front teeth. "At least you're here in one piece. If it was anyone else, we'd have started to worry."

"Thanks, *habibi,*" Yosef said.

"I thought you could only work twenty hours a week on a student visa," Varda joined in. "Rivka says you drove until two this morning and went back out again before eight." In striking contrast to her husband, Varda was fair-skinned and several inches taller. Her long blonde hair made her look more Scandinavian than Israeli, and most people were surprised to find out she was born and raised in Tel Aviv. "You must put in your twenty hours

76

each week by the end of the first day," she said.

"And so does everyone else," Yosef told her. "Figure it this way, Varda. I pay Yellow Cab for my insurance sticker every week to keep driving—and they take their money 'cash' or they don't give it to me—then I have to pay for gas and oil, whatever I use, so if I'm going to pick up enough fares to make back what it costs me, I have to put in the hours. It's illegal for me to drive more than ten hours a day, but everyone I know is a criminal then, driving at least twelve, sometimes fourteen, sixteen straight. Forget about the student visa and the twenty hours. It's the only way to make enough money to make it worthwhile."

"Make what worthwhile?" Varda asked. "How long can you keep it up, Yossi?"

"As long as I have to. It's not like I really have any choice. Look, back home if I was going to school, I'd be doing just about the same thing as here—working a six-day week, going to classes and writing papers, and on top of it all I'd be disappearing for six weeks of *milu'im,* reserve duty in *Tzahal,* every year. So the way I look at it, my deal here's not so bad. Not bad at all. Here I disappear, but only one day at a time."

"I don't know," Oded said pensively. "I think it's a curse we came with. We finally have a real weekend here, two days to sit back and just enjoy, but something inside won't let us. And what you just said proves my point. You're not working six days, Yossi, you're working seven. Why?"

"The seventh for me is like paying my dues," Yosef explained with a smile. "Every few months I count up those extra days and that's my *milu'im* while I'm here in America."

"*Milu'im* for whom?" Varda asked. "*Tzahal'*s not sending you 'call up' slips, are they? Who are you paying your dues to?"

"So far," he paused and started to laugh, "I'm paying them to Gimbels and Sears and Pathmark and Kiddie City." He paused again, looking at Oded. "And Yankee Doodle. How's business?"

"Not bad, not bad," Oded told him. Oded, who had finished his B.A. in psychology at Temple University last year, worked as a baker and counterman at Yankee Doodle Donuts across from the Ogontz Shopping Center. The store sold thirty-six varieties of donuts, baked fresh in continuous rotation on the premises every day. It was an all-day and all-night proposition, and the pay was only a few cents above the minimum wage, but Oded had found that he needed a graduate degree to qualify for any full-time position in psychology or the social services. "It's nothing to write home about," Oded went on, "but I still say someone could make a fortune by opening one of these stores in Tel Aviv or Jerusalem. Look at how many donuts people buy there every year just on Chanukah, and those are just jelly, only one flavor."

"Talk your boss into setting one up and sending you back to manage it," Yosef suggested.

"He doesn't think past the next batch of donuts. Maybe I'll do it myself," Oded told him. "Maybe you have a spare hundred thousand you could lend me?"

"No problem," Yosef said with a smile. "I'll just drive a few more Sundays."

"I wouldn't do it, Oded," Rivka said, walking back into the room carrying a tray of ceramic mugs filled with coffee. "That's the problem with America: too many choices. We don't need that back home." She set the tray down on the coffee table and placed a mug in front of each person. "I made them all with sugar and milk. I didn't want to give you too many choices."

No one voiced any complaint as the four of them sipped their hot coffee and watched the children.

"You're still working there every day, aren't you, Oded?" Yosef asked.

"Not anymore he's not," Varda answered for him. "He had to choose between keeping his job and keeping me." She cast a knowing glance up at Rivka, whose eyes met hers then looked away.

"And she would have gone, too." Oded said.

"I sure would have," she told both men, throwing her long blonde hair back, then leaning forward and flicking some ashes from her cigarette into the ceramic ashtray on the coffee table.

"Anyway, I kept them both," Oded continued. "I told my boss I'd work six days, take it or leave it. No way I was going to waste *every* day shooting dough full of colored creme. So now I don't work Sundays. *She* does. And we don't see any more of each other than we did before."

Varda shot a severe look at Oded. "I don't come home past midnight," she said.

"You're right," Oded said. "Just joking."

"How's the teaching going?" Rivka asked, taking a seat on the sofa.

"Other than the fact it makes me crazy, it's going fine," Varda told her. She taught Hebrew in the Sunday school at Congregation Adath Tikvah, a large synagogue in Elkins Park. "Like today. This morning was the *Yom HaAtzma'ut* party for all the children in the school. They played records, sang a few songs, had felafel. But what's the point? The felafel was cold, the pita was stale, and all of the kids made faces and spit it out into their napkins. Let me tell you, if it tasted like that at Melekh HaFelafel no one would eat it either. I don't know if any of the children really care about Israel, or if they even got a good feeling about it today. All I know is they don't want to learn Hebrew and they especially don't want to be going to synagogue on Sunday morning. They'd rather be walking through Cedarbrook Mall, spending their parents' money on makeup and Elton John albums."

"Kids here are so spoiled," Rivka said, looking across the room at the circle of children. "Just look at the presents in that pile. It's nice that everyone's so generous, but I've walked up and down the aisles at Kiddie City enough times to know that these presents cost a lot of money. I mean, we're talking about a five-year-old's birthday party here, not a bridal shower. She'll use them all, sure, but who in the world said she *needs* them?"

"What are you scared of, Rivka?" Oded asked. "That she'll enjoy them?"

"No," Rivka answered, "that she'll *enjoy* them and *think* she needs them."

"I don't know," Varda said, "I'm no psychologist like Oded, but I think American kids aren't as spoiled as Israeli kids are. I mean, American kids are spoiled all right, but back home we spoil them more."

"What're you talking about, Varda?" Rivka said. "Have you been walking around with your eyes taped shut or something for the past five years? Someone could really begin to wonder if you ever lived here."

"You can disagree with me if you want to, but I think it's true," Varda told her. "We're talking about kids, remember. Adults might be a different story but we're talking about kids, and I think kids get their own way more in Israel than they do here. When you were little didn't your family say, 'If she wants it, what's it going to hurt her, if she's asking already, give it to her?' My parents were always telling me you're only young once and even then for too short a time. People here talk about what they want to do when they retire; they map out their lives in five-year plans. No one in Israel talks that way. No one in Israel *thinks* that way. And they don't because no one knows how long they're going to be alive after they start in *Tzahal.* Here they tell the children to wait until college for this and until you're married for that, but back home everything's 'for now.' 'Do it now before it's too late,' 'spend your money today because it will be worth less tomorrow,' 'give the children whatever they want because who knows how long they'll be here.'" Varda let the gist of her theory register as she took a deep draw of her cigarette and, blowing the smoke out slowly, flicked more ashes into the ashtray. "Am I wrong?" she asked. "Am I, Oded?"

"No, when you lay it out that way," he began answering, "then I'd say—"

"Abba, Abba," Dorit interrupted, coming over to the leather lounge chair and pushing a toy in front of Yosef's face, "this one's broken. It's broken!"

"Wait a minute, sweetie," Yosef said calmly. "Let me take a look at it and see if I can't fix it for you. Stand right here and we'll check it out."

Dorit leaned against the arm of the chair and watched intently as her father inspected her new toy. It was a plastic doll, a model of the Six Million Dollar Man, the bionic hero of a popular American TV show. The doll was supposed to walk on its own power.

"I saw it in the commercial, Abba. It's broken. Can you fix it?" Dorit asked.

"I haven't done anything yet," he told his daughter. Turning the doll onto its stomach, he lifted up its little shirt and found a removable square of plastic covering a hole in the doll's back. He unsnapped the piece of plastic. The battery compartment was empty. "Okay, sweetie." he told her. "We found the problem. All he needs is batteries."

"Thank you, Abba!" she said with exuberance and, leaning over the arm of the chair, gave him a kiss on his shoulder. "Put them in for me now, okay?"

"I will right away, if we have any."

Rivka had been watching this interplay, a look of dismay and disapproval on her face. "Whatever happened to toys that only needed children?" she said. "Whatever happened to toys that ran on imagination? All those empty boxes, all those new toys, and nothing the children can play with. Everything's become so sophisticated that all kids can do is plug in their dolls and watch them. It's ridiculous already."

"Do we have any, Ema?" Dorit asked. "Do we?"

"I don't think so, honey," Rivka told her gently, then turned to Yosef. "Unless Abba keeps some in his cab."

"Do you, Abba?"

"No, sweetie, I'm afraid I don't but we can get some later, okay?" Yosef lifted her up over the armrest and onto his lap. "Okay?"

"But Abba," she whined, "I want to play with it *now.*"

"I know you do, but it runs on batteries," he told her.

"Just like your Abba does," Oded said with a grin to Dorit. "Isn't that what you run on, Yossi?"

Yosef smiled back at his friend. "Wish I did," he said. "I could use some new ones." Then he gave his attention back to Dorit. "You know what? I've got a great idea. What do you say we go open that present?"

"Yours, Abba? The big one?"

"The big one," he said, lifting her off his lap and standing her on the floor. "Take this six million dollar doll of yours and let's do some serious paper ripping."

As Dorit and Yosef walked back to the circle of children, Rivka sat with Oded and Varda. "Next year her birthday will be at *home,*" she told them. "I don't care if they have to mail Yossi's diploma to Haifa. We're going to be on the first plane out on the day he hands in his last paper."

"What's your rush?" Varda asked.

"I don't know if it's getting out of here so much as getting back there," she answered. "I look at Dorit and how she's developed and I say to myself it's been worth it, but then I look at Yossi and me and—" She stopped herself and switched gears in midsentence. "Excuse me, I've got to run upstairs for something." Quickly she rose from the sofa, left the room, and hurried up the staircase.

"Go ahead, open it, open it," Dorit's friends said, their expressions excited, expectant, ready to be surprised. Dorit hesitated before tearing the wrapping paper. The box was almost as big as she was, and for a moment the size of it scared her. "What is it, Abba?" she asked her father.

"You'll see," Yosef told her, "when you open it up."

"Okay, Abba," Dorit said, taking a deep breath to get ready. She looked across the room at the Hazons, then saw her mother come back downstairs and stand in the archway between the entrance hall and the living room. "Ema, look!" she said. "I'm going to open it."

Rivka was holding one hand behind her back and the present she had bought Dorit was in it, but everyone's eyes were focused on Dorit's smile and on the big box with flags and cracked bells on its gift-wrap.

Dorit began tearing the wrapping paper and kept tearing until she removed every piece. The gift was not packed in a box so the glass panels, the clear plastic tubing, the green and brown plastic toy mountains, and the clear bags of colored gravel were visible as soon as she opened it. Yosef watched her face, waiting for her reaction, but instead of her smile brightening, it faded into puzzlement and disappointment.

"What is it?" she asked, wanting to get excited but unable to.

"It's an aquarium," Yosef explained to her. "It's a giant fishbowl, and you can put a *whole* lot of fish in it, as many as you want, and no more of those cheap goldfish. We'll get special fish with blue tails and stripes and some that even glow in the dark. All right?"

"Wow!" one of the children shouted, "My cousin has one of them."

"I saw that at my doctor's," said another, "Wow!"

But Dorit was looking sadly up at her father. "Where are the fish?" she asked.

Yosef knelt down beside her, hugged her with one arm, and said, "We'll go to the pet shop this afternoon, sweetie, and pick out all you want."

This brought a wide smile to Dorit's face, and Oded and Varda smiled to watch her. But Rivka, looking on from the entrance hall, did not smile. She watched Yosef and Dorit continue talking, and her expression became an accusing glare. Extremes is all he knows, she told herself, everything or nothing. And not only didn't he tell me about it, but where did he get the money to buy it? Her eye moved across the living room and through the open louvered doors into the den where birthday cards stood on the mantelpiece above the fireplace. There was one from Barukh and Miryam, one from Nissim, and even one from Shoshanah who had always acted like an aunt to Dorit. The needlepoint of Haifa she had sent was already hanging over Dorit's bed. Each card was brightly colored and had the same message, written in Hebrew on the inside – "Dear Dorit: Whenever Israel has her birthday we think of you, and whenever we think of you we think of Israel. Happy *Yom HaAtzma'ut* and Happy Birthday, honey!" Rivka's eye swept across the bright cards and slowly returned to the living room.

To her the scene in front of her, with Yosef and Dorit and the empty aquarium, was pathetic, even more pathetic than a doll with no batteries. "*Our* present," she muttered to herself, still holding one hand behind her back and starting down the hallway toward the powder room at the far end.

Once inside the bathroom she closed the door and held in front of her what she had been hiding behind her back. It was a small clear plastic bag, tied in a knot so that the water it held could not spill out, and there was a goldfish swimming inside it, "a cheap goldfish." Rivka had bought it at the pet shop yesterday to replace the one Dorit had lost to this move, the one Yosef had not brought home from Spring Glen. This one would live in the other's bowl, she thought. "But an aquarium!" she muttered to herself. "All or nothing. How can he be so damn stupid?" Rivka could feel her body quivering, and she wiped the tears that had started to run down the sides of her face.

Through the door she could hear the children's voices growing louder. Rivka stood at the sink and looked at herself in the mirror. The touch of mascara she had put on this morning had smeared a bit under her eyes and a few strands of hair had fallen down across her forehead. She swept the hair back and studied herself in the mirror. What are we doing here? she asked herself. Slowly she lifted the toilet seat, held the plastic bag over the bowl, and tore the seal just below the knot. Then she poured the new goldfish into the toilet. "Happy birthday, Dorit," she whispered.

"Rivka," she heard Yosef calling to her, "Rivka, what should the kids do next?"

Tears were rising inside her again. "I'll be right there," she called through the door. "I'll be right there." Then she flushed the fish down.

BOOK TWO
Arrivals

"They were ashamed because they had had expectations."

JOB 6:20

Five

NISSIM LVOV STOOD UNDER THE METAL COVER outside the El Al terminal in the late afternoon storm, three large suitcases and a green duffel bag beside him. Where was his brother? he wondered. Nissim's flight had touched down on schedule, almost two hours ago.

Since landing, Nissim had waited in long lines to clear passport control, claim his bags, and take them through the U.S. Customs checkpoints. That had taken him the better part of an hour and then he had raced through the airport, searching for Yosef, looking at the throng of faces that had come to meet arriving passengers. Certain his brother was outside and waiting in the yellow Checker Nissim had heard so much about, he dragged his bags to the spot on the narrow covered walkway near the large El Al sign. Forty-five minutes and still no sign of Yosef. Raindrops hammered the roof above his head. Nissim drummed on the edge of his suitcase, the same unceasing beat as the rain.

If this were Tel Aviv and not New York, Ben-Gurion Airport and not JFK, Nissim could have understood Yosef's absence. It would have been "typical Yossi." But being late on a Friday evening to pick up a brother whom he hadn't seen for two whole years and who was stepping foot in America for the first time in his life — that seemed a little too much to dismiss.

Were Rivka and Dorit eating Shabbat dinner alone tonight, he wondered, not able to wait for Yosef to bring him home? A few minutes ago he had seen a yellow taxi drive by and slow in front of him, but the cabbie had not been Yosef. A large placard had been attached to the back of the cab, advertising America's celebration of its Bicentennial birthday. "1776-1976." America is two hundred years old and Israel is only twenty-seven, Nissim thought to himself, and the names of the airports he had passed through today struck him. David Ben-Gurion and John F. Kennedy. It was interesting – no, strange – that the young country had old leaders and the old country had young ones.

What could have happened to Yossi? What could be holding him up? At first Nissim worried that his brother had had car trouble and was stranded somewhere between New York and Philadelphia, or worse, that he had been in an accident. He debated going back inside the terminal and phoning Rivka to find out how long ago Yosef had left. But it made no sense to leave his bags unattended or drag them inside only to call and alarm Rivka by asking about Yossi. He would be there when he would be there.

For a brief time the worry subsided and Nissim began to enjoy being stranded. He liked the idea of standing here on this strip of pavement, under this sign, with these suitcases at his feet, knowing no one and no one knowing him. For the moment he was no one, a person with no context, no connections, no history. In Israel everywhere he went, anywhere he moved, he bumped into someone who knew him or his family. It was like living in a fishbowl. True, it gave him a feeling of belonging, but it also made him feel exposed. Here he was anonymous, and in his first unplanned moments in America feeling that way was freeing. This was why he had come, to be faceless for a while and enjoy it, to free himself from expectations. Here he would be accountable to no one. Here he could even be irresponsible and wound no one but himself.

"I come halfway across the world, on time," Nissim muttered to himself, "and my brother stands me up like a blind date." He looked out over the sea of cars that rolled in waves across the airport's curved, wet approaches. In the distance he could see a yellow cab driving along the circular route to the terminals. He watched it enter the curb lane and brazenly pass the first part of a long line of taxis that stretched back beyond the farthest lighted sign. The waiting cabbies began sounding their horns, their protest rising into a single blare. Quickly a traffic policeman in an orange raincoat stepped into the taxi lane, blowing his whistle and raising one forbidding hand in front of the nearing cab. When the yellow cab halted, the policeman walked to the driver's window and asked the cabbie for his license. The driver complied and gave a lengthy explanation of why he cut in front of the line. The officer stepped aside and waved the cabbie through.

A few moments later the yellow cab stopped at the curb in front of Nissim, and the driver opened his door and jumped out.

"How you doing, hero?" Yosef Lvov bellowed as he stepped out into the teeming rain and walked around the car toward his brother. "You're looking good," he said, slapping Nissim in the stomach with a stiff hand. "Welcome to America." He put an arm around Nissim's neck, pulled him close, and hugged him. "Hey, the beard, I like it! It almost makes us look like brothers."

Nissim freed himself from his brother's bear hug and stared up at him. He'd forgotten how big Yosef really was, not just tall but wide and broad. Standing next to him now Nissim felt as he had since they were children — small and stunted. After a moment Nissim shook his head and broke into a what's-the-use grin. "Right on time like always," he said. "You look damn good yourself."

"Ah, don't start with American bullshit. You just got here," Yosef said with a smile, gripping a fistful of his red plaid shirt and the soft flesh it covered above his waist. "I'm ten kilo fatter than when you last saw me. The good life's done me in."

"Ten?" Nissim asked, looking at his brother's girth and seeing that his stomach indeed had grown. Making a sudden move, he pushed two fingers into Yosef's midsection. "The good life, eh?" he said. "Take me to it."

Yosef reacted instinctively, grabbing Nissim's hand around the wrist before Nissim could pull away. "You don't know *how* to put on weight," Yosef said, Nissim's wrist still clamped in his grip. "You look like you're still doing those push-ups and sit-ups." He released his brother's hand. "So how was the flight? How late was El Al *this* time?"

"We landed on time," Nissim told him, rubbing his wrist and no longer grinning.

"On time? Great, so you've had a while to really take in the place. That's good," Yosef said.

Nissim looked at him in disbelief. "Yeah, I've had a great view of the rain and the traffic."

"Well, then you shouldn't waste any more time standing here," Yosef said. "Give me those bags and let's hit the road."

Yosef and Nissim, without raincoat or umbrellas, their hair and beards dripping wet, loaded the suitcases and duffel bag into the trunk, oblivious to the downpour. In no apparent hurry, they walked around to opposite sides of the cab and hopped into the front seat. Yosef released the parking brake and began to shift into gear but stopped himself. Instead he reached across the seat, slapped Nissim on the back of his head, and gripped him hard on the back of the neck. "Damn, it's good to have you here," he said. "Two whole fucking years! So where to, mister?"

"How about home to Rivka before dinner's in the trash?" Nissim answered.

"No problem, mister." Yosef released his grip on Nissim's neck and gunned the motor. "Let me just turn this thing on first," he said, lowering the meter arm. The meter started ticking loudly, keeping a faster beat than the whirring rhythm of the windshield wipers.

"What are you going to do, charge me?" Nissim asked, rubbing away the finger marks on his neck.

"Calm down, little brother. I may have been late to get you, but I'm no crook. I just want you to see how the money rolls in with this thing. And these are dollars, not liras," he said, pointing to the numbers that had dropped into place on the meter. "So how are Barukh and Miryam?"

"Fine, they're fine," he answered. Spots on Nissim's shirt had stayed wet with Miryam's tears long after the plane was airborne. He remembered the feel of her arms around him, almost constricting his breathing. The only time she had hugged him as hard had been at his homecoming after the war. He could still feel the imprint of her cheek on his chest, could still feel her trembling. Barukh, of course, had not cried at the airport. He had given a strong embrace and a kiss on both cheeks. "Take care of yourself, you're my Kaddish," he had said. Nissim knew from the stories Barukh had told him that these were the same words Barukh's father had told him on the transport to Treblinka. "They both keep working too hard in the store," Nissim told Yosef, "Ema's blood pressure has been acting up a little, and Abba is still out all night making housecalls. Nothing's really changed since you left. I didn't see them all that often during the past year. Just once a month for Shabbat. They miss *you,* though. I can tell you that. They're always talking about Dorit."

"I don't blame them. She's something special, that kid, and she's always talking about them."

"I can't wait to see her. How big is she now?"

"Twice the size since you last saw her. She's really sprouted. All the rain here's been good for her."

Nissim looked at the rain through the windshield and laughed. "Guess she can hardly wait till next summer and getting back to Haifa. Ema and Abba are counting the days," he said.

"So are Dorit and Rivka. I figure we'll be on our way in late May."

"Your studies going well then?"

"I've had a few rough spots, but I'm right on schedule. You'll see for yourself in another few months. The professors at Penn are supposed to be pretty tough, but you'll handle it. Everyone does."

Even during their childhood Yosef had never made more than small talk to Nissim, had never risked revealing himself. Yosef's envy had always been a wall between them.

Nissim leaned back in his seat, looking across at his brother. "It stinks in here. You know it?" he said.

"Stinks like what?"

"I don't know. Maybe it's from outside."

"Maybe. This place has its share of pollution. A lot of the time when it rains like this during a heat wave, everything starts to smell like fish. You know, pollution and all."

"Yeah, that's what it smells like," Nissim said. "Dead fish."

Still that damn fish, Yosef thought. One day he was going to disassemble the whole front seat and lift it out, and get rid of Dorit's goldfish, that putrid relic that refused to decompose and disappear. He reached into the glove compartment, took out his aerosol can of citrus-scented air freshener, and sprayed a quick burst toward the back of the cab. "Now it'll smell more like lemons," he said, "more like home. So tell me, how long have you been going?"

"Since five o'clock yesterday morning, our time," Nissim answered.

"Our time here or our time there?" Yosef asked.

"My time," Nissim told him. "I haven't switched my watch yet." He could still feel anger simmering inside him and felt sure he couldn't dispatch it without confronting his brother. It was a layered, compounded anger, directed not only at Yosef's being late to the airport. It was an anger that had been growing inside him, deepening inside him for almost two years, since the fall of 1973. Where were you then, Yossi? In America, living the good life. While real Israelis were getting killed, you were in America having fun. Nissim hated him for that. But I just got here, Nissim told himself. And he had promised himself he wouldn't fight with his brother, that there would be no confrontations, that he'd try to make this time different.

"Yeah, I remember how the trip here wiped *me* out," Yosef said. "I have an idea of how tired you are." He noticed Nissim fighting a yawn. "Go ahead and doze off if you want. You're not in *Tzahal* here, you know."

You're always in *Tzahal,* Nissim thought. But at least I don't have to worry about it for the next few years, unless another war breaks out. Suddenly images of the last war flashed across his mind, of tanks splayed into grotesque metal sculptures, of retreating personnel carriers loaded with burnt and bloodied bodies, of stretchers with limp, bouncing arms hanging over the sides. But I'm in America now, he told himself, shaking away the painful pictures. I'm with family here, with my cousin who left me standing outside in the rain for a solid hour, with my adopted brother who didn't come home for the war. "Who's not in *Tzahal?*" he said angrily, "and where the hell were you?"

Yosef knew Nissim couldn't let it rest, that he'd have to attack him for not having gone back to fight, that he'd accuse him and judge him. "Don't start judging when you don't know the whole story," Yosef told him. "I tried to go back, I wanted to, but —"

"Back where?" Nissim asked. "What are you talking about?"

"What are *you* talking about?"

"I'm talking about your leaving me stranded outside the terminal for a goddamn hour! Where the hell were you?"

"I was driving fares across Philadelphia," Yosef felt stupid for having set a trap for himself, but relieved at having been able to step back out of it. "And I thought one or two more wouldn't hurt anything because your plane would be late anyway. I figured

95

that by the time you got through customs I'd be there with time to spare. I figured wrong, but I didn't leave you stranded, did I? I mean, you *are* sitting next to me here in my cab, so I must've shown up to get you, right?"

Nissim looked at his brother and just shook his head. "America hasn't changed you a bit, Yossi," he said. "Still a master at covering up your messes. So how long will it take us to Philadelphia?" Nissim felt another yawn coming on.

"From here? About an hour and a half," Yosef answered, turning the radio to WABC. "A little of this stuff should wake you right up," he said, tapping his fingers on the steering wheel in rhythm to John Denver's "Thank God I'm a Country Boy." "Just sit back and enjoy the view, even if it *is* through rain and wipers. I'm going to show you Staten Island and a healthy chunk of the state of New Jersey." Heavy rain continued to fall, and the windshield wipers, swinging back and forth like two metronomes, seemed to keep time with the songs on the radio. Traffic was light and Yosef made good time.

"Everything all right?" Yosef asked his brother. "You don't look so good."

Nissim was slumped forward, his head resting in both hands, his eyes half closed. "It's just jet lag and the airplane food. I'm fine."

"You don't look so fine. Are you nauseous? Look, we can stop and get you something to settle your stomach down."

"No, don't stop," Nissim said, straightening up. "Keep driving. We're late enough as it is. I'll be fine."

"Don't worry about the time. It'll be okay, really. We'll stop, have a milkshake, it'll help you get your stomach back."

"It's not necessary."

"What's not necessary is you not throwing up in my thirty-five hundred dollar cab. Relax. I'll pull into one of the rest stops off the turnpike."

"What's a turnpike?" Nissim asked.

"A turnpike is what's taking us to Philadelphia," Yosef answered. *This is my chance to atone for being late.* He preferred starting off their relationship in America this way, with him being the caretaker. That's how it should be anyway, he thought, the older brother taking care of the younger, even though to this point in their lives the reverse had been painfully true. From the day of his adoption Yosef had felt like an appendage, like an extra limb grafted onto the family. His aunt and uncle had made them their son out of obligation, he thought, out of pity rather than love. He looked different from them, acted different from them, was different from them. His adoption had been more like a marriage than a birth. He spent his late childhood and adolescence feeling always an outsider, out of his real parents' home, out of context. And whenever he made strides toward acceptance within his new family, there was Nissim, their true son, his little brother, destroying Yosef's positive sense of himself by his very presence, by merely being. He had always measured himself against Nissim, and in his memory Nissim had always outdone him. Nissim had been the better student, the more responsible child, the more considerate son; he had become the better soldier, the higher ranking officer, the war hero. Yosef had been out of uniform for two years now. He had missed the war. Sure, he told himself, he had become the husband, the father, the university student, but Nissim had not entered any of those realms yet. Losing those advantages, Yosef had believed, was just a matter of time, and now here Nissim was, following him to America, enrolled in a university. "Come on, little brother," Yosef said, "even if you don't know what you need, I do. We're pulling into the next rest stop."

"I don't know, Yossi," Nissim protested. "We're late enough as it is. Rivka and Dorit are probably sitting around the table now, just waiting for us to walk in the door. I'll be okay.

Don't worry about it. If I were you—"

"Well, you're not," Yosef cut him off, pressing the gas pedal closer to the floor. "Don't worry about being late. Some things are more important. I'll take care of Rivka."

Nissim could see that arguing with his brother was pointless. "All right," he said, "she's your wife."

STANDING BESIDE THE RESTAURANT BOOTH, Yosef reached down, threw one arm around Nissim's shoulder, and squeezed him. "Damn, it's good to have family around. Real family, for a change."

Nissim once again felt overpowered and overwhelmed. "Yeah. It's good to be here," he said, waiting to extricate himself from his brother's embrace.

As soon as Yosef removed his arm, Nissim slid across the orange-cushioned seat and opened the large plastic menu. Yosef sat down on the opposite side of the booth.

"Order anything that looks good to you," Yosef said loudly, peering over the top of his menu. "I'm treating."

Nissim was looking over the beverages listed on the menu when the waitress came over to their table. She wore a white uniform that fit her slim figure like a bodysuit. She looked about nineteen years old. "You guys ready?" she asked with a smile.

"Yeah, I'm ready," Yosef leered. "You ready Nissim?"

Nissim nodded.

"A strawberry shake for me and a vanilla shake for him. All right?" Yosef asked, glancing at his brother.

Nissim nodded again.

The waitress quickly wrote down the order and walked back to the counter.

"Not bad, huh?" Yosef asked, watching her saunter away, her uniform clinging to her body.

"Maybe you've been here too long," he said. "Either that or driving that cab too much has taken away your eyesight."

"Come on," Yosef argued. "She's not that bad."

"Put it this way, Yossi. I wouldn't fight you for her."

Yosef watched the waitress push the kitchen door open then disappear as the door swung closed behind her. "Maybe you're right," he conceded. "But hell, *you* can afford to be choosy. Damn, do I ever envy you! You can take your pick of anyone out there. No wife, no kid, no claims on you. It's a goddamn candy store. Are you ever going to have yourself a field day here!"

"Day?" Nissim said, a smile breaking across his face. "What do you mean? I plan to have myself a field *year! Four* field years."

"I thought you were here to study," Yosef said with mock seriousness.

"That too," Nissim said, smiling wider.

"Here you go," the waitress said, returning with their milkshakes. "If you need anything else, just flag me." She whisked away the empty tray and hurried back to the kitchen.

"So tell me," Yosef said, "what's life like back home these days? And what's new with you, besides the beard?"

"The beard isn't new," Nissim said. "I've had it almost two years already. And life back home—well, you know it same as I do." Suddenly a rush of memories poured into his mind; midnight campfires with Shoshanah and Avi on Carmel Beach; walking downtown on Saturday nights, the three of them moving through the crowds, turning sideways to keep moving forward. He watched them pass the felafel stands and shuarma skewers, the long lines at the Ron Cinema, the teenagers perched on the sidewalk rails like birds on telephone wires, eating sunflower seeds from brown bags and spitting the shells into the gutter. He heard them whistle as Shoshanah walked past and watched how it made her smile. Then he was running into the sea, swimming toward the horizon, swimming as he always did on hot summer days when the heavy air stilled the waves and almost transformed the sea into a lake. Never before had he felt so connected to the world he had left.

"Everyone tells me that things have . . . changed," Yosef told him, sounding suddenly serious. "Have they?"

"It depends on *what* things. Prices are higher, but that's nothing new, and—"

"I mean since the war," Yosef said softly, seeming to measure his words, "since the war. People are saying it's like a different place."

"What people? Tourists? *Yordim?* Or Israelis?"

"Everyone." Yosef could feel the defensiveness rising inside him again. He could sense it coming up from his chest, into his neck, his face, his eyes. Could Nissim see it? he wondered. He could feel that same guilt overtaking him, the guilt he felt for not returning, for having waited, for having survived.

"The country hasn't changed," Nissim told him, "but anyone who was there's not the same."

Anyone who was there. The words flew like razor blades inside Yosef's head. *Not* being there changed me, he thought as he sucked hard through both straws.

"The mood has been a little down, but it's the same place it's always been," Nissim finished.

No, it's not, Yosef told himself. How could it be? He remembered the feeling of being locked out, of waiting for the call that never came. "That's good to hear," he said, putting on a smile. It had been a nightmare for him in America during the war. Even dying would have been better, he thought. At least death would have brought finality. Survival brought only excuses. "What made you decide to come now?"

"I just felt it was time," Nissim answered. "It was time and, to be honest, I was just plain tired."

"Of army life?"

"Tired of paying off everyone else's debts and not having any payoffs for myself. There's only so long anyone can put up with that. I needed to get away for a while."

"You've come to the right place to make up for lost time," Yosef said.

"Are you playing any ball here?" Nissim asked, changing the subject.

"Basketball? No, not much," Yosef answered. "Don't have the time. I get in a pickup game here and there, and once in a while I get in some swimming. There's a pool at the *Y* not too far from our house. I'll take you there, maybe this weekend. You'll love it."

"I just hope things go half as well here for me as they've gone for you," Nissim said.

"I hope so, too, little brother. Life here's been unbelievable for me. Unbelievable, period. I mean, look at my cab. I needed to work to pay for Dorit's program, not to mention my own school, and I didn't know what work I could do, you know, without a green card, so I applied to U.S. Immigration for permission to work on a student visa and they gave it to me. Do you know it only took me two weeks to sell my car and buy this Checker? The thing's a tank. All I added was a cruise light and a meter and for seven hundred more dollars I had a taxi. Just seven hundred dollars! Back home could I have touched anything like it? No way. And look at the extras I have on it—Blaupunkt AM/FM radio, Bose speakers, only the best stuff, top of the line, thermal strips on the rear windshield for defrosting—and it cost me half the price—half the price of the smallest Renault on the market in Haifa. The whole thing cost me thirty-five hundred dollars. That's all. Now is that unbelievable or what? All I have to pay for now, besides tuneups and stuff to keep the car running, is the insurance, and that I pay to Yellow Cab. For twenty-eight dollars a week they give me a sticker and everything's kosher."

"A Checker for thirty-five hundred," Nissim thought out

loud. "How much does she cost you in benzine?"

"It all depends on how much I drive but gasoline here is dirt cheap," Yosef answered. "Even with the gas shortage, which they're blaming on us—"

"They're blaming it on the cab drivers?" Nissim interrupted.

"No," Yosef said, a sudden glare in his eye, "on Israel, on the war. Gasoline just went up to fifty-eight cents a gallon and everyone here is squawking. What is it now back home? Ten times that in dollars?"

"Yeah, just about, if you figure it in liters," Nissim agreed. "So it pays to buy my own car here, you think?"

"No question about it. Here it costs more *not* to own one," Yosef told him. "Everyone here's got one or two, and they don't like to use public transportation so much." He flashed a wide grin. "And you can't afford to take a taxi everywhere, unless you own it."

Nissim stared out into the dining area a distant look came into his eyes. "I always dreamed of having a Chevrolet," he said slowly, "a four door, automatic, American Chevrolet."

"No problem. You'll find a million of them, any model, any color you want," Yosef told him. "We'll check out the paper for weekend ads when we get home. Believe me, you can pick up a used one cheap. People here buy and sell them in a day."

The straws made a loud slurping sound as Nissim sucked the last drops of his milkshake. Only foam remained in his glass. "Okay, let's go," he said to his brother. "That hit the spot, but I don't want to waste another minute. I just hope Dorit is waiting up."

"She's waited two years. She'll wait another hour. Don't worry. The main thing is you're looking better. Come on. Let's hit the road." He put down a dollar tip on the table, slid out of the booth, and walked over to pay the cashier at the entrance.

Nissim followed behind him and waited as Yosef paid the

bill. It was already after seven o'clock.

"There you go," Yosef said, opening his wallet and handing a ten-dollar bill to the cashier. Nissim caught sight of Yosef's wallet and stepped forward to look closer. "How many cards do you have there?" he asked.

"Let's see," Yosef said, inspecting the two tiers of plastic cards in his wallet as he waited for the cashier to ring up the bill. "I've got BankAmericard and Sears and one from Gimbels, then there's Mobil and Amoco and Sunoco and Gulf, and about a half dozen others. Back home they let you have overdrafts. Here you need these. Without them you can't even cash a check. Remind me we have to get you some, first thing Monday morning."

"Your change," the cashier said, holding out a palm full of bills and coins to Yosef.

"Oh, give that to my little brother here," Yosef said.

Nissim shot Yosef a look of displeasure, but stepped forward and accepted the handful of change from the cashier. Then he grabbed Yosef's sleeve and poured the change into his brother's shirt pocket. "What are you playing?" he asked as they headed outside.

"Santa Claus," Yosef answered.

"I see," Nissim said, walking again through the heavy rain, the wetness soaking his sandals, "then tell me what time we're due home."

"I'll have us there by 8:30," Yosef said as they reached the cab. He unlocked his door, opened it, and reached across to lift the latch on the passenger side door.

"New Jersey is that close to where you're living?" Nissim asked, getting in.

Yosef was already behind the wheel. "It is when I do the driving," he told him.

"A<small>NYONE HOME?</small>" Yosef called, entering the house through the side door in the garage. "A little late, but he made it."

Yosef was carrying two of Nissim's suitcases, and Nissim, walking behind him, carried the other suitcase and duffel bag.

"This place is a palace," Nissim said, impressed and surprised by the size of the garage, not to mention the house. "Where's Rivka, Yossi?"

"I don't know," Yosef said rather loudly. "This house is so big she could almost get lost trying to find us. Anybody home?"

"Shhh, keep it down," Rivka called in a loud whisper, coming downstairs from the bedroom. "Dorit just fell asleep, poor kid. She wanted so much to wait up to see her uncle, but—let me look at you, Nissim. Is it ever good to see you!"

"Same for me," Nissim said as Rivka came into his arms. He hugged her, then stepped back again. "And let me look at *you.*" Rivka was paler, more washed-out than he remembered, but otherwise he saw no marked changes. The straight black hair, the strong tight cheeks, those dark eyes that seemed to probe to the core of whatever she studied. "You look just the same as the last time I saw you," he told her.

"Come on, Nissim. You never lied, so don't start now," she said. "Either you're so tired that your eyes aren't working, or I leave an old impression." She moved over to her husband and gave him a quick peck on the cheek. "What took you so long?" she asked.

Yosef, who had been standing there holding Nissim's bags and watching his brother and his wife greet each other, looked surprised by this show of affection. He turned to kiss her, but she had already moved away. "Nissim wanted to stop," he told her.

What? Nissim thought. What's he telling her? He shot a sharp glance at his brother, but decided to remain silent.

"You must be starving," Rivka said to Nissim. "I'll bet it's been hours since the last meal they served you."

"It's been a while," Nissim said, still thinking about the vanilla milkshake, still able to feel it in his stomach, "and something sure smells delicious in here."

"It's been smelling like that for three hours already, and even if you're not hungry, I am," she said, "so let's not just stand here. Take those bags upstairs to the back bedroom and wash up for a real Shabbat dinner."

"Right away, sergeant," Yosef said, giving his wife a mock salute, then leading the way to the stairs. "And on the way I'll give our guest here a tour of our barracks."

"He's not a guest, he's family," Rivka corrected her husband.

"Don't worry, Rivka," Nissim told her. "I've kept you waiting too long already. We'll dump the bags, peek in on Dorit, and come right down."

Yosef and Nissim walked up the stairs as Rivka went into the kitchen. The brothers walked quietly through the upstairs hallway past Dorit's room to the large back bedroom, where they set Nissim's bags on the beige carpet.

"Bathroom's right over there," Yosef said, pointing to an open door across the hall. "And this room's yours for as long as you want it. Rivka and I already decided we're not letting you spend your money before you have to. We've got more rooms than we know what to do with, so why should you pay out rent when you can stay here free? In a month or so you might want to start looking, but we'd rather have you stay right here until we go back next summer. At any rate you don't have to decide anything right now. I'm going to kiss Dorit goodnight. See you downstairs."

Nissim hoisted the heaviest suitcase onto the bed, unzipped it and folded it open, then quickly picked out some fresh clothes. He took off his sweaty shirt, his rain-stained white slacks, and soggy sandals. Then he headed across the hall to the bathroom.

Nissim was not accustomed to having the tub and toilet in the same room, not to mention the sink. Back home the "bathroom" had meant the room where the bath was, and the "water closet," a small narrow room with a toilet and a window for ventilation. There was no sink in the water closet. Instead it was in the bathroom beside the tub, where he figured it belonged. Each room had its separate purpose: all washing was done in one room, something else was done in the other.

Another thing that bothered him about this bathroom was the design of American sinks. At home in Haifa the faucets were placed as separate fixtures in the wall above the sink, often as high as a foot above the sink itself, but here the faucets were attached to the sink and their spouts turned down into the center of the basin. Nissim cupped his hands under the faucet and brought them straight up to give his face a cold splashing, but the spigot got in his way. He didn't like it when things blocked him; he didn't like this sink or this spigot, but this was his brother's house.

He looked into the framed mirror over the sink and saw the strain of more than twenty-four hours of travel on his face, under his eyes. On the plane he had not had a minute alone, not one private moment, and so had not had time to perform the small act of remembrance which had become his daily ritual since the day after Avi's first burial. Closing the bathroom door, he removed a box of wooden matches from his pocket and lit one. Then holding the matchstick in front of him, he held a finger over the flame and kept it there, the yellow tip of the flame touching the quivering tip of his finger, scorching his skin until the pain became too severe for him to endure any longer. Nissim blew out the match and, sliding the box open, slipped the blackened match inside. Why aren't we both here? Why did I survive, Avi, instead of you?

He laid the burned finger across the palm of his other hand, and closed his fingers around it.

Leaving the bathroom, Nissim walked to Dorit's room. She was lying in her bed, taking up almost half its length. Last time he had seen her she had been little bigger than her pillow, a tiny, frail little girl whose future was uncertain. How big she had grown. How good America had been for her.

His eye moved above her bed to the framed needlepoint visible in the light from the hallway. It was a skyline of Haifa, the gold dome of the Bahai shrine highlighting the climb up the slopes of the Carmel. The needlepoint is beautiful, he thought, and so is my niece. He bent down over her and a smile spread across his face. I wish my parents were here to see her. Brushing the hair off her face with a gentle hand, he kissed her softly on the side of her forehead. "See you in the morning," he whispered. "Sweet dreams, little beauty."

Five minutes later the three Lvovs were sitting around the white-clothed table in the brightly lighted dining room, Yosef at one end of the rectangular table, Rivka at the other, and Nissim between them. In front of Rivka were two white candles, half-melted already, the paraffin running down into a wax puddle on the foil-covered tray that held the two silver candlesticks. The candlesticks seemed out of place, too elegant and too traditional for the other pieces on this Sabbath table. They had been a going-away gift from Miryam and Barukh when Yosef and Rivka had left for America two summers ago. "So at least Shabbat there should feel familiar," Miryam had said. Rivka kept them polished and gleaming, and used them every week. A fresh twist challah stretched across a white plastic plate, one end of the challah sticking out beyond the rim of the plate, the other end jaggedly torn and missing. Dorit had pulled it apart earlier and had eaten it with her dinner.

"Go on, Yossi," Rivka said, looking across the candle flames at her husband, then smiling warmly at Nissim. "It's so good to have you here."

Without standing, Yosef raised his glass and chanted the prayer for wine, just as he did every Friday night, just as his father Avram and his uncle Barukh had done every Sabbath eve of their lives. Nissim watched his brother recite the Kiddush and, noticing that Yosef's head was uncovered, thought of Barukh's beret. What were Miryam and Barukh doing now? he wondered.

Yosef finished singing the blessing and sat down. "So what did you make there for dinner?" he asked Rivka.

"Something for my daughter's only uncle," she answered, looking at her brother-in-law. Nissim and Yosef were so different, she thought, as different dispositionally as physically. Nissim had shaped his own personality by choosing only from among those traits his older brother hadn't claimed before him. Nissim had made himself the more reserved one, the more reliable, the more flexible one, and most important in her view, the more giving one. Never had she known him to covet anything so much that he wouldn't yield it to Yosef. Always he had cared more about his brother's well-being than his own, and Yosef had felt the same way, she thought, caring more about himself than anyone else in the family.

Nissim looked handsome to her now in his crisp white shirt and khaki slacks. Even his beard, neatly shaped and trimmed, became him, she thought. Yosef had washed before coming to the table, but he hadn't changed his clothes. His beard and hair were matted from the rain. Why did he have to look like that, especially on Friday night, with his shirt only half tucked in so that it billowed up when he walked, as though he were wearing a flag? Why did he let himself look that way? Nissim looked clean, fit, solid, with a strength more than just physical, and with eyes as intense as she remembered them. He seemed to be under control, in control, she thought, not like Yosef, not like her.

"Help yourself to some Philadelphia challah," Yosef said to Nissim, picking up the loaf in one hand and holding it out to his brother. "It's not bad really, even if it does look prettier than it tastes."

Like everything else here, Rivka thought. "So," she said with conscious enthusiasm as she began serving hefty pieces of sweet and sour chicken to Nissim, "tell us everything, about everybody. How are your parents? How are they feeling?"

"They're fine," Nissim answered, tearing off an obligatory piece of bread. "Not much is new with them, except that they've started crossing off the days on their calendar until you two and Dorit come home." He popped the piece of challah into his mouth, then picked up his knife and fork to taste a meatball. "The truth is they can't wait."

"Neither can I, let me tell you," Rivka said. She stared a moment at the candlesticks and as she did, she pictured Miryam and Barukh walking hand in hand to their little store in the Merkaz HaCarmel. She remembered the many days she had helped in the store, waiting on customers, taking inventory. In her mind Barukh hoisted the metal grid that shielded the door and front window as Miryam shook out the welcome mat. Then together they walked inside, he in his black beret, she in her paisley scarf, and like a veteran vaudeville team the two of them went into action. He tallied the receipts that lay in the drawer of their black, hand-crank register; she dusted the appliances that filled the bracketed wall shelves. He rolled reels of electrical wire and giant spools of laundry cord; she straightened the flimsy cardboard boxes which held assorted hardware. He stacked new light bulbs and batteries into large boxes; she cleared the clutter of lottery stubs from the small desktop counter. Rivka envied their working together, their intimacy, their interdependence. She envied the way they took care of each other and the weight they gave to values. Shabbat in their home was a special night, unalterable, non-negotiable. That was what Rivka wanted Shabbat to be in her home with Yosef and Dorit, no matter where that home might be. "I miss them more than they know," she told Nissim. "And how's Miryam's blood pressure?"

He repeated to her the same answer he had told his brother

earlier on the ride from New York, and they continued eating and talking for another hour around the table. There was so much for them to catch each other up on, so many questions, so many gaps to fill in after two years of living in different countries. Each of them knew it would take more than one night's conversation to fully answer the questions they were asking, so they focused more on information than on emotion, choosing first to bring each other up to date. Nissim explained about his program at Penn, when his courses would begin, why he had decided to leave Israel for his studies. Rivka told about Yosef's schedule, how busy and pressured he was, about Dorit's special preschool program, the progress Dorit was making, and about her own role in the program. Yosef sat largely silent, listening with interest but letting his wife do most of the talking.

"So you crossed with Sharon during the war?" Rivka asked.

"Yes, me and a few thousand others."

"And after the war you signed on for permanent service, until you felt you'd had enough for a while?"

"Right," Nissim told her. "And all the time I was hearing about you and Yossi and how good things were here, so it put the bug in my head, if you know what I mean."

"I know exactly what you mean," Rivka told him.

"And after hearing the stuff Yossi told me on the way here, and now seeing for myself what you've got here . . . ." Nissim looked around the dining room, then gazed across the hall into the sunken living room. Everything looked so spacious, so plush.

"It sounded like a fairy tale, didn't it?" she asked, seeing her husband's satisfied smile. "It did to me, too, when I first arrived." She looked across to the living room as Nissim did, and her thoughts turned to their own two-bedroom apartment in Haifa, the one she and Yosef had bought just before their wedding, the one they had been renting out for two years for a monthly income of one hundred dollars, the one to which they would be returning before this time next summer. How she missed it, with its small boxlike rooms and cramped kitchen, its uncarpeted floors and multiple little porches, its peeling paint and its nosy neighbors. She and Yosef had bought it with his inheritance from his father, money which Barukh had managed for Yosef since the time of Avram's death and money which Barukh had added to since the day of Yosef's adoption. Between the Deutschmarks paid as reparations for the murder of his family in Europe and the liras deposited in a savings account linked to the rate of inflation, the sum had been considerable. Yosef and Rivka had purchased their apartment outright as an investment in their future, and the cost of that apartment had left them little cash savings. But property was security, and no investment appreciated as quickly in Israel as urban real estate. Being away from the home they owned was the hardest part of living in this rented house for Rivka. Nothing here was hers, nothing. "The only thing that looks better to me now than it did when we got here," she told Nissim, "is Dorit."

Nissim smiled. "She's so big now," he said. "Will you tell her to wake me up in the morning?"

"I won't have to tell her. She'll be bothering you before six."

"No problem," he said already imagining her little hand poking his shoulder. "I like the picture in her room. Did you do it, Rivka?"

"The picture of Haifa? Shoshanah made it for Dorit's birthday. It was her favorite present."

Yossi frowned.

Nissim hadn't known that Shoshanah had kept in touch with his brother's family. He was surprised she even knew when Dorit's birthday was, even more surprised that she had spent all that time making her a present. He wished he had sent his niece more than a card. "It's beautiful work," he said.

Yosef tilted his wrist and glanced at his watch. "I can't believe it," he said, "after ten already. I have to leave in half an hour.

I thought about taking the night off but—"

"The only one making you drive tonight is *you!*" Rivka cut him short, glowering across the candles as she spoke. "You're your own boss."

"Look," Yosef shot back, "Nissim's exhausted, and one of us has to work now, don't we?"

On Shabbat? she wanted to scream. On your brother's first night here? But she said nothing, just turned to Nissim and smiled weakly.

Yosef also turned to his brother and explained to him what he wanted Rivka to hear. "Friday nights are good for big tips. The demand stays pretty steady into the small hours, you know, it being the weekend. And you can hardly hold your head up anyway." Then he turned back to Rivka. "You remember what the trip did to us. He needs to sleep it off."

And what about me? What about us and Shabbat and our sharing any real time together anymore? "You're going to get killed if you keep driving around picking up strangers at two o'clock in the morning," she said. "All it takes is one crazy with a gun and—"

"I'm going to work, Rivka, not to war," he said calmly. "Don't worry."

There was a cry from upstairs. The loud exchange had awakened Dorit. Yosef and Rivka stared at each other as Yosef rose to leave the table. "Don't worry," he said, "I'll go up. You two stay put. If she sees you now, Nissim, she'll never go back to sleep."

Nissim wanted to go with Yosef but he knew his brother was right. He and Rivka sat in silence as Yosef moved into the entrance hallway and disappeared up the stairs. Rivka looked despondent.

"Rivka," Nissim asked softly, "when does he finish?"

Rivka was staring at the pool of white wax on the foil between the candlesticks. She shook her head slowly as if clearing away a bad dream, then lifted her eyes and let out a breath that sounded more like a sigh. "Never," she told him.

Six

THE FORECAST FOR THIS LONG HOLIDAY WEEKEND is good, so expect an early exodus from the city, beginning this afternoon and evening, resulting in heavy traffic on the Walt Whitman and Ben Franklin bridges as people head for the Jersey shore. Enjoy your July 4th weekend this year, planners for the Bicentennial say, because next year the city will be so mobbed with tourists from all over the country, and the world for that matter, we won't be able to budge. Enjoy the sunshine, but if you have to be on the roads this Fourth, please drive carefully. Happy 199th, America.

Nissim half-listened to the radio as he drove Oded Hazon's car toward Cheltenham Avenue's intersection with Broad Street. Yosef had driven him to Yankee Doodle Donuts this morning to borrow Oded's car while Oded was working. The arrangement called for Nissim to return Oded's car to Yankee Doodle when he had finished his business, then catch a bus back to Louise Lane. Oded's car was a green two-door Datsun B210 with over 84,000 miles, dented in several places, a high mileage subcompact model. It had been new six years ago, but now the paint was chipped and peeling, the vinyl on the roof was tattered, and there were two large rust holes on the hood.

A just-released Harris poll shows President Ford's popularity among blue collar workers drop-

114

ping. The president's confidence rating has fallen a full thirteen points over the last three months with the sharpest decline coming from electricians and plumbers. The decline is attributed to the unusually slow housing starts this summer and to economic projections for a recession.

Nissim's ears perked up at the mention of electricians and plumbers. He thought of Barukh back in Haifa, fixing some broken appliance in the back of the store or making an emergency housecall to clear out someone's pipes. During these past weeks in America, though Rivka and Yosef and even little Dorit had tried to help him with American English, the radio and television had been his best teachers. He was always listening for new words and phrases that he could use in conversation. "Blue collar workers," he repeated to himself, trying to imprint the phrase in his memory.

On the bucket seat beside him lay a section of the morning's edition of *The Philadelphia Inquirer*. It was open to the "Automobiles — Used" section of the Classified Ads. One of the small-type entries was circled in red ink.

CHEV — '68 Chevelle, V-6 auto, a/c, ps, defog, am/fm, 63k ml., good cond., Pa. insp., $750, WA7-4938

Nissim had called the number before eight o'clock and had promised he would come over by ten. The car sounded like just what he wanted, and he was afraid of losing it to someone who might beat him to it. He turned right at Broad and Cheltenham then made the next right into Seventy-second Street and the "Smithfield Apartments." A sign spelled the name out in large letters above the entrance to a three-story brick apartment building which covered most of the small, side street block. Sitting outside in the sun on the steps to the entrance door was a woman in her twenties who seemed to be waiting for someone. She was wearing a red halter top, cutoff jeans, and dark brown sandals. Long sandy blonde hair, which was swept back off her face and held in place by flipped-up sunglasses on top of her head, fell to the rise of her breasts. There was an air of thrownback beauty about her. She held a can of soda in one hand and a lit cigarette in the other. Nissim decided to stop and ask her for directions, even though he knew exactly where he was going. The Datsun moved slowly down the street toward her, and came to a full stop in front of her.

"Excuse, Miss, but could you maybe to tell me where is Smithfield Apartment?" Nissim asked, leaning on an elbow through his open window.

"Sure," she said, standing up and walking toward the curb. "You're there." She turned around and pointed to the sign above the entrance behind her. "Who were you looking for?"

Now that he saw her more closely, she looked even more striking. "A Chevrolet," he answered. Her mouth had a sort of suggestive flare, a sensual elasticity to it that together with her bright blue eyes made her relaxed expression seem to hint at a knowing grin. She wore a blue shade of eyeshadow that matched the blue of her eyes. He could see that she was one of those women who men were always aware of, at parties, on the beach, on the street, and he figured she had to know it. "Do you know maybe someone called Neese?" he asked.

"Neese?" she repeated, flashing an amused smile that seemed to start in her eyes and spread across her lips. "If you mean Denise, I'm Denise." Her voice sounded different than Nissim had expected. It was not high-pitched and soft, but rather was raspy and full, giving her words a sort of bawdy quality.

"Yes," Nissim said, returning her smile. "I have never heard this name before. Hello."

"You're who I talked to on the phone, coming from Wynd-moor, right? You were the first to call. Well, why don't you park right over there; my car's just down the block. It's the green one with the initials on the license plate."

Nissim parked the car, then walked down the block to join her next to a green Chevelle whose vanity license plate read "I.D."

Denise watched him walking toward her. She watched how his body moved, his tight brown curls not bobbing or even blowing in the warm breeze, his tanned face and confident eyes giving him an aura of ruggedness. He was wearing a short-sleeved khaki shirt with three buttons open at the neck and with each sleeve folded twice to make a tight cuff just below his shoulders. She noticed the muscular definition of his arms, the mechanic's forearms and biceps. Rolled inside his left cuff was a pack of cigarettes, a thin gold chain around his neck. In his hand was a gray metal toolbox.

"How long you are having this car?" Nissim asked her.

"Three years," she told him. "It used to be my mother's, who bought it new. I bought it from her in '72."

"Bought it from your mother?" he asked, surprised.

"Right."

In Israel parents gave their children whatever they could afford, and many things they couldn't. With major purchases like an apartment or a car, parents often took out loans to finance their children's payments. No child could have earned enough money to afford such purchases, especially after losing three years in the army. It took a lifetime of working and saving. And it was understood that each child would repay his parents by doing for his children, their grandchildren, as his parents had done for him.

"I see," he said, thinking that perhaps she was older than she looked. "And why do you sell it now? It has problems?"

"No, nothing major," she answered, looking at the toolbox and wondering what he was going to do. "I figure it's still running well enough to bring a good price, and frankly all I want to do is make

117

back what I paid my mother for it. It's been real reliable for me, and except for a few nicks and scrapes, it's in just about as good condition as any six-year-old car I can think of. When I sell it I plan to go right out and buy myself a newer one. The price, as it said in the ad, is seven hundred fifty dollars."

"Yes," Nissim said, putting his toolbox down on the pavement and releasing the lock clips to open it, "this is what you call 'asking price,' no?"

"No," Denise said firmly, but with a smile, "that's the price, period. The 'blue book' price is fifteen hundred."

"I see," Nissim said. Yosef had told him the asking price was low. Either the car had a major problem or it was a genuine find. "You don't mind that I do some checkups?"

"No, I guess not," Denise answered, not at all sure. "Just don't damage anything." She watched him open the metal box and remove several tools, some pieces of hardware, and some sort of sophisticated gauge.

Nissim began to go to work. Raising the hood, he asked her to start the car, and ran a compression test on the engine, piston by piston. He checked the spark plugs and carburetor for dirt, and took off the distributor cap in search of condensation. He believed in doing things for himself. He checked the dip sticks for the oil and transmission fluid levels. The distributor and carburetor seemed to be in good working order, but the tire treads showed signs that the car tended to pull slightly to the right. He found a few rust spots on the body, but they were only a cosmetic concern.

"Do you mind if I ask you a question?" she asked while Nissim was under the car checking the oil pan and the axle alignment.

"Sure," he called out to her.

"You speak English very well, but are you new here?"

"Yes, I am here only two weeks."

"I see. And are you a mechanic?" She liked the way he handled his tools, how he handled her car, how he handled himself. There

118

was a confidence in his eyes when he looked at her, and that confidence attracted her. It was not the phony bravado or shy self-consciousness which she was used to seeing in the eyes of the other men she had met. She was watching him look her up and down, and she liked the way his eyes felt on her face, on her hair, on her body. Indeed, she was looking him over the same way, as brazenly as he was.

"No," he told her, sliding out from under the car and wiping his hands on a rag, "a student." It felt strange to Nissim to be known for only himself, to have no title in front of his name, no uniform to announce his rank, to define him. At once it diminished him and enhanced him, he felt. It set him back and pushed him forward. "I am studying in computers."

"Oh," Denise said, impressed, still curious about where he was from. "I know I'll guess wrong, but are you Spanish?"

"No, my accident is from Israel," he told her.

Denise could not help herself from breaking out laughing.

"This is funny?" Nissim asked, wanting to share her humor, but feeling defensiveness rise inside him. "From Israel is funny?"

"No, oh, no," Denise said quickly, forcing herself back to seriousness. "I've never been over there, but I'd like to go myself someday. I was raised Unitarian, but I'm half Jewish myself on my father's side. I wasn't making fun of anything, believe me. I was smiling because of your accent. I think it's cute."

"Cute?" Nissim busied himself with wiping the street dirt off the back of his shirt and the legs of his jeans. He thought he heard a seductive tone in her apology, but he wasn't sure. "What is 'cute?'" he asked.

"Cute is . . . I don't know how to explain it with another word . . . it's a . . . compliment," she told him.

He liked the way she looked straight into his eyes when she talked, and he liked the low raspy sound of her voice. "Thank you, then," he said, breaking into a friendly half-smile.

"How'd my car do?"

"A few problems," he told her as he closed the Chevy's hood.

"But you didn't even take it for a test drive."

"No need."

"You don't want it?" she asked, sounding surprised and disappointed. "It's a good car, believe me."

"It's okay," he said, returning his equipment to the metal box, closing the lid, and clipping it shut. His tests showed that the car was in good running condition, but needed a general tuneup, new spark plugs, filters, and a wheel alignment, all of which Nissim could do himself inside Yosef and Rivka's garage. "Seven hundred fifty?" he asked, wiping his grease-smeared hands on the rag again as he stood beside Denise.

"That's the price," Denise told him, "and I'm not coming down. Are you interested?"

"I'm interested," Nissim said, dispensing with flirtatious looks and getting down to business. He unrolled his left sleeve, removed the pack of cigarettes, opened the box, and took one out. A book of matches was tucked inside the cellophane wrapping of the cigarette box. He struck one match, lit a cigarette, and held it out to Denise. "Please, for you."

She hesitated, not used to taking anything from the mouth of strangers, and looked this Israeli over again. "Thanks," she said, reaching out one hand and taking the cigarette between two fingers.

Nissim lit a second cigarette for himself and replaced the matchbook and pack of cigarettes in his shirt sleeve. "This car is needing some work," he told her, taking a puff and patting the roof of the Chevrolet. "For sure it will cost money."

"How much work?" she asked, almost as interested to know what was wrong with her car as to know if this man was willing to buy it.

"This Chevy is needing garage work," he told her. "It is needing painting and some spraying on the rust spots. On the tires the rubber is not so good, and everywhere is needing new filters."

He paused to let her absorb what he had said. "I pay you cash, six hundred fifty for this car."

"Six fifty?" she asked, more offended than surprised. "You've gotta be kidding. The car's half-price to start with." She debated with herself about what to do. This whole business of selling her car bothered her. It was a royal pain, having to place the ad, having to answer the phone calls, having to stay around all day waiting for people who said they'd be coming. She knew how these things generally worked. Most of the people who called wouldn't show, and those who did would drive her car and ask her all kinds of questions and she would feel violated when they left with their "Thanks, we'll get back to you." Her friends at the bank had told her not to put it on the market this weekend. They said she would end up cursing herself for wasting away July 4th. Maybe she should just close the deal. Maybe a hundred dollars wasn't worth messing up her holiday.

"I know what is good car and I know what is needing work," he told her. "Seven hundred and fifty is fair price for this car *after* fixing; this is true, but fixing will cost maybe three hundred dollars in garage. If I pay you six hundred fifty, this car will cost me almost one thousand dollars. So I think this six hundred fifty is fair. And I will pay you cash dollars."

There was something about this guy Denise liked, something that made her believe what he was saying. "Even if you're right about the repairs costing that much, I still need the seven hundred fifty to put toward the car I'm going to buy to replace this one," she told him. "I'd like to sell it to you, but every dollar I lose in this deal is going to cost me two dollars — the dollar you didn't give me and the dollar I'll have to lay out for my new car."

"I see," he said politely. "Well, I should to keep on looking then. Thank you." He took his metal toolbox, turned slowly, and started walking back up the block.

She watched him head up the sidewalk and thought of how

she might call him back. "Wait," she shouted, before he had taken too many steps, "maybe we can make a deal."

When he heard her voice he stopped and turned. Slowly he walked back to her.

She stood beside her car and waited until he was next to her. "You're interested in buying my car and I'm interested in buying someone else's car," she began, "and you know cars and I don't, so I was thinking that maybe we could make an arrangement. I have an appointment this afternoon to check out a car from an ad in today's paper and if you'd come with me, you know, as my mechanic, and bring your trusty box there, then you could do the tests you did on my car on *that* car. I figure you'd give me enough ammo to bargain the owner down at least a hundred bucks. So if six fifty sounds fair to you for my Chevelle, and you'll come with me this afternoon, I say we have a deal. What do you say?"

"Okay. I am saying yes," he told her with a smile.

"Including the trip this afternoon, right?" she asked, wanting to make sure he understood the full deal.

"Including the trip," he said, glad to have the chance to see her again. "And don't to worry, we will get you a good one."

"Shake on it, then," she said smiling. "We've got a deal."

"When is this appointment?" Nissim asked, shaking the hand she held out to him. "And where?"

"Four o'clock, in Elkins Park," she told him, "just a few minutes from here. We can meet back here at a quarter to four, and I'll drive us there in my car—I mean your car."

Nissim's eyes moved over her face, her hair, her body. She looked more striking to him, more attractive now than when he had first seen her sitting on the steps. "Don't to worry. I will be here," he told her. "Fifteen to four, it's a date." Smiling, he turned and walked back up the block. For six hundred and fifty dollars and a favor he had himself a car, a Chevy. And a date with a beautiful American woman. It had taken less than a day, less than an hour. Six hundred fifty, he thought, a tenth of what it would cost me in Haifa. Reaching Oded's Datsun, he hopped in, and shooting a last look at Denise in his rear view mirror, he sped away to the donut shop.

JOCKO STUCK THE STOGIE BETWEEN HIS TEETH and hiked up his baggy slacks with both hands. Taking a large white handkerchief out of his back pocket, he blew his nose loudly. "I know what you're talking about, Joe," he said, more mopping than wiping the wetness from his nose. "Sometimes I think my cab's got a hole in it or something. I just keep pouring money into it and it just keeps leaking through. One year I laid out close to two grand on repairs, and the insurance didn't cover squat. Yeah, Joe, I know what you're going through. Took a big chunk out of every month till I paid the Company off. But the Company shop's got some good boys, and they treat you fair so long as you drive regular."

The line of taxis was growing longer by the minute, all the cabbies converging on Thirtieth Street Station to cash in on the heavy holiday traffic. They, like Jocko and Yosef, knew that when everyone else went on vacation, they worked double time. They also knew that working from a single base would earn them more money in a shorter time than cruising the streets of Philadelphia, waiting to be hailed. Already it was three o'clock. Within the hour the July Fourth crush would begin in earnest.

"How much you got to go yet?" Jocko asked, folding the hand-kerchief into a sloppy ball and tucking it into his pants pocket.

"Seven hundred," Yosef told him. His Checker had just needed a major overhaul. He had bought it used from a second owner who had turned back the odometer to make the car more saleable. The Yellow Cab mechanics said the car had at least 180,000 miles on it, but the odometer showed only half that many. A month ago, two weeks before Nissim's arrival, the transmission had given out. The Company garage had completed the repairs in two days, but while installing the new transmission, the mechanics had found

123

other problems. The bill for eight hundred dollars stunned Yosef. This was a full month's earnings. As a Yellow Cab driver, Yosef was entitled to pay off the bill in installments, and he had agreed to the monthly plan. One hundred dollars was due to the Yellow Cab Company on the first day of each month until the full debt was retired. This morning he had been greeted by his supervisor with a harsh reminder that today was the third of July and no one had seen any hundred dollars from Yosef Lvov yet. According to the credit agreement, if an installment payment was not made by the fifth of any month, then the entire balance was due in full – immediately.

It hurt Yosef to admit it, but at best cab driving had been a marginal enterprise for him. His Checker had been a serious disappointment, and a costly one. It seemed almost every penny he earned he had to reinvest in gasoline and maintenance. Sure, it was big and comfortable with a standard of luxury he could never afford in Israel, but it also was a gas guzzler and needed constant repairs. "I'll write out a check right now," Yosef told Jocko, "but then what do I do about this one?" He held up an envelope and removed a computer-prepared billing statement from inside it. "BankAmericard," he said. "I owe them for last month and this one."

A look of fatherly concern came over Jocko's face. He took his stogie out of his mouth and, waving it like an actor's prop, said, "You don't want to mess with them mothers. They'll nail you if you get behind. How much you into them for?"

Yosef held up the BankAmericard bill in front of Jocko's eyes and let him see for himself.

"A hundred bucks from the middle of May," Jocko read out loud, "and three hundred since the middle of June. Hell, that's only two weeks ago! What've you been doing? Taking your brother to the Bellevue Stratford every night?"

Yosef looked back at the station doors, checking to see if the next Metroliner had come in yet. It hadn't. "I've been trying to show him the sights," Yosef said, "but I didn't figure on falling behind this far."

"Yeah, you're in a fix all right," Jocko said. "If it was me I'd hightail it over to Broad and Sansom—I'd stick my face in front of theirs, and start talking—person to person." He paused and puffed on his stogie, then cast a quick glance at his watch. "And I'd do it right now, Joe, if I was you. It being the Fourth tomorrow, BankAmericard will probably be closing early. Better catch 'em before they all head out. You don't want to be dealing with no computers. Go talk to a live person who can bend some rules around and help you through the squeeze time. Just talk to them, and no poor-mouthing or they'll think you ain't gonna pay."

Yosef listened, then thought for a moment about what Jocko had said. He knew he should take care of his credit card debt, but he also knew that the only way he could pay it off was to drive his cab as many hours as possible. Taking time now to go to the BankAmericard office would mean money out of his pocket, lost time and lost fares.

"Well, what are you wasting time for?" Jocko asked. "You can lose an hour now or your good name later. And believe me, if your credit's gone, it's like no one wants to know you. Go take care of business, son."

Son? Jocko had never called him that before, and hearing it now surprised Yosef. He interpreted it as an admonition, as a sort of reproof for not having acted his age, for not having handled his affairs more responsibly. Without words, he folded the BankAmericard bill into the envelope, slipped it into his shirt pocket, and hopped into his Checker. "Catch you later," he said loudly through the open window as he started the motor and pulled away from the line of cabs.

PAYING MONEY TO PARK HIS CAB IRKED YOSEF. He figured the hackers of Philadelphia should be accorded special privileges when it came to parking, the same way policemen didn't get charged to park their patrol cars anywhere in the city. Muttering to himself about wasting good money, he tucked the claim ticket from the parking garage into his pocket and headed toward Broad and Sansom.

Even after two years, Yosef could not take this walk along Broad Street toward City Hall without looking up like a little boy in wonderment at the towering buildings. He found himself overcome by a sort of surrealist vision, the skyscrapers forming a tight walled cavern of stone and steel, of concrete and glass, the sky descending to seal the huge chamber. He could feel his self-confidence shrinking with each step he took down the crowded sidewalk. It seemed that everyone was dressed for a concert at the Academy of Music or a dinner dance at the Union League. Everyone but Yosef, who wore his red plaid shirt, blue jeans, and sneakers without socks.

Near the corner of Broad and Sansom he entered a large office building through one of the brass-plated revolving doors leading into the lobby. Inside he checked the glass-encased directory board for the BankAmericard Credit Office, and finding it listed on the eighteenth floor, moved quickly to the elevators. There were six elevators in the two-sided bay. When the first car returned to the lobby, he hurried in through the parting gold doors. No one entered Yosef's car before the doors closed. He pushed the button for the eighteenth floor and began his ascent alone.

The elevator had barely started up when it stopped and opened on the second floor. A delivery man in a green uniform entered the car pushing a hand dolly loaded with big boxes wrapped in brown paper and gumtape. The delivery man wheeled the dolly into a standing position between himself and Yosef, pressed the fourth floor button, and without acknowledging Yosef, stared straight ahead like a mannequin as the doors slid closed behind him. It's sad, Yosef thought, how people here avoid each other. Especially in public places—on the street, on the buses, in office lobbies, in elevator cars. The silence was eerie, unnatural. People seemed afraid of each other, couching their fear in the guise of politeness, confusing formality with consideration, respecting each other by zealously guarding their own personal space. In Israel everyone talked to each other, everywhere. Even strangers talked or argued like old friends about common concerns there, and the more public the place, the louder the conversation. Here the delivery man could stand in silence for as long as it took to reach his floor, never even making eye contact, let alone saying "Good afternoon."

Just then the sound of a fart reverberated in the elevator. Yosef stood startled. He looked at the delivery man for a clue, but the man had not even flinched at the noise. In fact, he had not moved at all. The car began filling with the smell of raw sewage. The stench spread like an expanding cloud until it enveloped everything. A second later the elevator stopped at the fourth floor and the doors opened. Maneuvering his dolly into position, the delivery man wheeled the packages out of the car. He turned for a moment to look at Yosef. "Sorry," he said, smiling sheepishly.

Yosef considered getting off and walking the rest of the way to the BankAmericard Office. It certainly seemed preferable to standing inside a sealed foul-smelling elevator. But if he got off now he would only lose time. He would have to walk up fourteen flights of stairs, so he decided to stay where he was. In Israel they didn't have many elevators. Electricity was too costly and there were too many blackouts to make them practical. Maybe it was a good thing, Yosef thought.

The doors slid closed again and the elevator began its climb. He winced at the odor.

Six floors later the elevator slowed again and its doors opened.

Two well-dressed women, both in their fifties, got in and pressed the button for the twentieth floor. The two women turned abruptly, and looked at him. Then one woman cast her eyes down, staring very hard at her shoes, while the other lady fixed her eyes on the lighted numbers above the door and kept them glued there. It was obvious they were going to look anywhere but at the big bearded stranger who stood beside them in sneakers, jeans, and an appalling stench. Yosef, however, looked only at them, studying their discomfort and their attempts to politely hide it. The elevator slowly ascended, and after a moment one of the women couldn't help looking again at Yosef. Catching her gaze, Yosef smiled at her. "After shave from Russia," he said.

Now both women were looking at Yosef and both wore mortified expressions. They turned away sharply, one staring up again, the other staring down. It had not been the greatest day, Yosef thought. He looked down at the floor and saw his sneakers, the laces more brown than white, smears of black grease on the tongues and toes. It's not my fault cabbies don't drive around in coats and ties, he told himself, feeling suddenly embarrassed at the way he looked. It's not bad enough that it stinks in here but that I have to look like the guy who did it. He touched his shirt pocket, reminding himself of the BankAmericard letter and garage claim ticket, then looked again at the two well-coiffed ladies standing with him in the foul-smelling car. He reached out and pressed the fourteenth floor button, and the car abruptly stopped. It wasn't his fault some schmuck farted, making him have to get off this elevator before he reached his destination. He hadn't done anything to be ashamed of. As soon as the doors opened Yosef hurried out into the hallway.

He would walk the four flights up to the Credit Office, he decided, rather than get back into an elevator. Across the corridor he saw a lighted EXIT sign. He walked over and opened the door that led to the stairwell, but standing on the fourteenth floor landing he paused to reconsider. Jocko had said to screw the computer and talk to a person, face to face. That had made good sense when he heard it, Yosef thought, but he'd do better with the computer.

He leaned over the railing and, craning his neck, looked up to the top of the tower-like stairwell. The Credit Office was so close above him. He patted the envelope in his pocket again, and a pained look spread across his face. Probably everyone's gone home already, he told himself. It wasn't his fault this was a holiday weekend. It wasn't his fault that BankAmericard was closing early. It wasn't his fault he smelled. He wasn't going to give some officious clerk in a business suit the chance to tell him "no," and he wasn't going to waste his time with some secretary. Next week he'd come back, when he was ready.

He headed down the stairwell.

"WE BOTH MADE OUT LIKE BANDITS, YOU KNOW?" DENISE SAID, smiling across the booth, a French fry in one hand, a cigarette in the other. A filet of flounder dinner was on the plate in front of her.

"Bandits?" Nissim asked, making a mental note of the word as he finished a forkful of salisbury steak.

"Robbers," Denise said. "You know, crooks."

"And this is good?"

"Yeah, it's good," she answered, smiling as she took a drag of her cigarette. "What I meant was that you got my Chevy for a song and thanks to your little toolbox, I got that Datsun for less than the man himself would pay me if he wanted to buy it back. We both got what we were after, for less than it should've cost us. Bandits is just an expression, Nissan."

"Nissim," he corrected her, his tone more amused than upset. In the past two weeks it seemed every American had mangled his name.

"Oh, I'm sorry," Denise said quickly, reaching across the table and putting her hand on his arm. "I'm thinking about my new car. Sorry." She gave a soft embarrassed laugh.

"Your car?"

"You know, Datsun . . . Nissan . . . the company," she told him, gently taking back her hand, her laugh now a warm apologetic smile. "I guess it goes without saying but—I don't know too many Nissims."

He looked at Denise and said, "Don't to worry. You can to call me Nissan. It's okay."

"I might just do that," she told him.

A half-hour ago they had finished looking at Denise's new car and now they were eating an early dinner at the Keystone Diner, a restaurant on the northern end of Broad Street with booths and chairs padded with dull red cushions and avocado-green tables. People dressed casually to eat there. Nissim was wearing the same clothes he'd worn this morning when he'd answered Denise's ad, but Denise had changed into a different outfit. She was wearing a strapless peach tank top and tight white pants. Her hair was different too. It fell in waves to her shoulders now, with bangs across her forehead. Her flipped-up sunglasses had been replaced by a colorful Indian-bead headband. Even the color of her lips and nails was different. She had put on peach lipstick to match her clothes, then had painted her nails to match her lips. From the moment they had walked in, Nissim had been aware that all the men, and most of the women, were looking at her.

"We've spent the better part of today together," Denise said, "and I still don't know anything about you. Of course, you don't know anything about me, either, so I guess that makes it even." She lifted her glass of diet cola, took a sip, then put it back down.

"Do you have family here?" she asked.

"My brother," Nissim answered. "He is here with his wife and daughter."

"And you two are close?"

"Close? Yes. We are living close, even in the same house."

Denise grinned, amused by Nissim's confusion. "No, I don't mean close that way," she explained. "I mean are you close emotionally, do you *feel* close?"

"We are brothers."

"I have a brother, too," Denise said, carefully picking some tiny bones out of her flounder, "and I hope you've got a better relationship with yours than I've got with mine. Well, actually you'd have to because our relationship's nonexistent. You have other brothers and sisters?"

"No. And you are having sisters?"

"Nope. My parents split up when I was two, so there's only my brother and me."

"What does this mean 'split up'?" Nissim asked.

"Divorced, broke up, wiped out their marriage," she told him. "It was definitely for the best, though, believe me. The two of them are impossible. I don't know how they lived in the same house as long as they did." Denise's father was a corporate lawyer with a large Washington firm. Her mother, a musician, had moved from their Bethesda home to Woodmere, Long Island after the divorce, joining a local chamber ensemble there and supplementing the alimony and child support payments by giving private lessons in her home. Denise had grown up in Woodmere with her mother. Her brother had grown up in Maryland, having moved back there to live with his father when his father remarried. Denise had been six years old at the time. Her mother had remained single.

"My mother comes from the school of 'they say,'" Denise continued. "You know, '*they say* nice girls would never use that word' and 'what will *they say* if you wear that dress?' and 'you know what *they say* about girls who go too far on the first date.' I always used to ask her who *'they'* was. 'The people who know about these things,' was what she always came back with. I must've heard that a million times and, God, did it drive me crazy! I can't stand that let-me-live-your-life-for-you stuff, you know?"

As Denise talked, Nissim was enjoying her animated gestures, her vibrancy, her attention. Never before had he met any woman as trusting, as open, as unconditionally candid as this woman across the table from him. For all she knew he could be a con man, a car thief, a good-looking bandit. Maybe he wasn't really new here. Maybe a lot of things. He hadn't paid her any money yet, they'd signed no bill of sale, she hadn't seen his passport or driver's license. Nothing. Yet here she was telling him intimate insights into her family and private details of her childhood. It contradicted the stories he'd heard about the women in America carrying tear gas in their pocketbooks and looking behind every door for rapists. She was taking him into her confidence after just a few hours together, a few hours spent on nothing more intimate than inspecting cars, and this instant trust of hers baffled him. More than that, it disarmed him.

"And my father's got his own problems," she went on. "It would be sad, really, if it wasn't so comical. He may be dynamite in the courtroom, but in real life he's not much to write home about. I think he realized both of his life goals before he turned thirty — to be a Washington lawyer and to have a telephone in the bathroom, not necessarily in that order." Denise paused, sipped her soda, and laughed, more at her words than at her parents. She was ready to continue, but noticed Nissim looking at her, his head a little tilted, a quizzical smile on his face.

"Come on," he said. "You're pushing my leg."

Denise let out a burst of laughter. "Oh, I'm sorry," she said, wiping tears from the corners of her eyes with one finger when she was able to stop herself. She debated whether to tell Nissim what he'd said, to correct him, but decided not to say anything for fear of insulting him. He was trying so hard to learn the language and was doing pretty well, she thought. "I really shouldn't make my parents out to be basket cases," she continued, not giving him a chance to ask what she meant. "I mean, I survived, right? We all did, somehow. What about your parents? What do they do?"

"They work in a little shop," he told her. "My father is a collar worker." He was pleased with himself for using another new phrase in his conversation.

"Oh," she said, "we call that a tailor."

"No, I know what is a tailor. My father is doing plumbing," he said, pronouncing the *b*, "and he is fixing the lights and things like this."

"Oh," Denise said, still not sure she understood. "And in Israel you call that a collar worker?"

"No," he told her, "you do, in English. I heard it on the radio." He quoted the broadcast he'd heard this morning. "Collar workers don't like Ford so much – the plumbers and electric workers and people building the houses. You know?"

"Oh," she said, "you mean *blue* collar workers."

"Right. I didn't to remember the color."

"And what are they like, your parents – as people?" she asked, finishing her last piece of fish, then lighting another cigarette.

Nissim did not answer right away. What would she say about Miryam and Barukh if they were her parents? he wondered. That Miryam was always waiting for the next tragedy, expecting it, planning for it? That she squirreled canned foods all over the apartment, in every closet, under the beds, for when she would have to bar the doors to avoid being dragged out into the night? Would she say that Barukh had his own problems, that he could never waste anything, never throw anything out? Would she say that he could leave nothing unfinished—no task, no argument, no newspaper? Would she tell about the back issues of *Maariv* piled on the little laundry porch, the stacks already reaching the ceiling, and no one being allowed to touch them until Barukh finished reading each page? Every family's sad and comical if you look at it closely, he thought. Every family's a caricature if you take it out of context. "My parents are married," he told her. "Crazy a little, sure, but they are good people."

Through the tinted window they could see the sunlight fading. Already the cars on Broad Street were driving with their low beams on. The fluorescent lights inside the diner seemed to shine brighter as the light through the window dimmed.

"So there's just you and your brother?" Denise asked.

"Yes," Nissim said, not wanting to go into a long story.

"And who came first?"

Nissim hesitated before answering. I did, he thought. My cousin came second. "My brother did," he told her.

"How many years does he have on you?"

"Five," he answered, aware of a sudden resistance inside him. The way she kept firing questions at him was making him feel interrogated. Were all American women so probing, so analytical? Was it part of the social foreplay here for them to bare their private lives and expect you to do the same?

"Which makes him what?"

Nissim did not answer, preferring to be silent and to see what would happen.

"Wait," Denise said, speaking almost immediately, "let me guess." She looked at Nissim, studying him, searching his eyes for a clue of his age. "He's five years older and you must be what, twenty-two, maybe twenty-three, so he's about . . . twenty-seven. Am I right?"

"Almost," he said. "He's thirty." Now he stared at her as she had just stared at him. "And how many years are you, Denise?"

She leaned back against the cushioned seat, acting horrified at the question, feigning offense. "Well, I shouldn't, but I'll tell you. I'm right between you and your brother. Twenty-eight . . . and counting."

Nissim had thought she was younger than that, a year or two younger than he was, so her answer surprised him. He noticed no wedding ring on her hand, no untanned band of skin on her finger. There had been no second name on her mailbox when he had checked it earlier this afternoon, and she had not mentioned the name of any man during these hours together. It didn't make sense to him. Yosef had told him to watch out because in America everyone married young, especially the women. Any woman past twenty-five was looking to trap a man into it, his brother had said. How could anyone who looked like her not be spoken for already? he wondered. Maybe it had to do with her work. "You are working full-time?" he asked her.

"Full-time. I work at Penn Savings. I've been working there since I was eighteen, since I moved to Philadelphia. Put myself through Temple that way. I'm the Assistant Branch Manager."

Nissim was impressed. "This is a big job, no?" he asked.

"Yeah, it's big all right," she said, "but I like it. Maybe because I've been there so long, maybe it's just a function of time, or maybe because I've been everything from teller trainee to investments counselor, but I feel it's really a part of me now and I'm in too deep to leave. And now with everything being automated, there's another new project every day. I like it when things keep changing like this. There's always something new to catch up with." She paused and drank the last sip of her soda, then continued. "I give it two years, three at the outside, before every bank is computerized. You're going into the right field, believe me. Are you going for your Master's or a PhD?"

"I am studying only for the B.A.," he told her.

"Twenty-five and a freshman, huh? You must have taken a

few years off after high school. Did you work?"

"Let's say I was taking care of business," he said.

Were all Israelis so guarded, so cryptic? she wondered. Were they guarded because they were sensitive, distant because they were vulnerable? She didn't know, but she wanted to get close enough for long enough to find out. He was so different from the American men she had known, and it was the differences between them that attracted her. His accent, his clothes, his foreignness. She liked unpredictable circumstances. The unfamiliar enticed her. Though he was soft-spoken, almost reticent, she could see that he was observing every nuance of his new surroundings. She liked how he filled the silences with his eyes, how the silences didn't threaten him, how his reticence seemed to draw her out and now was drawing her in.

Just then their waitress came to their booth, asked if they were done with their entrees, proceeded to clear their dishes, and asked if they would care for dessert. Denise asked to look over the menu again, but suddenly said, "I don't feel like dessert, at least not here. I know a better place. What do you say?" She slid out of the booth, took Nissim's hand, and led him toward the cashier.

"You're the driver," he told her.

NOTICING THE SINKING LIGHT, Yosef switched on his low beams, took a bite of his coconut donut, and pressed on the accelerator. Dusk for Yosef meant dinner time, and dinner time meant donuts. After paying to reclaim his cab from the parking garage, he had driven directly back to Thirtieth Street, had gotten in line, and had gone to work. For the past few hours business had been steady as travellers arrived by the trainload for the long weekend. Yosef's last passenger had gone to Yeadon. It had been a long ride, a profitable one, and now empty again he was ready to go home.

The Industrial Highway was less clogged with traffic than usual this afternoon. The cars on Yosef's right were moving faster so Yosef moved into the right-hand curb lane to make better time. After a few minutes the traffic thinned out until only one car, a red Plymouth Duster with mag wheels and a double tailpipe, stood between Yosef's cab and a traffic light about five hundred yards ahead. The Duster was doing fifty and speeding toward the intersection. Yosef pressed on the gas pedal, feeling an urgency inside him that would not accept his having to stop for a changing light. He didn't want to lose this momentum. Only fifty yards separated his yellow cab from the Plymouth. Just then the traffic light turned yellow, but rather than slowing down, Yosef pressed the pedal to the floor.

"Go through! Go through!" Yosef shouted in Hebrew as he noticed the distance between his taxi and the red car shrinking at an alarming rate. But the driver of the Duster was afraid. He slammed on his brakes while the signal was still yellow. The red Plymouth skidded across the asphalt and came to a stop several feet into the intersection.

"You fool!" Yosef screamed, shifting his foot from the gas pedal to the brake. The tires screeched as his wheels locked and the yellow cab rocketed forward. Pumping the pedals and gripping the wheel, he kept the cab from spinning out of control, almost stopping it in time, but Yosef could only watch in disgust as it slid forward the last few inches and kissed the Duster's bumper.

The driver of the Duster jumped out of his car and slammed the door closed. He was a lanky looking seventeen-year-old who stood about six feet tall and wore a torn black nylon jacket and black jeans. He looked angry. He walked hurriedly to the rear of his car to inspect it for damage. "You idiot! Where'd you buy your license?" he shouted at Yosef as he neared the cab. "You almost killed me!"

Yosef listened as the teenager loosed a barrage of insults, but he remained seated inside his cab. A little tap, no damage. What's the problem? he thought. I've got to get home. I don't have time for this.

"You fool! You imbecile!"

Yosef sat silent as the teenager kept spouting insults at him. This wasn't Israel, he reminded himself. There you could get agitated and exercised and verbally abusive over anything, as everyone did, and know that it would never come to blows. But he learned from driving his taxi through the streets of Philadelphia that behavior like that in America was equivalent to challenging someone, to laying down a dare. He could either sit tight and take the insults in silence, or get out of his car and meet the challenge head-on.

"What's the matter, you scared to come out?" the youth asked. "Look what you did here. I can't believe what you did. You dented my fucking bumper. Do you see this?" he said, pointing. "Let me see your driver's license."

"Why do you want to make a problem?" Yosef said through his open window.

"Make a problem! *You* made the problem. *You* ran into *me.* Where's your license?"

"What did you stop for?" Yosef asked, not moving. "We both would've made it."

"Look. Give me your information or I'm calling a cop," the youth threatened.

"Go ahead. You were speeding. The cops will see your skid marks."

"I don't need cops to settle this. Get your ass out here. I'll bash your face in." The seventeen-year-old pumped his shoulders and straightened his jacket.

"Take it easy. I'll take a look." Yosef opened the door deliberately and slid out from behind the wheel. Seated, he had appeared shorter, so his size surprised the teenager when he got out and began walking toward him. There was no fear in Yosef's eyes. "It's a scratch. It's nothing," he said.

"It's 'nothing' on *my* fucking bumper," the teenager shouted. "And hey, man, it'll cost me to fix it."

"Look, friend," Yosef said firmly, "I've got to get going. *My* bumper looks the same as yours and I wouldn't spend a penny on it." He reached into his pants pocket, opened his wallet, and handed the youth a bill. "Here's five dollars. Okay?"

The youth looked at the bill in disgust, "Five dollars!" he said. "What are you trying to do, jew me?"

"Pardon?"

"What d'you think I am? Stupid? Five dollars won't pay for nothing." He looked at Yosef more closely and noticed the star around his neck. "Right. You Jews think you can buy your way out of anything." Saying this, the youth stepped back, jerking his neck and shoulders as though his jacket were too small. "Fuck your five dollars, you cheap bastard." The youth walked back to his car and opened the trunk. He pulled out a rusty crowbar, closed his fist around its steel shaft, and walked back to Yosef. "Now give me your goddam insurance," he said.

Yosef didn't want to fight, but he also didn't like being threatened. He had let the slurs wash over him without responding, but now he could feel rage surging inside him. He moved forward toward the youth. As the youth raised the crowbar to strike him, Yosef grabbed the youth's arm at the wrist in one quick motion and squeezed with a vise-like grip until the crowbar fell to the ground. Then with another sudden motion he grabbed the lapels of the youth's leather jacket and pulled the teenager to him so their faces almost touched. In the army Yosef had been trained in hand-to-hand combat. One technique he had learned involved butting his head into the skull of an attacker. Gripping the uniform of your foe in your fists, you drove your forehead into his as you pulled him toward you. The skull was the hardest bone in your body.

As long as your head initiated the collision, you were all right. Yosef considered using what he knew. It was hard for him to restrain the urge to use his head as a weapon.

"I could break your head like a chicken egg," Yosef said, talking more to control himself than to say anything to the teenager, "or you could go back to your car and drive away. You choose." Thrusting his arms forward, he pushed the youth away. Yosef stood for a long moment with his arms extended, his palms open, staring coldly at him.

The teenager stood fixed there, staring back into Yosef's eyes for a few seconds, debating whether to pick up the crowbar, but looking at Yosef he decided not to. Instead he walked back to his Duster.

Yosef watched the high school boy get into his car. "Don't fuck with us, you know?" he said, loudly. Then collecting himself, he got back into his cab and drove off.

As the cab drove away, the boy made a mental note of its license. Pennsylvania plates. TX 16381. Two decals on the rear bumper also caught his eye and stuck in his mind—a U.S.A. decal on the left, an Israeli flag decal on the right. He reached into his jacket pocket, pulled out the crumpled five dollar bill, and stared at it for a long time. "No one gets off that cheap," he muttered.

"So you've only been here two weeks?" Denise asked, walking into the living room with two glass bowls of ice cream. Each bowl had a scoop of Abbott's chocolate chip sitting in the hole of a honey-glazed donut, and a spoon was stuck in each scoop, protruding up like a knife in the ground.

They had stopped at Yankee Doodle Donuts before coming back to Denise's apartment. After Nissim had introduced Denise to Oded, Oded pursed his lips, made a circle with two fingers, and nodded his head in approval. "Fantastic," he had mouthed to Nissim while Denise had surveyed the racks of donuts on the slanted shelves behind the counter. Oded had given them half a dozen donuts as a car-warming gift.

"You must still be in culture shock," Denise continued. "I envy you, though—everything being so new and all." She set the bowls down on the small walnut cabinets that doubled as stereo speakers and end tables on either side of her sofa. A lighted cigarette was balanced on the lip of the ceramic ashtray on the speaker at her end. "Do you miss it? Home, I mean?" she asked, picking up the cigarette and taking a deep drag.

He pictured himself travelling along the Haifa-Tel Aviv highway, palm trees bending against the wind, the Mediterranean Sea seductively blue, drawing his eye, not letting it go, sucking him into its undertow. "I am here too short to miss it," he told her as she sat down next to him on the sofa. "And America is getting always more interesting."

Denise watched his eyes as he said this last sentence. There was a light there, she thought, a certain glint that showed her he wanted her. She took off her sandals, got up again, and moved across the small room. A candle sat on a ceramic plate on top of the television. The candle was the size of a coffee mug, solid and wide, and made of rainbow-colored layers of wax. She lit the candle, gently cupping her hand around the flame, then moved to the stereo console on the bookcase near the front door. "Half of appetite is atmosphere," she said, "no, more like all of it." From the file of record albums she pulled one out, slipped the record onto the turntable, and turned on the stereo. "Do you like this kind?" she asked as the room began to fill with music.

"L-tone Joan? Of course," Nissim told her. "Who *doesn't* like him?"

With her back turned to Nissim as she played with the balance and treble knobs, she couldn't help smiling at his accent. She adjusted the volume setting, then walked back along the carpet and

141

sat down again next to Nissim. "If you had to pick just one difference, the first big difference that hit you between Israel and America, what would it be?"

"Just one?" Nissim asked, leaning forward on the sofa to reach his ice cream dish. "The biggest difference," he began, speaking as though he were about to make a major pronouncement, "is . . ." he thought a moment, "parking lots."

"Parking lots?" she asked. "That's it?" Of the many possibilities that had passed through her mind, that had not been one of them. "What's so shocking about parking lots?"

"For you maybe it is not something," he said, "but for me it is. In Israel we don't have them. No room. And also shopping bags we don't have. Paper is too much expensive."

"What do people do when they go shopping then?" she asked.

"Take many buses and bring plastic baskets."

"Oh." She took off her Indian-bead headband, pulling it back off her head. Soft strands of blonde hair fell onto her face. She tossed her head back and swept them away. "But they're just little things," she told him. "What's the biggest difference?"

Nissim thought a moment, finishing a spoonful of ice cream and looking pensively across the apartment. "The biggest difference," he began again, "is that everything here is big. Everything. It's like looking at things through a—how do you call it—a magnifying glass. The houses, the buildings, the roads, the trees, even the cars. Everything."

The sofa on which they sat was eight pillows, four laid flat on the carpeted floor, four leaning against the wall. It was virtually like sitting on the floor. Facing the sofa were three empty chairs. One was made of plastic, a fat yellow inflated tube that looked to Nissim more suited for the beach than for the living room; the other two were giant beanbags that conformed to the shape of your body when you sat in them. In the middle of the room was a white paper lamp that looked like a party lantern, and it hung so low from the ceiling that you had to either duck under it or walk around it to move from one side of the room to the other. Other than this lantern-lamp and the candle, no other lights were turned on in the apartment. Nissim couldn't help staring at the large-framed glossy poster that covered most of the half-wall between the kitchenette and the living room. It was a nearly life-size photo of a gorilla gazing out peacefully from its mountain habitat. There were no words or slogans on the poster.

"What is this monkey,?" Nissim asked, turning to Denise beside him.

"That monkey's a gorilla," she answered, "one of the few still left." A nature conservationist, Denise had made saving the mountain gorillas in Uganda her latest cause. "Doesn't he look human?" she asked, looking across at the framed poster as she spoke. "And gentle. They're the gentlest animals around, you know. So why aren't people screaming about what's happening to them? I swear, apathy's worse than murder sometimes, you know?"

Nissim nodded.

"Well," she went on, "what's happening is the gorillas are being wiped out. They're being pushed to the edge of extinction. I don't know about you, but a world that doesn't make room for animals, that takes away their natural space and takes away their dignity, isn't much of a world."

Nissim listened to Denise and watched her eyes flare as she spoke about this animal's plight. He listened about the gorilla, but thought about this woman beside him. Beautiful women have it hard, he told himself. They're almost always lonely because so few men feel equal to them, so few men feel at ease in their presence. They suffer from limited options, diminished possibilities, spiraling odds against them. The men they might find attractive don't seek them out for fear of feeling inferior, of being rejected, and the men who do seek them out are usually arrogant rather than confident, looking at them as ornaments and props rather than people. And their problems with other women are even worse than their problems with men, Nissim thought. Other women read motives into everything women like Denise do or say. Either they call them manipulative and calculating for using their beauty or else dumb for simply relying on it. Nissim wanted Denise to see he did not feel threatened by her beauty, that he did not feel self-conscious with her, that he had enjoyed today, tonight, now. He looked at her sitting next to him.

"But where's all the moral outrage?" she continued. "It's like everyone sees it and no one cares. Everything boils down to who's gonna give a damn in Washington, who's gonna raise his hand and do something about it. But how many gorillas live here in Philly, right? Or in New York or L.A. for that matter. Do you realize that whether or not they'll be wiped off the face of the earth depends completely on the whims of people who don't know anything about them?"

Whose fate doesn't? Nissim wondered. He was impressed by Denise's concern, by her sensitivity and activist sentiment, but he was also amused by it. Was she really so innocent, so naive? People don't care about people, he thought, so why should they care about apes? He spooned himself some chocolate chip ice cream, leaned back against the cushion behind him, and noticed another poster above his head. Slowly he turned his body around and pulled away from the wall to see it. This one was also a large-framed photograph, but of a woman, not an ape. Centered in an oval browned picture, the woman was dancing on a stage, her arms raised in a graceful ballet pose, a lace curtain behind her. Underneath the oval was printed in script letters: *All Of Her Gestures Left Ripples In The Air.* "This one is not an animal," Nissim said to Denise, looking at the poster as he spoke.

"No," she told him, "that's Isadora. Isadora Duncan. She was a great artist, just about revolutionized ballet and dance as we know it, and a great woman."

"Oh," Nissim said. He had never heard of this American dancer before. "It is a nice picture. I like it."

"Yeah, so do I," Denise told him. "Isadora was an original, the first 'modern woman.' I think she knew what life's about, you know?" She put down her spoon of donut and ice cream, exchanging it for her cigarette and changing the subject. "Do you want anything else to eat? I've got some frozen soft pretzels I could pop in the toaster oven if you want?"

"No," Nissim answered, patting his stomach. "I'm fine, believe me." Everything here was foreign to him— the music, the sofa, the chairs, the candle, the gorilla on the wall staring back at him, the donut in his bowl, Denise. But the very strangeness pleased him. It challenged him to explore and compare, to experience and remember. This was why he'd come to America, he reminded himself, to sample another world, a new world. As he listened to Elton John blaring his songs through the speaker-cabinet at his elbow, he looked at the row of half-windows that spanned the upper length of the wall to his left. It was already dark outside, the white venetian blinds were closed, and judging from the absence of fresh air, so were all the windows.

"You going to be living in the dorms?" Denise asked. "At Penn they're pretty nice really."

"No," Nissim answered, "too much money. I think I will live with my brother for a while, then maybe find some apartment." He stood up and moved over to the wall of half-windows that rose from just above eye level to the ceiling. "But one with a view, a nice one, you know?"

"What? You mean you don't like the view here?" she said, putting on an offended tone. "Where else can you look *up* at the sidewalk? I mean, really. This gives you a bona fide, real McCoy, roach's eye view. You don't find a basement like this every day, you know."

Nissim flashed a half-smile down at her, then spread two blinds and got up on his toes to look outside at the pavement. "I know. Do you ever open the windows?"

"Open the windows?" she said, sounding shocked. "Sure, I opened them up about four months ago." She stood up, carrying her cigarette with her, and walked to join Nissim at the windows. "See that spot?" she asked, pointing to a yellowed circle of carpet about six feet from the wall. "A German Shepherd did that. Honestly, when the steam cleared I was surprised it didn't eat a hole there. That was the last time I opened these windows. And, hey, when you find that apartment of yours with a view, let me know. Maybe I'll split it with you."

Nissim smiled at the idea, but didn't make any comment. Instead he looked at the yellow stain on the rug, then unfolded his shirt sleeve and took out a cigarette from the pack there. Before lighting it he turned back to Denise. "It's hot in here, no?" he asked.

She looked at him hard a moment, and then gave him a suggestive smile. "Maybe, but I'm a summer person, I guess—swimming, tennis, bumming out on the beach and all. I like it when things heat up. Don't you?"

"I come from the summer," he told her, "but I think I like better the winter."

"Meaning what exactly?"

"In Haifa all my life I spend in the sun, in the waters, always where it is hot, but now I like better the cold. This air conditioner, it works? In Israel we are not having these."

She switched on the wall-unit air conditioner which made a noise like a jet engine as it revved up to start cooling. "How's that feel?" she asked.

"Better."

"If you like it cold, wait till it snows."

"I am waiting very much for snowing. In Haifa we don't snow."

"In Philly we do. We get our share, but you'll have to wait till Christmas," she told him, "or should I say till Chanukah?"

"You should to say what you want," he told her, feeling a sudden easing inside him, a sense of comfort, of intimacy. But he did not want to overstep the bounds, to do something that might be misinterpreted by her, that might threaten her. After all, he told himself, he was a stranger, a foreign stranger. "When do you want to take me home?" he asked, checking his watch. Yosef had given him a ride to her place this afternoon and she had promised to drive him back to Louise Lane.

"I'm not sure," she said, touching his arm and putting one gentle hand on the waist of his pants, "I'm not sure . . . that I do."

THROUGH THE CLOSED SLATS of the venetian blinds a glow of street lamps entered and played on the walls as on water. Denise and Nissim lay in her high brass bed, visible in the glow from outside and in the soft yellow light from the candle which now sat on top of her bureau. The cotton sheet and soft blue blanket were bunched in a random mound at their feet. Denise pressed her thighs against him, then propped herself up on her knees and slid forward. Her hands were behind her, fingers spread flat on the mattress, arms supporting her. "Ah, Nissim." Straddling him she threw her head back, her long silken hair washing over his thighs like warm waves, then she leaned forward. Her hair cascaded down over him, gently running across his face, his lips, his eyes, as her breasts, round and firm, loomed above him. Reaching up he caressed them, kissed them, then took one nipple between his teeth and ran his tongue back and forth against it. He could hear her breaths growing shorter, more shallow, could feel the rhythm begin to control her even as it was drawing him in. She slid up further, beginning to roll her hips in wide circles, pressing him deeper and deeper inside her, her palms still flat behind her. He arched his back and began to roll with her, reaching his hands forward and stroking the inside of her thighs. "Yes, like that," she moaned. "Don't stop."

Nissim kept rolling his hips beneath her, stroking her legs and running his tongue across her breasts. His eyes were closed, but for an instant he opened them and saw the candle flame burning on the bureau. She had carried it in with her from the living room "for atmosphere," but for him it was not romantic. The atmosphere it created depressed him. It didn't give him appetite, either for food or carnal pleasures. To him candles were death lights, *yarh-zeit* flames. They were funerals and nightmares and Avi's grave. He took her nipple hard in his teeth and caressed it with his tongue. But how could she understand that? he thought. How? He closed his eyes again, listened to her breathing become spasmodic, and stroked her everywhere, feeling himself lose control. They rolled together in Denise's bed, locked and moaning in each other's arms. It was the Fourth of July in America.

Seven

HAIFA • JULY 4, 1975

AN EXPLOSIVE CHARGE hidden in an old refrigerator left on the sidewalk exploded today during the height of the pre-Sabbath shopping rush hour in Jerusalem's Zion Square. Thirteen Israelis are dead and seventy-two people, including two children and three women, have been wounded in the blast. Today's attack is the city's bloodiest terrorist incident since the founding of the State.

Government officials believe this attack is an attempt by Palestinian guerrilla organizations to disrupt the diplomatic negotiations presently underway for a new interim agreement between Israel and Egypt.

In Beirut the General Command of the Palestinian Revolution has issued a statement saying that the Jerusalem bomb attack, quote, "shattered the Zionist myth of security."

Mayor Teddy Kollek has appealed for calm and has urged both the Jewish and Arab communities in Jerusalem to display, quote, "mutual tolerance."

Reaction from around the world has been swift

. . . .

Barukh switched off the radio and returned to the Shabbat dinner table. "The murdering bastards!" he muttered to himself.

Shoshanah watched him take his seat, straighten the black beret

on his head, and try to ease the rage on his face with a slow sip
of Kiddush wine. Then she turned to Miryam. Miryam's hair was
in disarray with random strands hanging loosely, not neatly tied
in a bun at the back as usual. The white scarf on Miryam's head
looked like a bandage to Shoshanah. She had never seen Miryam
so drawn. The two weeks since Nissim's departure had taken a
visible toll, and this morning's news had not helped. Miryam wore
the tragedy across her forehead; it seemed almost to collapse her
brows. There were purple bags like wrinkled pouches under both
eyes, and even her smiles, short-lived as they were, didn't bring
any real light to Miryam's face. While blessing the Sabbath candles
tonight, she had stood with slouched shoulders, her movements
listless, her voice monotonic. Shoshanah knew these signs too
well. A physical therapist, she had seen them many times in her
patients, and seeing them now in Miryam concerned her. But that
was the reason she had wanted to come to dinner tonight, so that
Miryam and Barukh would not spend this Sabbath eve alone. It
had been a long, trying day for her at Rambam Hospital, it had
been a long, trying week for that matter, and when the terrible
news of the Zion Square murders had spread through the hospital
in the afternoon, it had left everyone in shock and in mourning.
But she was determined to help brighten the mood tonight at
HaTishbi 113. The Lvovs were like family to her, having treated
her as a daughter since she had been a little girl. Her parents had
complained for years that she spent more time in Nissim's home
than she did in her own.

"It's a wonder anyone's coming anymore," Miryam said,
ladling out a third bowl of soup from the steaming tureen at her
elbow, "and it's no wonder everyone's leaving."

Barukh listened to his wife's comment, disagreed, but decided
to say nothing. He looked across the room at the oak bookcase,
running his eyes down the line of gilt-framed photographs of family as he had the previous Shabbat. Where were the boys? he

thought. What were they doing right now? He wondered if they had heard the news yet about Zion Square. In the next letter he would send them clippings.

Outside there was almost no noise, except for the sound of the wind chimes from the downstairs neighbor's porch and the infrequent passing of a car. Shoshanah played with the Eilat stone pendant which hung on a thin gold chain around her neck, pulling on it as she listened to the Sabbath quiet.

"I've always been curious to know, and neither Nissim nor you ever told me," Shoshanah began, having thought of a way to change the subject, "what kind of a name is Lvov, besides a nice one of course?"

"I chose it. Not exactly out of the air, but I chose it," Barukh told her, "same as your father chose his." He looked across the Sabbath candles at Miryam, then scanned the frames on the bookcase again. "My family name was Leibovitch, and my father, who was a pious man—for all the good it did him—used to teach us a special prayer when we were little. *T'hillim kahf daled,* Psalm 24. One verse of it made a special impression on me. *N'kee khapayim u-var lvov.* It's the answer to a question: 'Who shall ascend the mountain of God and who shall stand in His holy place? He who has clean hands and a pure heart, and who has not set his mind on what is false.' Lvov was close to Leibovitch, so I picked it."

"I never knew that," Shoshanah, said, a warm smile spreading across her lips. "That's beautiful."

"When's the last time you had clean hands?" Miryam asked her husband, picking up the serving fork and lifting the platter of boiled chicken. "Whenever I see them, they're filthy, into some kind of mess. And your heart—who cares if it's pure, if it stops? Stop pushing yourself." She saw the look-who's-talking smile on Barukh's face. "I know what you're thinking, and yes I took my pills," she said, unable to fight smiling back at him. "Do you want some more kugel?"

"No," he told her, "I'm fine." Broken sentences of the reporter's voice from the radio replayed inside Barukh's head, interspersed there with verses of Psalm 24. Barukh listened to the strange tape in his mind as he looked at the peaceful table before him—the white cloth and braided loaves, the white candles in their silver candlesticks, the pewter winecups, the Sabbath foods, the faces.

Miryam began talking and put two pieces of chicken on Shoshanah's plate. "Shosh, you should start with a breast and a thigh," she said. "White meat and dark keeps a body in balance."

"One is really enough," Shoshanah told Miryam, protesting as she held up her plate. "Even if I could eat both, I don't need them."

"Shosh," Miryam said, holding the serving fork over Shoshanah's plate and debating whether to stab one of the pieces, "you're not on a diet, are you?"

"No, but I should be," Shoshanah told her. She liked when Miryam called her "Shosh." Miryam had called her that since Nissim and she were in first grade together. It was the nickname Nissim called her, and she couldn't hear Miryam say it without thinking of him, without thinking of him and of Avi. Avi had always called her "Shana." Together, she had kidded them when they were younger, the two of them had made her whole.

"With your body you don't have to worry," Miryam said. She looked at Shoshanah's full round face with those high cheekbones and deep brown eyes, remembering how they had made her seem womanlike even as a child. There was a voluptuousness about her, Miryam thought, the kind that couldn't accommodate thinness, the kind that always made girls like Shoshanah worry that they were a few pounds too heavy. Her fair brown hair was straight but layered around her face, giving her cheeks a certain softness. She was small, about 5'2", and pretty without the aid of makeup. Miryam liked her genuineness, the natural way Shoshanah presented herself, how animated she became when she spoke, always using her hands for emphasis, her eyebrows rising and her eyes widening with interest when she listened to you. And she liked the way Shoshanah dressed, modern but not too bohemian, in clothes loose fitting enough to hide any unwanted weight, but not too loose to hide her shapeliness. The top three buttons of Shoshanah's soft white cotton shirt were open, revealing the top of her breasts. Miryam looked at the tanned soft skin and watched Shoshanah play with the beautiful pendant which had been Avi's gift to her as the symbol of their engagement. Had that only been two years ago? Shoshanah and Avi had made such a handsome couple, she thought. "You're well enough put together to carry a few extra pounds," Miryam said.

"You can see the extra pounds then?" she asked, upset at the thought.

"No, no, Shosh. That's not what I meant at all," Miryam answered. "I just meant that you look prettier fuller, not like the emaciated girls the magazines call models. Anyway, dieting's unnatural; it's unhealthy to begin with." Hunger made you thin, she thought. Auschwitz made you thin.

"She's right," Barukh agreed. "From where I'm sitting I wouldn't worry about cutting out any pleasures if I were you, Shoshanah."

"Thank you, Barukh," she said, smiling first at him and then at the serving fork which Miryam still held over her plate.

"And you're sure you don't want this piece, Shosh?" Miryam asked, sticking the fork into one of the chicken breasts.

"Zeisa, she has what she needs," Barukh said, frowning and shaking his head. "Just let her put her plate down already so she can at least eat what she wants." As he looked again at his wife across the candle flames, glad to see her finally take one of the chicken parts away, he noticed the empty chair beside her on one side of the table. Yossi's chair. The sight of Yosef's vacant seat made Barukh feel that Nissim's was empty as well, though Sho-shanah was sitting in Nissim's place. How had it happened that both boys were gone? he asked himself. How was it that he and Miryam were alone tonight, except of course for Shoshanah who had come to take care of her best friend's poor parents? He thought back over the years when, instead of spending their hard-earned savings on themselves, he and Miryam had invested in their boys' future. After Europe, after the camps, their dream had been safety and permanence, and this they had achieved. The Central Carmel had been their home since their wedding day twenty-seven years ago, and 113 HaTishbi Street had been their sole address. For twenty-seven years they had not ventured outside Israel. Trips to Eilat, the Kinneret, Jerusalem, stays in the guest house at Kibbutz HaGoshrim had been their yearly vacations. World travel held no magic for them.

Instead of spending their savings on travel and other luxuries, they had invested in their children, in their future. Dividends from children are dearer than money, they believed. Weekly since 1950, since the day their store had opened, they had deposited liras into a savings account for Nissim. The balance was linked to the rate of inflation, which in Israel was astronomic. Avram Lvov had opened a similar savings account for his son, Yosef. Six years later, when Avram died, Barukh had started depositing money into Yosef's account.

What daydreams Barukh and Miryam had shared! How would the boys use those savings? they wondered. Perhaps they would buy adjacent villas right on HaTishbi Street. Maybe they would launch a joint business, making great fortunes together. And maybe then, as philanthropists, they would open a school or a hospital. Or would this money stifle their ambitions? Maybe they both would pursue simple loves rather than capital interests. Maybe, freed from financial worry, they would father larger families, raise more "sabra" grandchildren. All the options had been thrilling.

It had never entered Barukh's mind that both boys would use those savings to fly half-a-world away from him, a world away from home. Not that he begrudged them their freedom. The savings were theirs to use as they chose. But the thought of seeing them only in snapshots, of sharing their exploits only by mail, of hearing their voices only by phone and then just on special occasions, pained him deeply. The funds which he had dreamed would allow them more time with Miryam and himself had let them choose less instead. Barukh felt cheated.

Had it been worth the years of budget scrimping? Had it been worth the forfeited pleasures, the worries and the sweat? He thought of the reparations from Germany. What of the death camps, his time in Treblinka, those winters in the forest? Had his parents, his teachers, his people died to finance his sons' departures? Or were these Deutschmarks their legacy, the inheritance they would have willed had Auschwitz never existed? If they had lived, wouldn't they have been proud to finance their grandchildren's dreams? Shouldn't *he* be? Everything costs something else, Barukh told himself. Every breath is a trade-off.

The kitchen door to the laundry porch was open, and a breeze wafted down through the apartment from the direction of the sea, gently swaying the candle flames as it moved through the dining room and out through the open living room window.

"Why are so many leaving?" he said more than asked, turning to Shoshanah, a serious, almost severe look on his face. "What are they after?" He rose suddenly from the table and hurried into the living room. "Wait," he said as he walked away, "let me show you something." In a second he returned with a copy of that day's *Maariv* which he unfolded and held up in front of his face. All that was visible above the opened page was the black beret on

Barukh's head.

"Wasn't the radio enough for tonight?" Miryam said, not pleased to see him reading the newspaper at the Sabbath table. "But if you have to bring the headlines in here, read us already from the paper."

"I know you don't like it, Zeisa," he said, lowering the paper while he spoke, "but dinner is for having discussions, and this is for discussion." He watched Miryam shrug to Shoshanah in resignation, then turn her eyes back to him. He raised the page and started reading. "'Immigration Down; Emigration Soaring. Only six thousand new immigrants have come into Israel during the first five months of this year, which is less than half as many as arrived in the country during the same period last year. At the current rate, a total figure of less than fifteen thousand new immigrants is projected for 1975. The graph for the past three years shows a shocking decline: 56,000 in 1972, 55,000 in 1973, only 32,000 in 1974 – and now a projection of less than half last year's total for this year.' Do you hear these numbers? No one's coming. 'At the same time, figures from the Government Bureau of Statistics show that emigration continues to increase at an alarming rate. Approximately eighteen thousand Israelis, about .5% of the State's total population, emigrated last year. This was the highest number of *yordim* for any year since Israel declared statehood in 1948.'" Barukh peered over the paper a moment, pausing to look at Miryam and Shoshanah who were listening as they ate. "And that's not the worst of it," he continued. "It says here that even more Israelis – about twenty thousand – are expected to emigrate this year. You don't need a degree from the Technion to add up the numbers. If less than fifteen thousand *olim* come this year and twenty thousand new *yordim* leave, that's a net loss of five thousand people; and if that happens, it'll be the first time that's ever happened since before '48." He paused again, then gave a deep sigh and read the last lines from the article. "'Ten percent of our citizens have left Israel to live in other countries.' Ten percent of Israel doesn't live in Israel anymore! Do you believe it? One out of every ten! It's an epidemic," he said. "A national disgrace." Barukh folded the paper and dropped it onto the floor beside his chair. "What's happening?" he asked Shoshanah. "Maybe you can tell me."

"Why me?" she said, finishing a bite of cinnamon raisin kugel. "If I had the answers I'd be in the Knesset."

"No you wouldn't. They only know from questions," he told her.

Miryam served him some cholent and handed him back his plate, reaching around the candlesticks.

"Look," he continued after taking the plate from Miryam, "no country in the world gives a damn if Jews leave it. No country but ours. Everyone else only gets bothered when we come in." He looked at Miryam who was nodding in agreement. "I can understand people not coming," he went on, "but people already here *leaving,* people who were *born* here—that's another story. What are they after? Money?"

"I don't know," Shoshanah said, wanting to choose her words carefully so as not to further upset the Lvovs. "I'm sure that's part of it. But statistics can lie, you know. Look at Nissim. Why'd he go?"

"Nissim went to study, to get his degree," Miryam answered in a defensive tone.

"But I'm not talking about Nissim," Barukh jumped in. "He's coming back when he finishes, just like Yossi. I'm talking about all the young people who are living there and plan to stay there."

"Don't get me wrong," Shoshanah said, "I'm not saying Nissim's going to stay in America, of course—but everyone I know of who's settled in there said they were only going for a short time when they left, and all of them had what sounded like good reasons to be going at the time." Shoshanah paused, thinking how to change the subject to something more optimistic. "How are Yossi and Rivka doing?" she asked.

"Fine," Miryam answered. "This will be Yossi's last year. He graduates in May, then they'll be on the first plane home." She smiled to picture their return.

"I don't have to tell you how glad Miryam will be to have them nearby again, especially Dorit," Barukh said. "We're both tired of worrying ourselves sick over a fever that Dorit has and then realizing she's already been better for a week by the time we get their letter, probably has finished her full week of antibiotics, and the news is ten days old. Distance confuses everything."

"But they'll be back at the start of next summer," Shoshanah said. "I'll bet they're as anxious as you are."

"Judging from Rivka's letters, more," Barukh told her.

"They just got a new house, you know?" Miryam added cheerfully.

"No, I didn't," Shoshanah said. "I thought they were in a rented apartment."

"They were, until a few weeks ago," Miryam explained, "A professor of Yossi's went on sabbatical and rented his house to them. They're sending us pictures, but from the way Rivka describes it, it's a miniature mansion."

"Oh," Shoshanah said, trying to hide that she didn't share Miryam's enthusiasm. "I hope it doesn't spoil them."

Miryam's face became lined, defensive, then it eased again. "Maybe you don't know Yossi and Rivka," she said.

"They know exactly what they're there for," Barukh added.

"I'm sure they do," Shoshanah said, "and next summer is close."

"Yes, it is, thank God," Miryam said. "Then I'll be able to stop counting for at least one of the boys, and I'll have my baby Dorit to take care of."

"Your baby Dorit is five years old now," Barukh said with a

smile. "We probably won't even recognize her."

"That doesn't worry me half as much as the fact the *she* won't recognize *us,*" Miryam told him. "Check under that beret of yours. We're three years older too, you know, but she was only two when she last saw us, and she hasn't seen us for over half her life."

Shoshanah saw that this last comment had thrown Miryam into a new despondency. "Send them pictures of both of you," Shoshanah said. "Send them new ones every month."

"Don't worry, we do," Barukh said.

"Good. I just hope she doesn't get off the plane looking for grandparents who are two inches tall," Shoshanah joked.

Miryam didn't find the thought funny, but smiled weakly.

"Distance is distance," Barukh said. "There's no two ways about it. Which is why I don't understand these figures." He picked up the newspaper from beside his chair, rolled it, pounded it into the palm of his hand. "It also says in here that Pinhas Sapir is closing three Aliyah Centers in the United States because so few American Jews are moving to Israel. Not that enough ever came from America, but when the Jewish Agency starts closing them down because there aren't any takers!" He looked at the empty chair again and thought back to a few weeks ago. "You know," he said, speaking more softly, a distant light in his eyes as he looked at the women around the table, "before Nissim left, when I was trying to change his mind, I told him to think about something my father used to tell me—if you don't run so far away, the way back will be shorter. That's what I told him. He understood, but he didn't listen."

"And look at how well you listened to that one yourself," Miryam chimed in. "More chicken, Shosh?"

Shoshanah put up a hand and shook her head.

"I ended up far away," Barukh responded, his voice growing louder, "and so did you, thank God. But we had something to run from. And we ran *to* this country, not away from it."

"Things can change in a day," Miryam said, turning to Shoshanah and speaking in a voice that sounded almost too calm. "Look at what happened when Yossi and Rivka left. They weren't gone two months when the war broke out. And nothing's been the same here since."

Thank goodness Yossi had stayed in the States and absented himself from the last war, she said to herself. Nissim, somehow, had walked away whole. But if anything had happened to him, to either of the boys, Miryam did not know how she could have survived it. So maybe it's better that both boys are not here now, she thought. Maybe I'm selfish to want them both home with me.

Shoshanah looked down at her plate, thought back to the war, and pictured Avi. "You asked me why I thought so many young people are leaving," she said, lifting her eyes, "well, what Miryam just said is the reason."

"The war?" Miryam asked.

"Not just the war but the way it ended," Shoshanah explained, "if it ever *did* really end, and as far as I'm concerned it never did. This heading for the exits is just another battle."

"It's a retreat is what it is!" Barukh said loudly.

"I think that people are asking themselves for the first time what the point of risking their lives is," Shoshanah answered. "And I blame Kissinger for that. When he said to let the Egyptian Third Army go when we finally had them cut off in the Sinai, to feed them and not to shoot after they had butchered hundreds of our men for days and days, the message was loud and clear from then on: Our men can fight a war, die in it, but not win it. What soldier is stupid enough to put his life on the line for that?"

Barukh listened but said nothing. Miryam began stacking the soup bowls and dinner plates, readying for dessert. "That's the biggest thing," Shoshanah continued as she passed her plate to Miryam. "Add to that people being fed up with high prices, high taxes, low salaries, and stepped up *milu'im* and I think that's why a lot of young people are leaving for good."

"It's not for *my* good, or for theirs either as far as I'm concerned. I refuse to understand it," Barukh said with real anger in his voice. "They're choosing between freedom and freedom, not slavery and death camps like we did, and they're still ready to lie for a green card. What is this, a prison? If you ask me, the ones who stay over there are runaways, deserters. You can blame Kissinger or Nixon or Sadat if you want to, but I say it's because of the *yordim* that we have the problems they're running away from — the inflation, too many months in *Tzahal* each year, too few people, too few children — if they were here, holding up their part of the bargain, the strain would be less on everyone, and the problems would solve themselves."

"I just can't believe that both boys, both . . . ," Miryam said, almost to herself, her words trailing off before ending her sentence as she rose to clear the table. Then she continued talking, her voice clearer and louder. "I don't understand this fascination with America," she said. "We had our chance to go there and came here instead. And even with all we've been through here, even with the wars and the PLO Nazis, I'd still make the same choice tomorrow."

"So would I, Zeisa, so would I," Barukh said gently as he watched Miryam carry the dishes into the kitchen, "which is why it galls me to see the children who were born here, kids Yossi's and Nissim's age, going in the opposite direction. Sure, things are tough now, but they've always been tough. I can remember back in '48 and '56 when things were a hundred times tougher than now and no one was bailing out then."

"You were fighting for a dream," Shoshanah said, standing at her place, a stack of soup bowls in her hands. "Maybe that's easier to fight for than a state is." She carried the soup bowls into the kitchen, leaving Barukh alone at the table to ponder what she had said. Miryam busied herself at the kitchen sink.

"To listen to you, Shoshanah," Barukh said, lifting his eyes when she came back into the room to collect the serving platters, "I'm surprised you don't catch the next plane out. Why aren't you doing something like Nissim?"

"I've thought about it more than once, believe me," Shoshanah told him. She thought about it, but every time she thought of leaving, she thought of Miryam. For years she had listened to Miryam's deadened tone, had watched numbness overtake her, and she didn't want to find herself in the same condition. The world of Miryam's youth had vanished, she told herself, and Miryam could only reconstruct it in her memory, could only revisit it in her dreams. If she went away, she thought, she could lose Israel. It could happen to her. "I guess I'm not like those electric shavers with switches for different voltages," she told Barukh. "I only run on 220."

"I like that," Barukh said, nodding and smiling. "I agree with you one hundred percent. Leaving to me is like dying."

"I didn't say that," Shoshanah corrected him.

"I know, Shoshanah. I did."

Shoshanah loaded her arms with the large platters and started into the kitchen. As she passed the oak bookcase and the picture of herself flanked by Avi and Nissim on Carmel Beach, she stopped. She stood there a second, laden with dishes and heavy thoughts. All too vividly October 1973 flashed back in her mind. The fifth day of the war. The day she had learned of Avi's death at the house of Avi's mother.

SHE WATCHED TWO MEN walk down the Farkoshes' street, aware they were *Tzahal's* messengers, an officer in uniform and a doctor.

"Avi was buried two days ago," the office told Mrs. Farkosh. "In a temporary grave near Gaza, at Kibbutz Yad Mordecai. You can travel there whenever you choose. He will be reinterred in Haifa, after the war is over."

Reinterred? Shoshanah thought. How could they? How could they have buried Avi before I even knew he was dead? Where was I when they buried him? Showering? Shopping? Sleeping? She shuddered at the memory and walked into the kitchen.

"Do you miss him as much as I do, Shosh?" Miryam asked, washing dishes at the sink.

"Nissim?"

"Who else?"

Avi, for one, Shoshanah felt like saying, but instead she stayed silent, set the platters down on the marble counter, and waited for Miryam to continue.

"Do you miss him as much as I do?" Miryam repeated.

You have this way of doing that, Miryam, she wanted to say, and it always gets me. You have this way of setting up comparisons, of competing, and you always ask me before I'm ready, like tonight when you handed me my soup and asked me how it tasted before I could even put the bowl down, let alone pick up my spoon. Nissim's hardly gone two weeks yet. I haven't had time to miss him. "Yes, Miryam," she said, "I do."

Miryam wiped her hands on a dish towel and moved across to the little table with the two apple cakes on it. She cut one cake into generous slices and laid them on a serving plate. Then keeping her back to Shoshanah, she tore off a corner of one piece and put it in her mouth.

"Miryam, Nissim's only gone to study," Shoshanah said gently. "Even when he was here he wasn't home most weekends. You said yourself this was just his drop-off station. He hasn't disappeared."

Miryam finished the piece of apple cake and turned dramatically to face Shoshanah. "Gone is gone."

Shoshanah pictured the car rides to Yad Mordecai with Avi's father and mother. Nissim's gone but he's alive, thank God, she thought. He may not be here, but he's alive, and I'd rather have him there and breathing than here and dead like Avi. "The cake smells delicious," she said. "Let's take some into Barukh."

Barukh had overheard their kitchen conversation and as they reentered the dining room, he sipped some wine from his goblet and acted as though he'd heard nothing. "You haven't told us a word about work, Shoshanah," he said cheerily. "Now that you've got your degree, are things different? More interesting for you?"

Shoshanah had earned her certificate in Physical Therapy a few months earlier after completing a sixteen-month program which included intensive clinical experience under formal supervision at Rambam Hospital, and concurrent courses in anatomy, physiology, psychology, and physics. The academic and professional demands had been rigorous, allowing little time for any other activities. She had decided to become a physical therapist in 1973 during the war when, not called up to fight because she was not an active reservist, she had volunteered as a paramedic at Rambam and had treated the hundreds of wounded soldiers driven and helicoptered to the emergency wards.

"Having the certificate has made a difference," she said, "but I thought things were pretty 'interesting,' as you say, all along. They've given me greater responsibilities for the past six weeks or so, and I have freer rein now, but bringing a patient back from a heart attack or a stroke, certificate or not, is still the same challenge, and I love it. Just trying to give them the will to keep going, not to give up on regaining control of their lives – it makes me feel sort of doubly alive, like I'm part of their struggle. Not that everyone makes such great progress. Some don't make any." She tugged at the pendant around her neck, then put the gold chain across her mouth, running the stone back and forth across her lips, the light in her eyes dimming.

"And what do you do with them?" Barukh asked. "The ones that can't get better? How do you know it's not better *not* to help them?"

Miryam looked with alarm at her husband. "What are you saying? That she should just let them curl up and die, Barukh?"

Barukh combed his moustache with his fingers. "I'm saying that if people can't be who they were again, then maybe they don't want to be anyone," he answered. "If you ask me, losing your dignity is worse than losing your life. And if all the therapy and exercise in the world can't give it back to you, then you're better off dead. Who wants to be a burden, causing pain and costing a fortune for however long you linger?" He turned his eyes from his wife to Shoshanah. "You see it every day, Shoshanah. You see what it does to a family when someone's only alive on paper, with all the machines and tubes and pumps keeping him going, or when he's just breathing without a brain. You tell me if it's not better to let him die."

Shoshanah did not want to answer. This was not the uplifting kind of discussion she'd envisioned for tonight. But Barukh had asked the question and she would answer it honestly. "Yes, I do think it's better, Barukh," she told him.

Miryam's eyebrows lifted as she heard Shoshanah's statement. "I'm shocked, I really am," she said. "No one should play God."

"The way God plays Himself, *someone* else has to," Barukh retorted.

"You and your quips," Miryam continued. "There's so little we control in our lives to begin with, that to give up, to just throw up your hands and stop fighting . . . ." She stopped and looked down at her plate for a second, then raised her eyes and spoke more slowly. "If we'd done that thirty years ago, Hitler'd have had his victory."

"We're not talking about Hitler," Barukh said quickly, looking across at Shoshanah for support, "or even about Jews. We're talking about people, about any person who's so far gone that nothing can bring him back, and I'm just being a realist and saying—"

The ringing of the doorbuzzer interrupted Barukh's sentence. Miryam went to answer it.

"Shoshanah," she called, surprised, "it's for you."

"Ronni," Shoshanah said as she came to the door. "I didn't realize how late it was. Ronni, this is Miryam Lvov."

"Pleased to meet you," the young man said. "Ronni Ben-Dor."

"Shalom," Miryam said, surprised by the sudden appearance of this young man who was Nissim's age and height. Shoshanah had never mentioned him to her.

"Are you ready?" Ronni asked Shoshanah. "The line's already started at the Cinemateque."

"Just let me get my pocketbook," she said, then walked into the living room, grabbed her handbag, and headed out the door. "I'm sorry I have to run. Thanks for the wonderful dinner. We'll finish our discussion another time. Shabbat shalom, Miryam. Shabbat shalom, Barukh."

"Shabbat shalom," Barukh called from the table.

"Enjoy yourselves," Miryam called after them as they headed down the marble-tiled stairwell together. Then she closed the door and joined Barukh at the Sabbath table. Cake plates, the dessert platter, coffee cups, and silverware were scattered in random disarray, and only two of the four chairs were filled now.

"A date?" Miryam said, speaking as much to herself as to her husband.

"And what's wrong with that?" Barukh asked. "Did you expect her to live in a convent?"

"No, of course not," Miryam said, "I just thought that tonight—"

"Tonight what?"

"That tonight she would be more understanding."

"What's that supposed to mean?"
"I don't know myself," Miryam told him.

Eight

ODED REFILLED YOSEF'S AND NISSIM'S CUPS of coffee and handed them another French cruller. "Has Rivka calmed down yet?" he asked.

"No, you know how it is," Yosef told him. "It'll take a few days, maybe a week, then she'll come around." He took a sip of his coffee and winced at the taste. "What's an extra six months anyway? I would've dropped out *this* term instead of waiting till January, I would've stopped school right now to make up the extra money if the deadline for refunds hadn't already passed." He had asked the University's registrar last Wednesday if he could get his tuition back and was told that after the first two weeks of classes, payment in full was due whether you attended the rest of the term or not. "Rivka's upset about my dropping out, and I'm not exactly loving it either. Well, that's Rivka. When plans change on her she goes crazy."

Yosef and Nissim were sitting on the padded stools at the counter as Oded worked busily behind the long white counter, fixing the filter on the coffee maker, using a towel to wipe up some spots near the Spraymaster juice machine, straightening the wire racks of donuts on the slanted shelves, readying Yankee Doodle for the morning's first customers. Every Saturday for the past six months Yosef had made his seven-thirty A.M. "Shabbat donut run" to bring home breakfast treats for Dorit. It had become a weekly ritual, one which Nissim had shared with him for the past three months.

Yankee Doodle Donuts was a separate structure that looked

like a giant rectangular phone booth, with three glass walls and one solid side where the kitchen and bakery were located. Oded looked at the trees through the wall of windows and thought how beautiful the seasons were here. A row of tall trees lined the parking area on the left side of the building. Even under the overcast skies they looked to him like a colorful abstract mural. It was almost as if a beneficent fire had climbed up their trunks, swirling flames of orange and amber at the tips of each cluster. In Israel there were no changing colors. There was only summer or winter, heat or rain, and the two never mixed. The shifts back home were boring and abrupt, he thought.

"Rivka might not be too wild about your staying, but I am," Oded said to Yosef. "An extra six months means you'll be here next summer, and that means we can go cross-country. All of us, together." A car passed through the parking lot, but did not pull in. Oded watched it drive away. "I've got this idea that keeps growing on me, and now that I know you'll be here, we're going to do it. I'm going to sell my dying Datsun and buy a school bus and turn it into a leisure van, my style. We'll tear out half the seats, lay down mattresses on the floor, and sleep in the bus. The way I figure it is Nissim will recondition the engine, you and I will give the bus a new coat of yellow paint, and then we're set. Picture it! Orly and Dorit can play together in the back, nap on the mattresses whenever they want to, Varda and Rivka can shoot the breeze while they're stretching their legs out across the long seats, and the three of us can split the driving. Hell, Nissim, we've got room for that American dream queen of yours, if you're still together. You'll be our pit crew and she can be our tour guide. What do you think?" He looked at Nissim and Yosef with wide eyes. "And we won't have to pay for any parking from here to California— no trailer parks or camp sites— because wherever we are when it's time to sleep we'll pull into the local school and, believe me, no one will bother us. It'll be like a dream, like we talked about, Yossi, and now that you're staying I'm doing it."

"Sounds great," Nissim said, seriously considering the invitation. He smiled to think of driving cross-country, crossing state lines without a passport, crossing borders without fighting a war. And he liked the idea of Denise coming with him. Things were going pretty smoothly between Denise and him. They were spending a lot of time together, going to movies and dinners, having good talks, longer talks lately, about everything from the gorillas in Uganda to the carcinogens in decaffeinated coffee, comparing growing up in America to growing up in Israel, and they'd had no fights, no real disagreements to speak of. Nissim had expected her to start putting pressure on him, to start attaching strings to their relationship, but she was still as free and accepting now as she had been on the first day they met. Tonight they were going to the movies. *One Flew Over The Cuckoo's Nest* was playing at Market Square.

"Sounds great to me," Yosef said. "Cab, bus—I'll drive anything that's yellow. But Rivka'll never agree to it."

"Don't worry about Rivka," Oded told Yosef. "I'll have Varda talk to her. She'll go. Just give her time."

"Time," Yosef said, chuckling sarcastically. That's what Rivka was scared of, he thought. She didn't want the extra months to become extra years here as they already had for Oded and Varda, and neither did he.

"You know what she's scared of?" Oded said more than asked. "She's scared of liking it too much here, that's what she's scared of. She's scared of wanting to stay here. I know it. Varda went through the same thing two years ago. After we talked out all the guilt and she screamed at me for doing therapy on her, we cut through all the emotional garbage and came around to seeing that staying here isn't the worst thing that could happen. In fact, maybe it's a good thing."

"For whom?" Yosef asked quickly, surprised.

"I'd like to hear this one, too," Nissim said, eating the last small piece of his donut.

"Well, look at it this way," Oded began, taking a red plastic bread basket off the shelf, putting it down on the counter, and filling it two-deep with donuts. "Let's say this is a boat and it's holding more people than it can carry. What would you do to keep it from sinking? Take some of the people off, right?" He lifted out half of the donuts and put them back into a rack on the shelf. "Well, this is Israel," he went on, holding up the plastic basket, "and right now it's sinking. There aren't enough good jobs there to go around, not enough apartments for everyone, and there sure isn't enough money — so every person who bails out is doing the State a favor; every person who leaves for a while is easing the squeeze on everyone who stays."

Yosef couldn't believe his ears. Oded's leaving didn't make it easier for anyone, except maybe for Oded and Varda, and even of that Yosef wasn't certain. Oded's living in America meant someone else back home had to offset the taxes Oded wasn't paying, had to offset the time in *Tzahal* Oded wasn't serving, had to offset the ideas and energy Oded wasn't contributing. To Yosef, leaving Israel to settle somewhere else, not just to study there but to settle there, was shameful. It was like being born into a family, then leaving that family for one with a bigger house and more money. No one could trade in one family for another without feeling pain and great shame. Yosef stared at the bread basket filled with donuts on the counter in front of him.

"There's only one thing wrong with your theory, Oded," he said. "Bailing out might keep the boat floating, but someone else will own it."

Oded listened to Yosef then turned to Nissim when Yosef had finished speaking. "Am I wrong, Nissim? Are my facts wrong?" he asked.

"No," Nissim said, thinking before saying anything more.

There was some truth, maybe a lot of truth, in what Oded was saying. The housing situation in Haifa was terrible. A young couple couldn't begin to afford even a one-bedroom apartment in the city, and a single person coming out of the army could afford it half as well. Nissim himself had saved a lot of money by signing on with *Tzahal* after his national service. He had not had to pay for room and board since he turned eighteen, and even he couldn't afford an apartment of his own in Haifa. He remembered some news clippings Barukh had sent in one of the recent letters. Instead of writing anything, Barukh enclosed clippings from *Maariv* while Miryam wrote the family news. One of the articles had said that Israel's inflation was second only to Italy's as the worst in the world. Another said that Israel's cities were among the most crowded anywhere. Maybe Oded had a point. Maybe Israel had too much to carry, too many people with too many needs. Maybe the ship was sinking. "Your facts aren't wrong," he said to Oded. "I wish they were, but they're not."

"See, what did I tell you?" Oded said, turning to Yosef. "Tell Rivka not to punish herself about staying a little longer. Staying here's helping out."

Yosef gave his friend a crooked look, picturing Rivka bending a metal table leg around Oded's neck and heaving him out of the house. He debated whether to say something to him, unsure of exactly what to say but not wanting to let the statement go unchallenged, when a bell jingled and Yosef spun his stool around to see a customer coming through the front door.

As the man approached the counter and began surveying the racks of donuts, Yosef turned to Nissim. "Well, little brother," he said, slapping Nissim on the back again, "time to hit the road. Dorit's probably been sitting at the kitchen table for half an hour already."

"Please, I'll be right with you," Oded told the customer as he quickly picked up a waxed paper napkin and began filling a box with donuts for Yosef and Nissim. He selected an assortment of different flavors, folded the box shut, and taped it closed. "Have a nice day," he said to them in English, handing Yosef the paper box and flashing a formal, friendly smile, "and please to come again." Then softly he added in Hebrew, "Shabbat shalom."

Yosef did not reach for his wallet. The donuts were free this morning, as every Saturday. Oded went to wait on the man as Yosef and Nissim thanked him in English and headed outside to the cab.

Brown and orange and yellow leaves were scattered across the blacktop, blowing back and forth in the cool morning wind. Yosef and Nissim got into the cab and watched Oded through the windshield. Behind the glass walls he was unracking donuts like mortar shells and loading them into two boxes. Yosef thought about the school bus idea and imagined them motoring cross-country, all of them breaking free of their worries, leaving their debts behind them. "Nissim," he said, "do you think we should go?"

"Go where?" Nissim asked, still watching Oded.

"Cross-country, in that school bus."

"Yes," he said, smiling, "I think we should."

Yosef could feel the idea emerging inside him. More than a thought it was becoming an image, something he could visualize. If Oded was serious about selling his Datsun and buying a school bus, then Yosef was going to count himself in. Rivka he'd have to work on later. He watched Oded helping the customer and decided that he was going to buy him one of those white baker's hats. The watch on his wrist said 8:15. Dorit would be in the den now. Sesame Street had just started.

IT SEEMED TO RIVKA that every Monday here was either overcast or rainy. She looked through the kitchen bay window at the other split-level homes on her block and put on her favorite tape of Hebrew songs. Yehoram Gaon's voice crooned through the kitchen. In the center of the round white table was a colorful bouquet of silk flowers in a ceramic vase. Rivka and Varda were sitting across the table from each other, two cups and saucers in front of them, an ashtray beside each saucer. Rivka smoked very infrequently, only when she was upset about something. Already the bottoms of both ashtrays were covered with gray ash and butts.

"I knew it," Rivka said, running one hand through her uncombed hair, her eyes red from a restless night, "I knew this would happen sooner or later. If they're going to hand out credit cards to people like Yossi, they might as well pass out guns."

Varda looked at her friend with concern, her eyebrows slanting slightly inward, the corners of her mouth turned down. She put her cigarette into the ashtray, leaning it against the outer rim, then slowly lifted her coffee cup. "How much do you owe?" she asked evenly.

"Fifteen hundred dollars, before interest," Rivka answered dejectedly, taking another puff of her cigarette, then stiffly flicking some ashes into her ashtray. "I knew it would happen. Damn his cards."

"And how much do they want right away?" Varda asked.

"At least a third. The last letter said we had ten days to pay it, and that was already five days ago." Rivka paused and looked out at the gray clouds through the kitchen window. She would have been at school with Dorit, working with her as her parent-partner in the special stimulation program, but today was 'parents' day off' at the school. Dorit had taken the school bus alone this morning and would not be home until lunch time. "All we have left is a thousand dollars, total," Rivka went on. "If we pay out half of that now to BankAmericard, we'll only have enough left for rent and food, and we'll still owe them another thousand."

"Before interest," Varda added, taking a sip of her coffee. She had this way of reminding people what they already knew but were trying not to think about. It was how she empathized with them. She was a woman who thought out loud. For her it was easier to identify with a friend's situation if it sounded worse than it actually was. "And Yossi says there's no way you can come up with the difference?" Varda wanted to make sure she understood the full story.

"Oh, there's one way," Rivka said, an angry light coming into her eyes, "there's one way all right, and that's the heart of the problem." She thought back to an earlier scene, played out in front of Dorit at dinner, and lifted her cigarette to her lips almost against her will. "The only way we can pay it off is if Yossi drops out of school for a semester and drives his damn cab full-time."

"And what did Yossi say when you told him that?"

"Me tell *him?* It was his idea!"

"Oh, well that makes it simpler then," Varda said, looking relieved. "So he'll work for six months, pay off the debt, then finish up school in the fall. That ought to work out fine."

"For whom?" Rivka asked, appalled to hear Varda taking Yosef's side. "He only has one semester to go after this one. We're due back home in May for God's sake. I'd rather do anything to borrow the money, anything not to stay here one day longer."

"But Rivka," Varda said, sounding as though she were talking to a child, "that's what you've *been* doing, borrowing. That's what BankAmericard is. Another loan won't solve anything. If you don't pay BankAmericard what you owe them, they'll freeze your credit and you won't be able to cash a check, let alone borrow anywhere. They'll grab Yossi's earnings, tie up your bank account. You won't even be able to buy tickets home."

Rivka listened to her friend, hearing Varda's nasal voice and thinking it had never sounded so grating before. It felt strange to be talking to Varda about this because, after all, Varda and Oded had been in America for five years, and it had been three years already since Oded had finished his psychology degree. What were they waiting for? Oded was a donut man, still waiting for a job in psychology. They were *yordim,* she thought.

"What about your brother-in-law?" Varda asked, grinding out one cigarette and taking a new one out of the pack.

"What about him?" He was the reason they were in this mess, Rivka told herself. If Yosef weren't obsessed with impressing his little brother, if he weren't consumed by measuring up to him, they wouldn't be in such a deep hole now. Not that it really was Nissim's fault.

"Can't he lend you the money? After all, he is family, isn't he?" Varda said. She got up and walked over to the stove to put up the kettle again for more coffee.

Rivka had never thought of asking Nissim for the money, and she wondered for a moment why the idea hadn't occurred to her. She liked her brother-in-law. He was considerate toward her in ways that Yosef had never been. She didn't even mind the constant noise from his new computer. Most nights he stayed in his bedroom studying, coming down only at eleven o'clock to watch the newscast, then staying up to watch the late movie until two o'clock in the morning. It was nice to have a man in the house, she thought, even if it wasn't her husband. Yosef was busy picking up strangers off the streets and driving them all over Philadelphia, some nights till dawn. "Of course he's family, and he's got four tough enough years of his own ahead here," she said. "I don't want to drag him down, too. He's a good kid, and he needs every penny to pay for his studies. Penn costs a fortune, you know."

"What doesn't?" Varda spooned some freeze-dried coffee into her cup and, seeing the water was boiling, moved the kettle off the electric burner. "Want some more?" she asked, holding up the coffee jar.

"No thanks. Wait, okay, I think I need it," Rivka answered,

carrying her cup over to Varda and standing with her in front of the stove.

Varda fixed the two cups of coffee, speaking as she mixed in the sugar and milk. "Your brother-in-law's the key, believe me," she said. "You're just too close to it to be objective. He's staying with you in your house, right? So that's the income. Don't call it a loan. Call it rent."

Rivka could feel herself growing more uncomfortable, feeling more regretful for having begun discussing her problems with Varda. But what other friends do I have here? she thought. None. Who else could even begin to understand? No one. "He's already paying us rent," she told Varda as the two of them walked back to the table and took their seats. "We didn't want it, but he insisted. Pride. He's paying us more than we'd charge a stranger. No, if we can't pay BankAmericard, we can't pay him. Taking the money from Nissim would just be palming our own problems off onto him."

Varda took a sip of her coffee, then threw back her head. "You're right, Rivka," she said. "You're right. If you borrowed the money for Yossi to finish on schedule and then you all went back home, it wouldn't work. You can't pay off dollars with liras. You could never pay Nissim from there."

The voice of Yehoram Gaon continued to fill the kitchen with music. "*Ani ha-eesh asher tameed khozayr, khozayr,* I'm the man who always returns, returns," he sang. Rivka listened to the lyrics and felt at once like screaming and crying. She looked across at her Israeli friend, studying her blonde hair and blue eyes, and wondered if Varda would ever return, if she and Oded had plans to go back home.

"So you'll stay here another year," Varda continued after taking a long drag of her cigarette and blowing a cloud of smoke toward the window. "What would be so terrible about that?"

Rivka could feel her face growing hot. She wiped some beads

of sweat from her forehead and crushed her cigarette into the ashtray. "You really don't understand, do you, Varda? You really don't see it, do you?" she said, her tone both plaintive and angry. "This place is like quicksand. It swallows you up. The closer we come to leaving, the deeper we sink into staying."

"Maybe that's just the way life is," Varda said. "You do what you have to when you have to, and take the best it has to offer."

"That's ridiculous! Life is what you make it," Rivka said. "Yossi gave me the line last night about us not having any choices. We've got choices."

"Like what? Not paying? Going to jail?" Varda asked, frowning.

"Like sticking to our plans and heading home," she told Varda, "because if this is the best life has to offer, we're all in deep trouble."

Varda could hear Rivka's pain, but she thought that Rivka was being childish, unrealistic. "Tell me something, would you, because I don't get it. I understand you want to get back home and that the clock in your head was set for this summer, but take a look around this place. Maybe I'm missing something, but I wouldn't exactly call this roughing it."

Rivka looked through the narrow hallway that led from the kitchen to the den. From where she sat she could see the built-in bookshelves which covered one wall from the floor to the ceiling and which held Professor Barsky's home library. She could see the white Karastan carpet, the stereo console, the twenty-five-inch color television set, and one end of Yosef's fifty-five gallon aquarium. Little shapes of color were swimming through bubbling water against a background of tangled tubing and plastic props. Dwarf gouramis, six-banded barbs, glowlight tetras, Australian rainbows. Even from across the hall Rivka could see the whiskered catfish languidly licking the bottom clean. "You think this place is paradise?" she asked, almost spitting out the words. She didn't want to lose her temper, to lose control. "Do you? Yossi does, and if I were him maybe I would, too. Sure, why not? What does he know about living here? He uses this house like a hotel, just like he used our apartment before this. Bed and breakfast, if he can fit both in. Hell, he uses *me* like a hotel!" Rivka leaned forward as she spoke, looking across the silk flowers at her friend. "*I'm* the one who lives here, not him! And who cares how thick the carpet is, who cares how many rooms we've got? This place is a hell, it's a prison."

Varda shook her head and frowned. "Rivka, I know how you feel," she said, "because in a lot of ways I'm in the same situation you are. I've felt locked in plenty of times, and believe me I've given Oded his share of lumps for it, too. But look, Oded and Yossi aren't exactly walking down easy street either, you know. I remember when Oded was still at Temple, finishing up. He worked and worked and worked at school and when he came home I made him work there too, fixing up around the house and watching Orly. He didn't have a minute to breathe, a second to let down, and neither does Yossi. They're both doing the best they can, just like we are, and they're doing it for us and our girls."

Rivka glared at Varda, unable to hide her anger any longer. "You sound like Yossi, you know that? He always gives me that 'I'm doing it all for you, honey' line too, but it's bullshit and he knows it," she said. "He's been doing exactly what Joseph Lvov wants since day one when we got here. If he even gave me one thought, ever, he'd—oh, what's the use?" She turned away from Varda and stared out the window at the darkening sky. A downpour was imminent, she thought. "Maybe you ought to go," she told Varda, "and finish your shopping before the rain starts."

Varda reached over and laid her hand gently on Rivka's shoulder. "I'll go in a minute," Varda said. "But first I want to understand something. I live here, too, remember? And I'm not saying everything's perfect, but I wouldn't call it hell. What's so awful about it?"

"You want a list? I'll give you one. We don't have any family here, except now for Nissim, and holidays are like funerals for us, especially for Dorit. I don't know the neighbors, not even one, because none of them has a child under fifteen from what I've seen, and all of them keep to themselves anyway. Cars in, cars out — that's all life is here. Yossi takes the car every day, which leaves me locked in except for taking the school bus back and forth to Dorit's school. I've loved being with her every day, working with her and watching her move forward, but after two years of going to nursery school I feel four years old myself. She's growing, I'm regressing." Rivka paused a second, looking at Varda to see if she was still listening. "Whenever I do get the car, I can't even drive around the corner for groceries without someone flagging me down, thinking I'm a lady cabbie. I spend my nights alone, with Dorit asleep, Yossi out, and Nissim studying. Sometimes I watch television, too much of the time, but most of the shows just depress me or scare me. Most of them are about rape and murder, which makes the TV great company for me. And after the shows, I watch the news which is worse than the shows were." She looked through the hall and into the den again, focusing on the built-in shelves. "Only books and Dorit have kept me sane for the past two years."

Varda listened in disbelief. To her it sounded like Rivka was describing a different place, a different life from the one she was living. Thousands of people would pay to trade places with us, she thought. Some people just don't know when they've got it good. "Well," Varda said, grinding out her last cigarette and rising from the table, "I better get going if I want to do the shopping before Orly comes home." She walked to the front door with Rivka beside her. "And listen," she said, forcing a smile, "you and Yossi will work this out. You'll see. Oded and I always

seem to, somehow." She opened the door and started outside, turning around after only one step. "Rivka, if you want to talk," she
said, "just call me."

Rivka nodded, watched Varda get into her Datsun, then returned to the kitchen table. Her coffee cup was empty, but the
ashtray beside it was full. Had she really smoked that many
cigarettes? She thought about counting the crushed butts, but her
eye was drawn instead to the empty chairs around the table. Even
when Varda had been sitting across from her she'd felt alone.
Varda's parting words echoed in her mind. "If you want to talk
. . . ." No thank you, she told herself, I don't make the same
mistake twice. Maybe it's just me, she thought. Maybe I'm being too critical, too hard on everyone – Yossi, Varda, Philadelphia.
Maybe I'm the one with the problem. Yossi and Varda think so.
Maybe they're right. After all, Yossi's only in America because
I talked him into coming; it was even my idea that he should go
to school here. I made this hell for myself, she thought.

Cigarette smoke still filled the kitchen, hanging in a foot-deep
cloud across the length of the ceiling, choking the fresh air from
the room and making Rivka's eyes tear. She sat at the table, silent,
pensive, thinking back to last night's argument.

"Where are you running to?"

"I'm going for a ride."

"Don't run to your cab again. We have to talk."

"We've already talked. There's nothing more to talk about."

"Yossi, if you leave now, I'll leave. But when I leave, it will
be for good."

"Do whatever you want to."

Rivka looked at Varda's overflowing ashtray and half cup of
cold coffee on the table. She looked out through the bay window,
staring across the backyard at the split-level houses full of
husbands and wives and children. She pictured Yosef storming
out of the house, heard the garage door slam shut behind him.
Her neck muscles were so taut that her head seemed attached to

her shoulders by wires. Slowly she gripped the table from underneath and squeezed until her fingertips turned white. The cups and saucers began to rattle as she squeezed harder and harder. Do whatever you want to. Do whatever you have to. Letting go of the table she slumped forward, her body resting on her elbows, her face pressed into her open palms. And then Rivka began to sob, loudly and passionately, drowning out the music, drowning out everything, sobbing inconsolably as if she were a *Tzahal* widow.

THE METER ARM was in its raised position as the yellow cab sped along the New Jersey Turnpike. Rivka sat in the back seat with Dorit, who was laying down with her head resting on her mother's lap. It was already past her bedtime and she kept falling in and out of sleepfulness. Lights were flashing across the ceiling of the cab as she looked up at it, making a swimming pattern of changing shapes. The few times she had sat up and peered out the window, the traffic travelling toward her on the other side of the turnpike looked like a stampeding army, a giant battalion of blazing white lights. Yosef Lvov sat in front of them like a chauffeur behind the wheel, and as he drove he talked to Rivka in the rear view mirror.

"This is your last chance to call it off, Rivka," he said. "When you get on that plane, as far as I'm concerned everything's different. It will never be the same between us again. Tell me to turn around and let's figure out a better way. Together."

Rivka, who had been listening to Yosef talk like this for the last hour, sat stroking Dorit's head, trying to calm her daughter to sleep and not looking up at her husband.

"Let's be clear about who's leaving who," he went on after a moment. "You're the one pulling out and giving up, on me, on our life here, on *us*. Marriage is work and I know that, and I know

I haven't been especially available or even around most of the time lately, but I'm willing to work at it, to work at *us*. Are you?"

Rivka lifted her head and looked into Yosef's eyes in the mirror. She hesitated a long while before deciding to answer him. "Not here," she told him, "and not this way. I'm not leaving, Yossi. Leaving is what we did two years ago. Now I'm going home."

"Right!" Yosef came back sharply, jumping at the chance to engage her in any kind of conversation, even in another argument. "Just going home! Just taking our child and bailing out, deserting me when I need you most! Is she asleep? Dorit, sweetie? Are you asleep?"

"No, Abba," Dorit said softly.

"Good, honey. Do you feel okay?" he asked.

"Yes."

"That's good, sweetie. Tell me something. Do you want to go for such a long, long ride on that airplane, or do you want to stay here with Abba until Ema comes back from her visit?"

"Yossi!" Rivka said as loud as she could through clenched teeth. "Leave the child out of this."

"I'm not the one who involved her to begin with," he said, pleased to see that this last-resort tactic was drawing a strong response from his wife. "This was your idea, remember?"

Rivka did not answer him, but glared at him in the rear view mirror.

"Honey," Yosef said to Dorit, "do you want to stay here with me?"

Dorit, who was still lying down on Rivka, looked up at her mother's face and saw the tension and pain there. "I don't want Ema to be angry at me," she said softly.

Rivka gently stroked her daughter's long hair.

"Why can't we both stay here with Abba?" Dorit asked.

"Because there are a lot of things we have to do at home, and our home is in Haifa, honey. Not here," Rivka told her. "The house we've been living in is someone else's, not ours. We've just been borrowing it for a while, until they come back home to live in it. And just like they're going to come home to their house, we're going home to our house now, our real house."

"But what about Abba?" Dorit asked with real concern. "Abba, when are *you* coming?"

"I'll be there as fast as I can, sweetie," he said, "but I sure wish you and Ema would stay here with me so we can all go home together."

"So do I, Abba," she said, sitting up. "Ema, why do we have to go without Abba? I want to wait for him. Right, Abba?"

"If that's what you want, sweetie, it's sure what *I* want," he told her, beginning to smile.

"Ema, why can't we wait for Abba?"

"Because sometimes there isn't time to wait, honey," she told Dorit. "Sometimes you just have to pick up and go or you won't ever get there at all." Rivka was thinking back to the war, to how Yosef had waited for the phone that never rang, for the call that never came, and to all those nights she had waited for him to come home, to Dorit's party, to the night of Nissim's arrival, to Yosef's decision to drop out of school for next term.

"Oh," Dorit said to her mother, sounding as though that was an answer that made sense to her.

Yosef yanked open his glove compartment and, without looking at her, flipped an open envelope back over his shoulder to Rivka. "Here," he said, "look at this. It gives it to you in black and white. Look at it. Look at those numbers and tell me what I should do about it!"

Rivka took the letter out of the envelope and tried to read it in the darkness. She could see that it was from BankAmericard and was addressed to Mr. and Mrs. Joseph Lvov. She could also see that they owed almost eighteen hundred dollars, including interest, and that the balance was three months past due. "We've been through all of this before, Yossi," she said. "Another letter doesn't change anything."

"I said, tell me what I should do about it."

"Come home," she told him.

"Right, and that'll solve everything I guess. Hell, that won't solve *anything,* and you know it."

Dorit had put her head down again and was laying on Rivka's lap. Rivka was stroking her hair again. "Staying here will solve less," she said.

"You're really something!" he shouted back at her. "Really something else! I show you we're in debt, I show you that we don't have the money to pay it, I tell you that I'm sinking, and you go and spend a thousand dollars to leave me. A thousand dollars of my money. And you take my daughter away from me to boot. I'll tell you, you're a real help, a real hero in the trenches!"

Rivka did not even lift her eyes as she listened. There was nothing she could tell him, or at least nothing she wanted to say to him, that would make him see things as she did.

"It's perfect, you know? It's so typical, so just like a woman to do what you're doing," he went on, shifting his eyes back and forth from the road to the rear view mirror. "We *were* planning to be home in June and then I say we have to change that by about six months, that we have to push it back to next December, so you get all huffy and impulsive and push it *up* to this September! Tell me what *that* solves, will you? Tell me who wins *that* way? No one. Not you, not me, and most of all, not Dorit."

"Yossi," she said to the eyes in the mirror, "we've all been away too long."

INSIDE THE EL AL TERMINAL, people were dragging large suitcases and air cargo cartons of all sizes and shapes into the long lines that had formed in front of each check-in counter. Yosef

waited with Rivka in the line, holding Dorit in his arms as she
rested her head on his shoulder. The room was filled with choking smoke and people were jostling each other, pushing their suitcases into the back of the knees of the person in front of them.
There was a tenuous semblance of order, a tense commotion in
every corner and at every counter. Yosef and Rivka stood in
silence, not exchanging two words as they moved forward.

After checking the luggage, they turned and walked to a stair-
way that ascended from the middle of the "Departures" floor. An
El Al security guard was standing at the bottom of the stairs, and
when Yosef, Rivka, and Dorit approached, he stopped them
politely, saying, "Ticketed passengers only beyond this point,
please."

Rivka put her arms out, signalling Yosef to hand their daughter
to her, but Yosef was not ready to hand Dorit over. To him it
was like giving his daughter away, like putting her up for adoption. She was his, he heard himself screaming inside, and he was
going to keep her.

"Excuse me, sir," the security guard said, "you're blocking the
stairs for the other passengers. May I see your boarding passes,
please."

Rivka took out the two boarding passes from her handbag and
showed them to the guard. "These are for myself and my
daughter," she told him.

"Thank you. Go on up," the guard said. "And yours, sir?" he
asked Yosef.

"Oh, mine," Yosef said, "I should have explained. You see,
my wife and daughter are going home for a visit and my wife isn't
well so I'm sort of helping them get on the plane. I'm sure you
understand. I'd be travelling with them, and frankly I'd be happier if they weren't going at all, but I couldn't cancel some commitments I had in time. I'll just put them on the plane, make sure
my wife's okay, and then come down again."

"I'm afraid you can't do that," the guard told Yosef. "Only ticketed passengers can go upstairs. Sorry."

"Look, maybe you don't understand," Yosef protested, his voice growing perceptibly louder. "My wife is sick. I don't want to go into explaining what she has, but I have to be with her. The person I spoke with over there at the desk said it would be no problem."

As the guard and Yosef talked back and forth, Rivka became impatient, sickened to hear Yosef use her to manipulate the rules to get his own way. "I'm fine," she said to the guard, taking Dorit out of Yosef's arms. "Kiss Abba goodbye, honey," she told her daughter. "Our plane is going to leave in a minute."

Yosef did not try to resist when Rivka took Dorit from him. "I'll see you very soon, sweetie," he said picking her up one last time and squeezing her to his chest. "I love you more than anyone can tell you," he whispered into her ear.

"I love you too, Abba," she said, and held him tight around his neck. "Abba, I don't want to go."

"I know, sweetie, and I don't want you to," he told her, "but Ema and you will be with Sabba Barukh and Savta Miryam and I'll come back real soon. Okay?" He could feel her little body trembling, could feel her starting to sob against him, and tears started to well up inside him. It felt as though a gush was building from below his knees and was surging upward into his eyes.

"I don't want to go," Dorit repeated, sobbing into his chest.

"Come on, honey. We don't want to be late," Rivka said, feeling tears welling inside herself as she watched her husband and daughter embracing. Was this the right thing? she asked herself. Was she the one breaking their family apart as Yossi had said? Quickly she leaned over and kissed Yosef on the cheek, and when she pulled away her lips were wet. Never before had she seen him cry, and seeing the tears on his face now, she could not stay the flood that was rising inside her. If she did not leave quickly, she would not go, so she took Dorit's hand and started up the stairs. But after two strides she stopped and turned around. Yosef was still standing there, watching, tears falling from the corners of his eyes.

"If you want a family, come home," she called down, then, softly, "please, Yossi." Pulling Dorit, she turned quickly and ascended the steps to the departure gate.

DEAR SHOSH,

I got your letter yesterday. Work at the hospital sounds exhausting but you sound very good.

America is everything and nothing you imagine. The University of Pennsylvania is like a small city. I only have classes four days in the week so I have more free time than I ever had before in my life. It is funny to me to watch how Americans live. They skimp on time and money, trying to save them in wasteful ways. They go through the newspaper for an hour and clip out coupons that will save them ten cents on a bar of soap. They drive from store to store for "sales" and spend more money on gasoline than they save on what they're buying. They buy frozen dinners at the supermarket so they don't have to waste time cooking. Then they go home and waste the whole night eating their dinner in front of the TV set. Sometimes I think that too much time can be harder to handle than too little, too much freedom harder to handle than not enough. I have been spending my nights studying, but I also have been seeing the city and meeting people. I bought a car from a woman I am seeing. It has possibilities.

But not everything is perfect here. I walked into

the middle of something. From the moment I got here things between Rivka and Yossi started falling apart. Yossi was trying to juggle too many things – class time, schoolwork, driving his cab. He barely made time for Dorit, and none for Rivka. They were here, but they couldn't enjoy any of "the good life" together because Yossi didn't know when to stop running. Rivka spent most nights home alone, that is except for when I was there with her, and I wasn't there – I was upstairs working on my computer. She had no kind of life here, except for the work she was doing with Dorit at the nursery school, but Dorit doesn't need a special program anymore. Yossi had to be blind or stupid leaving Rivka all alone. I talked to him about it, told him what I thought he should do, but he just got defensive and tried to bite off my head like always. Yesterday Rivka left with Dorit. Please don't mention this to Miryam, but from what I've seen they're moving toward a divorce. By the time you get this they'll have been home a week.

My brother is a weakling. There is a clothes dryer in the basement of his house because people don't hang things out to dry here. Sometimes I think he is like that dryer. You turn him on and everything starts spinning, and no matter how much you put inside it, the middle is always empty. Everything gets thrown out to the rim. Nothing seems to fill Yossi up. He's always had a "thing" for America, and being here, he's let the place run away with him. You don't choose a country over your family. He's not in control, he's lost his perspective. Thank God he and I are so different. I'm enjoying this place, but I know how to control it. I know how to handle America.

The problem with my brother is he's been here too long. But for a short time America is healthy. I have been thinking that the Jewish Agency should take all the money it's wasting on bringing new immigrants to Israel and use it instead to send every Israeli to America for one year to live here. But after one year they would have to come home. It would be good for the country. Americans never have immigrated to Israel anyway, so all the money we're spending on them is wasted. They'll never come until they need somewhere to run to. For us it would be a good investment. After three years in the army it would be a real experience, a real education for the young people. Sometimes you have to leave a place to understand it.

I bought a camera, a Polaroid that cost me half what it would in Haifa. I took some pictures so you can see what I'm seeing and where I am, but they don't let you put enclosures in aerogrammes. Next time I'll write a regular letter and send them inside the envelope.

Looks like I'm out of room. I am thinking a lot about you and home. More soon.

Love,
Nissim

Tight-lined rows of black ink filled every side of the blue aerogramme. Nissim turned the sheet over to the main flap and began rereading what he had just written. "I bought a car from a woman I'm seeing." "My brother is a clothes dryer." "They're moving toward a divorce." "The government should send every

Israeli to America." I can't send this, he decided. He folded the flaps closed, tore the aerogramme into strips, and dropped them into the wastebasket.

From the drawer he took out a plain white envelope and a plain white piece of paper. Beside him was a short pile of Polaroids. One was of his brother's house, another was of his green Chevy parked next to Yosef's Checker. Others pictured City Hall, the River Drive, the Art Museum, some buildings on the Penn campus, a traffic jam on the Schuylkill Expressway. Nissim put the photographs into the envelope, picked up his pen, and began writing a few lines.

> Dear Shosh,
>
> I got your letter yesterday. Rambam Hospital hasn't changed.
>
> Everything is fine. Life here is soft. Lots of time and no worries. There are no words to describe America.
>
> Here are some pictures I took. I am thinking a lot about you and home. Keep writing, please.
>
> Nissim

Nine

GRANITE HEADSTONES LINED THE WAY along the wide stone path to Section Four. Those who fell in *Tzahal* lay here. 1948, 1956, 1967, 1973. Ronni and Shoshanah read the inscriptions and walked deeper into the graveyard. Some of the headstones bore dates that did not mark wars, and some of the dead were not soldiers. They paused beside two graves that were covered with small wreaths of flowers. One was the grave of a two-year-old girl; her mother lay beside her. Both had been killed a year ago in a terrorist blast in Jerusalem. Ronni repeated the *Tzahal* slogan to himself: Every Israeli's a soldier, and all of Israel's the front. "Shoshanah," he said out loud as she started to walk, "I'm going to wait here. You go ahead."

"All right, Ronni," she told him. "I won't stay long."

Section Four was just ahead. The section for those killed in the Yom Kippur War, October 1973. A turn in the path led to the section where Avi was buried, and she followed it until she was standing at the foot of Avi's grave. At the far end of the blanket of grass covering his grave a marble headstone lay like a pillow. At the end near Shoshanah a candle burned inside a small glass case. Its light was dim in the afternoon light, but at night its flame made the case a bright lantern. Around his grave a low brick frame only several bricks high supported several potted plants. Why do I believe it least when I stand here? she asked herself. Today marks two years, two full years. She wanted to deny Avi's death, to rewrite his epitaph so that it wouldn't read,

192

"Died 11 Tishri 5734, May His Soul Be Inscribed in the Book of Eternal Life."

Why is this place so pretty? she thought. The graves here are gardens, the paths colored stone mosaics, sea stones set in concrete. The largest part of her was buried here.

A jet roared overhead. Shoshanah lifted her eyes to see four planes flying in formation. She lowered her eyes to the row of tall cedars that bounded the cemetery on one side. The thin trees bowed, almost touching one another in the gusting winds. Beyond the trees was Mount Carmel. Shoshanah's eyes climbed the slopes to its peak. She looked at the green clumps of shrubs and trees, at the brown growth and the rocky crags, at the boxlike houses built on stilts that seemed to melt into the mountain. And she wondered how many doors up there bore family names etched in stone down here.

"Two years," she said softly, "two funerals, Avi." Today was the second anniversary of Avi's death, but he had been in this grave for little more than a year. Ten months after his first burial, his body had been exhumed from its temporary grave at Kibbutz Yad Mordecai and had been reinterred in the Haifa Military Graveyard. "I missed your first funeral," she whispered, wiping away a slow tear with the sweep of her finger. "I'm sorry." Tears ran down both cheeks as she sat down next to the glass case with the candle burning inside it. This was the memorial light, the eternal flame, the candle of memory that would always burn. She stared a long time at the flame through the glass.

"Daughters are raised to visit graves and sons are raised to fill them." That was what Avi's mother had said to her as they rode to visit the Negev grave of her son the year before. Was it true? What was true was what Nissim had told her of Avi's death, his death in the fire in the tank.

She stared at the small flame burning unattended. It seemed

wrong that fire should be the symbol to commemorate his death, or recall his life. Reaching down, she unlatched the top of the lantern case and lifted it open. "No more flames," she said aloud. "No more flames."

With infinite gentleness she leaned over and blew out the candle. Silently and slowly she closed the case. She sat there a moment, wiping her tears, and then with a proud throwing-back of her head, she stood up and started back along the stone path to Ronni.

"DAMN, I MISS HER," he said to himself, thinking about Dorit smiling up at him. Since finding the letter on El Al stationery in yesterday's mail he had read it nine or ten times. Rivka must have written it in flight and mailed it in Tel Aviv when she and Dorit had landed. The stamp was postmarked two weeks ago, just before Rosh HaShanah, but it had taken that long for the letter to reach Yosef due to the strain the High Holy Days put on Israel's postal system. Dorit had enclosed two crayon drawings, one of a girl standing with parents, the other of dark, angry dots and circles. Rivka had written three pages, continuing their fight on paper, begging him to come back. "She's in another world," Yosef told himself, "and I'm in this one – up to my neck in debt."

In the two weeks since Rivka's departure he had felt more burdened than when she had been here. Less free, not freer. He had more on his mind, more pressures inside him. In addition to BankAmericard and school and driving his cab, he had Rivka and Dorit tormenting him with their absence. Time had become more scarce since they had left. His courses at Temple had moved into high gear, the term's first major assignments coming due. This morning's history class, "Racism and Civil Conscience: Modern American Revolutions," was an especially challenging course for Yosef because the teacher, Professor Williams, acted as though his course was the only one, or at least the only important one, on his students' rosters. The syllabus was long and demanding, especially for Yosef whose reading speed was slow in English, and the projects Professor Williams assigned called for original thought. Yosef was still wrestling with what to write for that course's next paper. Professor Williams had read a sentence, and had asked everyone to write a ten-page paper "personalizing the experience of victimization." Yosef was still working on it.

Immediately after the "Racism" class he had dashed out of the Humanities Building and sped down Broad Street to Market Street, making his way toward Thirtieth Street Station. Now he and Jocko stood beside their cabs, warming their hands by rubbing them together as they talked, their cabs in the middle of the long curb-lane line.

Yesterday had been summerlike, high in the seventies, bright blue skies, but last night the heat wave had snapped abruptly. The temperature had plummeted to the mid-thirties, leaving a wintry bite in the air this morning. Octobers were like that in Philadelphia, forty degree swings in less than twenty-four hours, sudden shifts from summer to winter.

"She should've thought about *you* a little before she ran out half-cocked like a wild woman," Jocko was saying. "Like I told you before, that's *her* loss."

Yosef felt uncomfortable listening to Jocko criticize Rivka. It made him angry, though he agreed with what Jocko had said. But he and Jocko discussed everything: from family rifts to war stories to Monday night football, and he knew that Jocko was attacking his wife out of friendship for him. "Rivka, my wife, she never wanted to be here," Yosef told him. "She never felt at home here."

"Jesus Christ, that's no excuse," Jocko continued with aggression. "Everyone who ever came here could say that. You just don't feel at home in a year or two, or even after ten. Hell, even now after forty years here, I still feel like a foreigner sometimes. But that's how it is in America. Everyone's from someplace else not too far up on the family tree."

Yosef listened to Jocko but his eyes were fixed on the station's doors, counting the people coming through them. To conserve gas, he left the cab in neutral, turned the motor off, and stood on the driver's side with the door open. Every time the line shortened, he pushed his cab forward, maneuvering the steering wheel with one extended arm.

"Yeah," Yosef said, "guess so." He was listening to Jocko but thinking about Dorit.

Jocko took the cigar out of his mouth, dropped it into the gutter by the curb, and ground it with the heel of his shoe. "No, it ain't no lark being an immigrant at the start," he said, "'specially till you can shake your accent. But that's just a matter of time, you'll see."

For some reason everything Jocko was saying today upset Yosef. I'm no immigrant, he thought to himself, rolling his cab forward. I'm not building my home here. I'm finishing up what I came to do, which is to get my degree and get out of here, back to my family, back home. He remembered from his history studies that Hebrew had almost been chosen as America's official language during the American Revolution. In 1776 the colonists hated anything connected with the British monarchy, and a movement was launched to discard English in favor of Hebrew as the new nation's spoken tongue. After all, they argued, Hebrew was the mother of all languages and the key to understanding the Holy Scriptures. The names the colonists had chosen for their towns, like Salem and Bethlehem, were taken from the Bible, and it was family custom to name their children after biblical figures. A motion to adopt Hebrew as the national tongue was made on the floor of the new Continental Congress when Philadelphia was still the capital of America. Yosef wished the motion had not been defeated. Sure, I talk English with an accent, and sure, it bothers me. I get tired of wanting to say to everyone, 'I'm a different person in Hebrew.' I get tired of not being able to pick up the words to the songs on the radio. Sure, I talk with an accent. Why shouldn't I? I'm not from here.

"I don't know about you, but the first thing I took to was American music," Jocko went on. "Of course, back then it was the big bands and people whose names you've never heard of, but they were big stars back then. You like rock and roll? You like Elton John?"

"Of course," Yosef said, smiling at the naivete of the question. "Who doesn't? 'Philadelphia Freedom' I listen to all the time."

"Good," Jocko said, lifting his wallet out of his coat pocket and folding it open, "because I can't stand the guy. In my book he's just another fag from across the ocean, but if everyone else wants to make him a millionaire for it, that's fine by me." He pulled out two tickets from his billfold and handed them to Yosef. "He's coming to the Spectrum for one of them orgy concerts next week and someone gave me two freebies last night," he said. "I thought maybe you could use them."

"Thanks, Jocko," Yosef said with real enthusiasm. He had been listening to the radio spots advertising this concert and knew that tickets to it were both expensive and scarce. Even if he couldn't use them, he was sure that Denise and Nissim could. They'd love to go to the Spectrum to watch Elton John perform. "Thanks," he said again.

"Don't mention it." Jocko took a puff of his stogie and exhaled, following the smoke as it rose toward the pigeons roosting in the eaves overhead. There was a thoughtful look in his eye. "Joe," he said carefully, "there's something else I been thinking about. I know it's got to get a little lonely after a while—I mean, a married man gets used to a certain schedule—and what I'm saying is there's no reason to go without it, y'know?" He looked at Yosef to gauge his reaction, but couldn't read his expression. "Well, I know a place on Lombard Street," he went on. "Tell them I sent you." He twirled the cigar in his mouth and stared at Yosef with a lascivious light in his eye.

"Thanks," Yosef said, feeling put off by Jocko's offer and trying not to show it, "I can take care of myself." The first two taxis in line pulled out and Yosef rolled his cab forward. "Catch you later, Jocko," he said as he slid in behind the wheel and closed the door. His hands were red from the biting cold air. He rubbed them together, blew on them, and rubbed them together some more. Then he reached across to the glove compartment and took out Rivka's letter. He would read it one more time.

"AT IT AGAIN, EH?" Yosef said as he walked up behind Nissim, who was sitting in front of his computer and staring at lines of numbers on a black and white TV screen. "You didn't even hear me come in, did you?" he asked, slapping his brother on the back of the head.

"Dammit, Yossi! I'm right in the middle of something important," Nissim complained, trying not to break his concentration. He was finishing a pivotal section of research for Professor Clarendon, completing a section he had been working on for three nights already and which was finally taking the shape he wanted.

"What've you got there?" Yosef asked, leaning down to read the screen over Nissim's shoulder. "More robot mumbo jumbo?"

"Right," Nissim said, preoccupied with the idea in his head, not wanting to lose it before he could transfer it onto the TV screen. He had written a short paper about the computerization of military hardware for Professor Clarendon's course, and the professor had been so impressed by Nissim's "real-world thinking" that he had asked him to be a research assistant for a special study on the potential impact of automation on the economies of certain industrialized nations. Flattered and deeply interested, Nissim had accepted the offer. Now he was analyzing some figures related to the thesis of that first paper. "Look at whatever you want to, Yossi, but don't touch anything – including me," Nissim said without lifting his eyes. "I'm in the middle of something delicate."

Red lights were flashing above the toggle switches on the control board of the metal cabinet in front of Nissim, and the computer was making a lot of noise, its motor whirring and knocking and its pieces of hardware clicking like a used car. It had sounded this way since he had brought it home several weeks ago. It was an ALTAIR 8800, the first home computer sold in America. Its control processing unit made it functional, but its hardware design was poor, the instruction manual verged on being unintelligible, and it came completely unassembled. Professor Clarendon, a computer expert and electronics buff, had ordered three ALTAIR kits for four hundred dollars apiece direct from the small New Mexico manufacturer after seeing it in the February 1975 issue of *Popular Electronics.* After personally assembling one of them, he equipped it with a modem attachment which enabled his computer to interface with the university's mainframe system by telephone. The one assembled ALTAIR 8800 was in Professor Clarendon's home; the other two he had decided to leave in their original packing, saving them for the two students he would select to assist him on the "World Economy Impact" study. When he had spoken with Nissim several weeks ago about the research assistantship, he had invited Nissim home to see his computer and to demonstrate its use by putting it through several basic functions. After the demonstration, the professor had shown Nissim one of the unassembled kits and Nissim had asked if he could try his hand at constructing it. To the professor's surprise, Nissim had worked doggedly and methodically, solving the diagrams for the basic computer's four printed circuit board assemblies, then moving on to the front panel display board with its thirty-six LED indicators and their associated drivers and switches. Etching and drilling, following intricate component placement diagrams, attaching multiconductor ribbon cable that interconnected the circuit boards, Nissim had successfully assembled his own ALTAIR 8800. After bringing it home, he had constructed a special table to hold it. He had laid an old white Formica countertop across two wood horses. This was the only desk he could find large enough to hold the computer's bulky metal cabinet, the portable black and white television set, the black telephone, and the modem which Professor Clarendon had hooked up for him so that he could tie into the department's mainframe computer by phone. Tonight as every night Nissim had simply dialed the special phone number which Professor Clarendon had given him, and then had placed the phone receiver into the modem to effect the computer hookup.

"Don't worry about me, I just live here," Yosef said, smiling to himself. It amused him to see his brother so serious. Just like Barukh, Yosef thought, just like his father, always pushing, always seeing things through to the end. Yosef looked at the lists of figures on the monitor in front of Nissim. "What's all this?" he asked.

"It's my idea that Israel should establish a national Institute For Robotics and develop new state-of-the-art equipment as well as new industrial applications for sale to other countries. Haifa would be the best place to build the Institute because of the Technion. These are some cost projections."

Nissim continued explaining a detailed plan for the founding, funding, and operation of this Israel Institute For Robotics. Yosef saw his little brother had obviously done a lot of thinking to come up with such a blueprint.

"There," Nissim said, punching the last key on the keyboard and waiting for the red lights on his control board to go on, "now just to save it and I'm done."

"Pretty impressive, pretty damn impressive, Nissim!" Yosef

gave another walloping slap to the back of his stunned brother's head. "You think that up yourself?"

"Damn it, Yossi," Nissim shot back, "keep your hands off me! Yeah, I thought it up myself, and no one but you and me will ever see it if I don't lock it into the mainframe's memory at Penn."

"Don't let me stop you. Go ahead. I really just came in here to give you a present," Yosef said, stepping back from his brother's chair.

"A present?" Nissim said distractedly, toggling a switch on the front panel, still concerned about saving the work he had just written. "How about I get it from you in a minute, okay?"

"No problem, no problem," Yosef said, moving toward the door. "Just tell me, you going to be seeing Denise tonight?"

"Yeah, I plan to, later. Why?"

"Because the present I have is for both of you."

It was clear to Nissim that Yosef was not going to leave him alone until he delivered what was in his pocket and on his mind. "All right," Nissim said, hurriedly pushing down another switch then turning around to face his brother, "let's end the suspense. What money did you blow on me now?"

"Don't worry, I couldn't have afforded to buy these for you if I'd wanted to," Yosef told him, taking two tickets out of his shirt pocket and holding an outstretched arm to his brother. "I got them as a gift and I'm giving them to you as one. Since there are two of them, you can use them better than I can."

Nissim studied his brother a second and saw the deep sadness behind his smile. Refusing the tickets or protesting that Yosef should use them would only intensify Yosef's sense of aloneness, his growing sense of grief. "L-tone Joan!" he said with exaggerated enthusiasm when he read the tickets. "At the Spectrum. Fantastic! Thanks, Yossi."

"I thought you'd like them," Yosef said, gratified by his

brother's pleasure. He jokingly hummed a few bars of "Philadelphia Freedom."

"Next week. That'll be great," Nissim said, holding up the tickets. "Denise loves him. Thanks!"

"Thank me *after* you've heard the concert," Yosef said, walking over to Nissim's bed and sitting himself down. "Do you mind if I watch how you operate this thing?"

Nissim nodded, then turned his chair back around to his computer, and suddenly his face dropped. "Don't tell me!" he said out loud. "I didn't!" The screen in front of his eyes was blank. Pitch black. No numbers on it. Nothing. He felt as though his temper was tied to a heavy stone and someone had just thrown it down his throat. It was lodged now somewhere below his knees. Instead of depressing the switches that would have given the "DEPOSIT" command and stored his figures in the ALTAIR's memory, he had pushed down the switches for "RESET", instructing the computer to wipe the screen clean and start again from scratch. He had erased the "mechatronics" statistics that had taken hours to calculate. "Don't tell me I'm that stupid!"

"What happened?" Yosef asked. "What'd you do?"

"I lost it, that's what I did! I erased my goddamn source file."

"What's that mean?"

"It means I wiped out everything I wrote! A whole day of figures gone just like that," Nissim said, snapping his fingers. "Lost! I just can't believe I did that! Damn!"

"You can get it back, can't you?" Yosef asked. "I mean, it's at Penn, isn't it? I saw it myself right there on the screen a minute ago. It's gotta be in there, somewhere, doesn't it?"

"No, I hit the 'reset' switch. It's gone. As far as you and me seeing it goes, we might as well have seen a UFO. I can tell Professor Clarendon I had it all for him, ready to print out and put in his hand, and he can tell me it never existed, and he'd be right, not me."

Nissim looked at the blank TV screen, wanting at the same time to charm it into unerasing his work and to hurl it out the bedroom window. All that time, all that work. He looked at the two concert tickets which lay on the desk in front of him, and he thought of the picture he had seen of Elton John playing the piano while doing a handstand on the keyboard. Nissim was tempted to try that trick now, walking upside down across his computer's control board, doing a heavy hand dance there that would drive the whole system through the floor.

Yosef was no longer sitting on the bed. He was standing next to the computer screen, still looking incredulous, amazed to think that hard information could actually disappear like that. What are we dealing with here? he asked himself. Ghosts? Mirages? It made no sense to him. "Nissim, can your computer talk to — if that's the right way to say it — can it talk to *any* other computer?" he asked. "Or just to the one at Penn?"

Nissim was feverishly jotting down every key piece of data he could remember on a legal pad in front of him. "Any computer with a phone number and modem hookup," he answered, not even lifting his eyes from the page. "But I don't know what difference that makes now. No other computer's gonna help me get back what's gone."

Yosef listened and nodded his head. "Sorry," he said, stepping back then moving toward the door. "Well, you don't need me in your way. I'll be downstairs."

"HOW LATE ARE YOU?" he asked on the night of the concert. "Ten days."

"And this is not normal for you?"

"No," Denise said, "I'm usually on time."

Nissim was sitting in the brown leather lounge chair in the sunken living room, his feet propped up on the matching ottoman. Although it was only forty degrees outside, he was dressed for summer, wearing a maroon University of Pennsylvania T-shirt and gray gym shorts. He looked past Denise to the white candle burning in a glass holder on the bookshelf behind her. A stamp with the letters "Tel Aviv Memorial Lights" covered the front of the glass holder. Even with the floor lamps turned on, the candle cast a pale light across the room. It had been two days since Yom Kippur and tonight was Avi's *yarhzeit,* the second anniversary of his death. Nissim had lit this candle for Avi half an hour ago, just minutes before darkness had descended on Philadelphia, just minutes before Denise had arrived.

"How?" Nissim asked. "How are you late?"

"What do you mean 'how?' "

"I mean why."

"Why? Why is anybody late?" Denise said, choosing a question to answer him. Sitting on the sofa, she straightened her cream cashmere sweater, smoothed the brown wool skirt that barely covered the top of her knees, and crossed her ankles, lifting one suede midcalf boot over the other. She reached down to her pocketbook on the floor, took out a pack of Marlboros, and removed one.

Nissim could think of several reasons, none he especially wanted to hear. "Did you see a doctor?" he asked. He knew he hadn't taken any precautions, but he was certain Denise had.

"No, I don't need to yet." She lit the cigarette, leaning forward to place the match in the ashtray on the glass coffee table in front of her. "I will when I'm sure I'm pregnant."

"Pregnant?" He was totally confused. "What do you mean, 'pregnant?' " He looked at her sitting across from him, her legs bare from above her knees to the top of her suede boots, her sweater clinging to her body, the soft fullness of her breasts apparent through the cashmere. "When? How?" he asked.

"How do you think?"

"But you are taking pills, no?"

She did not answer immediately, choosing instead to flick some ashes from her cigarette into the ceramic ashtray on the coffee table. Through the open louvered doors to the den she stared at the huge aquarium with its bubbling water and tangle of tubes and its fish of all colors and sizes. How many babies were in there? she thought. How many mothers? "No," she said softly, turning her eyes to Nissim, "I stopped."

"You *what?*" Had he been sleeping with her, making love to her for the past month without her using any contraceptive? How? he asked himself. How could I be so stupid? He had simply assumed that any woman who jumped into bed on the first date would protect herself. His confusion intensified, turning into anger. "You didn't even say anything," he said, staring harshly at Denise. "Why? What is this to you? A game?"

She looked back at him, her eyes clear with an intimate light that sought to soften his glare. "No, Nissim, it's no game," she said evenly, her raspy voice seeming to give her words a deeper sincerity. "You're right, I didn't say anything, but I don't remember you asking."

Her words did little to ease his anger. "No," he said, almost shouting, "*you* didn't ask! *You* decided to play with *my* life and *you* didn't ask!" He sprang to his feet, looking as though he was searching for something to pick up and throw. "If *I* did that to *you* they'd call it rape!" His voice reached a crescendo at the last word, and he listened to it resound through the living room, through the hallway, through the many downstairs rooms. Denise just sat on the sofa across from him, looking sultry in the shadows of Avi's candle, watching him. It was a trap, he told himself, and he had walked blindly into it. He had let down his guard in America, had allowed himself to let down for a while, and look where it had landed him. I should have known, he told himself. It was too easy from the beginning, she was too pretty, we made love too soon. "I should have known," he said out loud. "I should have seen it. No one who looks like you could stay single. In America everyone marries early."

"Everyone in America doesn't do anything. It's too big a place for that," she told him, not sounding the least bit upset. "Everyone does something different." Denise was not threatened by Nissim's anger. In fact, on one level she was enjoying it. In the three months she had spent with him she had never seen him this animated, this agitated, this aroused, and she had never heard him raise his voice in her presence, let alone shout at her. It had bothered her that he was always so controlled, so measured in his responses, in his reactions, that he wasn't more spontaneous. It had seemed to her as though he had walled off a part of himself from her, the part of him that was in disarray. Every person had a part like that, she believed, and Nissim had boarded up that vulnerable part of himself as he would a broken window. So it pleased her to see she had happened into that private part of his being. However, on another level his anger concerned her. She hadn't meant to tell him anything tonight, not about being late, not about the pills, not about why she had stopped taking them, but seeing him just sitting there in that chair when she walked in, seeing him just staring at that candle, withdrawing into himself again and shutting her out as if she weren't there, she had been unable to stop herself. Something inside her had wanted to jolt him out of that shell, to shock him into acknowledging her. It had been a mistake, she knew, but it was too late now to undo it. "I'm still single because I want to be," she told him.

"It was a trap," Nissim said, cutting her short, sounding as though he were thinking out loud, not looking at her, shouting to himself. Then he turned to her. "You stopped taking the pills!"

Nervously she took a short puff of her cigarette, blew out the smoke, and concerned now about his growing anger, rose to her feet. She walked through the louvered doors to the aquarium and stood there a moment, watching the spectral fish swim inside the large glass tank. How many families were in there? she wondered. How many fathers? "No one said marriage is the only way to have children," she said slowly.

"What are you talking?" Nissim asked with a grimace, following her into the den. "Marriage is for families, and families are for children."

"Who said anything about having a family?" Denise asked, turning around to face him, her tone no longer dispassionate. "Marriage is the trap," she said, "not whatever you think I set up for you. I don't want to lock you in, I don't want to lock *myself* in. Marriage is the last thing I want, believe me. I can support a child on my own, I've got a good-paying job, a secure one, and I can raise her or him alone, without all the lies and without us inflicting pain on each other. Marriage makes liars out of everyone." Even out of people who never lied before, she thought herself. Marriage itself was built on lies. It began with lies and ended with them. She remembered the lies that she'd been told: that her father and mother loved each other; that one woman could satisfy one man and that monogamy was natural; that her father would take care of her, that he would always be there for her; and the biggest lie of all, that marriage itself was permanent. Where were you, daddy, for thirteen years? she asked herself. Where were you for all those times I needed you? It would have been easier for everyone, it would have been simpler and healthier and less painful for everyone, she thought, for everyone including herself, if she had been born to her mother only. "Marriage is a prison, Nissim," she said, throwing her head back to clear the film of tears that had started to blur her vision. "People come out of it bitter, less human than they were when they went in. The only way to stay loving is to steer clear of it, to live outside of it like Isadora did."

A quizzical, impatient look came across Nissim's face. He

remembered the poster of the ballet dancer in a graceful pose on Denise's living room wall, but he did not want to let Denise detour from the discussion at hand, even for a moment. "Isadora?" he asked.

"Isadora Duncan, you know, the dancer on my wall. She saw marriage for what it was. She never let herself get caught in it, but she still had children, two of them, and she had them by the men she chose." She looked at the fish in the tank and poked a playful finger at the glass, causing a rainbow-colored fish to dart away through the water. Having a child as an unmarried mother was no different than having one as a wife, she thought. Men were always deserting their women. She would protect her sense of self the same as Isadora had done—by not giving any man the chance to abandon her. You are always a single parent in the end anyway, she told herself. "I saw a movie about Isadora's life," Denise went on, "and she said in it that she wanted to have all her children by different men, beautiful men."

"So you chose me?" Nissim asked. "And I'm supposed to be flattered? Is that how it works?" He turned and walked back into the living room where he sat back down in the lounge chair, feeling not at all flattered or fortunate, but victimized, abused, exploited. A sense of powerlessness overwhelmed him, and the frustration it bred fed the fire of his anger. He pictured the other poster on Denise's apartment wall. "Like the apes," he went on, "is that how it is? Like animals in the jungle? You care more about them than you do about people!" More than she cares about her own child's life, he told himself, more than she cares about my life.

"Look, this whole thing is getting blown out of proportion," she said, coming back into the living room to join Nissim. "I don't even know I'm pregnant. And if it turns out I am, I won't make any claims on you. I promise." She sat back down on the sofa, flicking some ashes into the ashtray as she was seated.

"No claims? What's that worth now?" He looked across at Avi's candle, picturing the infernal war and his friend's face framed in a mane of fire. Two years ago, he thought, only two years ago, and by next year this time I may have a child, an American child. I won't have any bastards in my family. If she's pregnant we'll have to get married. But I won't marry a woman I can't trust, a woman I could never trust again. "Won't change my life? It will change everything," he said loudly. But how could I take her back to Israel? She could never survive there. What does she know about me, about Avi, about the war? Talking to her about life and death was like talking to a child. Had she seen the bloodied and rotting bodies strewn across the sands of the Sinai? Had she seen them lying spread-eagled on top of the retreating tanks, or stacked inside the gutted buses and armored personnel carriers? She couldn't begin to understand me, and I don't understand her. "It changes everything!" he said again, looking at the candle behind her. Her child will be my child, my seed. If I leave here alone and don't marry her, I'll be deserting my child. I'll be leaving a part of myself, an illegitimate part of myself, in America. "You selfish, thoughtless bitch!" he said, seething.

"Nissim, you don't understand," Denise said, her voice now plaintive. "It's easier this way. No one gets hurt."

No one gets hurt? he thought. Was she kidding? The picture of his child, their child, walking in the world here, growing up without him, without even knowing him, already began to haunt him. "The child will be a bastard!" he told her.

"Maybe in Israel that's still a big deal, but here it's nothing anymore. But look, I shouldn't have said anything to begin with. I'm probably not even pregnant. Everyone's late some time, for chrissake, and most of the time for no reason." She reached up and removed the hair clip from the bun on top of her head, looking softly at Nissim as her hair fell down over her back and shoulders. Placing her cigarette in the ashtray, she rose slowly and walked around the glass table to Nissim. "I like you, that's what matters," she said in her most seductive tone, standing beside his high-backed chair. She reached her hand down and began to let her fingers play in his curls, but the moment she touched him, he recoiled.

"It's over, Denise," he said, springing forward to his feet. "Whatever we had is over." He stared at her with a laser-like sharpness, his gaze seeming to cut right through her.

"Nissim," she said coyly, reaching out again, "don't do this. Please."

But again he pulled away. "I did too much already," he told her.

"What about the concert?" she asked. "What about the tickets?"

Nissim didn't care anymore about seeing Elton John tonight. He didn't care about seeing or hearing anyone tonight.

"Nissim, I'm sorry. I shouldn't have said anything. I shouldn't have worried you. It's nothing. I've been late like this before. Let's just forget about it. Okay? What we have is so—"

Denise stopped short as she heard the door from the garage open and slam shut. Heavy footsteps came through the hallway. The two of them stood rigid like two statues, waiting for the footsteps to reach them.

"So how's Denissim doing?" Yosef asked, peering into the living room as he walked through the hallway on his way to the coat closet. A lighted pipe was in his mouth and a sweet trail of cherry tobacco smoke followed him. He hung up his army jacket, then closed the closet door. His red plaid shirt was unbuttoned as usual, baring the Temple University T-shirt underneath. His blue jeans were wearing thin at the knees, and his leather Nikes were more brown than white. "Getting ready for Elton John?" he asked.

Denissim, Nissim repeated silently to himself. Yosef had combined their names by accident about a month ago, and had been calling them "Denissim" as often as possible since then. We're not part of the same world, let alone the same name, Nissim told himself. She doesn't begin to know where I come from, and I don't want any more to do with her.

"No," Denise said dejectedly, trying to make it seem to Yosef that the concert was the source of the tension between her and Nissim, "he says he won't go. Doesn't want to. Maybe you can talk some life into him. I'm sure not having any luck." She moved to the sofa and sat down, alone, taking another cigarette out of her pack.

"What do you mean 'won't go?'" Yosef asked, stepping down into the living room and sitting next to Denise on the sofa.

"He'd rather sit here and watch some candle melt," Denise said, turning to Yosef. "Elton John comes to Philly, he comes right here to our doorstep, and thanks to you we luck into tickets, and now he says he's not going! Maybe it's just me, but I don't get it."

"Come on, little brother," Yosef said, looking first at the *yarh-zeit* candle on the bookcase, then turning to Nissim, "you can't spend your whole life locked up in here, staring at some computer screen or standing around all night in your gym shorts. Get up, get dressed, and get out of here. You know you need it."

Nissim looked at his brother and sat down in the leather lounge chair. "Not tonight, Yossi," he said. "I'm not in a party mood."

"Not in the mood?" Denise said loudly. "That's an understatement if I ever heard one. Look at this place. It's so quiet and dark in here, it's dead. It feels like a morgue or something! Can't we turn on some lights, put on some music? God, lighten up, would you?"

Nissim's eyes were almost squinting, his lips a straight line as he studied Denise. He was enjoying the quiet, the dim light. He was listening to the silence, moving inside it, hearing himself think in it. Why did it always have to be so loud, so bright? Why did life have to feel like a carnival every minute, every day? Nissim wondered if Denise was aware of the constant noise in her life, if she was aware of how she always was filling the silence as though it were her enemy. He couldn't remember seeing her without the stereo or the radio or the television on as background noise, and he couldn't remember ever seeing her without some prop in her hand or in her mouth. Cigarettes, a drink, a magazine, some finger foods. He wondered why quiet scared her so, why she felt compelled to fill it with words and smoke and music. He looked at her now sitting there on the sofa, a lighted prop in her hand. She looked beautiful to him, she would always look beautiful to him, but she looked different to him now – seductive but dangerous, voluptuous but selfish, deceitful. "Don't play dumb, Denise," he told her.

Denise let out a dramatic sigh. "Did you hear that, Yossi?" she said, pronouncing Yosef's name with a long *o* as she always did, talking to him as though he were the judge. "Two days ago we did this whole religious thing and you didn't hear me complaining, did you? I took the day off from the bank, he dragged me to the synagogue, and I sat through it. I even fasted till lunch time. But that was about all of that trip I could take. And now he says he's staying home." She turned from Yosef and spoke to Nissim. "If you want to sit around all night staring at some candle, that's your problem. I'm not about to miss this concert." Denise crushed the butt of her half-smoked cigarette into the ashtray and stood up. "I'm sick of this morbid stuff, you know? What time is it anyway?" she asked Yosef.

"Six o'clock," he told her, checking his wristwatch.

"And the concert starts at seven-thirty. We should've been out of here fifteen minutes ago!" she said.

Nissim sat, unmoved and incredulous, in his chair. "No one's keeping you from going," he said, reaching into his shirt pocket and holding both tickets out to her. "Here."

"Both?" Denise said, walking over to him and taking them out of his hand. "What do you expect me to do? Scalp one at the door?"

"You don't expect her to go alone, do you?" Yosef asked, puffing on his pipe. "You know what goes on. I wouldn't let her go there alone. Come on, Nissim, go with her."

"I'm not going anywhere tonight," Nissim said firmly. "Why don't you go with her, Yossi?"

"I gave the tickets to you," Yosef said, still seated on the sofa, "for the two of you, not for me."

"What's the matter?" Denise asked coyly. "Are you embarrassed to be seen with me, Yossi?"

Yosef turned around and flashed her a smile. She was one of the prettiest women he'd seen and he'd told her as much more than once. Even looking at her now from only inches away she looked stunning to him. He ran his eyes slowly up and down her sleek body, and his mind filled with thoughts of Rivka. Denise was only two years younger than Rivka, but they looked like they belonged to different generations. Denise's skin was soft, her complexion creamy, and her figure was as shapely as any model's. Rivka's skin had become stretched and had lost its smoothness. Why was it that so many Israeli women lost their softness, lost their good looks as soon as they hit twenty-five? he asked himself. It wasn't only Rivka. The same held true for Varda and every other Israeli woman he knew. Maybe it was due to the hard water back home, he thought. The hard water and the harder life. And Denise's eyes were alive with excitement, open to new adventures, new discoveries. "Embarrassed?" he said to Denise, who had moved into the entrance hall and was taking her coat out of the closet. He watched her slip one arm into the coat sleeve. Her breasts pushed forward as she wriggled first into one sleeve and then the other. "Nissim, take the lady out, would you?" he said, turning back to his brother. "Elton John isn't going to be here tomorrow."

Neither will Avi, Nissim thought to himself. He looked at the candle, at his brother on the sofa, at Denise in the hallway. If she was carrying his child, then all of his plans would have to change.

He would be caught between two worlds, between America and Israel, between his child and his family, his progeny and his country. How would he tell Miryam and Barukh? In a letter? On the phone? The complications seemed infinite. Just thinking about them made him wince. There was a burning pain in his gut. Consciously he clipped the thought short as though waking himself from a nightmare. "You don't understand either, do you, Yossi?" he said.

"Yossi, are you coming or not?" Denise called, buttoning her coat and throwing a boa scarf around its fur collar.

Yosef stood up and looked at his brother again, asking without words if Nissim objected. Shadows washed back and forth across the living room walls and curtains as the flame of the *yarhzeit* candle quavered. A shifting light moved across Nissim's face, making his skin seem almost as dark as his beard, making his expression appear severe. He looked up at his brother, catching a glimpse of Denise beyond him as she waited near the front door. Neither he nor she had been in the Sinai, or in Israel for that matter, during the war. Maybe they deserved each other. "Go, have a good time," he told Yosef.

Yosef stood still a moment, puffing on his pipe again, looking at Denise who stood waiting for him. Rivka had never looked like that, he thought.

"Yossi, you coming?" she asked. "They're your tickets."

Nissim did not get up from the lounge chair when his cousin moved toward the door.

IT WAS TWO-FIFTEEN. Yosef parked his cab in the two-car garage and entered the house through the side door, opening and closing it gently so as not to wake his brother. Stepping softly, he walked to the hall closet to hang up his coat, but as he opened the closet he heard a voice behind him.

"Where were you?"

Yosef quickly turned around to find Nissim sitting in the lounge chair, in the same position, in the same gym clothes, even deeper in darkness than when he had left him. The *yarhzeit* candle still burned in its glass holder on the bookshelf. It was the only light in the room.

"Where've you been?" Nissim asked, not moving.

"With Denise. We went for coffee after the concert."

"It's after two o'clock," Nissim said. "The concert was over hours ago." He looked at his brother, a large silhouette in the hallway, and pictured him in Denise's bed, having her, making love to her. A sudden jealousy surged inside him. In the darkness Yosef could not see the pain etched across Nissim's face, nor could he see the tears that had dried on Nissim's cheeks several hours ago. "You didn't listen to the radio tonight?" Nissim asked. "You don't know, you didn't hear?"

Yosef stood in the hallway. "Know what, Nissim? Hear what?"

Nissim leaned forward, standing up slowly. "Yossi, Oded's dead."

Ten

YOSEF SAT IN THE SMALL OFFICE with the brochures of Mexico and Hawaii and Switzerland in a holder on the desk in front of him, glossy posters of the Parthenon, the Coliseum, and the Eiffel Tower covering the walnut-panelled walls. A small sign on top of a file cabinet in the corner read, "Sorry, no checks—We already have a good supply from last year!" They have to take mine, he thought. He had been the first client through the door this morning, having slept not more than an hour the previous night, and for the past few minutes he had been waiting anxiously for the travel agent to return to her desk.

"All set, Mr. Love," she said, coming back into the room.

"It's Lvov," he said.

"Sorry, Mr. Lvov. In light of the situation, Mr. Rosenbloom said that a personal check will be fine, so long as you have your driver's license and a major credit card with you. Does that present any problem?"

"No, no," Yosef said quickly, taking out his wallet and his checkbook. "I have everything right here." He removed his Pennsylvania driver's license and his BankAmericard from his wallet, laid them next to his car keys on the desk in front of him, and wrote out the check. Then he handed the check, his license, and his credit card to the travel agent.

"Thank you," she said with a smile, handing him an envelope. "And here are your tickets for Tel Aviv on the nine o'clock flight from Kennedy Airport tomorrow night. The earliest direct flight available on El Al. That is what you wanted, isn't it?"

"Yes," Yosef told her. "Thank you." He put the airline tickets into the pocket of his shirt, picked up his car keys, and hurried out to his cab.

THERE WERE NO WINDOWS on either side of the corridor, only closed doors. Nissim and Yosef stood silently in the dim alcove outside apartment 315. Yosef lifted the knocker and let it fall, remembering how he and Nissim had stood on this same spot at three o'clock this morning. Inside with Varda, he and Nissim had found two uniformed officers who were asking her questions and jotting down notes. She had cried in Yosef's arms, moving toward him as soon as he had entered. My friend dead, Yosef had thought, holding Varda, holding back his own tears. Murdered for what? Money? Less than fifty dollars! What a waste! What a tragic god-damn waste! He had felt like stalking the killer all night through the streets of Philadelphia, across America if he had to. Now he lifted the door knocker and let it fall again.

"Yes?" Varda called through the door, not willing to open it until she knew who stood on the other side. "Who is it?"

"Yossi and Nissim."

There were the sounds of dead bolts unlocking and chain locks unlatching, then the door opened and Varda Hazon was standing in the entranceway, still in her bathrobe, her figure backlit by the lamps inside the apartment, her daughter Orly in pajamas cling-ing to her with both arms wrapped around Varda's neck. Orly's head was pressed hard against her mother's chest. Yosef watched them silhouetted in the doorway and their shape, their intense and loving fusion, looked universal. They could have been any mother and child. They could have been primates or people. The two brothers walked into the apartment slowly. Yosef gently stroked Orly's head as he passed. All of them continued together into the living room. Varda eased herself down onto the sofa still holding

holding Orly, who curled into a fetal position on her mother's lap as soon as Varda sat down.

"Have you called yet?" Yosef asked as Nissim sat down in a stodgy armchair. Yosef chose to remain standing, for he knew he would not be able to stay long this morning because his first class would be starting in less than an hour. He studied Varda more closely now in the light, and she did not look good to him. Her straight blonde hair was disheveled and greasy, and there were dark circles under her eyes. Whatever makeup she had been wearing had smeared or washed away. The ashtray on the table at her elbow overflowed with butts and ashes, the remnants of a sleepless night. Yosef watched as she lit another cigarette now, careful not to let the match or the cigarette get too close to Orly's hair. Orly looked so small to him, curled up as she was on Varda. She looked so frightened, so wounded, her whole body tense and immobile, only her eyes moving back and forth, watching everything around her, seeming to dilate with every sound, every movement of light in the room. Yosef could not look at her without thinking of Dorit. He remembered back to Dorit's birthday party and saw Orly sitting in the circle of friends, sharing Dorit's gifts, sitting in the circle of children around his daughter. What if it had been me? he wondered. What if it were me? He thought of Rivka and Dorit in Haifa, of Barukh and Miryam. "Do they know?" he asked Varda.

"Yes, they know," Varda answered, averting her eyes as she spoke, "I told them." She had telephoned her parents in Israel before dawn this morning, not concerned about waking them. She had listened to herself say the words, "Abba, Ema — Oded was shot last night at work. He's dead." But it had sounded to her as though someone else was saying them and even that they were being said *about* someone else, someone else's Oded, someone else's husband. It was not until she had listened to the stunned silence on the other end of the trans-Atlantic line that she had started to cry again. It was her parents' silence that had shocked her into accepting the fact that Oded's death was real, that he was the man on the TV news and she was his stricken widow. Her parents had called Oded's parents as she had asked them to do. That was one call, she had told them, that she was unable to make. "They're waiting for me to call back," she said, taking a puff of her cigarette and looking up at Yosef and Nissim, "they're waiting for me to tell them the final arrangements."

Yosef, still standing, took the envelope out of his shirt pocket, leaned over, and handed it to Varda. "Here are the final arrangements," he told her. "Nissim and I took care of them this morning."

The two of them had split the cost of the passage home for Varda, Orly, and Oded's body. The body, as the undertaker had called Oded, would not be flying home with the family. It would be on board another plane, a container in the baggage bay, a ticketed piece of cargo. Since the airlines did not allow individuals to book the shipping of corpses by air freight, the funeral home had made the arrangements. There were rigorous health requirements and international regulations to be met. Oded would be travelling home separately and would be met at Ben-Gurion Airport by the Israeli *Chevra Kadisha,* the Burial Society. "The funeral parlor takes care of everything," he told her.

They had wanted to alleviate her suffering and to mitigate her anguish. She had told them at three o'clock this morning that she wanted Oded buried in Israel and that she and Orly did not want to stay in America "one minute longer than we have to. I want to go home," she had said several times. "God, I just want to go home." Yosef and Nissim had acted quickly, taking matters into their own hands, agreeing to underwrite whatever it cost to put the Hazons on the first plane out. Yosef didn't have the money to give, but said he would pay Nissim back as soon as he could. Nissim had brought with him a dollar reserve for emergencies in

America, and this, he said, was an emergency. Friends took care of friends even when they were no longer here, even when they couldn't repay the debt or reciprocate the favor.

Friends, Nissim thought. Dead friends. Avi's candle had not been burning yet for twenty-four hours. Now Oded and Avi would share the same *yarhzeit*. Nissim watched Varda crying, then focused on Orly's eyes peering out from under her mother's sheltering arms. When two parents look as different from one another as Oded and Varda, their child most often looks like either one or the other, Nissim thought, and Orly resembled her father. She had his dark hair and dark complexion, his Sephardic look, his deep-set eyes. Nissim looked at her and saw Oded, Oded whose dream for next summer had been to convert a school bus and take it cross-country, and Avi, whose dream had been to tour America on a three-person honeymoon with Shoshanah and him. Lost friends. Dead plans. Failed dreams. Orly would not be going to school today, he told himself. She would not ride the yellow school bus again, and neither would Oded.

Varda was still crying and Yosef moved over to her without words, putting a strong hand on her shoulder. He could feel her trying to control herself, trying to catch her breath. After a moment she raised one arm and squeezed his hand, holding it with a warmth that surprised him, a warmth that made him think of Rivka, of Rivka back in Haifa alone. "Thank you," Varda said, gradually composing herself. "Thank you, both of you . . . for being here, for the tickets. I'm sorry to fall apart like this." And she reached for a tissue to dry her tears.

"Varda," Yosef said, his hand still in hers, "don't apologize. You're crying for all of us." Gently he withdrew his hand and continued talking. "Nissim is going to stay here with you and Orly. I wish I could stay too, but I have a class that I can't miss any more of." Professor Williams had threatened to flunk any student who missed more than four class sessions during the term. Yosef had already missed four. Losing credit now would only extend his stay at Temple. He was already going to miss next term; he couldn't afford to lose any part of this one. "Nissim," he said, turning to his brother, "I'll be back as soon as I'm finished."

"No problem," Nissim said, standing up. "We'll see you when you get back."

Yosef leaned down and kissed Orly on top of her head. Nissim stood beside Varda and took her hand. I have a class too, he thought. Then Yosef, his beard brushing against her wet cheek, kissed Varda and hurried out into the hallway.

WHEN YOSEF ARRIVED, Professor Williams, in a tan three-piece Adolpho suit, was already standing in front of the students in his "Racism" course. A black man in his forties, he checked the time on his gold pocket watch, adjusted his dark-rimmed glasses, and looked out over his class. Slowly he put the watch back into his vest pocket, lifted out some pages from a manila folder on his desk, and began speaking. "I've read your papers and there were some excellent pieces, some truly outstanding efforts, especially for first papers of the term," he said, seeing the faces of his students ease as they listened to him. "But there's at least part of one paper I want to read you." He paused as he held several pages in front of his face and waved them back and forth. He straightened the typed paper and ran his eyes silently across the first page. Then, adjusting his glasses, Professor Williams began reading out loud:

> With the back of his hand the Gestapo guard struck the helpless woman across the face and threw her onto the bed behind her. She clawed and kicked and bit him, but he was too strong. Her clothes tore and fell. She could feel his fingermarks on her

flesh, his teethmarks on her breasts. "No! Not me!" the woman screamed. But he pinned her down and forced himself inside her.

Four months later, life was inside her, driving her to the edge of madness. "Kill it!" she screamed, "Rip it out of me!" But no one listened. The Nazi guards named her "the living dead one." She spent long hours facing the wall, staring and trembling and twitching.

"This is an example," he said, "of what I *never* want to see again. This is mere, cheap emotionalism, sensationalism masquerading as an analysis of racism. It reads like a screenplay of a *B* movie and is just as contemptible. Furthermore, it demonstrates complete disregard for basic research practices. It is presented out of context, has no footnotes or bibliography, and offers us nothing but hysteria. It is half the length I asked for, yet it goes on and on.

"She survives the rape but loses the baby, escapes the Nazis, lands in Cyprus, gets pregnant again, has a child . . . . Send this paper to *Reader's Digest,* please, not to me. And the paper closes this way. 'The days dragged on until one day the woman contracted pneumonia and died. Her new son was not yet six months old . . . . This is the story of more than one victim. I am that woman's child.'"

Professor Williams paused. In silence he scanned the faces of his students. "Apparently at least one of you needs to be reminded, so I'm going to say this only one time. This is a college course, not some high school class in creative writing." He folded the pages of the paper together and slammed them in the folder. "If that's understood, let's get on to something else."

Yosef, beet red in his seat in the back of the room, thought of tearing his teacher apart. He had never been this angry, this humiliated, this betrayed. He had watched his classmates, heard their laughter, watched the smirk on the professor's face as he had read.

What was I trying to prove? he asked himself. He would never have handed in this paper if time hadn't been running out on him. The professor should have spoken to him before making his paper public. He felt violated at not having been consulted, at not having been told.

Yosef had asked Denise if she would help him with his school work one night when she was over and Nissim had been upstairs working on his computer. When the deadline had been only two days away, Yosef had still not written a word. The afternoon before it was due, he had sat down and finished the assignment in one sitting, writing in longhand. Denise took it home and typed it for him just as Rivka had done for him during the past two years. His handwriting in English was terrible and typing services were too expensive. Denise had been happy to do it for him.

For this "Racism" paper he had thought it would be easier to use what he already knew and not have to do any new research. He had thought that the story would speak for itself. Denise had told him that it had moved her deeply, that she had been on the verge of tears while typing it.

Hearing his story from the lips of a stranger, hearing it read out loud to a group of strangers, had made it seem more real to him, more immediate, more painful. It had made him think of the hole inside him since Rivka and Dorit's departure, of the hole inside him since his father Avram's death, of the void inside him for never having known his mother, of the jagged hole inside him today after Oded's murder. These were wounds that would never heal, he thought, holes that would never reseal themselves. "I knew I shouldn't have turned it in," he muttered to himself. "I should never have told the truth. I'd have been better off if I'd lied."

The professor closed Yosef's paper into the folder on his desk, took out some new notes, and continued. "Last week we were talking about the pre-Lincoln roots of the abolitionist movement . . . ."

DIRECT FROM HIS "RACISM" COURSE Yosef drove to the Yellow Cab office to purchase his insurance sticker for the coming week before heading back to Varda and Orly. It was Pennsylvania law that all cabs had to bear a current insurance sticker and that every cabbie had to carry personal liability and collision coverage for himself and his vehicle. Yosef had paid his six month premium for the private coverage and each week it cost him twenty-eight dollars for the Company sticker.

"Six thirteen, Lvov, Joseph," the secretary repeated. She was a gray-haired woman with glasses and she was running a finger down the long list of names and numbers on the clipboard in her hand. "Number six thirteen. Yeah, I see you, but it looks like there might be a problem." She showed Yosef the red check next to his number and name. "See Mr. Hendrick."

"A problem?" Yosef asked, perturbed. "There is something wrong. Someone made a mistake."

"I only know what's written here," she said. "I wish I could help you out, but I can't. If it's a mistake, there'll be no problem. Mr. Hendrick's right in there." She pointed to the door of the office just behind her.

"What problem?" he asked, working hard to control himself, feeling more dismay than concern, wondering why today of all days something couldn't be easy. "I am sure there can be nothing wrong," he said.

"Then that's fine," she told him, "and as soon as he gives you the say-so, just come right back in here to me."

Yosef scratched his head, put away the twenty-eight dollars which he had counted out before coming inside, and walked to the supervisor's door. Knocking but not waiting for an answer, he opened the door and walked in.

"Yes?" Mr. Hendrick said, lifting his eyes from the papers on his desk, a ballpoint pen in his hand. He did not look unduly surprised or disturbed to be interrupted this way. "What is it?"

"My name is Lvov. I came to get my sticker and there is a red mark next to my name. I am sure it is someone else's."

Mr. Hendrick slid his chair out and pulled open a file drawer on the right side of his desk. He lifted out a folder labeled "CLAIMS" and leafed through the sheets of paper inside. "What number are you?"

"Six thirteen."

The supervisor continued thumbing through the pages, then stopped, lifted out a single printed sheet, and set it down on top of the other papers on his desk. "Here it is," he said, rolling his chair back in and propping both elbows on his desk. It was clear from his expression that he believed this paper contained no new news for Yosef. "Says here you rear-ended a Plymouth to the tune of four hundred dollars."

"What?" Yosef said, leaning over and trying to read the page upside down.

"Here it is in black and white," the supervisor said, handing the written claim to Yosef. "Have a look for yourself."

Yosef read the claim slowly. On July 3 he was said to have collided with a Plymouth Duster, having driven at an excessive speed approaching the traffic signal at a major intersection. The driver of the other car had claimed not only rear end damages, but also physical injury to himself from the impact of the crash. The driver of Yellow Cab #613 was being held liable for all expenses incurred in connection with both the repair costs for the Plymouth and the medical costs for whiplash and related ailments suffered by the driver. "I don't believe this," Yosef said loudly. "This guy tried to pick a fight with me. I never touched him and

I never touched his fucking car. No policeman ever showed up, and no one who saw what happened even got out of their car."

Mr. Hendrick took the form from Yosef and read it over once more. "It says here he has witnesses," he told Yosef, pointing to a little box in the bottom corner of the form.

"Well the kid's a liar!" Yosef said, his eyes turning to slits with rage. "I should've busted his head when I had the chance. Check my cab. There's no damage on it. And I do all my repairs in the Company garage. You've got all the records. Check them."

Mr. Hendrick looked at Yosef carefully, studying his eyes, sizing him up, trying to decide if he should believe him. Then after a moment he said, "All right. If you say no cop was at the scene, that means they're can't be any report in their files, which means the kid doesn't have a real case, so tell Sally out there to sell you your sticker. But listen, you're driving with the wrong papers to begin with—y'know what I'm saying? So I'm gonna make a note this time. Next time you won't be so lucky. Next time I'll have to can you."

"I understand," Yosef said. "There won't be a next time." He headed back into the outer office, paid the secretary in cash, and walked out with his sticker. You never know, he told himself, from which side they're going to get you. Some days life was an ambush.

YOSEF TURNED OFF HIS LIGHTS and parked his cab at the curb. Walking inside the brick apartment building, he headed down the stairs to the basement. A moment later he was standing at a door, ringing the bell.

"Yes?" a voice asked suspiciously. It was after ten o'clock. "Who is it?"

"Yossi."

"Yossi?" Denise opened the door slowly. "Is everything all

right? Come on in." She was wearing a blue silk kimono robe with a sash tied around her waist and opened in front. Her long hair cascaded between her breasts.

Yosef looked at her, unable to keep his eyes on her face. "I wanted to see you," he said in a sullen voice.

"You look like something's wrong. What happened?"

"I just left my friend's wife. Her husband was killed last night. Someone shot him," he told her. "Maybe you read it in this morning's paper. Maybe you met him. Oded."

"The donut man?" she asked, remembering when she and Nissim had gone to his donut shop on their first night together. "I'm sorry," she said, her brows suddenly heavy with sympathy and concern. "I'm really sorry." She looked at the pain on Yosef's face and remembered the paper she had typed for him. He had begged her—his paper was due, he didn't type, and Rivka, his typist, was gone. She had agreed reluctantly, but what a different Yossi she had seen. Sensitive, vulnerable, and now he was here, grieving in her presence.

Yosef stood in the small living room, listening to the music from the two cabinet speakers on either side of Denise's sofa.

"Sit down, Yossi. Please." Denise said, moving an open *Vogue* magazine from the cushion. "Can I get you something to drink?"

"No, thanks. Nothing," Yosef answered, looking at the sofa, but not moving toward it. He had never seen a sofa without legs before. This one looked to him like no more than pillows laid next to each other on the floor. His eye was drawn to the glossy poster of a gorilla hanging on the wall to his right. It moved to the framed poster-sized print above the sofa. The inscription written under the oval photo of the ballet dancer intrigued him. "Who is this woman?" he asked Denise.

"Just a dancer," she answered quickly, remembering her fight last night with Nissim. "Just a dancer. Are you sure I can't get you something to drink?" she asked. "Something solid maybe? You hungry?"

"No," Yosef told her, no longer looking around the room, looking instead at Denise, running his eyes up and down her body. The night she had typed his story he had thought he had seen a certain look in her eyes. Last night after the concert, when they had sat and talked so long over coffee, he had seen that look again, and he was looking for it now, searching her eyes to find it there. But so far he could not see it. "I really just wanted to stop by and see how you were," he told her, "and tell you how much I enjoyed last night. But I ought to be getting back to work now, you know?"

"No, I don't," Denise said brazenly, fixing Yosef with a gaze. "I really enjoyed last night, too." She looked at Yosef standing across from her as she moved to the stereo turntable, lifted the needle from the record, and turned off the system. Yosef almost looked like a bodyguard to her. He was such a big man, so different from his brother. Nissim would never touch her again, she thought. He had said that. Well, what would he say if she slept with Yosef? How would he feel if she and his brother became lovers, if she made love with him in the same house where Nissim was living, if she moved in with Yosef and the three of them lived under one roof? She found vengeful pleasure in imagining the torment, the jealousy Nissim would suffer. "Yossi, please don't go yet," she said coyly.

Yosef no longer was uncertain about her feelings for him, but he was having second thoughts about his feelings for her. Nissim had told him that whatever had been between Denise and him was finished, but still Yosef felt uneasy. In his seven years of marriage he had never been unfaithful to Rivka, and there was something secure, if not sacred, in knowing that. But Rivka had walked out on him. *She* had deserted *him*. Why should I be celibate? "Look," he said, "you were going to bed when I knocked.

I don't want to keep you up."

"Oh, don't worry about that," she said, moving over to him and taking his hand. "I still plan to go to bed." She undid the sash around her waist. "It's just that tonight I thought that maybe both of us could use a little company."

"DENISE," HE TOLD HER as he lay beside her, "there's something else beside Oded's death that's pushing me down."

"What are you talking about?" she asked, pulling up the sheet to cover herself.

"I'm in trouble," he told her. "I have to . . . some way . . . I don't know."

"What's wrong?" she asked in a soothing tone, her head resting on his chest as she drew with her fingers on the inside of his thighs.

"Forget it," he told her, running a gentle hand over the contours of her back, stroking her hair with the other.

If he was going to finish his degree, he would have to find the money to pay off his credit card debt now, he thought. Otherwise the interest would compound and he might never dig his way out. He wanted to go back to Israel with his head high, with at least a degree in his suitcase. When he went back home, he would go in style. "I'm past the point of choices," he said, massaging the small of Denise's back.

"What did you say?" she said, curling the hairs on his chest as she spoke.

"Nothing," he said. "Nothing."

Eleven

"'AND DENISE,' I SAID, 'Denise, we can walk up and down these aisles all day and spend more on clothes for that doll of yours than it'll cost to put you through college, or we can buy just one thing that'll save this poor tired aunt of yours a lot of time and money and will take care of little Barbie here for the rest of her life.' And don't you know that I walked right up, picked a Ken doll off the shelf, and paid for it right there on the spot. Then I put that Ken doll into Denise's little hand and said, 'Denise, now Barbie can have anything in the world she wants, so long as *he'll* pay for it.'" With this, Denise's aunt, Mrs. Jenkins, laughed a properly muffled laugh, covered her mouth with a white linen napkin, and patted her lips with it.

Yosef sat across the small elegantly set table, straightening his necktie and smiling stiffly. He served himself a roll from the basket next to the small vase of flowers and looked around at the other diners. The elegant restaurant was filled with well-groomed men in black, pinstripe suits conducting business over lunch. For the past twenty minutes Yosef had been listening to stories about members of Denise's family. There was one about an aunt who held dinner parties where each person was asked to bring a specific food so that she didn't have to do a thing but set the table and wait. And there was another about an uncle who was so scared of his wife that every year, a few weeks before her birthday he sent all the relatives a blank birthday card and a stamped return envelope so that all they had to do was sign the card and mail it back to her. Mrs. Jenkins had been reeling off anecdotes about almost

every member of Denise's family, but she hadn't yet asked Yosef a single question about himself.

"Yes," she went on, "people still tell that story at our table."

Yosef was becoming uncomfortable dressed up in a suit and
tie. Everything about this meeting, this interview, felt constricting to him. Even the table was too small; he had to squeeze his
knees between two leg posts. This restaurant, this food, these people, these clothes. His tie felt so tight around his neck. How could
these people walk around all day and keep breathing? But Denise
had told him that he would have to dress up to meet her aunt if
he wanted a shot at securing her help. Until yesterday he had
owned no suit. Never had there been a need for one. In Israel no
one ever wore a coat and tie. Even the Prime Minister, model-
ing himself after Ben-Gurion, went around in an open-necked
shirt. During the past two years Yosef had never needed a suit—
not to drive his taxi, not to go to classes at Temple, not even to
go to synagogue on Rosh HaShanah and Yom Kippur. A sweater
and dress slacks had been fine. So he had gone out and bought
a suit for this lunch, a grey herringbone suit to impress Denise's
aunt. Why was it that you always had to risk more to make more,
that you had to spend what you didn't have to get what you
needed? It all seemed backwards. He had also gotten his hair cut
and beard trimmed for the first time in two months, for the first
time since Rivka and Dorit's departure at the end of September.
"Dashing" was how Denise had described the way he looked that
morning, but he felt like a man in a monkey suit, a big ape.

Mrs. Jenkins was eating artichoke leaves in a vinaigrette dressing. "But enough about me and my family. Denise has told me
a little about your situation, Joseph, but only a little. She said that
you needed money to pay off some debts and finish your school-
ing. So I guess we should get right down to brass tacks. How much
money are we talking about?"

"Twenty-five hundred dollars," he told her, figuring in his share

231

of sending Oded's corpse and widow back to Israel. He waited for Denise's aunt to wince or flinch or show some surprise, but the sum didn't seem to trouble her.

"I see," she said calmly, lifting an artichoke leaf to her mouth. "And if you got the twenty-five hundred dollars, what would you do with it?"

"I would pay off my debts, finish my studies at Temple University, and return home to Israel, to my wife and daughter." A brown crust of baked cheese covered the onion soup in the crock before him. He punctured it with his spoon and watched as steam jetted up in front of his face. He straightened up again and leaned back in his chair.

"I see," she said again, probing Yosef's eyes, studying his face. "But haven't you been — what shall we call it? — 'seeing' my niece for the past month or so?" She paused and lifted her tea cup. "Am I wrong?"

Yosef tried unsuccessfully to control his face from losing color. He cleared his throat, leaned forward, and preferring not to answer, dipped his spoon into his hot soup. Strings of melted cheese hung from the spoon as he lifted it toward his mouth. He pictured himself suspended there on one of those strings, dangling there like a marionette. "Your niece is a wonderful girl," he said. "She and I are alike in many ways."

"Yes," she said, "she is a wonderful girl, and that's why I'm asking you what your intentions are."

Denise's aunt continued talking, but Yosef did not hear another word she was saying. He put down his spoon and pushed his chair slowly away from the table. "Excuse me, please," he said, interrupting Denise's aunt and rising, "but can we continue in one minute?"

"Of course," she said.

"Thank you. Excuse me."

Mrs. Jenkins watched Yosef walk across the dining room and

232

disappear into the alcove where the rest rooms and lounges were.

Inside the men's room Yosef walked to the bay of sinks and looked at himself in the section of long mirror that covered the wall above the sinks. He was sweating and the tie around his neck was choking him. This was not going to work, he told himself. Her aunt was not about to help out some married guy who was screwing her niece, and he couldn't think of a reason why she should. Since the night after Oded's murder, Denise and he had been seeing each other regularly. He had even driven directly to her place and spent the night with her after driving Varda and Orly to the airport for their flight home to bury Oded. And during the past week she had shared Yosef's bedroom. What kind of lie could he tell her aunt? Maybe if he took his time and didn't think too hard the line would come to him. He leaned down and turned on the cold water, cupped his hands under the spigot, and splashed two handfuls onto his face. The cool water refreshed him. He reached for a towel to dry himself. A metal towelholder hung on the wall beside him, but it was empty. So was the metal holder on the opposite wall. Yosef cupped his hands under his face, trying to keep the water from dripping off his beard and onto his shirt and suit jacket. Then he noticed a hot air dryer on the wall. Yosef pushed a large silver button and a loud whirring sound like that of a small jet engine filled the bathroom, sending a hot stream of fan-forced air out through the shiny pipe. Yosef held his hands under the pipe's opening, rubbing them together to help them dry faster, but water still dripped from his beard. A restaurant like this should have towels, he complained to himself, but there were no towels. Not seeing any alternative, he turned the short curved pipe so that it pointed upward, and put his face directly above the opening. The force of the hot air blew his hair in all directions, making his hair stick straight up in front. When his face had dried he walked over to look in the mirror. His hair and beard looked electrified; he looked to himself like a wild man, even in his suit. He tried to smooth his hair with his fingers, but that did little to improve his unkempt appearance.

In utter frustration he walked out of the men's room and paused at the edge of the alcove that separated the rest rooms from the dining room. From where he stood he could see Denise's aunt running an artichoke leaf against her teeth. Yosef ran his hand once more through his hair. He looked around the dining room at all the men in their business suits, cutting their steaks on bone china plates, and he straightened the crooked knot of his tie. He had never worn a tie before and he wouldn't have ever worn one today if it weren't going to improve the odds that a generous woman was going to hand him a check and solve his problems. *How could I have been stupid enough to tell her the truth?*

Denise's aunt finished her artichoke leaf, put it carefully onto her plate, and wiped her mouth and hands with her napkin. *Everything was so proper here,* he thought. *So foreign.* This was a different world from the one he moved in, a different city from the one he had come to know. He was out of his element, out of his league. *These are not my people,* he thought. *I have as much chance of winning over Denise's aunt as I do of bringing back Oded.* He cast a last glance at Mrs. Jenkins. Then reaching up and loosening his tie, he headed out of the restaurant.

TALL POLELIGHTS LIT THE SPRAWLING LOTS surrounding the Philadelphia Spectrum. A sea of cars filled the parking areas though tonight's basketball game would not start for half an hour. Nissim parked his green Chevy in the first vacant space, turned up the collar of his down Army jacket, and followed the stream of people up the concrete steps to the box office. After waiting in line several minutes, he bought a ticket in the cheapest section and walked inside the sports complex.

The Spectrum was a large round building capped with a massive domed roof. Nissim stopped inside the door and let his eye sweep over the milling crowds, the barking vendors, the long snaking lines at the food stands. He looked up at the towering canopy of painted steel that loomed so high above him. It felt like being outside inside, he thought. There was the same sense of freedom and space here. The sky was the only thing missing.

Nissim checked his ticket stub to find his row and section number, then he walked into the huge arena. At the entrance to Section G, one of the ushers pointed him to his seat in the gathering crowd. Tonight's game was expected to be a near sellout because of the 76ers' acquisition of a new star. George McGinnis, an all-star power forward from the rival American Basketball Association, had just signed a six-year contract with the Philadelphia team for a reported sum of more than three million dollars. Last season the 76ers had finished last in their division. This year they hoped to turn the standings upside down. Tonight they were playing the New York Knicks, a team studded with established stars – Walt Frazier, Bill Bradley, Earl "The Pearl" Monroe, and their own new multimillion dollar acquisition, Spencer Haywood.

Nissim watched the players finishing their pregame warmup drills. These were the same players he had heard so much about in Israel, the same athletes he had watched in taped segments on Israel Television's weekly sports magazine. These were the best athletes in the world, and he thought of the best team in Israel. It also had an imported star, a black center, not from another league like McGinnis and Haywood were, but from another country. He was American, and so were a growing number of other players, both black and white, on the best teams back home. The Americanization of Israeli basketball, or of Israeli sport for that matter, was already an old story, but Nissim still had strong feelings about it. Sure, basketball was born in America, and sure, Americans knew the sport better, coached the sport better, played the game better, but that didn't mean that Israel's teams should buy American players to help them compete in Europe. Sure, it lifted the level of play in the country, and sure, it hiked up the gate receipts, but there was more to representing a country than just putting on a uniform. One day an Israeli team would win the European Championship, he was certain. His only question was how many Israelis would be members of that team.

As he looked down at the brightly-lit court he saw vendors of popcorn, hot dogs, and ice cream walking up and down the steep steps in the aisles. They would run farther in the course of the game than the players themselves would, he thought to himself. Rows of seats ringed the sunken court in expanding, rising circles and every row was filled with fans. Colorful banners hung from the scoreboard and rafters, celebrating past championship seasons for Philadelphia's professional sports teams and announcing the upcoming celebration of America's bicentennial year. Almost everything seemed to be red, white, and blue here, from the glossy programs to the popcorn bags.

This was Nissim's first time inside the Spectrum, having cancelled out on the Elton John concert the month before, and he was glad he had decided to pick up and come tonight, even alone. He knew he needed the diversion, and he also knew he had earned it. After six hard weeks he had completed his Robotics Institute research paper last night and had handed it in to Professor Clarendon that morning. Now he wanted some time away for himself, some time to do nothing but sit back and watch, some time to be passive and be entertained.

GARBLING THE WORDS of a Hebrew song, his hands unsteady, Yosef steered the cab into the wide garage, turned off his headlights and motor, and tottered into the house through the side door. The house was dark, and he stumbled over a chair in the kitchen, barely keeping himself from falling by grabbing onto the island counter in the middle of the room. Everything was blurry, and Yosef thought that was funny.

Fed up with driving, he had gone to Hank Burton's party at Temple and had stayed there until he was drunk out of his mind. He had spent the night talking to several women, none of whose names he remembered. "You're okay, Hank. *You* came through," Yosef muttered out loud, thinking of that afternoon's lunch with Denise's aunt. "Stingy bitch! I'm – an – *IDIOT!*" he shouted. Then he lifted three limp fingers to his lips and said, "Shhh!"

Not turning on any light, he walked into the narrow hallway to hang up his jacket in the front closet, his head bobbing, his body lurching from side to side as he moved. "Nothing's simple," he mumbled to himself, still thinking about Denise's aunt and feeling his frozen smile fade. "Nothing. No one sticks a blank check in your hand. Not in mine, not in this lifetime."

The closet door creaked loudly when he opened it and the wire hanger fell noisily onto the floor when he lifted it off the rack. "Shhh!" he said in a loud whisper, fitting his jacket onto the hanger with difficulty. "Not enough hours to make enough dollars," he mumbled, "not this month, not any month." After several tries he succeeded in hanging up his coat, fitting the hook of the hanger over the rack. The door creaked even more loudly when he closed it. "Shhh! They're sleeping," he whispered again, imagining for the moment that his wife and child were home.

The louvered doors to the den were open and from the entrance hall where Yosef stood a muted light was visible. It spread like a dim haze from the den into the living room. Out of the corner of his eye Yosef saw it and began walking toward it, not knowing what it was but feeling as though it were drawing him to it. Yosef took two strides and fell forward, landing on one elbow on the living room rug. "Damn that step down," he muttered to himself, staggering to his feet. "They ought to put it outside." He kept moving forward unsteadily, walking a crooked line through the louvered doors to the den.

The bookshelf in front of him caught his attention. It was as though he had never seen it before, as though he were seeing it for the first time. Some of the titles on the book spines were visible in the glow of the aquarium bulb. Hardback volumes filled every one of the built-in shelves that covered the walls of the spacious den. In a daze, Yosef scanned the books on the shelf in front of him, staring at the English names more than reading them, then lifted his gaze to the next shelf and scanned it the same way. One tier at a time his eye moved up until it reached the top shelf where the books almost touched the ceiling. Looking up he felt dizzy. His mind grew fuzzy a moment and his vision blurred. These books in Professor Barsky's den made him think of the books that filled the bookcase in Barukh and Miryam's apartment. He imagined that all of the titles on these shelves were written in Hebrew, and he heard the volumes talking to him. A jumble of voices filled his head, all familiar but none recognizable. They were pouring sayings down on him, the proverbs he'd heard as a child.

Looking up at the highest shelf, with the voices and noises and words swirling in his head, Yosef felt himself losing his balance. A second later he was falling. By reflex he reached out to save himself, woozily groping for something to grab, for something that might soften his fall, but his hand could find nothing. He toppled sideways like a felled tree, his body crashing into the fish tank and sending water and fish and tubing flying off the metal stand. He and the aquarium thudded onto the white carpet.

THE GAME BEGAN. "Fray . . . zure," the P.A. announcer bellowed, his voice echoing and reverberating after Walt Frazier had driven to the basket for a graceful reverse layup. The lead changed hands with every change of possession, and Nissim found himself enjoying the game even more than he had expected. Too bad Yossi couldn't be here to see this, he told himself. He had waited until almost seven o'clock for Yosef to return home this evening. Often Yosef stopped home after his last afternoon class before heading out to work. Nissim had planned to convince his brother to take the night off and come with him to see the 76ers. Yosef would surely have come, if only he had come home.

Nissim could not watch basketball without thinking of his brother, without remembering the dozens of games he had watched while they were growing up in Haifa, games in which Yosef had been a star player, games which Nissim still pictured all too vividly. Being 6'4" in Israel was like being 7' tall in America, and Yosef had been among the tallest players. Yosef had been good, Nissim thought, but he had been physically, more than athletically, gifted and Nissim could see that his brother knew it. Yosef had always acted impulsively and unwisely under pressure. It seemed that he was forever coming up short in the closing seconds, taking some rash action that not only left his problem unsolved but made his predicament worse. Too often frustration had exploded inside him and he had resorted to physical force in misguided efforts to save himself, to save face. Nissim remembered the pain he had felt when Yosef had started fighting in the final seconds of too many games, always after he had missed the tying or winning basket. He pictured that desperate look in his brother's eyes, the look that came only when Yosef felt himself crushed in the fist of failure, and he saw his brother throwing an intentional elbow into an opponent's chest or lashing out with a forearm. It hurt Nissim deeply to see Yosef resort to violence, to brute strength to hide his weakness.

THE FLOURESCENT BULB HAD GONE OUT when the wire and plug had been ripped from the wall socket during the crash, so the room was now pitch black. "Shit!" Yosef whispered as he pulled himself to his feet and searched in the darkness for the table lamp near the stereo. Finding it, he turned it on. Fifty-five gallons of smelly water, dozens of tiny tropical fish, a silenced air pump, yards of clear tubing, five pounds of colored gravel, and four collapsed panes of shattered glass covered the carpet beside him. "You idiot." Quickly he bent down to clean it up, to put it back together, to save his investment. The little fish wriggled and thrashed desperately on the carpet; Yosef watched them helplessly, thinking of Dorit's goldfish and of the move from Spring Glen. "It wouldn't be a real move without a casualty," Rivka had said. Her words echoed now in his mind. With his hand he scooped a fistful of gravel and emptied it onto the base of the shattered aquarium. Shards of glass were scattered across the rug, their sharp forms reflecting the light from the table lamp. This was Dorit's aquarium, he told himself, reaching over and picking up two jagged pieces of glass. He could not help thinking of Spring Glen, of the broken window in Dorit's room there, of the lost security deposit. "Four hundred bucks!" he muttered to himself. "They robbed me of four hundred bucks, and that place was clean!" This was his daughter's present, he reminded himself, the one he'd brought home for her birthday, the one he'd spent so much money on. He clutched his wrist a moment with his hand, and when he pulled the hand away it was covered with blood. Large drops had spattered on the white carpet. This was Dorit's aquarium, he thought, and this was the Barsky's Karastan rug. The stain would never come out.

EARL MONROE SWISHED A JUMPER from deep in the corner for the Knicks, then the 76ers started back down court. Collins passed to Cunningham at the top of the key, and Cunningham squared to shoot. But instead of taking a shot, he lofted a soft high-arching pass a foot to one side of the basket, and McGinnis, timing his leap perfectly, caught the ball above the rim and slammed it down through the basket. Nissim sprang to his feet, cheering wildly. The roar of the crowd shook the hanging banners that waved like flags from the rafters. The 76ers had mounted a comeback, pulling even on McGinnis' score after trailing by twelve at the end of the third quarter. Less than five minutes remained in the game.

Bradley used a screen to break free for a jump shot and banked it off the glass to put New York back in the lead by two. Slowly, deliberately, Lloyd Free dribbled back upcourt and worked the ball into McGinnis who had set himself in the low post. Haywood stood behind him, keeping a hand on McGinnis' back and leaning against him to block his path to the basket. With a fake to one side, McGinnis turned and tried to go over Haywood for a slam dunk, but the two players collided. Haywood went flying out of bounds as McGinnis lost his balance in midair, missing his dunk, the ball caroming wildly off the back rim and sailing beyond the foul line. McGinnis landed awkwardly, coming down on the side of his ankle. In obvious pain, he fell to the floor. A hush of concern came over the crowd, as the team doctor and trainer came onto the court and assisted the center back to the bench.

Nissim's eye moved to the official scorer's table where a player was reporting in to replace the injured star. Wearing the 76ers' red, white, and blue uniform, the player turned around and trotted onto the court. He had a beard and wore a Jewish star. It was Yossi, star of Israel's National Junior Team at sixteen, Yossi, whom *Maariv* had called "a rising star."

Nissim watched in dazed surprise as Free inbounded the ball to Collins. Minutes had ticked off the clock. Only seconds remained and the score was tied. Haywood bodied up against Lvov who was trying to muscle himself into position near the basket.

241

Nissim could see Haywood's forearm pressing into the small of Yosef's back, trying to keep him outside. The game clock was counting down. There were less than ten seconds remaining, time for one last shot. Collins dribbled around the key and passed the ball inside to Lvov. Wheeling quickly, Lvov launched a shot over Haywood's outstretched fingers. The ball fell short, bouncing off the basket's front rim and floating back toward Yosef. The clock showed two seconds. In desperation, Lvov hurled himself toward the backboard, crashing into Haywood, who had established inside position for the rebound, and knocking him to the floor. Haywood got up and walked over to Lvov, pushing his face toward him and scowling. Lvov did not back down. Staring coldly into Haywood's eyes, he grabbed the straps of Haywood's jersey and readied to fight. *Yossi, don't foul him! The game is tied!* But instead of using his head, Lvov threw Haywood backward into the courtside seats. Only the shrill, sudden sound of the referee's whistle kept Haywood from retaliating. Both benches emptied. Players from both teams rushed toward the two centers. The referee restored order and called a foul on Lvov. The scoreboard clock was all zeros, as the referee walked the length of the court for Haywood to shoot two free throws. *Why, Yossi? It would have gone into overtime.* Oblivious to the jeering crowd, the New York star sank both shots. New York won by two.

A buzzer sounded and Nissim looked up at the scoreboard. Four and a half minutes still remained in the game. The 76ers' backup center was trotting from the scorer's table into his spot near the basket. He was seven feet tall. He had no beard.

"A WHITE RUG NO LESS," Yosef said in disgust. That made about as much sense to him as having white sneakers. They ought to make things the color they're going to become, he thought.

Carpets and sneakers should be brown or black. It would save everyone a lot of grief.

"I've got to get this mess out of here." Quickly, impulsively, he began ripping up the carpet, tearing it off the strips of tacks that ran around the room's border. Minutes later he had torn the whole piece loose. He rolled the carpet up, folding the glass and dead fish inside, and dragged it through the narrow hallway as if it were a corpse. Reaching the side exit to the garage, he pushed the door open and lugged the rolled rug out. The exertion of ripping up the rug and dragging it through the house had left him dripping. A red smear ran across his forehead as he wiped away the sweat. Blood from his wrist trickled down his hand. Breathless, he hauled the rug down the long driveway and left it at the curb.

"LAST NIGHT WAS THE FIRST FRIDAY in weeks that she didn't sleep here," Nissim said. "What's wrong? She have her period?"

"No," Yosef told him, buttering a toasted muffin, "she went to New York for the weekend, to visit her mother."

"Oh," Nissim said, hiding his disappointment. It had been more than a full month since she had told him about the chance of her being pregnant, and she had been with Yosef since, so if she didn't have her period yet, Nissim figured that the pregnancy was a virtual certainty. He had been telling himself that it could be a cyst, that women can miss periods for many reasons. A friend he had asked had told him that stress alone could stall menstruation. He would ask Denise what was going on as soon as she got back. "So when are you going to buy the new carpet?" he asked, lifting his mug and sipping his coffee.

"Maybe today," Yosef answered, checking the scab on his wrist. "I guess I'd better not put it off any longer." Yosef was still in his underwear as he sat across the kitchen table from Nissim.

"The Barskys' friends haven't been by to check on things yet this month. They could drop by any time, and I don't need any more trouble."

The "weekly top forty" countdown was playing on the radio that stood on the island in the middle of the bright kitchen. Its long antenna stuck up at an angle that threatened to poke out someone's eye. Dishes and coffee mugs, pieces of toast and butter knives, ashtrays filled with the previous night's cigarette ashes and pipe tobacco lay on the kitchen table. Nissim and Yosef were listening to Diana Ross and eating Saturday breakfast.

"I don't have anything pressing to do," Nissim said, glad to hear his brother say he was going to take care of the carpet. He still couldn't believe he had come home to that a week ago. Nissim was worried about his brother. He had watched Yosef sink into depression since Rivka and Dorit's departure. Last week, just before the accident, he had caught his brother mumbling to himself when he had come down to breakfast. And since the day after the accident Yosef had been acting strangely. He had grown more quiet, going through each day as though he were sedated. Nissim knew the pressures that were weighing against him, pushing him down. "I'll come along and give you a hand," he said. "We can lay it this afternoon."

"Thanks," Yosef said, not sounding very enthusiastic. Laying the rug was only a minor worry; the major one was paying for it. "Let's see how the day goes." Today was Saturday, he told himself, he'd been working and studying every day for the past month, and he didn't feel like spending all day battling traffic. In fact, he had other plans. Today he would solve his problems, he thought, most of them anyway, and he'd do it his own way. There was no reason to involve Barukh and Miryam as Rivka had suggested. He would take care of his problems in his own style, without humbling himself to Barukh, without upsetting Miryam. And he would go home in his own time, not empty-handed, not in debt, and not in disgrace. If things went according to his plan, the world would seem a different place by afternoon. "Hell, Nissim," he said warmly as he looked out the window to the back yard, "we both finally have a day to blow, it's a beautiful one, why should we waste it working? I don't know about you, but I could do with some real exercise for a change. Let off some steam, you know? The only work I feel like doing today is working up a sweat. What do you say we go play some basketball?"

Nissim looked at his brother quizzically, holding his coffee mug in front of him. The warmth in his brother's voice surprised him.

"We don't spend enough time together, you know?" Yosef went on. "We're both working ourselves into the ground, and we don't make enough time for each other, like when we were little. We don't do any messing around anymore. Let's get out of here. Come on, we'll go play basketball, get the kinks out. I've got a ball in the trunk of my cab, you won't even have to change your clothes, and the rug can wait till this afternoon."

Nissim, wearing gym shorts and a white mesh jersey, wondered where this sudden brotherly sentiment was coming from. But he had to admit he was glad to see it. Yosef and he had been living in the same house for the past five months, but saw as much of each other as tourists staying in the same hotel. "I don't mind playing, but basketball," he told his brother. "What's the point? You'll just kill me."

"I just want some exercise," Yosef said. "You pick the sport."

"Feel like swimming?" Nissim had not gone swimming once since the weather had turned cool in September, and he missed the release it gave him. "I've been waiting to try out the *Y,*" he said.

"Then let's go. We'll shoot some hoops in the gym and head right into the water." Yosef put down his mug, got up from the table, and started upstairs. "Be down in five minutes."

ALTHOUGH IT WAS JUST ABOVE FREEZING OUTSIDE, the temperature of the indoor air was in the eighties and the water temperature was not much cooler than that. The giant windows at the side of the olympic-size pool were steamed with condensation. In the shallow end, several old men were wading. The youngest among them looked to be in his seventies. They were talking to each other as they walked through the water, their voices echoing damply in the closed, high-ceilinged room. At one side of the deep end, two grown men had been roughhousing and shouting, racing in the water like rowdy young boys. Now they stood poised to dive at the edge of the pool.

" . . . Get set, go!" Yosef shouted as he and Nissim leaped headlong into the water, their arms churning and legs kicking powerfully as their bodies moved across the pool. Each of them stayed in a separate lane which was marked by a string of red-and-white plastic buoys. The thrust of their bodies sent rippling waves through the water as they raced across the pool's length. Yosef took the early lead, his long body and long strokes giving him a decided advantage over his smaller brother. Nissim needed to manage almost two strokes to match every one of Yosef's, and he knew it. But he also knew that Yosef was not in good enough condition to sustain a fast pace over the full fifty yards. At the midpoint of the race Nissim pulled even; by the three-quarter mark he was pulling away. His hand touched the wall in time for him to watch Yosef finish after him.

"Damn!" Yosef said, shaking the water from his hair and beard and seeing his brother's smile. "Thought I had you this time." He was panting. His voice was almost breathless.

The brothers climbed out of the pool and stood beside each other, both of them slightly bent over, their hands gripping their sides, their palms braced on their hips. This was the seventh full length they had swum. After only a few seconds, they looked at one another, nodded, and took their positions at the edge of the water, their toes curled around the curve of the pool's ledge.

"On your mark," Yosef said, then stopped himself. He stuck out an open palm and straightened up. "Give me a second," he said, wincing as he still breathed hard through his teeth. "I'm not going home till I win one." He took some deep, slow breaths. "But don't let up, you hear me, Nissim?"

"I hear you, Yossi," Nissim said, watching his brother compose himself.

A second later Yosef was ready. He barked out the signal to start and the two men stretched through the air to full extension, their bodies hitting the water at the same instant. Again Yosef led at the start, faltered in the middle, and faded in the end. Nissim's hand touched the tiled wall several full seconds ahead of his brother.

As soon as Yosef's hand touched the wall, Nissim lifted himself out of the pool and, catching his breath, stood on the deck waving his hands back and forth. "That's it, no more," he said, hunching over. "No more races. Not today." He was debating with himself about not having let his brother win this last race or any of the races before it. If Yosef had won, he told himself, they would both be going home happy. What difference did it make to *him* whether he won or lost? No difference, none at all. But to Yosef it made a big difference. He should have let him win one. It would have cost him nothing to make his brother feel good, to give him this small victory, to let him believe that he had outdone his little brother. But he also knew that letting Yosef win was worse than beating him. Yosef would have known he had not gone full speed. He would have interpreted his victory as an insult, a calculated condescension, a cheap sign of pity. Winning and losing would have brought the same result, Nissim figured. Both would have left his brother defeated. But it had never been any different.

Yosef raised himself out of the pool but did not stand up. Instead he spun around and sat on the blue-and-white tiled deck, his feet hanging down into the water. His breaths were so deep that they sounded like wheezes, and he waved his hands in a sign of surrender. "Okay," he said after a moment. "You win."

Nissim sat down beside him, his feet also dangling into the water, and gave his brother a long look. "You're in better shape than I thought," he said after Yosef had caught his breath. "Eight laps is more than I thought either of us could handle."

Yosef was still hunched over, looking down at the water, watching the lights reflecting on the surface. He lifted his eyes without lifting his head and turned to Nissim. "You hardly broke a sweat," he said.

"Sure," Nissim said sarcastically, shaking his head. "You just can't see it in the water." It would never change, he told himself. Yosef would always believe things were easier for him, that his little brother had it better than he did.

"When's the last time, Nissim," he asked, "when's the last time we did this?"

"Too long ago to remember," Nissim told him. Even in Haifa they hadn't made much time for each other. Nissim had been in the army and Yosef had gotten married and, before they knew it, had left for America. The last time they had done anything like this, Nissim figured, was about eight years ago at the outdoor HaPoel pool.

"Too long is right," Yosef said, looking across at the old men who now sat half-immersed in water on the steps at the shallow end. "We've wasted too much time, you know? Too much god-damn time." He looked at his brother and thought how little he knew about him. He wasn't a little brother anymore, he was a man. It was hard to remember that.

"How's the paper coming?"

"I finished it last week."

"That's great. Congratulations! I know how hard you worked

on it. Hey, that calls for a celebration. Let's go somewhere together. My treat."

"Thanks, I already celebrated. I went to the Sixers game. Remember?"

"Right." The night of my stupid accident, he thought. "Who won?"

"New York Knicks by two. Haywood won it on free throws in the final seconds."

"Good game, eh? The Spectrum's an amazing place, isn't it? There's no place like it back home."

"What about Yad Eliyahu?"

"Doesn't compare," Yosef answered. "And in America every city has a stadium like that. We have Yad Eliyahu in Tel Aviv and that's it. One arena for the whole country."

"You sound like you prefer it here," Nissim said.

"While I'm here I enjoy being here. Don't you? I take what America has to offer. Why not? I miss Israel, but I'm here for now. I'm doing the best I can—just like you—but it's hard having one foot in two countries."

Nissim turned and grinned at his brother. "The crotch pains are incredible, aren't they?"

Yosef laughed. He splashed the water with his feet, kicking gently in a slow rhythm. "Nissim," he continued, his voice becoming serious, "I like America, but I've made a real mess of my life here, you know? I lost sight of the bigger picture even before Dorit and Rivka left. I wasn't spending enough time with them, not with either of them. They didn't have me here. I see that now. Well, now all I want is to finish up what I've got to do here and get back to them. Back to the family, you know?" Yosef had been looking at the water, at the old men, at his swinging feet as he spoke. "I could cut everything loose here and not miss any of it. My thing with Denise came from nothing more than my being alone and her being alone. Family's all that matters in the end.

I always knew that."

Nissim wondered if the look on his face showed the pleased surprise he felt inside. He could not remember ever hearing Yosef talk this way before. Maybe he'd come around. Maybe the hardships and the failures had benefitted him in the end. Apparently Rivka's leaving had forced him to take a long look at himself. Maybe even Denise had been good for him. His affair with her had helped him handle Rivka's absence as he pieced his life back together. Maybe, Nissim thought, this was a new Yosef sitting beside him.

Yosef looked out over the pool again, swung his legs to ripple the water, and continued speaking. "Which is why I feel I can talk to you like I can't to anyone else. I've only got one brother. Right?"

It took Nissim a second to realize that Yosef expected an answer. "Right," he said.

"No one knows me like you do, Nissim. I need you to help me think something through." Yosef paused a moment, studied Nissim quickly, then turned back to the water and continued talking. "Let me lay it out for you. I owe a lot of money, a *lot* of money. I'm working as many hours as I can, you know that, but I'm hardly making up any ground. It's like I'm running in place. I owe BankAmericard twenty-five hundred dollars, Nissim, and I owe Yellow Cab's Body Shop another four. The new carpet's going to cost me another six, and all of that's got to be paid before I can think about paying another thousand to Temple to finish up my degree. All together I'm looking at what? Forty-five hundred dollars, closer to five thousand if you figure in the interest I'm going to have to pay before I'm done. Part of the money's already due. I'm running out of time, Nissim."

"How much do you need?"

Yosef hesitated before responding. He looked at Nissim, then looked down again, his large feet still swinging in the water. "I need a thousand dollars," he said softly, not wanting the words to echo through the pool area. He put his hands on his knees and, lowering his head, fell silent.

"A thousand dollars," Nissim repeated slowly, nodding his head as he spoke the sum. None of us ever really changes, he thought. We just sink deeper and deeper into who we really are. "A thousand dollars. And what will a thousand dollars solve, Yossi?"

"It will pay off the body shop and buy the new carpet."

The cab and the rug, he thought to himself. And what about what he already owes me? In Yosef's list of outstanding debts he had forgotten to mention the seven hundred dollars Nissim had loaned him to pay for the plane tickets for Varda and Orly and for Oded's corpse. The gift of the tickets had been a noble gesture, Nissim thought, but it had also been extravagant, overgenerous, unnecessary. It had been far more expensive than anyone but Yosef would ever have considered giving, let alone have expected to receive. Even splitting the cost of those tickets had been more than Nissim had intended to do. He had not wanted to deplete his emergency dollar reserve for a family he'd known for only a few months, especially when he had been here himself for so short a time. But Yosef had been persuasive as always, and Nissim had known that his brother would have gone ahead and bought the tickets without his help if he had to. So he had said yes, agreeing to pay half the fourteen hundred that the tickets had cost. Look where it had landed him—he had had to underwrite the full expense, paying both his half and Yosef's. Of course, his brother hadn't paid him back a cent yet. And now he wanted more. Every time they did anything together Nissim paid the damages. "And what about the credit card debt? How are you going to pay that, Yossi?"

"I'm taking care of that one on my own."

"How much do they want from you now? The minimum?"

"They want it all."

"Twenty-five hundred dollars?" Nissim thought of the many times he had heard Barukh tell both of them, "Don't let your eyes run away with your wallets. Be satisfied with what you've got." Even as children, they had been different — Nissim saving and Yosef spending. "And how do you plan to come up with that much money?" Nissim asked.

"I'll get it. Don't worry."

Nissim stared skeptically at his brother. Who does he think he's kidding? Even if I give him the thousand dollars, it's not going to solve his problem. Someone some time is going to have to cut the cord and make him pay the costs. Bailing him out will just let him keep right on living like he always has — first class at all costs, even when it breaks the bank, even when it breaks the family, even when it breaks the man. We're not kids anymore. Why should I foot the bill for *his* accident, *his* indiscretion, *his* poor judgment? He shouldn't have been on a drinking binge to begin with. He shouldn't have broken the aquarium. He shouldn't have tried to pick up jagged glass with his bare hands. All those dead fish and gravel and the water stains would have washed out of the carpet. There are rug cleaning services. He didn't have to go bleeding all over it and throw it out. Maybe it would have been fixable, cleanable if he hadn't ripped it up like he did and thrown it out. That was typical Yossi, he thought, impulsive and unthinking, making things worse by looking for quick solutions. "Yossi," he said, "I don't have enough dollars to bail you out. Look, I want to help but I don't want to do something that's just going to set us both back for nothing."

"For *nothing?* I'm talking about going under and you call that *nothing?*"

"I'm not sure a thousand bucks is going to make any difference. It might be the worst thing I could do for you."

"Oh, so now you're deciding what's good for me? Who do you

think you are? My banker? My father? Why don't you just not help me, or better yet, if you're so smart, why don't you tell me what *you'd* do." Yosef knew that Nissim would have no solution this time.

"I'd go home right now," he said. "I'd go back to Haifa tomorrow."

"Home, eh? Brilliant. You think I haven't thought of that. There are just a few small problems with that one – it's taking me too long to pay off BankAmericard when I'm earning dollars; it would take me a lifetime to pay them off in liras, especially with what I'd make back home, and they want the money yesterday. Any other bright ideas?"

"You're wrong, Yossi. You could pay them off before you leave," Nissim said, a smile spreading across his face. "You want to be home with the family, right? To be with Dorit and Rivka? Well, you could go home owing nothing."

"How? I can't drive any more hours than I'm doing."

"That's the problem," Nissim said. "You shouldn't be driving your cab. You should be selling it."

Yosef's face froze. He had never thought of selling his cab.

"You owe BankAmericard twenty-five hundred dollars, the body shop and the carpet together are another thousand, and your cab is worth about thirty-five hundred you told me. Well, you can sell your cab and get the thirty-five hundred, pay off the credit debt and the body shop and the carpet, ask Abba to send you a one-way ticket, hop on the plane and go home. You can transfer to Haifa University for your last semester, finish up your degree at the same time you were planning to finish it here, get a job, and pay back Abba the price of the ticket over the next year or two. That's what I'd do if I were you."

"Well, you're not me," Yosef said loudly, his words carrying over their heads and echoing across the pool. "I'm not asking Barukh for anything. I don't want him to know anything about this.

And I'm not going home without that degree."

"You asked me what I'd do. I told you."

Why did Nissim always have to interfere? Yosef asked himself. Every time he helps me, he judges me, he shames me. Just like he did with Rivka. Yosef had never forgiven Nissim for shaming him in front of her.

Rivka had met Barukh and Miryam at the very beginning of her courtship with Yosef, and she had liked them. She had told him that she could see how he had come from such lovely people. Embarrassed, he had not told her about his real parents or about his being adopted. When he and Rivka had decided to be married, they had needed to present their birth certificates to receive their marriage license. Yosef had stalled for several months, not wanting Rivka to see the names of his real parents on his birth certificate, not wanting her to discover his lie. Rivka had become distraught. Yosef was delaying because he didn't love her, she thought. He wanted to cancel their engagement but did not know how to tell her. The strain had grown unbearable between them until Rivka finally decided that she would call off the wedding herself. Yosef had not known what to do, and he had turned to Nissim for advice. That same night, Nissim, without asking Yosef's permission, had gone to see Rivka and had told her the true reason why his brother had been stalling. Nissim had told her about Yosef's adoption, about their being cousins before they were brothers. And Rivka had understood. She and Yosef had reconciled and the wedding had taken place shortly thereafter. But Yosef had never forgiven Nissim for telling the truth and exposing his lie.

"I asked you for a loan," Yosef said now, looking down at the water. "Are you going to help me or not?"

"Yossi," Nissim said slowly, "what if you can't pay BankAmericard back quick enough?"

"I will."

"But, Yossi, what if you can't?"

"I said I *will!*" Yosef shouted. He saw the old men turn their heads and look at him, then watched them turn away. He was glowering at his brother.

"What are you talking about?" Nissim asked.

"I'm talking about are you going to help me pay for the goddamn carpet."

Nissim kicked the water with his feet. Is this what I should use my army savings for?. To pay off the debts of accidents rather than finance dreams? Looking down, he gave his answer. "No, not this time, Yossi."

"You know what you can do with your goddamn money — keep it! Keep your fucking money and keep your fucking answers and keep your fucking judging! I'm drowning and you won't even help me!" Saying this, Yosef brought his arm around behind Nissim, grabbed him on the back of the neck, and pushed him into the water. "See how *you* like it." Then he jumped in after him.

The attack caught Nissim totally by surprise and he swallowed a mouthful of water when he fell into the pool. The gigantic wave from Yosef's large body breaking the surface rose up around Nissim's head and engulfed him. Yosef was on him before he could breathe, pushing him down before he could come up for air. Nissim tried to poke his head up, but his brother kept him submerged. Often when they were little they had roughhoused like this with each other, sometimes in anger, sometimes in jest. They had always had their dunking contests to see who could stay under longest, and as with the races across the pool, Nissim had always won. You're the swimmer, Yosef thought as he wrapped his legs around Nissim's thighs and clamped them into a scissors hold that he locked by crossing his ankles. You can take it, you always could. I'll let you up in a second, but not until you see how it feels to be going under. He could not tell the difference between Nissim's desperate struggling now and their childhood games under water.

Nissim was unable to speak or breathe. He was unable to tell his brother that he was drowning. His eyes were open as he tried in vain to wriggle free. With his hands he reached for Yosef's face, but could only grab the star of David on the gold chain around his brother's neck. He pulled it with all his strength, and the force of Yosef's resistance caused the chain to break. The gold star sank to the bottom of the pool and lay there under eight feet of water. Nissim reached up again and tried to grab a fistful of Yosef's beard, but Yosef jerked his head back and continued to hold Nissim down. Nissim's eyes began to bulge. There was little time left to fight his way free. This was the enemy, not his brother, he told himself. The only thought in his mind was survival. His cheeks were deflated and had begun to cave in. There was a terrible weight in his chest. His heart and lungs felt so inflated that he thought they would explode. He pictured his heart and lungs erupting. His head began throbbing; his mind became fuzzy. There was time for only one last thrust, one more lunge. Summoning his last bit of strength, he bent his body forward as far as he could in Yosef's leghold, reached down to where Yosef's ankles crossed, and closed his hand around the big toe of his brother's foot. Then he grabbed the smaller toes of that foot with his other hand, and began pulling his hands apart, trying to tear Yosef's big toe sideways until it broke or popped out of its socket. Nissim's eyes were white and bulging, like grotesquely painted ping-pong balls, as he tried to break his brother's will with every ounce of his being. Suddenly there was a brittle snap, and Yosef's ankles shot apart. Nissim wriggled his body free and rocketed to the surface. Gasping for air, he swam to the nearest side of the pool and, struggling, choking, almost retching, he hoisted himself up the ladder.

Yosef was still in the water, flailing one arm and clutching one foot with the other, his screams of pain echoing through the steamy room. Nissim watched as his brother lumbered to the edge of the pool and hoisted himself with great difficulty onto the tiled deck. Quickly the old men gathered around Yosef as he writhed in pain on the floor.

Nissim had not yet caught his breath. His chest was fitfully heaving, the rhythm of his breaths irregular. With every inhalation, his eyes stretched wide open. The large form writhing and moaning on the deck across the pool wasn't his brother, he told himself. It wasn't his cousin. It wasn't a new Yosef or the old one. It wasn't anyone he knew.

The old men huddled around the wounded man and began talking about a hospital. One of them would drive him there. Another would bring the man's clothes. Moans continued to echo through the steamy room as the old men tried to figure how to lift the man up, how to manage to carry such weight and bulk. Nissim watched a moment, turned away sharply, and disappeared into the locker room.

The Star of David was invisible under the eight feet of water.

Twelve

DEAR YOSSI,

Next week it will be two full months that we've been apart. I can't keep up this charade for your family anymore. I'm tired of spending my nights alone. I need you here.

I've been reading a lot since I've been back. I've been reading books mostly about spiritual things, trying to keep everything in perspective. "Life goes wrong when the control of space, when the acquisition of things of space, becomes our sole concern. Judaism is a religion of time. And the meaning of the Sabbath is to celebrate time, not space." A rabbi wrote that. In America we lost Shabbat. We lost time. I don't want to lose you.

Some things are unknowable before you step into them. It's time to cut our losses, Yossi. You know if you stay you'll just sink deeper. You never could budget anything—not money, not time, not love. You can work just as hard here as there to pay off the debt. Work is work and money is money, no matter where you are. Forget your degree, forget finishing it on time. You're not going to finish it on time as it is, even if you stay there. Come back and finish it here. So what if it takes you a little longer?

I know you're saying what about the money we

owe. The debt is in dollars, not liras. Well, we don't need BankAmericard or Bank Leumi or any other bank to give us any special consideration. All we have to do is tell Barukh the truth, just tell him what happened to us. I'm sure that if you said you'd come home right now, he would loan us the money to pay off the debt—even if he had to take out a loan himself to give it to us. You could pay *him* back over as many years as it took and you could handle it all from here. But I can't tell him anything, I can't ask him anything, until you say you're ready to come home.

Nissim can sublet the house from us for the rest of the year, and he can take a roommate if he needs to. Maybe his girlfriend would move in with him and split the rent.

I've racked my brain for months already and this is the only solution, Yossi. We have to ask Barukh. Dropping out of school to drive a cab fulltime isn't going to move either of us closer to what we want to do. Israel doesn't need another cabbie, Israel doesn't need another family without a father, and Israel doesn't need another *yorade*.

Yesterday a child in Dorit's class asked her if you were killed in the war. She said no, that you were driving home from America and that it took a lot longer to get here that way.

Please say you'll come home and I'll talk to Barukh. Write as soon as you get this.

Rivka

P.S. America is a disease. The cure is coming

home. Every time I write to you, every time I think
of you, I can't help thinking of Oded. If you'd been
here for the funeral you would have . . . .

The last three lines of the letter had been crossed out, but the
words were legible through the strike marks. *"Yorade!"* Yosef said
out loud to himself as he stared at the onionskin pages in his hand.
The word rankled him so deeply that he couldn't contain his anger.
A *yorade* was an Israeli who walked out on his country, on his
responsibilities. A *yorade* was a deserter. "Where the hell does
she come off calling me that?!" he shouted, angrily folding the
handwritten pages and stuffing them back into their envelope. He
looked through the windshield of his cab at the line of taxis in
front of him, but saw them only as a long red and yellow blur.

Already it was dark outside and Thirtieth Street Station bustled
with hundreds of travellers. The yellow cabs traced a snaking line
around the station, their engines running and their red brake lights
shining. People were moving in and out of the station doors so
steadily that none of the doors ever fully closed. But this was as
Yosef had expected, it being Thanksgiving eve. America's
Passover, thought Yosef, America's seder night.

"Come home *now?*" he said out loud. "Who's she kidding?"
It's always the same with her, always wanting me to be wherever
I can't be. Nothing's ever right with her. Everything's always too
much for her, but nothing is ever enough. I'm killing myself in
the land of opportunity just to make a living for us.

Yosef had been making small payments to BankAmericard
each week since Rivka's departure. He had not used his credit card
since she left, but these payments were not even covering the interest on what he already owed. Then yesterday a letter from
BankAmericard arrived, saying that his account was being
transferred to a collection agency. He knew what that meant. The
agency could take away his cab and he had worried all night about

waking up in the morning to find his Checker gone. Between the threat of losing his right to drive because of the accident claim from the high school kid and the threat of having his cab repossessed, he felt under attack from all sides. But he had always found his way out of tight spots before. This was his responsibility, not Barukh's, or anyone else's.

"Hey, Joe!" a voice bellowed through the closed window. "How's the foot?"

"Freezing, Jocko," said Yosef, glancing at the fiberglass cast which covered his left foot to mid calf, his jeans split at the seam to accommodate the cast.

"That's too bad," said Jocko. "When's it come off?"

"Not until Christmas."

"Christmas? Nice present! Hey Joe, this is going to be my last run. I have to get home for Thanksgiving dinner with the family. How about you?"

"I'm in no hurry," Yosef answered, still thinking about Rivka's letter. "I don't have any wife to rush home to."

Jocko looked away. "Yeah, I know," he said. "Come to my house. Have Thanksgiving dinner with us."

"Thanks, but no," Yosef told him.

"I'm sorry you won't be joining us."

"What's there to be sorry about? I never even heard of Thanksgiving before I got here. For me it's just another night."

"Yeah, well, whatever it is, have a good one, Joe."

Travellers kept pouring out of the station doors and the taxi line moved steadily forward. Yosef watched the stogie hanging from one side of Jocko's mouth as Jocko walked back to his cab, the round mound of his belly still visible under his heavy winter coat. There had been no classes at Temple University yesterday or today and Yosef had been driving for almost forty-eight hours without more than a few hours' break. Jocko was making this his last run. He would do the same.

4 NOVEMBER, NEW YORK—

PLO delegate Farouk Kaddoumi opened the UN General Assembly debate yesterday on the Palestinian question with a warning to the United States that his organization has the endorsement of "our friend, the Soviet Union." In a reference to last year's address by PLO chairman Yasir Arafat to the Assembly on November 13, 1974, ("I come with an olive branch and a gun") Mr. Kaddoumi said that the United States and Israel "were determined to let fall the olive branch that we held in our hands last year." "We are closer to war than to peace" in the Middle East, he suggested. The USSR, he asserted, "maintains a responsible and constructive stand in opposition to Israeli aggression" while the United States has "moved nuclear weapons into Israel." Calling for the UN machinery to consider Israel's expulsion from the United Nations, he denounced the Egyptian-Israeli Sinai agreement as conducive to war.

In rebuttal, Israeli delegate Chaim Herzog welcomed the Sinai agreement as the only approach that "gives any hope for an advance toward peace." Mr. Herzog also characterized the draft resolution equating Zionism with racism as "the first major international anti-Semitic attack on Jewry since the days of Hitler."

13 November, Jerusalem—

A bomb concealed in a porter's luggage cart left on the sidewalk exploded today on Jaffa Road, the center of Jerusalem's main shopping thoroughfare, leaving six persons dead and forty wounded. A second explosive device hidden in a tin can was detected in the Mahane Yehuda food market and defused by police.

Wafa, the Palestinian press service, called the Jerusalem explosion a "heroic and daring operation" which caused a large number of casualties "among the settlers."

Also today, Arab students staged demonstrations in towns on the West Bank to celebrate the first anniversary of the speech to the United Nations General Assembly by PLO leader Yasir Arafat. A near riot erupted in Nablus when high school students stoned passing patrols of Israeli military policemen.

13 November, Washington, D.C. —

Christopher Columbus was not the first person to set foot in the New World. Upon reaching America, he decided to send one of his crewmen ahead in hopes of conversing with the Indians who he thought might be members of the Ten Lost Tribes. The man he chose to send was Luis de Torres, a Jew and interpreter for his fleet. Obeying Columbus' instructions, de Torres greeted the natives in Hebrew, uttering "shalom aleikhem," the Hebrew phrase for "peace be with you."

13 November, Cairo —

Arab League Boycott Director Mohammed Ahmed Mahjoub declared today that the League will blacklist all foreign vessels that pass through the canal carrying goods for Israel. Blacklisted vessels will not be allowed to anchor in any Arab port and will not be serviced. The Greek freighter Olympus,

the first Israel-bound vessel to pass through the canal
since the signing of the Israeli-Egyptian Sinai ac-
cord and the first Israel-bound cargo ship to travel
the canal in fifteen years, has already been
blacklisted in Egypt, Mahjoub said.

Nissim finished reading the clippings from Barukh and slipped
them into the manila folder on the glass coffee table before him.
Every other news clipping that Barukh had sent during the five
months since Nissim's arrival in Philadelphia was there. Nissim
had kept them all.

"Nissim," Denise called, stirring the vegetables in pots on the
stove, "this is insane. I'm not waiting a minute longer. Where is
he?"

"Start if you are wanting to," he called back, not looking up
as he straightened the papers inside the folder. "I'll be upstairs."
He picked up the folder, stood up, and headed to his bedroom.
There was work he could do while they waited for his brother to
come home for Thanksgiving dinner. Anything would be better,
he thought, than sitting alone over dinner with Denise. Yossi and
she deserve each other, he thought. A maniac and a rapist. It had
been two weeks already since Yosef had come home heavily
medicated from the hospital, his foot in a temporary soft cast until
his horribly deformed toe returned to its normal size. Yosef had
come in on crutches, his face lined as much with embarrassment
as with pain, his eyes downcast. "I don't know what . . . I lost
control . . . It was an accident, a misunderstanding . . . I didn't
know . . . ." Nissim had listened but said nothing. Only pity and
some deep-seated sense of connectedness kept him standing there
to look at his large, hobbled brother. Then he had turned and
walked away. For the past two weeks they had stayed out of each
other's way, barely exchanging two words, both of them hoping,
if not believing, that time would work its healing.

Just as Nissim started up the stairs he heard the cab pull loudly into the driveway. A second later he heard the sounds of doors opening, the sounds of crutches tapping, and the sounds of a moccasined cast scraping across the kitchen floor.

"It's about time," Denise said with hands on hips as she watched Yosef hobble in from the garage. "You said you'd be home an hour ago. This turkey's dry as a log now."

"Sorry," Yosef said, swinging on his crutches as he continued toward the hallway.

"Sorry? Is that all you have to say? The banks are closed so I take my whole day off to fix you a special meal, to give you more of a family feeling and show you what Thanksgiving's like, and you walk in after everything's either overcooked or cold and say, 'Sorry!' And I'm supposed to say, 'Oh, don't worry about it?' You said seven; it's already after eight."

"Where did you think I was? Atlantic City?" Words he had said before, in this same house, in this same kitchen, but to another woman. "They ought to make clocks illegal," he said.

Denise, saying nothing, shot him an angry glare, let her hands drop from her hips, and checked the oven.

"Everything smells delicious and you look very beautiful," Yosef told her, answering her anger with a boyish smile. He watched a moment and waited until her look softened. "It's Thanksgiving, no? Be thankful I'm home. I'll take off my clothes and let's eat."

Denise smiled. His clothes? Then watching him carry himself into the hallway, she started carving the turkey and called to Nissim to come downstairs.

A few minutes later she and the brothers sat around a formally set table in the dining room. Maroon linen napkins were folded at each place, a candle was lit at the center of the table, the lights in the room had been dimmed.

"If neither of you is going to make a toast, then I am," Denise said, raising her wine glass and motioning to the two men to join her. "It's a tradition in my family, wherever they are." She paused a moment to collect her thoughts, then looked at Nissim and Yosef and spoke. "To new beginnings, for all of us," she said, clinking each brother's glass in turn.

"New beginnings," Yosef repeated, smiling at Denise.

Nissim said nothing. It was enough of an effort for him to sit at the table with these two people, let alone to hold his glass up as they clinked their glasses against it to celebrate a dubious toast. He had seen how Denise had looked at him and how she had looked at Yosef as she had said the words. Her meaning had not eluded him.

She served them turkey with gravy and stuffing, warm cornbread muffins, marshmallow and yam pie, and a large tossed salad. The two Israelis ate, complimented her on her cooking, and began talking about a recent speech by Idi Amin at the United Nations where he had called for "the extinction of Israel as a state."

"Amin's a black Hitler," said Nissim.

"And we trained him!" Yosef interjected. "When no other country in the world would talk to him, when no one else would deal with Uganda, we sent people there to work with him and to train his people as farmers and soldiers. We helped *him,* and look where it got us."

"Ruwanda's in Uganda," Denise said, sipping her wine. "That's where the nature preserve is with the mountain gorillas."

"Yes," Nissim told her, picturing her poster, "and they are doing better than we are."

"Things are pretty bad over there, in Israel I mean, aren't they?" said Denise.

"How do you mean?" Yosef asked.

"I mean with all the bombings and stuff. It seems every time I pick up the paper some more people are being blown up while they're shopping. What is it, three bombs in the last four months in Jerusalem?"

"Yes," Nissim said, thinking of Barukh's clippings and looking down. The bombs keep exploding, we give back the oil fields in the Sinai next week, the world is calling *us* racists. He thought of Avi. What did we fight for?

"It's part of life there," Yosef added. "You get used to it. It bothers you and maybe frightens you, but you get used to it after some years."

"I wouldn't," Denise said. "Never. I mean, if it were me I'd be on the first plane out. It's all so senseless, you know. Killing doesn't solve anything."

Nissim could feel the blood rushing around his ears as he listened to Denise talk. What did she know about it? he asked himself. What did she know about living in a country under siege? What did she know about war, about how it changed people, how it haunted soldiers? It irked him to hear her analyze everything, judge everything the way so many Americans did.

"It's tragic is what it is," she went on. "I mean, okay, people are always going to disagree over things, and countries are going to also, but that doesn't mean they have to destroy each other. Countries are no more than people in the first place, and they ought to sit down, put it all on the table, and reason it out. You know?"

Right, just like us, Nissim thought to himself. Sit down and reason out your being pregnant, make it go away by talking, reason away the baby. It wasn't that simple. Life didn't work that way.

"It would be nice if people were sitting and talking," Yosef said, choosing to keep the conversation superficial.

"I'm serious," Denise said. "I mean, if the only answer is bombs in the streets and wars then there's not much of a future for anyone over there. Not in Israel and not around it either. Face it—they set off a bomb in Jerusalem, you send planes to bomb the refugee camps, they set off another bomb. It never ends. I've been reading about it for ten years now and nothing's really changed. The same thing is still happening. Children are being killed on both sides and the ones who are living are losing their fathers. If you ask me both sides should sit down and talk before there's no one left to do the talking."

"Talking?" Nissim asked, unable to keep silent any longer, bitterness obvious on his face. "And when the first bomb is going up in Jerusalem, what? And after the second one, and the next?" Why did Americans believe that everyone in the world was rational, or even wanted to be? Whenever we've trusted reason, whenever we've signed papers, we've found a new bomb in a baby carriage. "What would America do?"

"Not go down to their level."

"Meaning what?" Yosef asked.

"There are other ways of fighting back. We'd go to the UN and get the other countries behind us for starters. Public opinion, world opinion, plays a big role. When the terrorists see they're not getting anywhere and that they're only ruining their reputation in the eyes of the world, they'll stop."

"The UN?" Yosef said loudly. "The UN is a joke. The UN hates the United States as much as it hates us. It only has words, and they mean nothing. Where we come from people only understand power." He looked at Denise and thought about America. "Let's say Cuba is putting terrorists in Mexico across the border from Texas and they are shooting Katyusha rockets into the Texas towns and cities, and the rockets are killing the school children and the mothers. What would America do? Wouldn't President Ford send your air force into Mexico to send the murderers a message? If he knew their headquarters and where they were camping, wouldn't he teach them a lesson from America?"

"No one said anyone should get off scot-free for killing people. I'm just saying that there's got to be a better way. You set a higher example."

Nissim looked across the table at his brother, and the two of them exchanged knowing glances.

"It sounds nice," Yosef told her, "but if you are not fighting back you are dying. It is not a better example to be lying under the ground, you know?"

"What's the answer then?" Denise asked. "You tell me."

"I wish I knew this answer," Yosef said gently.

Nissim sat silent. The only answer is staying strong, and never giving up, he thought.

"Well, if it's that hopeless," she went on, feeling frustrated, "then it's no wonder people are leaving to come here, or go anywhere else for that matter. I would, just like both of you did."

Yosef and Nissim straightened abruptly in their seats.

Nissim thought about saying something but remained silent. Before the last war he would have told her she was wrong. Before the last war he would have told her that everyone made a difference, a critical difference. But everything had changed.

"We came here for studying," Yosef said. "That's all." But as he said it, lines from Rivka's letter raced through his mind. 'Israel doesn't need another *yorade.*' The Hebrew word spun in his head like a sputtering star sending white-hot sparks of light flying against the inside wall of his eyes. Every spark that hit the wall scorched it. Yosef winced in pain. To calm himself he focused on the word *yorade. Yorade, yordim,* he thought. They were just temporary titles, not like 'doctor' or 'father' or 'Israeli' for that matter, not like titles that defined you forever once you had them. *Yorade* and *yordim* were titles that you lost as soon as you moved back home. "But anyway what is so bad about it?" he asked Denise. "Always Americans are leaving and no one is saying this is a crime. We are going back. Just because someone is born someplace doesn't mean he has to stay there."

Denise thought of her baby as she listened to Yosef and her hands instinctively touched her stomach. "True," she said, "but almost everyone who's born here stays here. They travel but they don't leave, if you know what I mean. People don't run away from America."

"This isn't so true," Yosef responded. "For maybe thirty years at the beginning of this century many people were coming into America and many were also leaving. This we know from history. It happens the same to every country when they ask for immigrants. And America was even worse than Israel. More than thirty percent of the immigrants were running back from America to the countries they came from. In Israel the number is not so big, only ten percent maybe. It is not such a surprise."

He thought of his own situation. He had not run away from anything. He had tried to go back for the war, just as he was trying to go back now. "We don't know for sure if people were running away from here and we don't know for sure if people are running away from Israel," he continued. "All of them are not staying away because they want to."

Nissim was eating his turkey, looking down at his plate as he cut another piece. He lifted his eyes and looked at his brother. It was painful to see him, painful to listen to him. Even if I wanted to help him I'd only end up hurting him, Nissim thought. Every time I've tried to help him it's ended up with him wounded. He looked at the wooden crutches propped against the wall behind his brother's chair, then looked down at his plate again and cut another piece of turkey.

"Maybe," Denise said softly, studying the two brothers a moment and feeling the tension around the table. "Maybe you're right. Citizenship's an accident of birth."

Nissim's head lifted sharply as he heard the phrase. His eyes locked with Denise's until she looked away. Accident of birth. That's what life was, from start to finish. He stared at the candle burning at the table's center, then looked above it to see Yosef sipping wine. Brother, cousin. Accidents of birth. Denise: pregnant, unwed. He pushed his chair away from the table and excused himself for the rest of the night.

"Where are you going?" Denise asked. "It's Thanksgiving. Nothing's open."

"Everything's closed," Yosef told him in Hebrew. "It's a holiday. Even the malls are locked up. Where are you going?"

Nissim didn't care if he spent all night just cruising the streets in his Chevy. All he wanted was to get away from this table, from this holiday, from this mockery of a family. He wasn't going to waste all night listening to some American discuss the future of his country, to watch his brother sink in self-pity. Before he spoke he was at the hall closet putting on his army jacket. "Out," he said.

THE CLOSED DOOR plunged the room into darkness. She was somewhere near him, moving across the carpet toward him, stopping at the foot of the bed. Yosef lay on the soft sheets, naked except for the cast on his leg, straining to see her more clearly in the crack of light that squeezed under the door from the hallway. Something rustled over Denise's shoulders, over her knees, and fell onto the carpet like a whisper. His senses lifted to hear the sound of one foot and then the other stepping out of a soft heap of silk. She came to him and stood beside him, leaning over him so that her hair fell forward and washed like a warm wave across his body.

He reached up and gripped her gently by her shoulders. Just her touch excited him. He felt her breasts pressing warm against him as his large, strong hands massaged her neck, her shoulders, the delicate sway in the small of her back. His fingers moved in soothing rhythms, exploring her body in widening circles, building into more sweeping motions as his hips and thighs rolled beneath her.

"Yossi, I really like you . . . You know that."

"I am getting that idea," he said, hugging her to him and

271

smiling in the darkness.

"I'm sorry my aunt couldn't help you," she said, arching her back a moment and slipping one hand between their stomachs as she felt him swelling.

"That makes two of us," he said, his mind flowing back and forth from the feel of her hand to the memory of that lunch, that disappointment, that night's accident. His hands moved up and down her back, passing over each other as they traced the smooth curves of her body.

With two fingers she made a ring and, taking him in her hand, moved it gently up and down him. But instead of feeling his passion rising she felt less desire in him. His thighs were not stiffening. His hips were barely rolling. "What's wrong, Yossi? What happened?" she whispered. ·

"Nothing," he told her. "Nothing." He continued stroking her back, consciously keeping the rhythms going in his hands and in his body, but his mind was somewhere else. It was on her aunt and the aquarium and his money problems.

Maybe she felt different to him, she thought. Maybe he could tell. Denise continued trying to arouse him, but after another minute to no new effect, she stopped. "You can tell, can't you?" she asked. "I thought so. I wanted to tell you before but you came home so late and . . . ."

Yosef's hands went still as he listened. Tell me what? he wondered, but decided to remain silent.

"I was going to tell you tonight, after this," she went on. "The doctor confirmed it yesterday. I wondered if you'd be able to tell, if I'd feel different, and you could. It doesn't have to change anything, Yossi. I still want you, Yossi. I still want you . . . now." Her fingers started gliding, stroking, exploring him again.

Doctor? Confirmed? He was certain he hadn't heard her clearly. Such soft hands, such knowing hands.

Her hips started rolling on top of him as her nipples and full breasts moved in paired circles across the dark curled hair on his chest. She threw her head back then swung it forward so that her long hair washed over his face and shoulders, but his hands remained unmoving. "Yossi," she said, "don't stop, please. I'm still me. I want you."

"Still you? You're pregnant! How? We haven't been together long enough for it to be mine."

"What are you saying?" she asked softly.

He lifted her off of him and rolled her onto the empty space beside him on the bed. Pulling away, he sat up and turned his back to her as he swung his legs over the side of the bed. "I'm saying I've been a goddamn fool and whatever we had is over. I've got my own child and my own wife, and I don't need to sleep with the mother of my brother's bastard!"

"What?" Denise asked, unable to understand him. "What?"

"I can't say it any clearer," he said sharply. Suddenly he realized he had been speaking in Hebrew.

"Yossi, look at me. What are you saying? I don't understand you. Where are you going? Come back, let's talk," she said, pulling the covers over her as she watched him take the crutches from the wall.

"Talk," he said in English, turning back to her in the darkness. "Talking won't change anything, talking never solves anything."

"Yossi?" Denise called, not moving from the bed. "Come back, please . . . Where are you going?"

"I need some time to think."

"About us?"

"Yes, us." He stopped in the darkness and turned around to face her.

"Yossi," she said softly, her raspy voice especially seductive, consciously vulnerable, "that number you asked for? I brought it home for you, Yossi."

Yosef had never thought she would do it. "You're giving it

to me?" he asked, swinging himself toward the bed on his crutches.

"I already did," Denise told him. "It's on top of your dresser, on an envelope."

"Thank you," he said, feeling himself overwhelmed, almost speechless with gratitude, with hopefulness. He knew the risk she had taken for him, the trouble she would find herself in if Penn Savings ever found out. She could lose her job for something like this. Leaning his crutches against the wall, he came back to the bed, lay down beside her, and pulled her to him. "Denise," he said, "you always surprise me." And taking her with renewed desire, they made long and passionate love.

Afterwards, Denise kissed him gently on his chest and went into the bathroom. He rose quickly out of bed, pulled himself up on his crutches, and made a straight line to his dresser. Two envelopes were on top of the bureau. One contained his last BankAmericard statement; the other had a number written across its front. Quickly he opened the top drawer and fished out a pair of underpants. Then taking the envelopes in one hand and the underpants in the other, he wrapped them around the handles of his crutches and moved his naked frame to the doorway. Light flooded into the bedroom as he pulled the door open and started down the hall.

Inside his brother's room he went quickly to Nissim's desk. His brother's ALTAIR computer sat on the long countertop in front of him. He looked at the metal box, the complex control panel with all the switches, and remembered the night he had come upstairs to give his brother the Elton John tickets. If Nissim could lose everything he had worked on, if his work could be made to disappear as though it had never existed, then why couldn't someone's financial records, his credit card charges for example, disappear too? There were only a handful of these computers around and almost none of them had modems, he knew. How hard could it be to get inside the BankAmericard system? They would never expect it, and they would never even realize it, if he could do it right.

Still naked, he sat down at the desk and put the BankAmericard bill and the second envelope from Denise in front of him. He turned on the computer, watched the power lights on the control panel brighten, and lifted the receiver of the telephone at his elbow. His bill was computer-prepared, the figures all computerized, and every code was clearly marked on the statement. His customer account number, credit and debit codes, dates of transactions, bank branch numbers. If Nissim's computer could talk to the mainframe at the University of Pennsylvania, it could talk to the mainframe at BankAmericard's central office, he reasoned. With one proper entry he could wipe out his debt and put himself back on his feet, back on schedule, back to Dorit. With one false transaction he could reclaim control of his life, of himself. All he needed was the phone access number and Denise had given him that tonight. It was his only chance, his last avenue of escape. He refused to go home in debt, in disgrace. He would not go back until he had paid back every cent he owed and had finished his degree. If this failed he might never go home. He hooked the telephone receiver into the rubber shoe modem next to Nissim's computer and, thinking about his family, began dialing BankAmericard's number.

BOOK THREE
Open Window

*"For death is come up into
our windows."*

JEREMIAH 9:20

Thirteen

Dear Rivka

I found a way to pay off the debt. Don't ask me how but I did, and now there's nothing standing in the way of our being together again. I've had some time to think, to really think for the first time since we came here, and here's what I've decided. The way things were, I was planning to miss next semester and finish up my B.A. some time next year. It was beginning to look like I'd be lucky to be able to scrape up the tuition for the *last* semester of next year, let alone the first, so I would have been here another eighteen months from now any way you figure it. Well, now that money's not a problem, I've registered at Temple for next term so I can graduate on time like we originally planned, and I've applied there for the one year Master's degree program in history for next year. If I get in, which I figure I will with my 3.0 average, then I'll finish next year with not just a B.A. but with an M.A. in my pocket, too. I don't have to tell you what that'll be worth in Haifa. A Master's here will be worth a Ph.D. there. I figure this is my one chance at it. Once I come home there'll be other pressures and I'll never have the time again to go back to school like this for my Master's. Staying the one extra year will save us four years of my working full-time

279

and studying part-time in Haifa.

I don't want us to be apart any more. We're a family and we need each other. It's that simple. Please come back just for another year. It would be no problem for me to find the money to send you and Dorit tickets to come here right away. I know you were unhappy here, but it will only be for a short time and we will be together. Dorit can go into a regular first grade class here in the public school so it will not cost us any money—not like the fortune we were paying for her special nursery program—and her English is already good enough to handle it. First grade is an important year for learning a language, for learning to read, and the English she would learn would be a real asset for her when she grows up. And I don't want *you* to be sitting around this time, either. I've been looking into courses you could take at Temple or through the Montgomery County Adult Education programs, and there seem to be more than a few that might interest you. I'll send you the catalogue and the forms in the next day or two.

It will be hard for you, and for me, in some ways, but anything would be easier than what we're doing to each other right now. If we help each other through the next eighteen months, I know we'll really have something. We will have done it together, and most of all we'll have each other. I don't want to lose that. Now there's not any need to.

Kiss Dorit for me and tell her how much I love her. And think over what I'm suggesting. I need your answer soon. The catalogue should be coming tomorrow. Rivka, come back to me.

Yossi

What kind of story is he feeding me? Rivka asked herself as she sat in the shade on a bench in Gan HaEm, the municipal park near the Haifa Zoo. What did he do? Rob a bank? Was the Barskys' house sitting on an oil field or something? He's too proud to face asking Barukh so he's making up stories again, and every one he makes up leads to another that's even bigger. B.A., M.A., me go back there.

She was worried about him. There was a euphoric tone to the letter, a tone that almost made it seem he believed what he was saying. Maybe he had lost touch with reality. Maybe the pressure had been too much for him and his mind had snapped in his desperation. Someone who knew Yosef less well might read this letter literally, but the real meaning was clear to her. She knew the extent of their debts. There was no way he could have paid them all off. He might do anything if he was cornered, if he became convinced there was no good way out. How would she feel alone in America? she asked herself. How would she feel if he and Dorit had left *her* there? It was her fault he was there now, she told herself. It was her fault he had gone there to begin with.

A cool December wind blew across the park, blowing some strands of dark hair across her face. She listened to the laughter of the children playing on the small playground just beside where she was sitting, and she thought of Dorit, in *gan* with her own age group since September, thriving but missing her father terribly.

"Kiss Dorit for me . . . ." Dorit was spending the day with her Savta Miryam and Sabba Barukh. Rivka didn't have to go back to HaTishbi Street to pick her up for several hours. She folded the letter and stuck it into her coat pocket. Yosef needs me, she thought, but I can't go back there now with Dorit. My parents can't afford to pay our way, and I can't ask the Lvovs. Anyway Dorit is finally settled here. Her *gan* is on the same street as our apartment. She's with children her own age, children who talk her own language. Groups of friends come into our home without needing to make an appointment to play and without having to make their mothers drive them every place they want to go. I couldn't uproot her again, not now.

But he needs me, I can hear it, he's in trouble. And I need him, she admitted. I need him. I didn't get married to live alone, certainly not to live half-a-world away from my husband, and I didn't marry to get divorced. If we were together we could work things out. I'm not sure anymore that it matters where, so long as we're together. But then she remembered the Yossi she had seen there, the Yossi in America, the Yossi in this letter. I have to convince him to come home *now,* she thought as she started up the steep curved path to the street. What would it cost for her to fly back to see him? she wondered. A travel agency's offices were just a block away on HaNassi Boulevard in the central shopping district. I should go there, she thought, make sure he's all right, bring him back. He sounded imbalanced, almost psychotic, maybe suicidal. Money's not worth our marriage. It's not worth his life. It's not worth anything.

THE WIND WHIPPED across the gravel parking lot, empty except for two cars. Sounds of passing traffic from the Haifa-Tel Aviv highway mixed with the wet thrashing sounds of the surf on Carmel Beach. Clusters of clothes and shoes dotted the sand like lost laundry, and in the water, beyond the rough winter waves three bobbing heads were visible. Miryam, dressed in a sweater and pants, sat on a towel and looked out at the Mediterranean, watching Barukh swimming there like the young man he used to be. It had taken her several months to convince him to take a day off but she had finally succeeded, and today was that day. He had been resistant to the idea for several reasons, she knew, but there was one that overshadowed the others. It was the legacy of Nazi Europe, of Hitler's camps, and having been there she understood. In Treblinka or any of the other so-called labor camps, when you stopped working you died. If you couldn't work you were killed. After what he had seen in his youth, even the prospect of a single vacation day, of an open window to rest and relaxation, no matter how brief or how fleeting, caused him more anxiety than rest. Yet this was Israel, not Poland or Germany, she had reminded him continually. There was no commandant here, no cadre of Gestapo guards. He was his own taskmaster, his own boss. He could control his own schedule, his own life. Only he could say "stop," she had told him, and finally he had yielded, saying that even if *he* didn't need any rest, at least *she* did.

They had started the morning with a late breakfast, then had taken the long walk up HaTishbi Street to Merkaz HaCarmel. It had been therapeutic just to spend a few pressureless hours together, a few hours without the constant interruptions. From there they had continued leisurely along the length of Panorama Road, looking down over the port and the bay as they walked, looking all the way out over the northern coastline up to Rosh HaNikra. Then they had walked home, enjoying the ease of the downward slope on the return trip. Miryam had fixed a picnic lunch, packed it into the basket which now sat at her elbow on the sand, and they had hopped into their Fiat to drive down the mountain to Carmel Beach. Barukh had said that if the water were warmer than the air, he would jump right in. After testing it with one sockless foot, he had stripped to his bathing trunks and had done just that.

Miryam felt the cool wind in her face as she looked out at the water. The sea with its soothing rhythms and white-capped waves, with its changing moods and constant tides always had the same effect on her. She could not look at it without becoming pensive about life, without being overcome by a sense of timelessness, of history, of mortality. She could not look out toward the endless horizon without reflecting on herself. Turning her attention back to the shore, she let her eyes run over the long expanses of empty beach that extended to either side of her for as far as she could see. The sand was smattered with rocks and the relics of the long summer months when this beach was crowded every day to overflowing – food wrappers, fruit pits and peels, soda cans and bottles, countless popsicle sticks. A group of sparrows were probing around a buried peach pit whose tip poked through the sand. They hopped around it, their little feet moving quickly over the soft grains, their little beaks intermittently pecking at it, sending tiny splashes of sand into the gusting wind. As Miryam watched them try to unearth the pit, working silently to loosen it peck by peck from the sand, she wondered what they would do with it when they had dug it out. Would they try to carry it off, fly away with it, drag it for miles across the sand? Collectively they pecked away at it, none of them ready to admit the task was too big an undertaking. Just like Barukh, thought Miryam, like Barukh and both of the boys.

What were Yossi and Nissim doing right now? she wondered as she made sure Barukh's head was still visible beyond the waves. The horizon was stark this afternoon, a rulered edge between sky and water as in a child's picture, exactly the way Dorit would draw it. Each summer this beach had been the boys' playground, and in winter it had been their retreat, a gateless place, their separate sanctuary. Often on days like today, she remembered, they had come here to swim or just to watch the surf. Yossi and Nissim could just as easily be the two strangers beyond the breakers with Barukh now, she thought.

After a moment one of the swimmers rode a wave in toward the beach and, coming quickly out of the water, hugged himself against the cold air and raced to his towel. He was young, clean-shaven, and reminded Miryam of Nissim before the last war. Watching him on the deserted beach, Miryam thought more about Nissim and Yosef. She loved both boys and had done her best to make them each secure in her love, but she had not been wholly successful, she told herself. For she had gotten in her own way. By wanting to be too fair, by wanting too much to convince them that she loved them equally, she had done them both an injustice. She had cheated them both with her evenhandedness. From the moment of her brother-in-law's death, Nissim had been cheated out of his birthright, denied his special status as her and Barukh's firstborn, their only child. How strange, she thought, that her firstborn son should be her younger child. He had survived the confusion, but still she felt guilty for giving him less than she had wanted to, less than he deserved. Yosef's adoption had forced her to hold herself back with Nissim. It had forced her to love him consciously instead of naturally. It had been like loving and raising her child with a hand tied behind her back. And Yosef had been cheated also. In trying to give him security, to give him a message of loving support, she had given him instead a message that had hurt him, one that had left him questioning her love. "You have so much natural ability, so much to contribute," she had told him throughout his childhood. Almost against her will she had always compared the two boys, and the comparison always favored Nissim. "Yossi, I don't want to hear any more of that from you. You're a part of this family, just as much a part of this family as Nissim," she remembered saying too often. "We love you just as much as we love him." As much perhaps, she thought now as she looked out beyond the waves, but not the same, not in the same way. It was unfair but it was a fact that Nissim had always been the barometer of her love for Yosef and that Yosef had come to define himself only in comparison to Nissim, that he had come to view Nissim's achievements as devaluing his own worth. Her relationship with Yosef was different. It had required work and constant nurturing. In her desire to make things right between Yosef and her, in her desire to compensate for his losing his parents, she had gone out of her way to be there for him in ways that she wasn't for Nissim. Maybe she had gone too far. Maybe she had over-compensated, had interfered, had made Yosef feel more distant rather than more included. Maybe her concern for him, her over-concern, had made him remember that he was Barukh's and her son on paper only, by an act of law, and not an act of God, that he was their nephew, not their child. She hadn't prepared him well enough for life, for marriage, for raising a family of his own. She had done her best, but apparently that hadn't been good enough. Both boys had run away from her at their first opportunity. Both of them had run as far as they could, punishing her in their own ways for the deficiencies of their childhoods. That much she could understand and deal with, but to see little Dorit suffering for what *she* hadn't given Yosef—that was more than she could stand to watch. Fathers were meant to be with their children as long as they were alive.

Barukh was swimming back toward the shore, churning his arms through the first tier of waves. Miryam smiled to watch him moving so freely in the winter sea. It made her happy to see him enjoying the day, and she was enjoying it through him. He had been working too hard for too long. It was critical to let up once in a while, to let your mind unwind and your body recharge. Only Barukh would have felt guilty for having hung the "CLOSED" sign on the door of the store today. If she hadn't nagged him for the past few months he would never have closed the store on a weekday.

Barukh emerged from the white-capped sea, walking slowly through knee-high waves. Miryam watched lovingly as her husband came out of the water. How strangely he was walking, she thought, or was it her imagination, magnified by distance? It seemed to her that he was moving with a slight limp. Perhaps it was his bad leg, the one he had wounded at Bet HaNajadda almost thirty years before. It had probably stiffened up on him when the cold wind hit it after being immersed in the warmer water. She was concerned that he might catch a virus swimming on a day like this, and so she lifted the extra towels out of the bag beside her and readied them to bundle around her husband. Barukh walked out of the water, across the wet sand. She watched him nearing and noticed something different about him. He was smiling at her as he approached, still moving with that tilt to his walk, with that mild limp, but the smile somehow was not his smile. The angle of it was different. It seemed slanted a little more than usual. It seemed less conscious. But she was always worrying and imagining things, not just about Barukh but about everyone in the family.

"So how was it?" Miryam asked as he came within earshot. "Wake you up?"

Barukh nodded as he walked toward her, his smile unchanging.

One at a time she unfolded and handed him his towels, which he took from her, slowly wrapping them around himself.

"Isn't this a dream, Barukh? Dry off and sit down. Hungry?" Miryam spread another large towel on the sand, opened the picnic basket and began lifting out plastic containers, paper plates, and plastic bags. Humous, tehina, sliced tomato, cucumber salad, pita bread, and two cans of soda. With the silverware which she had brought from home she prepared a plate of lunch for Barukh and handed it to him as he sat down next to her.

"Thanks, Zeisa. It looks good," he said.

"What? I couldn't hear you."

"Thank you," he said again.

"Oh," she said, straining over the noise of the waves to understand him. "Enjoy. I'm just glad to be here. When's the last time we had a picnic down here? It's been so long I can't even remember."

Barukh began eating as Miryam fixed a plate for herself. He picked up his knife to spread some humous and tehina onto his bread, but the knife fell out of his hand and landed with the sticky side of the blade in the sand. Ignoring the grains of sand stuck there, Barukh picked up the knife and continued smoothing the spread onto his pita. Having finished preparing her own platter, Miryam turned to talk to her husband who was sitting beside her, fumbling with the knife, white tehina sauce running down onto his hand and in between his fingers, a smile on his lips and a look she had never seen before in his eyes. He looked to be on the verge of tears, but he was smiling. This was not Barukh, she told herself. He was not even trying to wipe the sticky rivulets of sauce from between his fingers. The knife looked like it might at any second slip out of his hand. This was not the same man who could fix anything, who could maneuver a screwdriver or any other tool at angles which would cause any other man to lose his grip. This was not the same man who only yesterday had run around tirelessly with his granddaughter, only stopping when Dorit couldn't keep up with him. "Barukh? What's wrong?" she asked him softly, trying to control the frenzy she felt suddenly building inside her.

His only answer was that slanted smile and those frightened eyes.

"Barukh, answer me, please. What's wrong?" Her face was beginning to quiver as tears began to well in the corners of her eyes. She reached out and took his face in her hands, but he did not lift his arms to touch her. "Barukh, should I call a doctor?" She looked at him, wanting to pull him to her, to rest his head on her breast. It looked to her as though he wanted to speak to her but couldn't, as though his skin were a plastic mask behind which his true lips were taped shut, leaving his eyes with a terrified, vacant gaze.

Miryam, he wanted to say, I hear you. I'm okay, I'm just tired, please don't worry. A film was playing in his mind and he was watching it. I hear you, Zeisa. But it was playing in reverse. The reels were being rewound and he was watching the images race backward across his eyes, forcing him to strain to capture every image, every detail. The background sounds and the voices were garbled. It was his life he was watching and he watched it as he would a dream, entranced but powerless to direct it, powerless to change anything, curious beyond memory as he watched himself grow younger frame by frame. The film was filled with small moments that had shaped his life. His father at the Lodz shul, teaching him and his brother Avram how to lay tefillin. His father in the lineup at Treblinka, telling him goodbye without words, telling him to run when the guard gave him the chance. His British cousins answering the door of their Manchester home, their shocked, wide-eyed, silent faces, their arms grabbing him inside with wordless embraces. His wedding day with Miryam, standing under the wedding canopy, no member of their families alive to attend except for his brother, Avram. His visiting Miryam in Rothschild Hospital on the morning after their son's birth when they had decided to name him "Nissim," the Hebrew word for "miracles." Avram's funeral on a rainy day at the foot of Mount Carmel, his body rolled out of the white shroud and plummeting with a chilling thud into the muddy grave. Yosef's adoption, the wedding to Rivka, the birth of Dorit, Avram's grandchild whom Barukh loved as his own. The film continued rewinding itself, gaining speed so that Barukh kept falling behind, missing months, missing years, then suddenly it stopped. Everything went dark. Too suddenly silent. It was as if the film had snapped in half. It had torn and left his mind suspended, his memory hanging, his life incomplete. What had been the last image he had seen? He couldn't remember. Was that Miryam speaking? She sounded as though she were calling through deep water. He wanted to answer her, at least to blink his eyes for her, but his lips would not cooperate, his eyelids would not obey him. I'm all right, Zeisa, he wanted to say. It's just a dream, a dream. How far away was she? he wondered. Shouting couldn't be so soft, could it? He struggled to restart the torn film, to unstill the reels, but his mind stayed silent, its motor refusing to whir.

"Barukh! Barukh!" Miryam shouted. "It will be all right. I'll drive us there. We're going now, Barukh. Barukh?" She put her hands under his arms and lifted him bodily to his feet, struggling to keep her footing in the sand as she stood up. The sparrows scattered, abandoning their peach pit and taking flight as the people rose. Miryam propped Barukh up on herself, throwing one of his arms over her shoulder and dragging him as quickly as she could to the parking lot. Rambam Hospital was only five minutes away. She hoped it wasn't too late already.

Even before the sand had settled, the sparrows circled above the peach pit and fluttered back down to surround it. Spurts of sand flew into the cool wind as the birds resumed their pecking.

TEARS ROLLED DOWN HER CHEEKS as she sat next to the phone in the living room, her hand quivering on the receiver, uncertain whether to pick it up. The poster of Isadora Duncan stared at her mockingly from one wall, a gentle mountain gorilla stared compassionately from another. Except for them, Denise was alone in her apartment this afternoon. Except for her tears, she imagined, no one would know that anything was different here, that anything had changed. Her long blonde hair felt dirty and she wanted desperately to shower. But that would have to wait, she told herself. That would have to wait until she could stop this crying, until she could talk to someone who would understand, until she could make one call. Her clothes were the same ones she had worn to work at Penn Savings yesterday – a white cotton blouse with a navy blue jacket and skirt. Underneath them she felt ugly, unclean, nauseous. "It's my fault," she said softly to herself, fighting back the nausea, fighting back the sobs. "It's my fault . . . ."

Slowly she stood up and walked over to the wall of high half-windows. The venetian blinds were turned up as usual so that no one could peer down from the pavement into her apartment. She reached out and wound the cord of the blinds between her fingers, trying to control her mind. Holding the cord taut in one hand, she moved the tip up and down with her other hand as though she were sliding a loosely strung bead. But horrible pictures kept flashing in her mind. She was unable to stop them, unable to stop her mind from going over and over the trauma of yesterday and today.

The spotting had started intermittently, painlessly. She had noticed it for the first time last week, but it had cleared up. The doctor had told her not to worry, that there was no call to take any time off from work or otherwise change her schedule. Everything would be all right. Then two days ago the spotting had started again, but this time it had continued, the faint streaks of dried brown changing to bright red stains. Denise had been terrified, feeling possessed by a strange sense of dread. By nightfall the bleeding had become a red, heavy flow and her abdomen began cramping. Soon the pain became so severe that she couldn't breathe. She lay on her bed, certain that something horrible was happening to her baby and wondering if she would survive it, if she herself were dying. Unable to speak, unable to remember her doctor's phone number, unable to think clearly, she dragged herself across the floor and through the short hall to the bathroom. There she propped herself onto the toilet and sat there screaming, expelling the life inside her. The toilet bowl had filled with blood, the sides and rim splattered with the red death of her child.

She wasn't certain how long she had sat there sobbing or how much time had passed before she phoned the doctor. All she remembered clearly was his saying "spontaneous abortion" and telling her to call a cab and come to the hospital immediately. He had examined her there last night, trying to calm her with empty words and statistics. "Nature's way . . . one out of every five pregnancies ends in miscarriage . . . it's not so rare, not your fault, all for the best . . . you're fine, and next time . . . ." He had acted like she had simply lost a thing, not a baby, not her child. The world was set up like hell, she had thought. It was set up so that women always were forced to suffer at the hands of men. But what did they understand about a woman's feelings or a woman's thoughts? The doctor hadn't even realized that she had lost a child, a child she had started to love even before conception, a child she had loved already for eight long, lovely weeks. From the moment the pregnancy was confirmed, she had begun to envision what her child would look like and what kind of parent she would be. She had thought about all the things her parents had done that she was resolved not to repeat. She even had designed the nursery, decorating it in her dreams. But what did a male doctor know? Only enough to give her a sedative to help her stay sane through the night, only enough to perform the D & C late this morning. She had considered the miscarriage the worst experience of her life — until undergoing the D & C. Never before had she felt so demeaned, so dehumanized. It had been as though she were a piece of faulty machinery recalled to the factory, recalled to be cleaned out and reassembled. Something was wrong with her body, with her being. She was in need of correction.

"All for the best." The doctor's words reverberated inside her head, rankling her now as she continued to slide the plastic tip up and down the cord. How did he know that? He wasn't God. Since walking back in from the hospital a few short minutes ago she had felt lost, disoriented, still desperate. She felt lost inside her own apartment, lost inside her own private world of grief, a place that knew death but had no rituals to mark it, a place with no grave and no service and no gathering of family and friends. It was a world that offered no consolation, no comfort. She had never imagined such pain, such despair.

Dropping the cord so that it swung back and banged against the metal blinds, Denise swept away some tears with the side of her hand and walked slowly back to the telephone. It was four o'clock in the afternoon. Maybe her mother would be home. She sat down in the chair and lifted the receiver, but then she put it down again. Her mother, she remembered, had not been as excited about this pregnancy as Denise had expected. Of course, her mother never was as excited as Denise expected or wanted her to be, but that hadn't made this time any easier to handle or any less disappointing. "You're not married," her mother had said to start, and then had said those same words in answer to every question Denise had asked, to every comment Denise had spoken. So she hadn't phoned her mother from the hospital, afraid that the call might leave her feeling more desolate, more alone. Her mother didn't know yet about the D & C, about the miscarriage. Denise thought of packing a suitcase, calling a cab, and heading straight to the station to catch the next train to New York. Maybe she would move in there for a while, just show up at the door and stay. She would call Penn Savings tomorrow morning and tell them she needed a leave of absence. Her mind was too clouded to focus on work or plans. All she knew was that she needed to be held and cared for, to be babied for a while. She pictured her mother and imagined two voices, the one she wished for and the one she knew. Fearing the familiar, she decided not to phone her yet.

Instead her thoughts were of Nissim. He was the only person to whom she felt connected at this moment, the only person with whom she had felt a oneness during these last ghoulish days, and she wanted to talk to him right now. He was the father, she told herself. Their baby was dead and he should know it. Her pain would be less if he shared it, she thought. She had needed him, had wanted him in her bed, caressing her, protecting her so many times these past weeks, but he had not been there for her. He had

293

crossed her off, had discarded her. He had rejected her, and so had his brother. Once Yosef had gotten the number he wanted, he no longer had wanted her. Both brothers had left her because of her baby, and now she had lost it. They both had used and abandoned her. What were they doing right now? she wondered. Living it up in America.

Anger surged inside her as tears rolled down her cheeks. Before Nissim, it had always been she who had ended her involvements. It had always been she who had controlled the flow of her relationships. First Nissim and then Yossi, she thought. Just like my father.

There was a loud ringing. The phone. She looked at it a second. Slowly she picked it up. "Hello?"

"Denise, where are you? We have a big problem here. We've been trying to reach you all day. Just because you're a woman doesn't mean you don't have to call in like the rest of us."

It was Mr. Richards, the manager at Penn Savings.

"I'm sorry, Mr. Richards," she said. He doesn't even ask what's wrong, not that I would tell him. What does he think, I'm faking it? Insensitive bastard. "I'm not coming in today," she told him. "I'll be in tomorrow."

"Tomorrow?" he asked incredulously. "This is a serious matter and it's been on your desk since Monday. A deposit on Thanksgiving. Several thousand dollars. I haven't seen any report from you."

Not that, not now, she thought. I told him I was working on it. Back off, Mr. Richards. I'll be in tomorrow.

"Are you there?"

"I'm here," she said weakly. She wondered what she could have been thinking to have given Yosef that access number. The truth, if discovered, would cost her her job. But what difference did that make right now? What did anything matter right now?

"I need that report, Denise. The regional office is on my back.

And if my job's on the line, so is yours."

There was no hiding it any longer. Yosef was probably still making fraudulent entries, she thought, Nissim was probably still staring at candles, and her baby was still dead. "Okay," she said, feeling tears trickling down the side of her nose but not lifting a hand to wipe them away, "let me tell you about that deposit . . . ."

Fourteen

A SUDDEN, LOUD RINGING invaded Yosef's dream. Groggily he reached for the telephone on the table beside his bed and fumbled with the receiver. "Hello?"

No one answered.

"Hello?" he repeated, rubbing his eyes with his free hand and focusing on the digital clock beside the phone. Ten o'clock in the morning already. Still no voice answered him, but through the earpiece he heard a sound like that of a pebble plinking into a deep well. He cleared his throat and braced the receiver between his pillow and his beard. "Hello?" His voice echoed loudly back into his ear.

"Yossi? It's Ema. Did I wake you?"

"Miryam?" There had been a delay between each phrase she had spoken. To him she sounded a world away. "What's wrong? Why are you calling? Is everything all right?"

"What? I can't hear you very well," Miryam said. "We must have a bad connection."

"I hear you fine," Yosef said, propping himself up quickly in the bed, deep worry now etched across his face. "What's wrong? Is everything okay?" He was screaming so that she could hear him and his words were shouting back at him.

There was a long, hollow pause. "Yossi," Miryam said in a quavering voice, "I'm calling from Rambam Hospital."

"Rambam Hospital? Who's there? What happened?"

"The doctors say he'll be all right . . . ." She stopped herself, fighting back the tears. "Barukh was swimming and . . . the doc-

296

tors say he had a . . . stroke. His signs are stable now, and they say it was . . . mild, but they're watching him, Yossi, and . . . ."

"Nissim!" Yosef shouted, covering the mouthpiece with his hand and not getting out of the bed. "Nissim, it's Miryam!" But he heard no movement either from Nissim's room down the hall or from downstairs. No one called up the stairs or picked up any of the downstairs phones. He must have gone out, Yosef surmised. "Where's Barukh now?"

"They have him in Intensive Care . . . they told me that if there's no change through tonight he should be all right . . . but it's minute to minute . . . and I hate to see those tubes hanging . . . ."

Yosef heard the delayed echo of her crying. "Is anyone with you?" he asked loudly. "Are you just there by yourself?"

"Shoshanah is here, she works here . . . she's come up every few minutes to check on me . . . Rivka just left . . . I'm spending the night here . . . in the waiting room . . . I'm holding up . . . the best I can."

Yosef wondered how much of the quiver he heard in her voice was simply due to distortion over the international phone lines. Often he had heard Miryam overreact to illnesses, exaggerating their severity because she feared her nightmares were coming true. He was used to seeing her moved to tears by medical complications that never materialized. So he was unsure how to judge the despair he heard in her voice now. Minute to minute, she had said. Barukh, his uncle and his Abba, his father's brother and his father lay in the hospital in intensive care. Barukh, the one man who had always been there for him, the one person who—busy and time-pressed as he was—had come to every basketball game in which Yosef had played, had come to every school event and every Israel Scouts outing, that loving man was hooked to monitors and machines and was being fed through tubes. And where am I for him? Yosef asked himself. On the other side of

297

the world. But Miryam had said that by morning he should be out of danger. "What should I do?" he asked her.

"I don't know, Yossi," she said, sounding numb, exhausted, powerless. "I don't know what any of us can do right now. I just called to let you know . . . and to let you and Nissim decide."

Decide, he repeated silently as he listened to Miryam's words echo and fade. Should he fly back right away or wait? Wait for what, for Barukh to die? Should he wait to fly back for the funeral? Life was no less of a reason to return, was it? Would Nissim hesitate? He had to find him. "Miryam," he said loudly, "just take care of yourself, and tell Barukh that we love him. He's a fighter, and he'll pull through. You'll see."

"I hope so . . . *Ribbono shel olam,* I hope so."

"I'll get hold of Nissim and we'll check back with you tomorrow, your time. What's the number at the hospital?"

"Hold on a minute. I know I wrote it down somewhere . . . there's a phone right in the waiting room. I wrote the number on a slip of . . . here it is." She read the telephone number to Yosef.

"Okay. I'll check back with you tomorrow. It will be all right, Miryam. He'll be all right, you'll see."

"Whatever . . . it's out of our hands now. Yossi, other people are waiting to use the phone. Goodbye, son. I'll wait for your call."

"Goodbye, Ema."

Yosef hung up the phone, bolted out of bed, and got dressed. It was Saturday and he had decided to sleep late this morning, just as he had last weekend, now that he no longer had impossible debts hanging like boulders around his neck. Life had become manageable. He could work human hours knowing he only needed to earn enough money to cover his current expenses. It allowed him to live from this week to next week without having to enlist the help of Nissim's computer again. Things had been going smoothly, yes smoothly, and now this call out of nowhere.

After washing his face he went downstairs, grabbed a toaster pastry from the kitchen cupboard, and headed out the side door into the garage. Nissim's Chevy was not parked next to the Checker. Yosef figured that his brother had probably left an hour ago for Penn campus. Maybe he was in the library now, maybe he was in the computer lab, maybe he was studying with a classmate in the dorms. Yosef hopped into his Checker, gunned the motor, and left tire burns on the blacktop as he backed out of the driveway to find his brother.

IN PHILDELPHIA, black skies turned afternoon into night. Snow alerts had been issued that morning, but the forecast had been revised by noon and now they were only calling for showers. There was enough of a bite in the afternoon air to make the steering wheel of Nissim's Chevy uncomfortably cold to the touch. Nissim, wearing gloves, pulled his car into the empty garage and walked quickly into the house through the side door.

He had driven to the Student Center at Penn this morning to do some studying for his final exams which were coming up in the next few days. But there were distractions there. Other students were milling around, joking and laughing loudly, not wanting to think about schoolwork on a Saturday morning. And the Student Center had another distraction, one that especially bothered Nissim. In addition to all the American Bicentennial banners, the Center was decorated with Christmas symbols and holiday signs, and they weakened Nissim's concentration. It seemed to him that Santas, carols, and manger scenes had followed him everywhere since Thanksgiving. There were Christmas sales, Christmas foods, Christmas shows, Christmas savings plans. On radio and television, at the market, in the malls, at the bank. He had caught himself whistling Christmas melodies more than once that week.

The Christmas season troubled him. It forced him to sort out his identities, to rank them all of a sudden, to acknowledge and rearrange them. He felt as though Christmas in America had lit a thousand fuses that snaked along behind him everywhere he went, their sizzling flames moving toward him to scare him out of hiding. He felt threatened, visible, a minority Jew for the first time in his life. In Israel, there had been dreidls, menorahs, candles, and donuts. There had been Chanukah parties, Chanukah vacation, Chanukah songs on television and on the radio. But here everything was Christmas first, and Nissim felt more a Jew than an Israeli.

Sitting in the student lounge he had been reminded again that there were very few places he could go where Christmas didn't wait in ambush. So he had left the Student Center and had sat in a park off of the West River Drive where he had studied outside on the grass for several hours, enjoying the open air and disregarding the winter winds. Just being by the water calmed him. It was one of the few places where yuletide didn't pursue him. It made him think of Haifa instead of Jesus Christ, of home instead of Christmas. And he had thought about Denise as he sat there by the river. Since her call last week he had felt like a free man again. It had restored his sense of infinite possibility, his vision of an open future. He was sorry to hear Denise in such pain, in such despair and desolation, but it had been of her own doing. He wished he could have disguised his relief, his pleasure at hearing of her pregnancy's termination, but he had been unable to, and he knew that had only compounded her pain. But her call had ended weeks of rising worry for him. It had wiped clean the slate of his life and had revitalized him. He had attacked his schoolwork with new energy and with renewed interest.

Entering the kitchen now, he unloaded his pile of library books on the island counter, took off his gloves, and continued into the entrance hall. His cheeks were red from the biting winds along the river, and he was glad to be indoors again. Moving to the hallway closet, he hung up his down army jacket, then walked into the den and turned on the television. It was four o'clock in the afternoon and the college football game of the week was still on. Nissim settled into the high-backed leather chair, readying himself for some uninterrupted viewing. He took off his shoes, socks, and shirt, and sat there in his jeans. Then he took a deep breath. This is the life, he told himself. Weekends in America, two days every week. What a dream. No huddling around any kerosene heater to dry out from the winter rains and keep warm. Outside it's cold enough to snow and in here you could go swimming.

The volume on the television was too low and the color of the artificial grass was too blue, so Nissim got up to play with the knobs. As he was adjusting the color setting, the phone rang and he went to the kitchen to answer it.

"Hello?"

No one answered on the other end.

"Hello?" he repeated, hearing his voice echo back at him. There was the sound of a vacuous blip, then he heard the voice of a woman.

"Yossi?"

"No, Ema. It's Nissim."

"Nissim . . . oh, Nissim, he's . . . ." Miryam could not speak through her sobbing.

"Ema, I can't hear you very clearly. What's wrong? Where are you?"

"I'm at the . . . Nissim, Yossi didn't tell you?"

"Tell me what? I haven't seen him today." As he held the phone, he moved across the kitchen, checking the refrigerator and the table and the countertops for any note Yosef might have left for him. He found no slip of paper. Nothing. "Ema, what's wrong?" he asked her. "What happened? Tell me."

"Nissim . . . I'm at Rambam Hospital . . . with your father

301

. . . he had to make it through the night but . . . he just had another stroke . . . ." Again unable to speak, she stopped talking. Her body tensed and heaved, making it hard for her to hold onto the phone, wanting instead to let it drop and curl herself into a tight ball on the hospital floor. She tried desperately to catch her breath, to control her gasping, and almost choked on the swallowed air.

"Ema, calm down. Just talk to me. I'm here, I'll wait. Just collect yourself and talk to me," Nissim told her. Another stroke, he thought. Another? When did Barukh have the first one?

"When I spoke to Yossi this afternoon . . . things looked hopeful . . . Barukh was swimming and something happened . . . but the doctors said it was mild . . . he would be all right if . . . if he made it through the night being stable . . . but Nissim, dear God, Nissim, he didn't . . . and they say . . . they say this one was . . . ."

"Ema," he said, fighting back his own tears, "Ema, I'll be there as fast as I can. I'll come straight to the hospital. Tell Abba I'm coming, Ema. Tell him I'm coming."

"Nissim, I never thought . . . I mean, I always thought that I'd be the one . . . ."

"Ema," Nissim cut her off, "Ema, we'll talk when I get there. Is Shoshanah with you? Does she know?"

"Yes, she's here with me, and she's helping . . . Nissim . . . they don't know if . . . ."

Nissim felt the tears rise inside himself as he listened to his mother's voice dissolve into sobs, her cries echoing into his ear over the long-distance phone lines. Her pain and despair penetrated his mind, made his body tremble as the sound waves travelled through him, sending quivers down his chest and legs. He could not control his emotions any longer, but he didn't want Miryam to hear him cry, so he decided to end the conversation. He had already heard enough to know what he had to do. "Ema," he said,

"I have to pack. I'll be there by tomorrow, as fast as I can get there."

"Nissim . . . ." Miryam said, barely able to speak, "I love you."

"I . . . will be there tomorrow." Unable to say goodbye and not even trying to wipe away the tears rolling down his cheeks into his moustache and beard, he hung up the phone and slumped onto the counter. Barukh, his father, the victim of a massive brain hemorrhage, was dying and there was no way to get back to him quickly. Not quickly enough. There was no way to cut out the cabs and planes, no way to make the travel time shorter, no way to abridge the distance. How many hours ago had Miryam called Yosef about the first stroke? he wondered. How much time had he lost in his race to his father's bedside because of his brother's stupidity? How could Yosef not have left a note, not have told him in person? If he saw his cousin again before he left, he would kill him. For this one Yosef could have no excuse. This was no accident, no misunderstanding. Nissim wondered what he would find when he rushed into Rambam Hospital, now that he'd lost such crucial hours. He wondered if his father would be gone before he reached him. "Abba," he cried out through his tears, "Abba . . . wait for me . . . I'm coming . . . wait . . . ."

The sound of a car pulling into the garage caused Nissim to fall silent and straighten up. He listened to the engine wind down and wiped the tears from his face with both hands. Yosef walked into the house through the side door from the garage to find Nissim standing in the middle of the kitchen, blocking the way between the counter and the kitchen table.

"Nissim, where've you been?" he asked loudly and quickly, then looked more closely at his brother's face and noticed the redness around his eyes and the wet streaks on his cheeks. "What's wrong? What happened?" he asked, moving forward.

"You selfish bastard!" Nissim said through gritted teeth. "You goddamn selfish bastard!" Staring into Yosef's stunned eyes, he slowly closed his right hand and punched his brother in the lower stomach with great force.

Yosef let out a guttural groan and doubled over from the blow, clutching his stomach with both hands, not even thinking about striking back. Nissim watched his brother's pain a second, then turned and started out of the room. He was halfway up the stairs, heading to his room to start packing, before Yosef managed to utter a word.

"Nissim . . . what the hell's wrong with you? I've been looking for you . . . since eleven this morning." Still holding his stomach, he straightened himself up and started slowly into the hallway.

Nissim stopped on the staircase when he heard his brother's voice, but he did not answer.

"I drove to Penn," Yosef continued, holding on to the banister and talking up to his younger brother. "Where were you?"

"There, but I left early." Nissim could feel his anger easing as he realized Yosef must have just missed him. His brother had tried to find him, had searched for him. Nissim figured that he had been home for less than fifteen minutes before the phone call had come, so even if Yosef had left him a note, it wouldn't have made any difference, it wouldn't have saved any time. "Ema called."

"How did you know? I was looking for you to tell you."

"She called five minutes ago."

"What?" He tilted his wrist to check his watch. "It's the middle of the night there. Is Barukh all right?"

Tears trickled down Nissim's cheeks as he swallowed to answer. "He had another stroke."

"Another? But he only had to pull through the night."

"He damn well better pull through the night, and the next one too," Nissim said, his voice shaking, "because I plan to be there to wake him up."

Yosef felt tears welling in his eyes. Barukh? Another stroke? "What do you mean? You're going? Just like that? What about your exams, your semester?"

"Some things don't wait, Yossi. I'm catching the next plane out. It might be too late already."

"Nissim?"

"What is it? I've got to get moving."

"Nothing . . . ."

Nissim hurried up the stairs to pack. Yosef walked slowly to the hall closet, still holding his stomach. Barukh was there and he was here. Silent tears streamed slowly into his beard.

From the hallway Yosef heard the roar of a crowd in the den. He walked into the room to find the television blaring and a football game entering its closing minutes. The score flashed onto the screen; Penn State was leading Pittsburgh by three points. Yosef sat down in the high-backed chair and settled back to watch Pitt try to pull out a victory by mounting a final drive down the field, but he was unable to concentrate on anything except thoughts of staying and leaving, of waiting and not delaying. I'm going too, he thought. But leaving is not that simple. There were many considerations, many costs. He couldn't afford to leave here and then come back again. How could he leave now with everything finally coming together? How could he leave now when he was so close to accomplishing what he had come for? Final exams would start next week. If he missed them he would lose this semester, the one semester he had counted on completing. And if he lost this one, then all the progress he had made would be nullified, negated, neutralized. He would still have two more semesters to complete before he could graduate, and he would have to withdraw his application for the Master's Degree program, deferring that until the year after next. Leaving now with Nissim would mean that these past months had all been for nothing — the separation from Rivka and Dorit, the working double-time

driving his cab, the computer fraud with BankAmericard. They
would all have been no more than empty exercises in frustration.
He had commitments here, commitments to himself and to his
future, to his family's future. His courses, his cab, this house.
Commitments. Could he afford to forfeit the money he'd already
spent? Could he afford to forfeit the time? The semester's tuition,
the months of classes, the rent he would still have to pay for this
house, the income he'd lose by not driving his cab for however
long he'd be gone? Life is *always* minute to minute, he told
himself. Don't think so much. Decide.

His thoughts turned back to the last war. If only he had been
there, he thought. If only they'd called him. But what difference
would his return have made to *Tzahal*, to his friends who had
fallen? Who could know that he could have done anything to help
them, to save them, or that his being there would really have mat-
tered? All he did know was the difference it had made to *him*.
His *not* being there had changed everything. It had locked him
in his own private hell, a hell of exclusion and disconnection, of
shame and self-indictment. It had made him an absentee casualty, a wounded veteran of that war. He considered the wound
of his absence more serious than the loss of an arm or a leg. It
had not cost him his life, but sometimes he felt it had cost him
his soul. Not being there had crippled him, and only now was
he getting back on his feet. Leaving now would turn the clock
back, but so—he knew—would staying. There was no way for
him to arrange what he would have to arrange in order to leave
with Nissim tonight, but if Nissim would agree to wait till the
morning, then maybe tomorrow . . . .

A knock at the front door jolted Yosef from his private
thoughts. Getting up slowly, he walked through the hallway to
see who was knocking.

"Joseph Love?"

"Yes?" Yosef said, surprised to find two policemen standing

at his door. How do they know my name? Yosef wondered.

"Mind if we come in?" the older officer asked as politely as he could in a rough-edged deep voice. He had black hair that was graying in spots, very broad shoulders, and a paunch that threatened to pop the lower buttons on his uniform.

"No, not at all, officers."

The policemen put their caps under their arms and walked inside, stopping in the entrance hallway.

"Your brother in?" the younger officer asked. He looked to be Yosef's age, had square strong features, and was only an inch or so shorter than Yosef.

"Yes, he's upstairs," Yosef answered.

"On his computer?"

"No, not now," Yosef told him, wondering how they knew about Nissim, how they knew about his computer, wondering what they were doing here.

"Mind if we go up?" the older officer asked, his voice making the request sound too authoritative to deny.

"No," Yosef said hesitantly, "sure, go right ahead." Then stepping in front of the officers, he led the way up slowly.

As they reached the top of the stairs, Nissim called out from his bedroom in Hebrew, "Yossi, who was it?"

"Police," Yosef called back. "We're coming in to you."

Following Yosef as he walked through the upstairs hallway toward Nissim's voice, the officers frowned at one another when they heard the foreign language. The younger officer, suspicious of what the brothers were saying, put his hand on his gun. A moment later they stood in the doorway to Nissim's room.

"Going somewhere?" the older officer asked in his gravelly voice.

Nissim, who was bent over the open suitcase that lay on his bed, looked up. The drawers of the dresser behind him were open. The suitcase was already half filled, and in Nissim's arms were a pile of folded sweaters. "Yes," Nissim said, laying the pile down neatly on top of the open suitcase, "I am going home."

The officers looked at each other.

"Why? Something wrong?" the older officer asked. "You look like you're in a hurry."

"My father is in the hospital," Nissim answered, stopping his packing.

Again the officers looked at each other and exchanged disbelieving looks.

"In the hospital, eh?" the older policeman said as he moved further into the room and walked over to Nissim's desk. "Nice machine you got here, Mr. Love," he said, inspecting the top of Nissim's computer. "Know a lot about these, do you?"

Yosef stood silently, growing increasingly apprehensive as he listened to the officer questioning his brother. He wondered how much they knew. He hoped they knew no more than Nissim did because he had told Nissim nothing of his crime; he had told him nothing about phoning BankAmericard. In fact, he figured, Nissim wasn't even aware that Yosef knew how to use his computer. So Yosef remained silent, trying to hide the concern inside him as he watched the policemen probing.

"I am learning at Penn about computers," Nissim answered. He did not want to be disrespectful, but he was in a terrible hurry. "Why are you asking me these questions? I am sorry but I have too little time."

"Well, Mr. Love," the older officer said, speaking slowly as he looked across at his partner whose hand pressed against his holster, "I'm sorry to throw a wrench into your travel plans but I wouldn't plan on going *anywhere* too soon, if I was you. You see, we have a lot of talking to do before we're gonna finish here, so why don't you just close up that suitcase and let's you and your brother go where we can talk."

Nissim's face was more angry than confused. "I don't have time for talking now," he said, straightening up but not moving. "My father is dying and I must go to him."

"You don't have any choice, buddy," the heavier officer said, any trace of politeness gone from his voice. He put his hand on the rubber shoe next to Nissim's computer and continued talking without taking a breath. "You put the phone in here and just dial? That how it works? Just turn on the brain here, pick up the phone, set it right in here, and break into any bank you want without ever having to leave the house? Not too shabby, not too shabby at all. Unless of course you get caught at it."

Nissim looked at Yosef. Their eyes locked across the room as Yosef spoke to his brother in Hebrew.

"Don't say another word. I'll handle this," Yosef said.

Nissim could see in his brother's eyes that these officers had not come without cause. What had Yosef done this time? he wondered. But all he could really think about was not losing any more precious minutes in his race back home to Barukh.

"What was that?" the younger policeman asked Yosef gruffly. "What did you say?" His whole body was braced and his right hand was on the black nub of his pistol.

"I told him that he should not answer these questions, that I would answer them for him, Yosef said."

"And why's that?"

"Because I'm his big brother."

"I see. And which one of you came up with the idea in the first place? Him or you?"

"What idea?" Yosef asked innocently.

The younger officer looked across at his partner with impatience. "Jack, this is gonna take longer than we thought."

"Maybe so, maybe not," the older policeman said. "Let's move on downstairs, boys—all of us."

Yosef motioned to Nissim to come, and Nissim, leaving his suitcase open on the bed, reluctantly walked out of the room with his brother. The two officers followed closely behind them.

Downstairs they entered the living room, and Yosef and Nissim sat down on the sofa; the two policemen stayed standing.

"Let me lay it out for you," the senior policeman began, "and save us all a lot of time. This house has two phone numbers. One's in the name of the people who own it, the other's in yours," he said, looking at Nissim. "The second line goes to your computer machine up there, and we did some checking through the phone records to see what numbers you called out to. Seems you mostly called only one number on that line—the computer center down at U of P, but back around Thanksgiving time, seems you dialed yourself a new number—one you never should've known. You following me?"

The officer had been talking to Nissim, whose face was growing more and more confused. Nothing the officer was saying was making sense to him, but he was listening to every word. Nissim looked at Yosef. Deep lines of worry were carved on Yosef's face.

"So then we checked with the BankAmericard people," the officer continued, "following up on a lead we had, and sure enough, their records showed that a lot of money had appeared, just like magic, in your account." Now he was looking at Yosef. "And the number of dollars that someone punched in there just happened to exactly match the amount you owed them. You really ran up a tab for yourself there, didn't you, Mr. Love? Tell me, where does a cabbie driving twenty hours a week on a student visa come up with that kind of money?" The officer paused and stared at Yosef, waiting for his answer. "Huh, Mr. Love?"

Yosef did not answer.

The older officer waited, his thick arms propped up on his belly and folded across his chest. His expression turned impatient.

"Let's just read these guys their rights and take them down to the station," the younger policeman said as he walked over to his partner. "They're not the only ones in a rush around here."

"Hell, Don," the heavier cop whispered, "these white collar jobs are a bitch. You can't rush 'em. We don't have enough solid stuff on these guys to make it stick yet. Let's keep 'em talking. I'm in no hurry."

The younger officer looked at his partner, nodded, then moved to the other side of the room from where he watched the conversation continue.

Turning his attention back to Nissim, the senior policeman said, "Look, fella, we can sit here all night if you like, but if you want to see your father—it was your father, wasn't it?—well, if you want to see him, you better start giving me some answers."

Nissim did not know what to do. This was no game. If he said anything against his brother, he could be sending him to jail. But if he said nothing, he could be denying himself the chance to see Barukh before he died; he could be losing his chance to save him. Miryam hadn't said he was dead. She hadn't said there was no hope. He had to get home. "Officer, I don't know anything about—"

"That's right, officer," Yosef cut his brother off, "he doesn't know anything about this. It was my idea. He had nothing to do with this. His father *is* dying in Israel. It's minute to minute. Let him go. I'll answer your questions, but first let him go."

The officers exchanged congratulatory looks.

"Not so fast, brother," the older officer barked angrily. "We're the ones holding the cards here, and we don't take kindly to ultimatums. You want to make a deal, make it with the judge."

Yosef remained obstinate. He figured that if they already had enough evidence to convict him, they wouldn't be asking so many questions. They'd simply be hauling him in, arresting him—and perhaps Nissim with him. So he decided to gamble, figuring he couldn't lose more than he might have lost already. "Let him go or arrest us," he said. "It's your choice."

Nissim looked at his brother in shock. What the hell is he doing? he thought. He'll land us both in jail before he's finished.

The officers walked over to one another, conferring in hushed tones in the middle of the living room. Then the older officer spoke to Yosef. "Here's the deal," he said in a gruff and angry voice, fixing Yosef with a squint-eyed glare. "The deal is no deal. You're both subjects in an ongoing fraud investigation. You'll both come down to the precinct to make statements and you'll both be staying put for a while. Leave the city and you're risking a jail sentence. Am I understood?"

Neither Yosef nor Nissim responded. Instead they both sat on the sofa, absorbing what the sergeant had just said.

"Understand?" the policeman repeated, much louder. "Let's go, we're going downtown." With that, he motioned to his partner, and the two of them walked the brothers quickly to the front door.

The brothers stared at each other, as they put on their jackets.

"Nissim," Yosef started to say in Hebrew, "this had nothing to do with you . . . ."

"What did you do?" Nissim asked, disgusted, as they walked toward the squad car where the two officers awaited them. "Use my modem to hook into BankAmericard?"

"Yes."

"How?"

"Denise gave me the access number."

"Denise?" Nissim lifted his eyes and paused a second, looking knowingly at his brother. He could see in Yosef's eyes that he, too, understood how the police had found out about the fraud.

"But she would have had to implicate herself," Yosef said, as much to himself as to Nissim. "She'd lose her job. Why would she do it?"

"Yossi," Nissim said, not willing to waste another second on questions, "I don't care why, and I don't care what the officer said.

I'll make the statement and then I'm going — tonight. I don't even care what they do to me."

Yosef studied his brother a moment, then nodded. "Okay, little brother. I'll drive you."

Fifteen

TEL AVIV • DECEMBER 1975

THE METAL ASHTRAY on Nissim's armrest bulged with crushed butts. A cigarette dangled between his lips and stereo music flowed into his head through earphones that looked like the stethoscope in Dorit's toy doctor kit. The "no smoking" signal flashed on. Nissim ground out his Marlboro, flipped the little metal lid of the ashtray shut, and pressed the button on his armrest to straighten his seat. "It's one thing if he fucks up his own life," he told himself, "but it's another if he ruins mine."

Nissim had pictured his return home many times during the past half-year, but never had he pictured it like this – with him returning as a fugitive, running away from the law in America, running to his father's sickbed in Israel. His mother had called him to come back home; he wondered if the Philadelphia police were calling him back also at this very moment. He had never imagined such complications, such entanglements. For a moment his thoughts focused on Denise, but shifted back quickly to Barukh. It seemed much longer than six months ago that he had taken his flight in the opposite direction. Seen from the clouds, New York at night had looked futuristic. The neon glow of its skyline and the rivers of light coursing its highways had made it appear surreal. The land he looked down on now was much different, less glittering, more real.

Through the oval window beside him, Tel Aviv's shorelights were vivid colored dots tracing a crooked line along the coast. The El Al jet began its descent and as the colored lights grew larger, Nissim found himself forgetting how long he had been away. A warm sensation flowed inside him, a sense of anticipation. Coming home to Israel this time was like coming home to a lover.

Nissim checked his wristwatch. It was already 10:00 P.M., Israel time. "Abba, be alive," he said silently to himself, cursing the stop to refuel in Paris. What had been scheduled as a forty-minute operation had become a five-hour ordeal, being made to wait in a special wing of the DeGaulle Airport terminal for security reasons until the plane was readied. He had felt as though he were under house arrest, as though the planeload of passengers were being held hostage in that terminal, being held hostage by time. He had been powerless to make anything move faster, though he had certainly tried. "Just be there when I get there, Abba." He reached into his coat pocket and felt his passport, making sure it was accessible to speed him through Passport Control.

"Minute to minute," Miryam's words repeated in his head. Through the oval window the coastal lights were replaced by strings of lights on the landing strip as the jet engines revved down loudly. Shortly the plane touched down to a collective cheer of "mazel tov" from the full load of passengers, then taxied to a stop far away from the terminal. The cabin filled noisily with fresh air amid the whirring din of decompression. Even before the plane had come to a full stop, Nissim stood up, took his jacket from the overhead storage compartment, and hurried into the aisle toward the exit. Looking down through the windows on either side he saw a fleet of forklifts and security buses approaching. Long metal stairs were rolled into position and attached to the plane's front door. Nissim was among the first in line when the plane began to empty into the damp Israeli night.

After the shuttle ride to the Arrivals hall, he moved quickly through Passport Control. His suitcase and green duffel bag had already been unloaded and were circling on the luggage conveyor belt when he reached the Baggage Claim area. He threw his duffel bag over one shoulder, lifted the suitcase in his other hand, and hurried through a maze of luggage carts to Customs Inspection where he walked through "Nothing to Declare." No Customs official stopped him to check his bags.

Directly ahead of him were metal doors. They swung open as he neared. Beyond them, a large crowd waited in the raw December night and he watched the anxious eyes look him over as he strode down the path that guardrails cleared through the sea of faces. No one was there to greet him, he knew. Six months ago when he had left, the whole family had come to see him off. Six months ago he had pictured his return home, coming back to the same faces, the same loving smiles. This was nothing like he had envisioned. "Just be there, Abba."

Moving quickly, he walked straight to the line of Mercedes taxis that waited at the curb beyond the guardrails. "Haifa," he told the driver as he hopped into the first cab in line. "Rambam Hospital." Not wanting to lose even one second more, he put the duffel bag and suitcase beside him on the seat and sat back as the taxi sped out of Ben-Gurion Airport.

No streetlights lit the long flat road leading from the airport to the main interchanges, and few headlights shined into the driver's eyes as he turned on his high beams and pressed the throttle to the floor. Driving this access road at night was like driving along a drag strip in pitch darkness. The landscape whizzed past Nissim's window in a dark unending blur.

The taxi merged onto the main road, ignoring the speed limits as it raced through the outskirts of Tel Aviv, through Hadera and Hod HaSharon and onto the coastal highway. Towering street lamps cast a warm yellow light all the way from Country Club Junction north to Haifa. Nissim listened to the Mediterranean Sea rolling toward the shore on his left, but he could not see anything there through the darkness. On the other side of the highway were darkened houses and quiet apartment buildings. There was a tranquility to the darkness there, a sleepy peacefulness to the absolute absence of movement. As the taxi sped northward, Nissim held his wrist out in front of him and waited for the glow of the next street lamp to light the face of his watch so that he could read the time. It was already past 11:30 P.M. "Be there, Abba, be there," he said to himself.

"What?" the cabbie asked. "You say something?"

"I'm just in a hurry," he answered.

The driver pressed the throttle down even further, exceeding the speed limit by yet another twenty kilometers per hour. A half-hour later Nissim looked through the window on his left and a wash of memories filled his mind. Suddenly the sea became visible, lit not by the highway lamps but by the hazy midnight glow of the moon and stars. He watched the soothing rhythm of the waves and listened to them pound like boards clapping together as they crashed against the shore. He imagined himself running into the sea, swimming out toward the dark horizon somewhere beneath the lowest star. He remembered the hot summer days when he had come here with Avi and Shoshanah, days when the heavy air stilled the waves, transforming the sea into a massive lake, and he remembered the winter days when no one else would have ventured in, days when he and Avi and Shoshanah had shivered and laughed their way out beyond the last breaker, looking back together at the empty beach. Avi was dead, and Barukh had swum here just the day before yesterday, Nissim told himself.

He turned his eyes sharply away from the sea and looked out the opposite window. A deep sense of guilt and longing came over him as he saw Mount Carmel rise up beside him like a mythical mountain. Ribbons of light traversed the mountain, winding and intertwining as they climbed toward the peak. Nissim pictured himself climbing down the steep wadi behind HaTishbi Street, climbing down to the secret spot where he and Avi had played. How many plots had they dreamed up there while looking out across the mountain, while looking down on the glistening sea, out to the line between sky and water, out to the line between real life and dreams?

The taxi approached the traffic light just beyond the "Welcome To Haifa" sign. This was the route Nissim always took to get home. He thought a second about asking the driver to turn here and take him up to HaTishbi Street, to take him to Miryam, but she would be asleep by now, so he said nothing as the driver raced through the changing signal. Tonight home was a hospital. A minute later they had turned off of the main road at the new Central Bus Station, and the gate to Rambam Hospital was visible through the windshield.

The taxi pulled into the hospital driveway and stopped in front of the guard's booth. The guard, his Uzi slung over one shoulder, came out to conduct a security check.

"Yes?" he asked the driver, gripping his gun with one hand as he leaned down to talk through the rolled-down window.

"My passenger is here to visit his father," the driver explained. "I am bringing him straight from the airport."

"The airport?" the guard repeated, shining a flashlight into the backseat of the dark Mercedes and seeing Nissim's face as well as his baggage.

"Shalom," Nissim said in his most military voice. "My father is here. The doctors expect me."

The guard eyed him suspiciously. "With a suitcase and duffel?"

"They called me. I just got in from America."

"America, eh?"

Nissim did not like the sudden change of tone in the guard's voice or the judgmental look in his eye.

"You living there?"

"Studying."

"Right," he said with a sarcastic smile.

"Look," Nissim said, "my father's here, and I have to see him, immediately."

The guard eyed Nissim suspiciously a moment, shining the flashlight into the car one more time. Then he lowered the beam, opened the gate, and waved the Mercedes through.

The main entrance to the hospital was closed. Following the ambulance route away from the parking area and around the huge square structure, the taxi slowed as it neared the emergency entrance. Nissim looked into the hospital through the glass sliding doors of the entrance and saw a young guard sitting with an Uzi across his knees. Getting ready to move, Nissim combed his hair with his hand, zipped up his jacket, leaned forward, and paid the driver. Jumping out of the taxi, lugging his suitcase and his duffel bag with him, he watched the Mercedes' red taillights pull away into the darkness.

The young guard stood when Nissim marched in through the automatic sliding doors. The clock on the wall near the entrance showed the hour was past midnight. "One minute!" the guard said sternly as he watched Nissim approach. "Where are you going?" He eyed Nissim's luggage with suspicion.

"Up to see my father."

"Visiting hours ended three hours ago. I don't know who let you in, but unless you need a doctor yourself, you'll have to come back in the morning."

Nissim had no time — and less patience — for any more barriers. He had jetted halfway across the world to get to Barukh and now he was here. His father was just two floors above him. Nothing and no one would stand in his way. "Talk to the guard at the gate about it," Nissim said angrily, as he started past the guard.

"Wait, not so fast," the guard shouted, grabbing Nissim around one arm. "Let me see those bags." He ordered Nissim to lift his suitcase and duffel bag onto the table for a security inspection.

Nissim obeyed and waited as the guard gave the pieces a perfunctory checking.

"What room is your father in?" the guard asked when he had finished.

"Intensive Care. This is an emergency."

"His name?"

"Lvov. Barukh Lvov," Nissim said quickly, taking his suitcase and bag from the table.

"Lvov," the guard repeated slowly as he picked up a clipboard from the table next to his chair and wrote down the name. "And yours?"

"The same. I'm his son. And I'm in a hurry." With that, he threw his duffel bag over his shoulder and started quickly down the hallway.

"Come back, friend," the guard shouted after him, "before you make me stop you."

Nissim did not slow down or even turn around. "Do whatever you have to," he called back as he strode down the wide blue hallway.

Reaching the elevators he pressed the button on the wall, wondering if the guard would come, but no angry footsteps echoed through the empty hallway. When the door opened, Nissim rushed inside the car and pushed the button for Barukh's floor. Minute to minute, he thought to himself, and please, no more checkpoints to run through.

As the doors parted, Nissim rushed out and stood in the hallway, surveying the floor, realizing he didn't know exactly where to go. Minute to minute. The corridors were deserted. There were no nurses, no doctors, no orderlies in sight. There were no sounds of squeaky-wheeled carts, no echoes of loud or hushed hospital voices. Everything was white and still, and all the props were silent. The wooden benches, the white fire hose next to the extinguisher, the standing ashcans with silver tops that seemed

to keep a silent vigil, the wall clock with hands but no numbers —
all of these were soundless, lifeless. The floor resembled a wide
tunnel with fluorescent tubes running down the center of the ceiling. Nissim walked to the nurses' station, dragging his luggage
with him. He stood there at the vacant counter a moment, but no
one came. Should he scream? If he shouted for assistance he would
wake up everyone on the floor, and for all he knew, the nurse
would block him from seeing his father. He decided not to stand
around. His steps resounded loudly as he walked through the
hallway past the half-closed doors of several rooms. Finally he
found a sign to the Intensive Care Unit. It was just ahead, with
a waiting room adjacent to it.

He walked faster now, almost running to see if Miryam was
still here waiting. His face was ready to smile and wince, to release
the swell of conflicting emotions as soon as he saw his mother,
as soon as he could see the pain and worry in her eyes. He rushed
into the small waiting room, ready to drop his suitcase and duffel and to throw his arms around his mother, but the room was
empty. She must have gone home to get some sleep, he thought
as he ran his eyes over the blue-gray benches, the light blue walls,
the emptiness. Above his head a bare bulb in the center of the
ceiling scattered his shadow across the pale walls. He studied the
room a second, comparing its desolation to his own, then headed across the hall to stand in front of a closed green door.

A forbidding white sign with black letters was glued to the
door.

NO ADMITTANCE
Family Only
One Member At A Time
This Rule Is Enforced In The Patient's Best Interest

Underneath these words the visiting hours were posted. Nissim decided he would just walk in, just push the door open and enter. He had waited long enough already. Barukh was in there and he was going to him. But instead of rushing in, he hesitated. "In The Patient's Best Interest." Maybe, he thought, if he walked in unannounced like this, the shock and the surprise would be too much for his father. Maybe the excitement, the emotion would injure Barukh and set him back. But I'm here, Nissim thought, and no choice seems right through a closed door. Minute to minute. I'm going in.

Across the hall a door to a patient's room opened and a nurse came quietly out, writing something down on the clipboard in her hand. She saw Nissim reaching for the I.C.U. door and moved quickly toward him. "Wait!" she called in a hissing whisper.

Nissim froze, stepping back and staring at her as she neared. She was short and heavy, looked to be about the same age as his mother, and the black-gray hair that framed her face like a headscarf also reminded him of Miryam. He noticed her stern expression and watched her eyes grow suspicious as she looked at the luggage which he had left beside the door. Another wall, he thought. Another delay.

"Who let you in here?" she asked officiously, approaching him, the clipboard tucked under her arm.

"My father is in there," he told her, pointing to the green door.

"Your father?" she said, her tone softening. Family were given special consideration. She smiled at Nissim and took a relaxed breath. "You look like you've come a long way," she said.

"I just got in from New York."

"New York," she repeated, nodding as she said the name. She could see the travel weariness and the pain in this young man's eyes. "I see. Well, you came far enough not to have to wait until morning. When did they call you?"

"Yesterday."

"Let me just check to see if your father is still in the I.C.U. What is his name?"

"Lvov, Barukh." Nissim waited anxiously as the nurse lifted the clipboard and leafed through some pages to find the list of patients. A sudden frenzy overtook him, a frenzy of not knowing, a frantic fear about family, about losing his own flesh and blood. He was afraid that his father was not in this room, that Barukh wasn't here any more. He was afraid that he had returned too late, that Barukh was already dead.

"Lvov," she whispered, lifting her eyes when she found the name. "Yes, he's here. And sir, they've told you?"

"Told me?" he asked. "About the second stroke, you mean?"

"Yes . . . the second stroke."

"Yes," he said, "they told me."

Nodding, she pushed the green door open and motioned Nissim forward. "Third bed on the right. Take as long as you need."

Nissim thanked her and straightened his shirt collar as he moved hesitantly into the Intensive Care Unit. A doctor who looked to be Yosef's age was sitting at a desk in the corner of the windowless room. He lifted his head distractedly to see Nissim enter, then returned to reviewing the medical files on his desk. In front of Nissim were flasks and machines, high-tech monitors and blipping scopes. For a moment it reminded him of his robotics research and of his feelings during the war. Everything looked mechanized, impressive, technologically consummate – everything but the patients who lay lifeless in high white metal beds, looking mortal and incidental. The accouterments of medicine were cloth or metal, plastic or glass. Tubing, pumps, inverted bottles. It seemed an inorganic jungle and there was something inhuman about it. Nissim's first thought was to carry his father out of this place, to carry him home up the mountain.

Nissim walked to the third bed on the right and stopped behind the metal bars at the foot of the bed, pausing a moment to study

323

the man who lay there. "Abba?" he whispered, seeing his father was sleeping but not wanting to wake any of the other patients. "Abba?"

Barukh did not move. He lay on his back, his mouth distortedly open, his arms resting limply across his stomach, a piece of tape covering the long needle in his left arm on the inside of his elbow. A clear plastic tube rose from the taped needle up to the bottle of glucose water hanging upside down from the stand beside his bed. His left arm was discolored an angry purple above and below the strip of white tape. Two large white pillows rested under his balding head, and the pillows made his head seem small, smaller than Nissim remembered. In fact, there was much about Barukh that looked different than Nissim remembered. Without his black beret, the bald spot on top of his head seemed larger. And Barukh's hair had whitened, making him look years beyond his age.

Half a year, Nissim thought as he moved around the side of the bed and leaned down beside his father. I was only gone half a year. "Abba, I'm here," he said into his father's ear. "It's Nissim. I'm home."

Barukh lay still, breathing audibly through his mouth, not acknowledging Nissim's presence. His eyes twitched beneath their lids as though he were dreaming.

"Can you hear me, Abba?" Nissim said louder, causing the doctor to lift his head once again. He placed his hand into Barukh's right palm and closed his father's fingers around it, hoping that touching him might gently wake him, but Barukh's body did not stir. "Abba, you sleep. I'm here now, Abba." Tears began rising into Nissim's eyes, but he stopped himself; he did not want to cry here, he did not want to have his father wake up to find his son sobbing at his bedside. Gently he slipped his hand from his father's limp grip. He was straightening up to turn and leave when he saw the young doctor standing beside him.

"Excuse me," said the doctor, fixing his glasses as he spoke, "this is your father?"

"Yes."

"And you are trying to wake him?"

"I'm sorry, I know I shouldn't disturb his sleep," Nissim said softly. "I've been away and I just want him to know I'm here. I was just going back outside."

"Yes," said the doctor, pausing a second and regarding Nissim seriously. "Mr. Lvov, I'm afraid you can't wake your father now. He's in a coma."

"A coma?"

The doctor adjusted his glasses and nodded. "As of this morning," he said, looking down.

This morning? The world can change in six months, Nissim thought. The world can change in a day. As the doctor walked back to his seat at the desk, Nissim knelt down again beside Barukh's bed. "Abba, I'm here. It's Nissim. I know you can hear me." He leaned over and lifted his father's right hand, bringing it close and pressing his bearded cheek against it. This was the hand which had trained him, the hand which had rested on top of his own, guiding his small fingers in the assembly of a bicycle, in the fixing of a tube radio, in the soldering of a toaster. This was the strongest hand he knew, the warmest hand he'd ever held, that had ever held him. "Abba, I'm back. It's Nissim." He felt the loose skin and the lifeless grip that made Barukh's hand seem boneless, and he moved the limp hand across his own face, tracing the contours of his bearded chin, his mouth, his nose, his eyes. "I flew back tonight," he whispered. "When you wake up, I'll be here." He pressed his face into his father's hand. His tears trickled down through the fingers.

Nissim rose slowly, laid his father's hand across his stomach, and wiping his own eyes, left the room. Outside the door he picked up his suitcase and duffel bag and carried them across the hall into the waiting room, where he hoisted them onto one of the benches. Standing in the small empty room he stared up at the lonely bulb in the ceiling and at the shadows which its dim light cast on the drab walls. Alone in this room he was alone with his thoughts, and he listened to them echo inside his head, flowing into one another, talking back to one another. Where was Miryam? Where was Shoshanah? Where was Yossi? The scene from last night replayed in his mind:

At Kennedy Airport a full moon, stars, and highway lights glowed brightly in the darkness. Yosef followed the color-coded signs to the El Al departures terminal. "How long do you plan to stay?" he asked.

"As long as it takes," Nissim told him.

At the curb in front of the El Al check-in, they got out of the Checker, unloaded Nissim's bags from the trunk, and stood facing each other.

"Safe trip," Yosef said. "And listen, when you see Rivka and Dorit, tell them . . . ." He stopped and looked down at the pavement. "Tell them I'm working on coming."

Nissim nodded silently, wondering if it would take a funeral to bring his brother home. Yosef gave him a sudden embrace, gripping his shoulders and pulling him to him.

"Safe trip, tell them," Yosef said again as Nissim rushed into the terminal.

Last night, this morning, then, now, here, there. Time was a blur, a dark blur like the landscape on the road from Ben-Gurion, a blind concept, a meaningless measure. Minute to minute, six months, a day. All Nissim knew now was that he was late, too late to see his father conscious, too late. Guilt like a ghost stood in front of him, clouding his vision as did his tears, clouding his vision and his mind. On the wall near the doorway was a public phone. Nissim stared at it and thought of his mother. She was waiting for him to come home, he told himself. She would cry to hear his voice, she would answer him when he spoke to her, she would wake up. He checked his watch and saw that it was already one in the morning. She would be sleeping, she needed her rest. Tomorrow would be another hard day. He decided not to phone now. Instead he lay down on the long plastic bench, folded his down army jacket into a pillow, and stretched out, waiting for morning.

"NISSIM?"

Slowly he opened his eyes, feeling the soft touch of a hand on his shoulder and the stiff boards underneath him. "Ema?"

"I was waiting for you all night at home. I was worried sick." Miryam looked lovingly at her son, convincing herself he was really here, just waiting for him to sit up to hug him. "You came alone? Where's Yossi?"

Nissim sat up and embraced his mother. "He's working on coming, Ema," he said softly.

Sixteen

"NISSIM," SHOSHANAH SAID, "you've been in those clothes for two days already, you haven't had a chance to wash the trip off you yet. Why don't you and Miryam go home, unpack, get cleaned up, have a meal, then come back. I'll stay here and look in on Barukh."

Nissim knew that Shoshanah was right. His hair was matted from sleeping on his jacket, his shirt and his jeans were badly wrinkled, and his face was drawn from travel and worry. There was little he or Miryam could do now to help Barukh, whether they were across the hall from him or at home just up the mountain. The distance made no difference now. It only made a difference to *them*. Earlier this morning Shoshanah had explained to him the medical meaning of Barukh's condition, describing to him what had happened to his father during the past two days. Barukh had first suffered what was called a transient ischemic attack, a brief episode of numbness, tingling of his arm and leg, slurring of his speech, and disturbances in his vision. The obstruction of blood flow had been due to a clot in a diseased artery. Then, less than a day later, the carotid artery in the neck had become so blocked that closure had occurred, causing a massive second stroke. Barukh was not "brain dead" but the damage to his brain from the second stroke was so extensive that he could never regain the faculties of speech or memory. Just yesterday she had been working with him, helping him move his affected arm and leg. He had been awake and aware, depressed but cooperative. She could still see the frightened light in his eyes

328

that showed he knew that things were not stable, that something was about to explode, to rupture like a hot water heater. For two hours she had talked to him, trying to interpret his garbled attempts at speech, giving him a small chalkboard so that he could write his words. But he had scrawled unintelligible letters. Tears of frustration oozed down his cheeks like honey over stone.

"Ema, she's right," Nissim said. "We ought to go home, I'll unpack, shower, and then we'll come right back." Gently he helped Miryam to her feet and smiled softly at her. "It's a good idea, we'll go in a second. I just want to see him once more."

Miryam did not protest. The past two days had weakened and aged her. Her skin was pale, ghostly. She looked haggard, disheveled, her hair in disarray, her life in disarray. Her eyes were red and swollen; the purple bags under them looked like pockets of internal bleeding. She moved with obvious effort and pain, her shoulders hunched forward from the weight of her grief. It was as though her soul were lying in that other room and only her body was with her. She wiped her eyes with a handkerchief as Nissim stood up and disappeared through the doorway. Shoshanah walked over to Miryam and sat down beside her, taking her hand.

Across the hall Nissim opened the heavy green door and walked into the Intensive Care Unit. Barukh lay unmoving, a balding frail form in a white bed. Tubes ran in and out of him everywhere, and the long clear cord that ran from the plug inside his ear to the transistor radio on the table beside his bed looked like just another section of tubing. Music. Shoshanah's idea. She had read that doctors in California were treating comatose patients with classical music which they claimed helped stimulate the brain and keep the flow of blood constant.

Nissim stood next to his father a moment, studying him. Such a proud man, so vibrant, so virile, he thought, and yet here in this bed he looked like someone else.

Maybe music could help bring him back. Maybe music could

save him. Leaning over, he removed the earphone from his father's ear and put it into his own for a moment to listen to the music his father was hearing. Through the cord came only static, sounds of live wires touching. No music. Nissim looked at his father's still form and tears again filled his eyes. Of course, nothing could come in here clearly, he told himself, not with all this electrical equipment, not with all this machinery. He shook his head and wiped the beads of sweat from his father's brow. Then he turned off the radio and put the earphone back into Barukh's ear. "Abba," he said softly, "sleep in peace."

He walked back to the waiting room where Shoshanah and Miryam sat talking. He walked to the end of the bench, picked up his suitcase and duffel bag, and stood in front of them. He looked at Shoshanah in her white uniform as she nodded at him and his head filled with thoughts of her. I've known this woman all my life. She's beautiful, sensitive, caring. She loves my father like her father. She's family. We know things about each other that no one else knows.

Why had he written to the University of Pennsylvania requesting an application for admission? Why had he decided to leave *Tzahal* for a while, to go away for his studies? Why had he decided against the Technion in favor of Penn, decided against Israel in favor of America, decided against the familiar in favor of the unknown? It was because of her, because of last Passover. It had been a warm clear night in April, just after the Passover seder, and Nissim, home on holiday leave, had come over to her apartment when his family's long meal and celebration had ended. She herself had just come back from her own family's seder, attended that year by the Farkoshes. No one's mind was on the exodus from Egypt. All anyone thought of was the absence of Avi. She had left as early as she could.

When Nissim had knocked, she had almost been asleep on her sofa. They sat together and talked about grade school and high school, about *Tzahal* and the hospital, about Avi and the war, about family in America. Suddenly Shoshanah laid down across the sofa and put her head in his lap. He had been surprised, utterly surprised to feel her on him. "Stay with me tonight," she had said. "I need you." With that, she had leaned forward, pressing her body against his, pressing her open lips against his and kissing him passionately with her tongue. He was afraid, not of Shoshanah as a woman but of Shoshanah as Avi's fiancee. He felt her soft hair on his face, her gentle hands around his neck. The Eilat stone pendant brushed against his shirt, the same pendant he had picked out with Avi to give her for their engagement. She wants Avi, not me, he felt. His hands had pulled back, his body had frozen. He had left her that night without explaining and the next day had made his decision to leave.

Now looking at her he wondered what he had run away from. I love this woman. She's perfect for me. How many women do I need to make love with to know who I really love? I should ask her to marry me. But can I ask her now, with my father dying? It would be too much. Maybe I should wait . . . wait for what? I'll ask her. Will you marry me, Shosh? Avi is dead, my father's dying, but we're alive, I'm back, you're here. Will you marry me? I'll ask her now. I'll ask her when we come back.

Shoshanah stood up and Miryam rose slowly with her. He put his arm around his mother and the two of them started into the hallway with Shoshanah walking beside them.

"Don't worry," Shoshanah said softly, "I'll stay here and mind the store."

WAITING FOR MIRYAM to finish in the bathroom so he could shower, Nissim walked through the small apartment, stopping for a moment in the narrow kitchen. Through the two vertical panes in the white door to the laundry porch Nissim gazed out at the dreary day. Driving rains pelted the bushes and brown overgrowth in the wadi below. The cold winds and the dampness penetrated even into the kitchen. He felt raw and exposed as he stood there, naked but for his towel. This was so different from Yosef's house, so different from America, but this was a different world.

A box radio sat on the little shelf which Barukh had built above the row of spice jars at one end of the kitchen counter. Nissim looked at the radio and thought of his father, of the transistor at his bedside and the static in his ear. As soon as he got back to the hospital, he thought, he would go straight to the medical library and read everything he could find there about stroke. He would check every book, every journal, every clipping for some obscure treatment, some unrespected school of thought that might give hope for Barukh's chances of recovery. Barukh had never given up. He wasn't even giving up now, even though the doctors had said his body had outlived his brain. Barukh had taught Nissim that nothing was beyond fixing. Not even my father, Nissim thought.

A gust of cold air slipped under the laundry porch door, causing Nissim to shiver. He turned on the radio. The dial was set to *Galei Tzahal,* the army station. Nissim listened to a haunting song by Naomi Shemer and wondered what Yosef was doing. It was strange and good to be home. Just then four beeps signalling a news bulletin interrupted the singing.

> This is Israel Radio from Jerusalem. Three terrorists attacked an apartment building in Nahariya just before dawn this morning and took two families hostage. *Tzahal* forces moved to the scene, and just minutes ago a special unit of our forces stormed the building and killed the terrorists. Two *Tzahal* soldiers have been wounded in the rescue action. One hostage, a seventeen-year-old boy, is dead. In

Beirut, the PLO has claimed credit for this terrorist
act. This has been a special report.

As the music resumed, Nissim reached up and turned off the
radio. He felt hot blood rush into his head and circle around his
ears. When will it stop? he wondered. Abba would have sent me
a clipping about this in next week's mail.

Miryam was opening the door as he walked from the kitchen
to the short, dark hallway outside the bathroom. "The heater's on,"
she said, letting him squeeze past her. "I wanted to warm it up
for you. And there's plenty of hot water." She had turned on the
hot water heater last night for her son and the red light above the
boiler switch was still lit. The electric coil heater on the wall inside the bathroom was set on "high" and the coils were glowing
red hot now.

"Thanks, Ema," he said. He would not tell her about the terrorists in Nahariya. She had enough worries. "I'll shower and be
right out."

"Take your time," she said, standing there and talking to him
as he went inside, "but close the door before all the heat leaks out."

Nissim nodded and pulled the door closed until it clicked shut.
Wasting no time, he turned on the water and stepped into the
shower. Two minutes later he stepped out into the small steamed-
up room. Standing in front of the fogged mirror above the sink,
he dried himself with his bath towel.

Quickly the heat escaped from the room, the steam dissipated,
and the mirror cleared. Nissim wrapped the towel around his waist
and looked at himself in the mirror. Water dripped from his hair
and beard, falling in silent beads into the white basin. He felt clean
again, renewed to have washed off the long plane flight and the
taxi ride and the night in the hospital. He stood at the mirror and
looked at himself but he was thinking too hard to see. He stared
at his beard and thought of his brother. Where's Yossi? I see my

beard and I think of him, I think of him and of Avi, of both of them and the war. Where are you, Avi? Where were you, Yossi? He pictured Yosef's cab, the flag decals on the bumper, Israel on one side, America on the other, and the back of Yosef's head seen through the Checker's rear window. Avi was driving their Patton down Broad Street and Nissim stood exposed in the turret as they rolled in procession behind Yosef's Checker, rolling toward City Hall. One side of the street was Philadelphia; the other side was Haifa, the Sinai, Jerusalem's Old City. When's Yossi coming? Suddenly the tank disappeared, he and Avi vanished, and the yellow cab drove on. Did you hear about Nahariya, Yossi? Did you hear about Abba's coma? Rivka and Dorit are waiting.

Nissim thought back over the past six months and saw himself in America, in his brother's house, sitting at his computer, working with Professor Clarendon, watching the 76ers play at The Spectrum. For him America had been a chance to start over, to build his own history in a place where no one knew him, where no one knew his family. It had been a clean slate. No one but Yosef and Rivka had known what titles he held, what ranks he had achieved, what battles he had survived.

America had been good for him, he thought. In every way America had been more than he had hoped it would be. At first it had excited him, enticed him, titillated his senses, but soon the stimulation had been too much. Too many great shows, too many stars, too many grand openings, too many stores, too many movies, too many malls, too many channels, too many choices, too much freedom, too few rules, too much graffiti, too many murders, too much talking, too little caring, too many people, too few friends. Nissim could see how just the visual allure of life there could seduce people, how America, like the undertow of a warm sea, could suck them in, draw them in as it had drawn in Oded, and Yosef, and as it might have drawn him in. He pictured the deep green lawns and thick green trees, the wide smooth

roads and big sleek cars, the huge heated malls with the sprawling stores and acres of parking spaces. It was impressive. It was
beautiful. He saw himself in his Chevy, the car which he had
bought from Denise, saw himself in Denise's apartment, in
Denise's arms, in Denise's bed. Denise. She was too attractive,
too easy. Everything was too good, too fast. Nothing is as simple as it looks, nothing is as innocent, as open as it appears. The
more innocent it seems, the more dangerous it is. Yossi, if you're
not in jail, get on a plane before it's too late. Get on a plane and
come home. You're no *yorade*. Come home.

Yorade. Nissim heard himself think the word and noticed he
had thought it with a different inflection than he had six months
ago. *Yordim,* a national tragedy that he had begun to understand.
Yossi has a "thing" for America and so do I, so does every Israeli,
so does everyone else in the world. We played cowboys and Indians on the Carmel as children. Cowboys and Indians in Israel?
From where did we get the idea? From the movies is where we
got it, from the American movies. From *High Noon* and *Gun-
fight at the O.K. Corral* and *Shane* and *Butch Cassidy and the
Sundance Kid.* The American message was the message everyone
loved. No one could watch those movies without longing for wide
open spaces, for a horse ride into the sunset.

In Nissim's mind the cowboys became police detectives. Gary
Cooper became Steve McGarret, Shane became Kojak, the wild
west became Hawaii, the frontier was Manhattan. But the message
was still the same: you can do it, you can control your life, your
destiny, you can make a difference, you can live your dreams.
America was everywhere and all-pervasive. American movies,
American television, American music, American clothes. You
didn't have to leave Israel to find America. It was all around you,
on you, flooding your consciousness, shaping your perceptions,
your desires, your dreams. The world had become one country,
one culture, and all of it was America.

Nissim pictured his brother pulling into the two-car garage and walking into the big empty house. He could hear the echoes, the hollow sounds of being alone as Yosef walked through the creaking side door. Yosef's world had crumbled around him and Nissim had been there to witness it. He thought back to the fight at the *Y*. If America had given him anything it was insight into his brother's life. I'm sorry I broke your toe, Yossi. I'm sorry I punched you, Yossi. I'm sorry I added to your pain, I'm sorry my coming reopened old wounds.

America had not changed Yosef really; it simply had given him the chance to become more the way he was.

Yosef was a sad study, a complex study. It had taken six months in America for Nissim to comprehend his brother's way of looking at life and the world. Yosef's dilemma, the deterioration of his situation, the splitting apart of his family—these had preceded Nissim's arrival in Philadelphia, Nissim knew. It had started years ago during their childhood, possibly even before Avram's death, and any chance Yosef may have had of avoiding self-defeat had been wiped away by the Yom Kippur War. The war had started two years ago, but its real effects were only now being realized. The war had not ended. It was still going on, still leaving casualties in its wake, and Yosef Lvov was one of them. He was another missing soldier, lost but alive in America. Every new *yorade* was another casualty from that war.

It wasn't your fault, Yossi. Life doesn't work out according to plans. It doesn't unfold into neat squares. Not here, not anywhere. America taught me that. Just half a year there taught me that. You tried to come back for the war. You tried but things didn't turn out the way you had wanted, the way you had expected. I understand that now. You tried to be a good father, a good husband, a good citizen. No one's condemning you for not having been there. No one's blaming you. Stop the punishing, Yossi. Stop the running away from your country, from your family, from

336

yourself. You didn't make the war happen, you didn't keep the Consulate from calling, you didn't put your friends in their graves. It wasn't your fault, but living with it is your responsibility. Getting beyond it is your responsibility.

I feel just as much guilt as you do; it's just that it's of a different kind. I look back at the war just like you do and I wish I could turn back the clock and change it, wish I could change the nightmares in my mind. But I can't, you can't. We both survived, we're both alive. The war wasn't your fault, it wasn't mine, but it's all our responsibility. And it's still going on. Maybe you can't see that in Philadelphia. I know. I was there. Things look different in American mirrors. What are you doing? Barukh is dying. Your family needs you. Be a good son, a good father, a real soldier. Come home.

Nissim looked in the mirror again. His heart was pounding inside his chest and his head was throbbing. Fault and responsibility, guilt and duty. Shosh understands those things. Shosh understands me. She knows me. She and I are perfect for each other. Even the work we chose is similar. Hospitals and armies are virtually identical. Working at Rambam is no different from working in *Tzahal*. Soldiers and doctors are in the same business—survival. That's why so much army R & D turns up as new hospital equipment and new medical technologies.

I'm here now and I don't see going back. It shouldn't be too complicated to let Penn know my change of plans. They'll understand. An illness in the family, I was called back home, my family needed me, I regret I won't be returning. They'll let me write papers instead of taking final exams. I'll be able to finish this term by mail. Yossi can pack up and ship me my things. He can sell my Chevy and send me the money. I'll transfer to the Technion, stay right here in Haifa, live with my mother. She'll need me near her for a while. So what if I have to wait until next fall to transfer? So what if I lose a semester? At least I can look after Miryam, at least I can be with Shosh. It had been a strange mix of emotions, of pleasure and of grieving, seeing each other the way we did—me just home from America, home too soon and too late, come home a visitor for the first time, a visitor to both my country and my father. It had been Shosh who had cried in comforting *me, she* who had been overcome by emotion to see me again, to hold me and be held. I'll ask her as soon as we get back. She'll need some time. And I want Abba to know about it, even if he can't understand, even if he can't hear me.

Miryam walked back into the dim hallway outside the bathroom and stood staring at the closed door. It was a comfort just to know that Nissim was behind it. "Nissim," she called through the door.

"Yes?"

"Are you out? What's taking so long?"

"Everything's fine."

"It's warm enough in there?"

"Yes, it's fine. It's perfect."

"Nissim?"

"What, Ema?"

"I'm glad you're home," she said, brushing her hand absently with her fingers. "Thank heavens for you. And thank heavens for Shoshanah. She's been really wonderful to me. She's a special, wonderful girl."

"I know, Ema," he said, "I know."

"Ronni's a very lucky man."

"Ronni?"

"Didn't she tell you?"

"Tell me what?"

"They're planning to get married. They're talking about a summer wedding."

Stunned and confused, he opened the door and poked his head out. "Planning to get married?" he said to his mother. "No, she

338

didn't tell me."

"Of course not," Miryam said softly, seeing her son's distress. "There wasn't time. It wasn't the right time at the hospital, not in the waiting room. But she will. She's very excited about it."

"Why didn't you tell me? You never wrote me a word about it. How long has it been going on? Months?"

"I'm sure I wrote you about it," Miryam said, not at all convinced she had. "I'm sure I mentioned it in one of my letters."

"You didn't, Ema. Not a word. If you had, I'd remember, believe me."

"Nissim," Miryam said quickly, a mother's concern on her face, "I'm sorry if I didn't tell you before this. Shosh started dating Ronni just after you left. I only found out about the wedding plans myself a few weeks ago." Miryam knew her son too well, and she could hear in his tone what was on his mind. But she also knew how difficult it had been for Shoshanah to decide to become engaged again, to decide to become engaged to *anyone* after Avi. She didn't want to see Nissim make the decision more difficult than it already was for her, to weaken her resolve to move beyond mourning. And she didn't want to see Nissim get hurt.

"Forget it, Ema. It's no problem, really," Nissim told her. "I didn't mean to jump at you. I'll be out in a few minutes."

Closing the door, Nissim moved back to the sink and stared at the bearded face staring back at him in the mirror. The face in the mirror looked like Yosef. It looked like Avi. Nissim reached into the pocket of his shirt hanging on the metal hook on the back of the door. He took out the matchbook and, lighting a match with one hand, held it up in front of his face. Solemnly, he lifted his other hand and held one finger directly above the flame. Avi, I haven't missed a day, I haven't run away from the pain. His finger touched the tip of the flame and he looked at the pain on the face in the mirror. This is the last time, he thought. I can't do it any more, Avi. His finger pulled back, his face stopped shaking. He blew the match out quickly and held it a moment. Scenes from the war flashed behind his eyes. The Patton was burning, his hair was on fire. The vision shrank to a candle flame.

Nissim picked up a pair of scissors and watched in the mirror as he lifted them to his chin. Who's Ronni? How long has she known him? He closed the scissors and watched a clump of curled brown hair fall into the white sink. She's gone beyond Avi. It's time. So should I. The scissors opened and closed again as more beard fell into the sink. This beard is his, not mine; him, not me. From that day in the Sinai two years ago when Nissim had started growing this beard as a tribute to Avi, he had worn it as a symbol of the friendship that had bound them together. Each time he looked at it he remembered two images—the bright days on Carmel Beach, diving headlong into the tallest waves, and Armageddon in the Sinai with Avi's head in flames. The beard had become a symbol of grieving to him, and shaving it had seemed tantamount to erasing Avi's memory. Even the thought of removing it triggered tremendous guilt. Shoshanah wants to get married, Avi!

The white basin was littered with curled hairs, and a sprinkling of clipped ends covered the sink's rim on all sides. Avi's not dead *because* I'm alive. If I had died, he wouldn't have lived. It's no different than Ema and Abba felt after surviving their families. Not everything is within our control. It wouldn't have kept him from burning. I'm not guilty for being alive, I'm responsible for living.

He snipped his beard till the drain became clogged. Patches of skin on his chin and his cheeks were visible now. It's time to stop confusing the way you died, Avi, and the way you lived. I need to go back to before the war, to see you and me as we were all those years, to remember both of us from before. I need to keep us separate. You don't have to live through me to be alive. I don't have to be you to remember you.

He set the scissors down on the back of the sink and reached into the medicine cabinet, taking out the shaver which Shoshanah had given him. It was where he had left it before leaving for America. "I like you clean shaven," she had said.

It had been different for him in America. He had been surer about who he wasn't than who he was. He was not a soldier there, not a citizen, not at home. Being faceless there for a time had been good. But now he was back, he was himself, he was home. He turned on the electric razor and began shaving the sides of his face.

Shosh likes me better clean shaven. I'll ask her to marry me as soon as I get there. She didn't tell me yet. It's not too late to ask her. She knows we ought to be together, that we shouldn't be apart again. She knows I wanted her that night, that she's the reason I went to the States. Why should I give her up in silence? She can't know this Ronni long. When she sees me it will take her back. She knows. She understands.

With one last series of buzzing strokes he ran the razor across his cheeks, around his chin, and under his neck until the last traces of stubble were gone. All that remained was a brown moustache.

He turned on the faucet, cupped his hands underneath it, and splashed cold water all over his face. The water cooled and burned him. I can't wait to see Shoshanah's face, I can't wait to see her surprise at having me back. He looked in the mirror and smiled dryly at himself. It was like turning the clock back two years, turning it back to set it forward, going back to reclaim himself. Time by itself doesn't heal anything. Time by itself only dulls things. Time only covers them over, like my beard did, only buries them. Time by itself doesn't *do* anything. Time is all *undoings*. Avi taught me that. Yossi taught me that. Abba taught me that.

Nissim splashed more cold water on his face. Hundreds of short brown hairs covered the white basin. Shoshanah's razor lay next to the scissors on the back of the sink. Abba, I'm back. It's me. I'm here. Turning on the faucet, he swept the dark hairs from the rim and sides of the sink and watched them disappear down the drain.

Seventeen

MIRYAM LEANED HER UMBRELLA against the waiting room wall. Two young soldiers with Uzis slung over their shoulders stood talking to each other in one corner of the room. Miryam glanced at them as she took off her wet raincoat and laid it across an empty part of the plastic bench. Nissim too glanced at the soldiers a second, thinking how long he had been away, how long it had been since he'd been in uniform, then he moved out into the hallway and stood next to the pay phone.

"Go on, Ema," he said, putting a hand on his mother's arm, "you go in first. I want to make a call. Go on."

Miryam nodded. Seeing him clean shaven was like having him back twice over, she thought. It was her Nissim, the one she hadn't seen for two years. He had come home and he had come back. She headed across the hallway and disappeared through the green door of the Intensive Care Unit. Nissim lifted the receiver and dialed.

"Hello?" the voice on the other end answered.

"Rivka, it's Nissim. How are you?"

"Nissim? Where are you?"

"At Rambam. I promised Yossi I'd call."

"When did you get back? How's your father?"

"Yesterday. There hasn't been any change."

"Yesterday? I was there yesterday till dinner time. I must have just missed you."

"No, I got here late," he said. Too late, he thought.

"At least you're here. Is Yossi coming?"

"I know he wants to be here," he told her after a momentary pause. "He's working on it, Rivka."

"Then he knows about the coma? He didn't call here last night. Did he call you?"

"No, I haven't spoken to him since he drove me to Kennedy Airport," he said. "He misses you, Rivka."

"How was he when you left, Nissim?"

"Upset. He's killing himself to get back. He wants to be here. He'll be here. How's Dorit?"

"She wants to be with Barukh—and she wants her father with her."

As Nissim listened to Rivka he saw the green door swing open and Miryam come toward him. Her face was drained of color. Her mouth was open but there was no sound. "Rivka," Nissim said urgently into the phone, "something's wrong, I'll get back to you, I have to go."

"Nissim? Nissim?" Rivka called, but he had hung up the receiver and moved toward his mother.

"Ema, what is it?" he asked as she came into his arms. "What happened?"

Miryam stared at him with horror. Silent tears were running down her cheeks. "He's not there," she said.

"What are you talking about, Ema? Where is he?"

"I don't know."

Nissim wanted to rush into the unit and grab a doctor by his hospital suit. He wanted to pick him up with one hand and hold him there as the doctor explained what had happened, explained where his father was. But he didn't want to leave Miryam alone. "Where's Shoshanah?" he asked. "Did you see her in there?"

Miryam shook her head, her eyes still wide and white with dread. He pulled her close and held her as the quaking tears poured forth.

"Ema," he said gently after a moment, "we've got to find Abba.

I'll get our things. Wait here." Quickly he went into the waiting room and picked up their coats and his mother's umbrella. Seeing a young doctor, he called out to him, "My father—Barukh Lvov—he isn't in the Intensive Care Unit. Where is he? What happened to him?"

The doctor walked over to Nissim. "Some patients had to be moved to the fourth floor to make room for two soldiers wounded in the rescue this morning. Perhaps your father's there."

Nissim nodded and noticed the soldiers in the corner, talking. He walked over to them and asked if they knew anything about the wounded soldiers being treated at Rambam. Yes, they told him. They had brought them in themselves this morning, by helicopter, from Nahariya. Nissim remembered the news bulletin about the terrorist attack. A soldier in exchange for my father, he thought.

Coming out of the windowless room, he took Miryam's arm and they hurried down the hallway to the elevators. A car came quickly and, rushing in, they rode up to the fourth floor. Nissim led his mother through the long corridor, checking every room for Barukh, opening each door, wondering who else had been displaced and how many other fathers were dying.

The next room was Barukh's. Miryam and Nissim paused in the hallway, acknowledged the fear in each other's eyes, and walked in. There were two beds in the room, but the one near the door was empty. A lone wooden chair sat next to the wall across from the foot of each bed. Barukh lay in the bed near the window, his face turned away from the hallway. Nissim spread their coats across the seat of one chair as Miryam moved around the bed and stood between Barukh and the window. She bent down and stroked his brow as a mother would touch a sick child. He felt chilly; his skin was cold.

"It's cold in here," Nissim said, feeling the cold metal bars of the bed. Nissim's eye moved to the window behind Miryam. It was open. "Stupid idiots!" he shouted, looking out at the rainstorm.

Miryam turned to him with a start. She said nothing as she watched him stride to the window and close it.

"Can you believe it?" he said a little more softly. "They left it open, the idiots! He could catch pneumonia." He stood at the window a second, gazing out, trying to control his anger, trying to figure out who to blame.

"You'd think they'd have more sense," Miryam said. She leaned over and stroked Barukh's forehead.

Nissim turned away from the rainstorm and looked at his father. There was no radio by Barukh's bed, no cord or earphone in his ear. There was no arsenal of high-tech monitors as there had been in the Intensive Care Unit. And there was no waiting room. All that remained, all that had been transported with Barukh was the IV stand with the glass bottle hanging upside down on it. The patch of tape still covered the needle that entered his arm just below the inside of his elbow. Under the tube that rose to the bottle he could see the tattoo from Treblinka.

"Ema," he said, watching her comfort Barukh, "Ema, I'm going to find Shosh. I want to know what's going on. I have to ask her something."

Miryam lifted her eyes without standing up and nodded at her son as he walked out into the hallway. "Barukh," she said softly, "Barukh, just rest, we're here. I know you can hear me." Back and forth she moved her hand as she looked at her husband, so frail, so peaceful. After a minute she closed her eyes, and the white sheet on the bed became a linen cloth on a Sabbath table. A lavender canopy gently descended over Mount Carmel and apartment windows lit the mountain like candles. Barukh was standing in front of her, chanting the Kiddush prayer, his goblet in his raised hand, his voice full with song. Soup simmered on the kitchen stove. Chicken baked in the oven. She smoothed her apron across her lap and straightened the white cotton scarf on her head.

How many times she had studied Barukh's face above the candle flames, had listened to his melodic chant, had stared at the black beret on his head. She remembered when it had covered dark curls instead of a balding head. Twenty-seven years, she thought to herself, almost three decades together. There were patches of gray above Barukh's ears and a gray moustache above his lip. He looked fit as a soldier. Miryam was fifty-five years old, two years older than he, and in his image she saw herself. She felt the deep half-circles under her eyes and the deep grooves across her forehead. Barukh is my looking glass; Barukh, my Shabbat. Twenty-seven years on HaTishbi Street, twenty-seven years of Sabbaths around this table, twenty-seven years of kindled lights, of kindled dreams. Before reaching Palestine, if she had spoken of having even one such Sabbath, her friends would have called her mad. I have known more joy than is possible, she told herself, looking at Barukh across the white table. Her eye moved around the table and a proud, loving smile spread across her face. Nissim and Yossi, Rivka and precious Dorit were there, looking above the candles at Barukh. Everyone had come home, everyone had come back for this Sabbath.

Her hand was still stroking Barukh's brow as she looked at him lying there, so still, so unmoving. With a wistful sigh, she straightened up and walked over to the window. Through the pane she watched the cold rain pour out of an overcast sky. She stood there, gazing out at the storm, waiting to start crying. She stood there a long time, thinking, and then turned around to look at Barukh. "Barukh, what do you want me to do?" she asked aloud. "Please help me." The December winds gusted fitfully, changing the angle of the rain's descent so that some drops pelted the window. She turned back to the window and reached out to open it. A cold, wet wind blew across her fingers. It whipped through the room, rippling the section of untucked sheet at the foot of Barukh's bed. There was no greater injustice, she thought, than for a proud man to outlive his dignity.

Stepping back from the open window, she sat down in the chair near Barukh's bed. In all their years together it had never occurred to her that Barukh would suffer a lingering illness, that he would suffer the torture of something killing but not fatal, something permanent but not final. Wars, death camps, terrorists. That was how people died, she thought. In her experience it had always been black and white, perish or survive. Yet here she was, here Barukh was, his brain mostly obliterated, a fractional man with a fractional mind. A virus would be a blessing, she thought.

The bareness of Barukh's head upset her. She didn't want to see him this way, she didn't want to remember him like this. She lifted her handbag from the floor, stood up from the chair, and took out the beret she had kept there since the first stroke. Moving to the bedside, she lifted Barukh's head and put it on him so that it covered his bald spot. Now he looked like the man she had married, the man she had spent the best years of her life with, the man with whom she had made a family. "Sleep, darling," she whispered as she straightened the beret. "I love you."

Stepping back slowly, she moved to the chair and sat down again. A cold wind gusted in through the window, blowing some graying hair onto her forehead.

Nissim did not notice the chill in the room as he entered. His mind was focused instead on Shoshanah and on what she had just told him. "I found her," he said, sounding short of breath as he walked toward Miryam. "She was called away for another patient about half an hour after we left; when the helicopter came in from Nahariya she didn't know. No one told her. They moved Abba up here just a few minutes before we got back." Nissim had not broached any proposals. It had not been the right time to talk of marriage. But he would ask her later today, as soon as he got the chance. "She said she'll be right up," he told his mother.

Miryam sat listening in her chair, looking wistfully at Nissim, a sad soft smile on her face. "What did she say when she saw you?" she asked.

"Nothing," Nissim said, moving to the side of Barukh's bed as he spoke, "she didn't say anything. She just stood there and smiled."

Miryam nodded and began rocking almost hypnotically back and forth in her chair. She continued rocking that way as Nissim leaned down beside Barukh and put his father's limp hand in his own.

"It's me — Nissim," he said softly, lifting his father's hand and touching his fingers to his smooth cheek. "I'm here and Yossi's coming . . . everyone's all right, everything will be fine . . . ." He turned his head to look at his mother as he held his father's insentient hand. His eyes lowered back to Barukh. "Abba," he said, "I've got news that'll make you smile. Shoshanah and I are getting married, and I wanted you to know, Abba . . . I wanted you to know." He lifted his eyes and turned slowly to look at Miryam again. "I've made up my mind to ask her today," he told her.

Miryam kept rocking, pursing her lips and nodding, but saying nothing. A cold wind blew into the room, displacing loose strands of her hair.

Nissim felt the damp draft on his neck. Instantly he looked to the window. "Who came in here while I was gone? Idiots! Goddamn idiots! What are they trying to do to him?" Angrily he strode to the window and reached out both hands to slam it closed.

"Nissim," Miryam said softly, "don't."

He turned around slowly, his hands still touching the window frame, and, horrified, stared at his mother. What was she saying? Barukh could catch pneumonia, he could die, he wasn't ready yet, he was still fighting, still holding on. He was a man who left nothing unfinished, no work, no project, no dream. He was still alive because he hadn't finished yet, as if anyone ever did, as if anyone ever could. Nissim gazed out through the rain-streaked

349

pane as cold, wet air blew across his knuckles. The Barukh we know is already gone, he thought. He can't come back to finish. The time is never right for dying.

Miryam stood up without words and walked over to the bed. Gently, she lifted the black beret and began stroking Barukh's brow.

Slowly, Nissim pulled his hands away from the window and stood there, staring distantly out. The winter downpour had not abated. He could feel the cold wind penetrate his shirt above his waist. He could feel the damp chill against his skin. Tears rose into his eyes as he looked out at nothing in particular, at the driving rain, thinking of his father, thinking of death, thinking of his Uncle Avram and of Avi, thinking of his family, thinking of the future they hadn't lived to see. Shoshanah would be up any time now. He stared out blankly through the glass, but instead of seeing beyond the pane, he caught sight of the hospital bed behind him. His father and mother looked so peaceful, so serene, reflected there in the glass.

Eighteen

THOUGH IT WAS ONLY NOON, the airline signs were turned on. Sleet poured down from a dark Philadelphia sky, glazing the pavement and the curb lanes at Philadelphia International Airport. Yosef Lvov sat in the back seat of the Checker, sleet flying toward him in a constant bombardment, attacking the glass, turning into raindrops as soon as it crashed against the pane. He watched the storm through the fogged window beside him. Was it raining in Haifa now? he wondered.

"You don't believe in Christmas, do you, Joe?" Jocko asked from behind the wheel. He was puffing on his cigar, his eyes shifting back and forth between the windshield and the rear-view mirror where he saw Yosef's face. "Y'know, myself I've always wanted to be in the Holy Land around this time of year. Take the grandkids to Bethlehem. They'd love it. But this year they'd rather be home because they're calling for three inches."

"It never snows in Bethlehem," Yosef said, half-listening to what Jocko was saying. The rear side window had become so fogged from the heated air and the smoke from Jocko's cigar that Yosef could hardly see through it. With the sleeve of his jacket he tried to wipe it clean, but he smeared the glass instead, and the images he saw through it were blurred. Red and blue lights on a jet's wings and tail blinked on and off as it ascended. They looked to him like the Christmas lights that had been strung across Center City since Thanksgiving.

"Yeah, Joe," Jocko went on, tapping some ashes from the tip of his cigar into the open ashtray under the radio, "remember last

351

year we didn't get our first real snowstorm till damn near the end of January?" But Yosef heard Jocko's talking as a voice with sound but no words. He was listening to his own thoughts as the yellow cab motored toward the Overseas Terminal.

It had been three days since Nissim's departure, since Yosef had driven his brother to New York to put him on the first flight home, and during these past three days there had not been a minute without urgency, not one minute when Yosef could pause without paying for the delay. It had been as though a meter had been ticking, charging him for every second, charging him for every move as he tried to speed his passage home.

From the moment two days ago when he had called Rivka and found out about Barukh's coma, he had worked even more furiously to try and put his American affairs in order. That same afternoon he had driven straight to Temple University and had met with the Registrar, explaining about the illness in his family and requesting an extension of time to complete his work for the current term. The Registrar had approved his request and had made notations on his student record that guaranteed his credits would not be affected by his sudden leave of absence. As soon as the situation stabilized itself, he was told, he should notify the University and arrangements would be made for completing his coursework. He had thanked the Registrar and headed straight home to clean the house.

When he got there, the police were waiting for him. And for Nissim. He told them that Nissim had driven to Penn to study in the library for his final exams.

"Then give him a message for us," the heavy set officer had said, moving into the living room. Usually in cases like this one, the officer explained, Philadelphia judges ruled for restitution over time and immediate deportation. But *voluntary* deportation would save the taxpayers money and save the city time. The money would have to be accounted for, but the brothers could save themselves from having criminal records if they left on their own accords. If Yosef didn't pay back everything he owed *and* leave within the next few weeks, he would not only lose his job and be expelled from school, but would also face criminal proceedings. "The choice is yours and your brother's," the officer said as he and his partner walked slowly out the front door.

As soon as the police had left, Yosef picked up the phone and dialed Denise. A tape came on. Her line had been disconnected. It was Denise, thought Yosef, who had turned him in to the police, but at what price? Even if she had been granted immunity from prosecution for agreeing to testify at the trial, she would have lost her job at the bank. Was revenge worth that? What had he done to her? Perhaps she had gone home to her family. He would have, he thought.

"You taking anything back for Dorito, Joe?" Jocko asked.

Yosef's arm was propped up on the suitcase which lay across the seat beside him. His second suitcase was in front on the passenger seat. He patted the suitcase under his elbow and smiled to himself at the thought of seeing Dorit, feeling her little face pressing warm against his beard, the squeeze of her little arms around his neck. He pictured how she would beam when she saw the giant decal which was packed in with his clothes. It was a decal of Cookie Monster, all blue fur and ping-pong ball eyes, for her to put on the wall above her bed. "Yes," he told Jocko, "I am bringing her something."

"Good," Jocko said, "I always say don't come home empty-handed." He reached his arm back over the seat and handed Yosef a small plastic bag. "Here's something from me that I want you to give her."

Yosef reached into the bag and slid out a shiny, plasticized paper. It was a red, white, and blue Bicentennial sticker, with

353

stripes running like ribbons around a silver Liberty Bell. "Thanks, Jocko," Yosef said to the eyes in the rear-view mirror. "She loves stickers."

Jocko smiled, reached up to the visor above him, and took an envelope out of the plastic sleeve. "And this is for you," he said, handing it to Yosef. If my son were still alive, I'd be doing the same thing for him, he thought. His son Frank had been killed in Vietnam near the end of a year's tour of duty. Had he lived, he would have been twenty-five. Jocko had talked to Yosef about it. Yosef understood him. He could talk to Yosef about the army, about serving your country, about patriotism, about laying down your life in combat, about war. And Yosef knew what it was to face death, to bury friends and family. "Merry Christmas, Joe."

Yosef took the paper and read it. It was a personal check. *Pay to the order of Joseph Lvov — Two hundred and xx/100 dollars.* Yosef squinted and tilted his head at a slight angle as he looked at Jocko in the mirror. He was surprised and moved by the generosity of the gesture. Jocko already had given him the money to replace the rug, and just yesterday Jocko had given him thirty-five hundred dollars, payment in full for Yosef's Checker — the cab in which Yosef was riding now, the cab which Jocko was driving. Jocko had driven a rented cab for years, having decided that it was simpler and less expensive in the long run to pay the weekly rental fees and buy his weekly sticker. But he was aware of Yosef's situation, of his problems with money and with the police. He wanted to help. Wasn't it about time for him to own the cab he drove? After thinking it over, he bought Yosef's cab from him on the spot. Together he and Yosef had gone to his bank to draw two checks. One had been for twenty-five hundred dollars made out to BankAmericard. Jocko had promised to hand it over to the police this afternoon as soon as Yosef was on the plane. That would clear up all matters involving Penn Savings Bank. It would also keep the Philadelphia Police from calling the Immigration authorities, Yellow Cab, and Temple. The other check was for one thousand dollars. Yosef had cashed it and had bought travellers' cheques. "Jocko," he said, holding the two hundred dollar check in his hands, "this isn't necessary. I have what I need."

"Don't argue with me. I want you to have it. I gave it to you. Use it for something you need."

Yosef combed his fingers through his beard and smiled. He could see there was no point in protesting. "Thank you," he said, trying to think of what he could do to repay his friend. He knew that the check was an extravagant gesture on Jocko's part. Jocko didn't need to buy his cab—he only did it to bail him out. Jocko had saved some money over the years, but he was no rich man. The cab he had rented for so long also had served as his family car. And this was Christmas. Yosef was sure the money given to him would have gone to someone else. Keeping his hands in his lap and making sure that Jocko couldn't hear, he slowly began to tear the check into little pieces and stuffed them into the ashtray on the back of the front seat.

"Which airlines?" Jocko asked.

"Northwest Orient."

"Northwest Orient?"

"I switch in London."

The Checker slowed to a stop as it reached the curb in front of the Overseas Terminal. Yosef and Jocko opened their doors and jumped out. The sleet continued to fall, pelting their heads as they moved onto the sidewalk. Yosef put his two suitcases down on the pavement and extended his right hand to Jocko.

"Have a safe trip," Jocko said, squeezing Yosef's hand in good-bye. He stepped back, slapped Yosef on the shoulder, and smiled.

"Thanks for the ride," Yosef said. "Thanks for everything."

"Don't mention it. After all, it's your cab," Jocko told him. "And listen, don't be worrying. I'm heading straight from here to the police station. Just let me know what's with you."

Yosef nodded as he watched Jocko head back around the Checker and slip into the driver's side. "Thanks, *habibi,*" he whispered. The red taillights of his Checker, of Jocko's yellow cab, pulled away in the winter storm. Yosef saw himself in that moment as a man without a home, a citizen in self-exile and a voluntary deportee. He lifted his suitcases in his large, thick hands and walked forward onto the black plastic mat. Large glass doors parted in front of him and he walked into the terminal.

Directly ahead of him a crowd of people stood in lines at baggage check-in counters. A bay of public phone booths was down the corridor to Yosef's left. He paused a moment just inside the doors, headed toward the check-in lines, then turned and walked to the pay phones. Only one booth was not occupied. He entered the vacant booth and slid the glass door closed. From his jacket pocket he removed two five-dollar rolls of quarters. Lifting the receiver he dialed "O" and waited for assistance.

"Operator. Mrs. Martin. May I help you?"

"Yes, I want to call long distance."

"Certainly. What city, please?"

"The city of Haifa. In Israel."

"Station-to-station or person-to-person?"

"Station-to-station, please."

"Yes, . . . eight dollars and eighty-seven cents for the first three minutes, please. Did you wish to make this a collect call, charge this to your home phone, or pay by coin?"

"I will pay with money," Yosef said. "I have quarters."

"Fine, sir. Then please deposit nine dollars in quarters and give me the number you're calling."

Yosef pulled out a slip of paper from his wallet and read the operator the number which was written there. Then he broke open each of the rolls of quarters as if he were breaking open an egg and deposited thirty-six coins in the coin chute.

"Thank you, sir. I'll dial that number for you now."

As Yosef waited for the number to ring, he looked out through the glass door at the bustling activity in the airport, the caravans of travellers passing by him, men and women and children leaving and coming, arriving and departing, all hauling cartloads of luggage. Suddenly he heard Rivka's voice. "You can't face going home. That's it, isn't it, Yossi?"

"What are you talking about?" he shot back. "What do you mean, that's it?" Of course he wanted to return. She knew that, didn't she? She knew he dreamed of Haifa, of the Haifa of their youth with the outdoor dances on Friday nights and the campfires on Carmel Beach. He remembered his friends, the friends he had last seen before the war. Some of them had been killed in action, others had lost limbs. He had not written to them, to any of them. He had not been able to. What could he say? How could he explain his absence? He had not been there. Nothing would change that, but the only good excuse for his absence would be coming home in style. Then maybe he wouldn't have to explain.

"If you're not afraid to go home, then let's go. Like we planned and when we planned. You're so close, so close . . . ."

The ringing on the other end of the line brought him back to himself. Yosef pressed the receiver to his ear and listened. The phone rang five times before someone answered.

"Shalom, Rambam Hospital."

"Hello," the operator said, "this is the United States calling. Go ahead, please, sir."

"Hello," Yosef shouted into the phone, speaking now in Hebrew. "Hello, my name is Yosef Lvov. I am calling to check on a patient there. Can you hear me?"

"Yes," the receptionist said, "I can hear you."

"I am calling to find out the condition of Barukh Lvov. *Lamed, vet, yud, vov.*"

"One second, please. I am checking."

Waiting for the receptionist he thought of Barukh. Barukh

telling him stories, Barukh at his basketball games, Barukh at his wedding. "I love you like my own son," he had said. Like his own son.

A full minute had passed and now the receptionist came back on the overseas line. "Hello, I have that information," she said, "but I am sorry, I can't give it over the phone."

"What do you mean you can't give it over the phone?" Yosef screamed. "I'm calling from America! I'm his son!"

"His son?"

"Yes, my name is Yosef Lvov. I want to know my father's condition."

Again there was a long pause before the receptionist spoke. "Mr. Lvov, I'm sorry . . . Your father died this morning."

Barukh dead? This morning? Yosef's face went white. Weakly he hung up the receiver. How could I not have been there for Barukh? How could I not have been there for Miryam? Yosef had lost his own father the same way, to a sudden death. He had been notified. Miryam had told him. "Yossi," she had said, tears rolling down her cheeks, "I have something to tell you, something sad, something . . . ." He had not had the chance to have hugged and been hugged by his father, to have cried and said goodbye. And now it had happened again, again.

Slowly he opened the phone booth door, steeling his face against yielding to tears. His jaw muscles tightened and bulged underneath his thick beard. He stood up, lifted both of his suitcases, and started walking slowly down the corridor to the passenger check-in counters. His thoughts dizzied him as he moved through the throng of other travellers, oblivious to their rushing, their urgency, their presence. His thoughts were of the two phone calls that had changed his life: the one that never came from the Consulate in Philadelphia, and the one that did come with the news of Barukh's stroke. Both of these calls had blown holes in his being. All he could fill them with was guilt, but these were wounds he held no hope of closing. He had not been there for his friends, for his country. He had not been there for his uncle, for his father, for his family. He had not been there when he was needed and going there now, he thought, would only bare the fact of his absence. It would mean having to answer the questions that letters and phone calls had let him ignore. He had spent too long with one foot in two worlds. He had been away too long, he thought, and this was no way to go home.

I should have paid my way back to fight, back to the war, back to Barukh at Rambam, back to Dorit and Rivka. He moved into the line at the ticket counter. I can't be everywhere. No one can. You have to make choices in life. People have to understand that. Rivka and Dorit have to, and Miryam . . . and Barukh.

"Yes, may I help you?" asked the ticket agent.

"Yes. I need to buy a ticket. The fastest connection to Israel."

"Tel Aviv?"

"Yes."

"And will this be just for one, sir?"

"Yes." He took the travellers' cheques out of his pocket.

"The first flight with availability would be via London and will depart here in one hour and forty minutes. Is that satisfactory?"

"Yes, fine." As the agent began checking the flight information and the times of connecting flights from Heathrow to Ben-Gurion, Yosef lifted his suitcases onto the metal scale beside the counter.

"Will this be cash or credit?" the agent asked.

"Cash," he said, beginning to sign his name on the cheques.

"Sir, is this one way?" she asked.

Yosef looked at the ticket agent, then turned from the counter and stared out through the glass doors. A string of cabs lined the curb near the entrance. "No, round trip," he answered.

EPILOGUE

*"And all this people shall go to
their place in peace."*

EXODUS 18:23

EPILOGUE
HAIFA • JULY 5, 1976

PUTTING UP HER HAIR, Rivka looked out the open window at the sunlight glinting off the sea. It's so beautiful here, she thought. Across the wadi, sand-colored porches of terraced buildings, bathed in warm light, seemed pieces in a familiar painting. The wedding would start in less than an hour; it was hard for her to believe that the courtship had lasted less than a year.

"Dorit, are you putting on the blue dress?"

"I don't like that one, Ema. I want one with sleeves."

"I put out the blue one because I want you to look really pretty today. Let's not waste time arguing. Just put it on, honey. I'll be in in a minute."

A song by Ilanit played on the transistor radio she had brought from America. Rivka walked over to the night table and turned up the volume as the music was interrupted by a series of short beeps signalling a news bulletin. When she heard about the daring rescue and return of the hundred skyjacked hostages from Entebbe, she shouted out loud. "*Kol ha-kavod lanu!* Good for us!"

"What, Ema?" Dorit called.

"Nothing, honey. Here I come."

"Ema, does Ronni have a beard?" Dorit asked as her mother entered the room.

"No, honey," Rivka answered, "and your dress is on backwards. Let me help you turn it around."

"I can do it myself," Dorit said, lifting her dress over her head. "How come he doesn't have a beard?"

"I guess he likes himself without one."

"But Ema, then he can't get married."

"Sure he can, sweetie."

"But Ema, he can't be an Abba," Dorit said with genuine concern. "Does Aunt Shoshanah know that?"

"Know what, honey?" she asked, an amused grin on her face.

"That he can't be an Abba because Abbas have to have beards?"

"No, honey, she doesn't know that," Rivka said, "because Abbas just have to be Abbas. There are a lot of Abbas who don't have beards."

Dorit fell quiet a moment, thinking about what her mother had said as she reversed the light blue sleeveless dress and slipped it back over her head. "Right, Ema," she said, getting tangled. The dress looked like a pillow case over her face. "But our Abba has a beard."

"Right, honey. Your Abba does."

Dorit's little head poked through the head hole. "Right. And Uncle Nissim doesn't, but he can be an Abba, right?"

"True, Dorit, true. But if you don't hurry and finish dressing, we're going to be late for the wedding."

"Okay, Ema." Dorit wriggled one arm and then the other through the sleeve holes until the cotton dress flowed smoothly down over her six-year-old body. "Ema, if we're late, does it still count?" she asked her mother.

"Does what still count, honey?"

"Does the wedding still count? Are they still married if we aren't there?"

"Of course, honey. We're not getting married, they are."

"Ema, did Abba see you get married?"

"Of course, sweetie. We couldn't have gotten married without him. Hurry up now, put on your new sandals. Aunt Shoshanah is counting on us."

Dorit reached under her bed and pulled out her shiny new pair of sandals. "Ema, can Shoshanah start if Abba's not there?"

"Yes, honey. She's marrying Ronni, not Abba."

"I know that, Ema," she said in a huff, putting her hands on her hips as she straightened up. "And you know what?"

"What, Dorit?"

"When I grow up *I'm* going to marry Kobi." With that, Dorit sat down on her bed and began putting on her sandals.

"Kobi's a very nice boy," Rivka said, moving next to her daughter and sitting down on the bed. "I think you have good taste. And I think you look beautiful, honey."

"So do you, Ema."

Her mother reached over and gently stroked her on the head. "Thank you, little friend."

"Ema, is this the right foot?"

"Yes."

Dorit leaned far forward as she tried to pull the buckle strap and close it on the fourth hole. "Ema," she said as she held her foot out for Rivka to help her, "when I marry Kobi will you be there?"

Rivka pulled the strap through and buckled it. A warm smile was in her eyes. "I wouldn't miss it, honey. I wouldn't miss it for the world."

Dorit smiled and slipped her second foot into her new sandal. "Ema?"

"Yes, honey?"

"Will Abba be there?" She held out her foot to her mother again so that Rivka could fasten the buckle.

"Be where, Dorit?"

"At my wedding."

"Of course, sweetie. Of course he will." Rivka had a brush in one hand, a blue ribbon in the other. She fixed Dorit's hair into a neat ponytail and tied the ribbon around it. Dorit had grown four inches since December, since her father had left to go back to America to finish his studies. The taller she grew, the more she resembled Yosef. He would hardly recognize her, Rivka thought. So much can change in the space of six months. "Your Abba loves you, sweetie."

Dorit touched her shiny new sandals, smoothed her blue summer dress, and stood beside the bed. A few steps from her, the Cookie Monster decal brightened the wall above her pillow. She ran her hand over the blue cellophane body. "Ema," she said, "you know what?"

"No, what, sweetie?" Rivka watched her daughter's hand on the decal her Abba had put up for her six months earlier.

"When I get married," Dorit said softly, "I'm not starting without him."

A sad smile came across Rivka's face as she thought of what she might say to her child. Dorit was growing beautifully. How far she has come, she thought. Before America, Rivka had never considered that Dorit might be an only child. Her thoughts turned to Shoshanah who two weeks earlier had confided to her that she had just missed her second period.

A loud knock at the front door pulled her from her thoughts. Quickly, she stood up from the bed, gave Dorit a squeeze, and said, "Uncle Nissim's here, come on, we don't want to be late."

Dorit stood beside her bed and stared blankly at the wall.

"Come on, honey," Rivka called from the door. "It's time. Uncle Nissim's here."